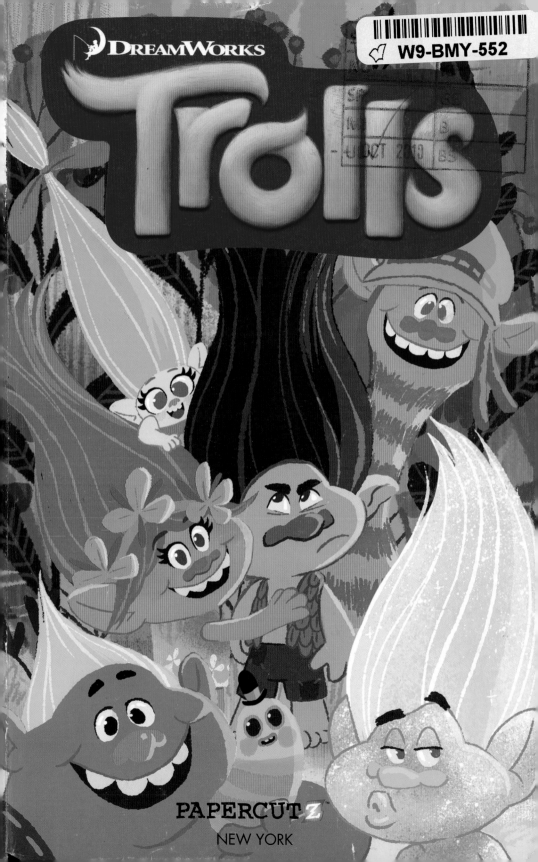

DreamWorks
Trolls

PAPERCUT*Z*

NEW YORK

MORE GREAT GRAPHIC NOVEL SERIES AVAILABLE FROM PAPERCUTZ

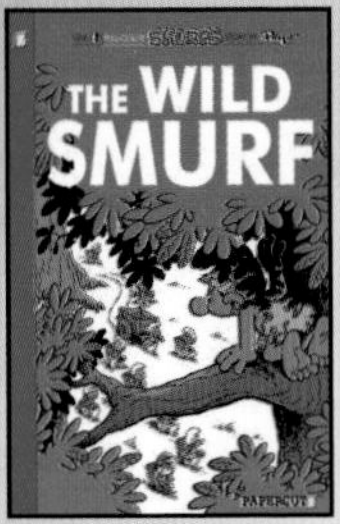
THE WILD SMURF
THE SMURFS #21

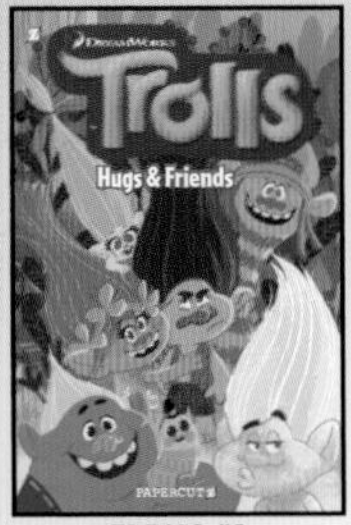
Trolls
Hugs & Friends
TROLLS #1

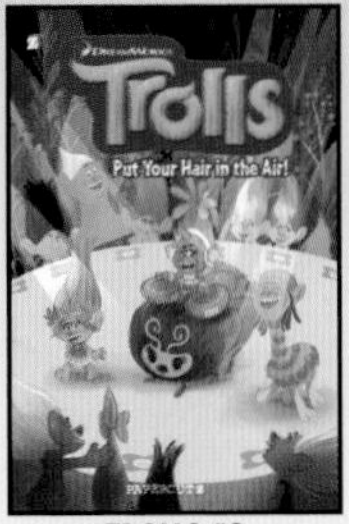
Trolls
Put Your Hair in the Air!
TROLLS #2

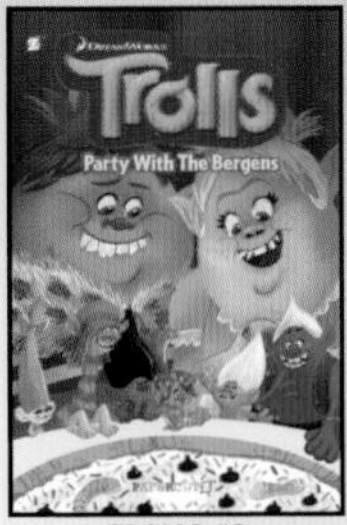
Trolls
Party With The Bergens
TROLLS #3

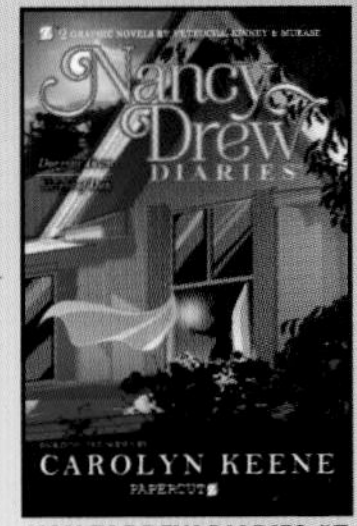
Nancy Drew
DIARIES
CAROLYN KEENE
NANCY DREW DIARIES #7

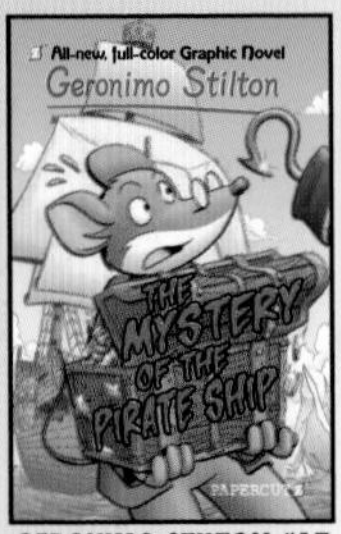
All-new, full-color Graphic Novel
Geronimo Stilton
THE MYSTERY OF THE PIRATE SHIP
GERONIMO STILTON #17

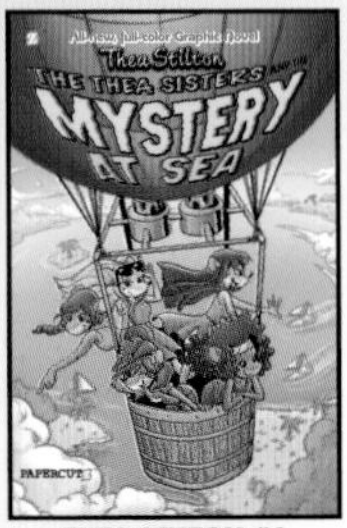
Thea Stilton
THE THEA SISTERS
MYSTERY AT SEA
THEA STILTON #6

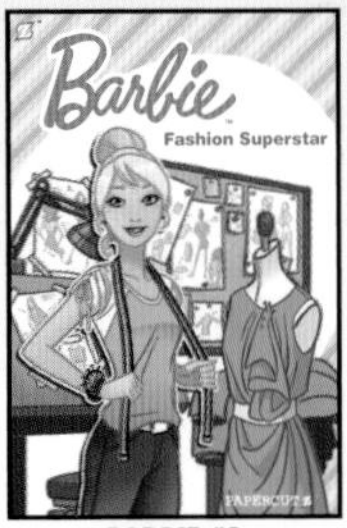
Barbie
Fashion Superstar
BARBIE #1

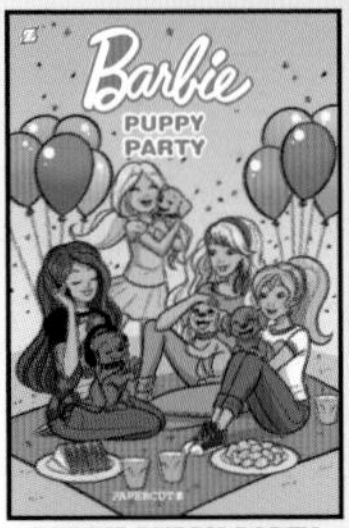
Barbie
PUPPY PARTY
BARBIE PUPPY PARTY

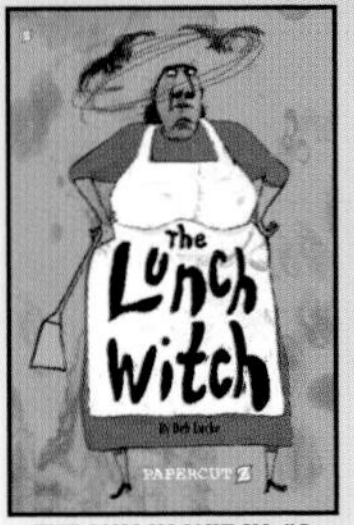
The Lunch Witch
THE LUNCH WITCH #1

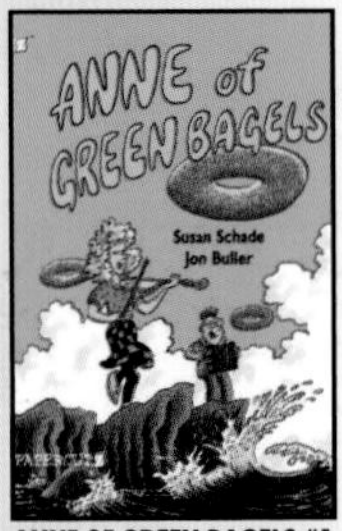
ANNE of GREEN BAGELS
Susan Schade
Jon Buller
ANNE OF GREEN BAGELS #1

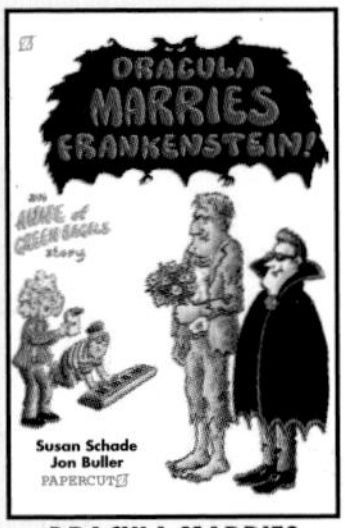
DRACULA MARRIES FRANKENSTEIN!
Susan Schade
Jon Buller
DRACULA MARRIES FRANKENSTEIN!

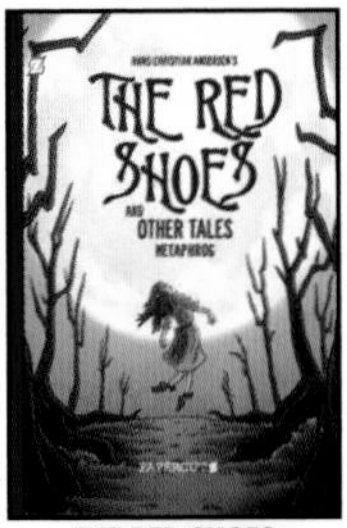
THE RED SHOES
AND OTHER TALES
METAPHROG
THE RED SHOES

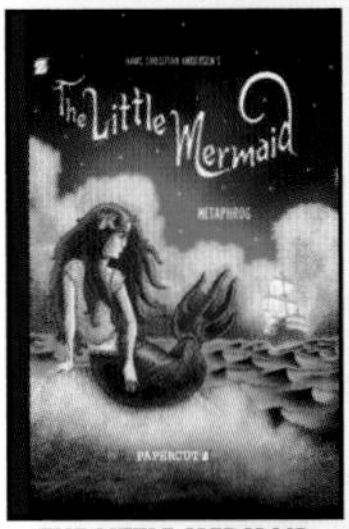
The Little Mermaid
METAPHROG
THE LITTLE MERMAID

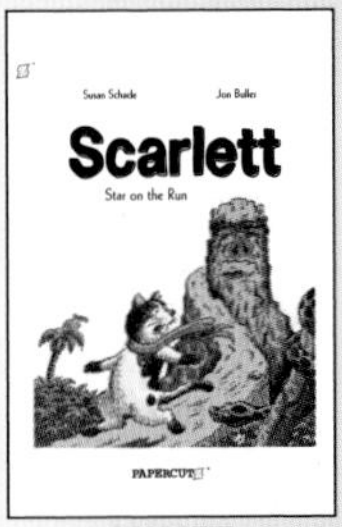
Scarlett
Star on the Run
SCARLETT

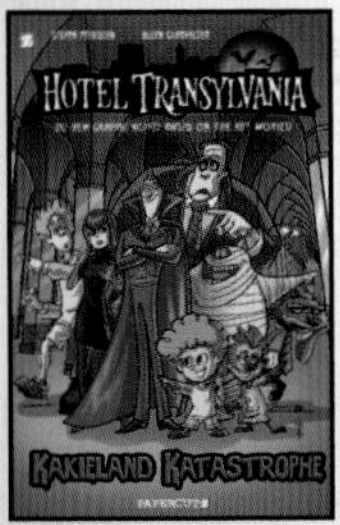
HOTEL TRANSYLVANIA
KAKIELAND KATASTROPHE
HOTEL TRANSYLVANIA #1

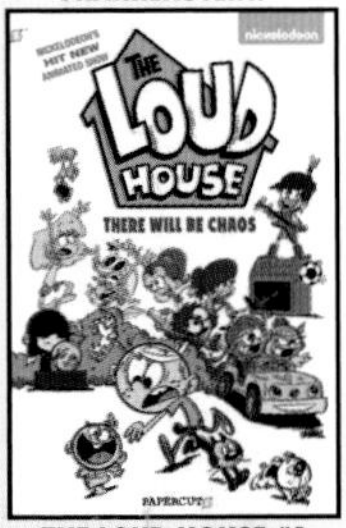
THE LOUD HOUSE
THERE WILL BE CHAOS
THE LOUD HOUSE #1

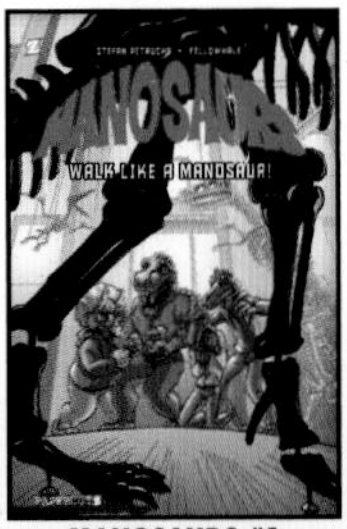
MANOSAURS
WALK LIKE A MANOSAUR!
MANOSAURS #1

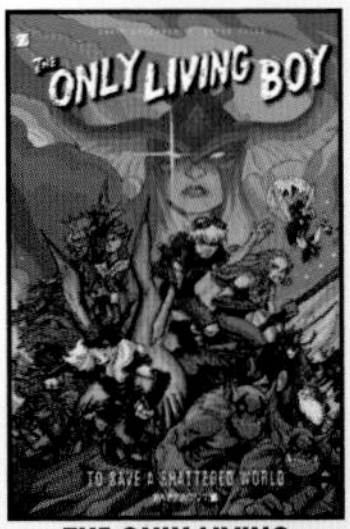
THE ONLY LIVING BOY
TO SAVE A SHATTERED WORLD
THE ONLY LIVING BOY #5

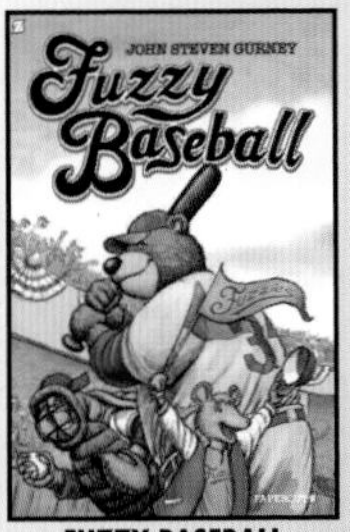
JOHN STEVEN GURNEY
Fuzzy Baseball
FUZZY BASEBALL

THE SMURFS, BARBIE, HOTEL TRANSYLVANIA, MANOSAURS, THE LOUD HOUSE and TROLLS graphic novels are available for $7.99 in paperback, and $12.99 in hardcover. THE ONLY LIVING BOY graphic novels are available for $8.99 in paperback, and $13.99 in hardcover. GERONIMO STILTON and THEA STILTON graphic novels are available for $9.99 in hardcover only. FUZZY BASEBALL and NANCY DREW DIARIES graphic novels are available for $9.99 in paperback only. THE LUNCH WITCH, SCARLETT, and ANNE OF GREEN BAGELS graphic novels are available for $14.99 in paperback only. THE RED SHOES and THE LITTLE MERMAID graphic novels are available for $12.99 in hardcover only. DRACULA MARRIES FRANKENSTEIN! graphic novel is available for $12.99 in paperback only.

Available from booksellers everywhere. You can also order online from www.papercutz.com. Or call 1-800-886-1223, Monday through Friday, 9–5 EST. MC, Visa, and AmEx accepted. To order by mail, please add $5.00 for postage and handling for first book ordered, $1.00 for each additional book and make check payable to NBM Publishing. Send to: Papercutz, 160 Broadway, Suite 700, East Wing, New York, NY 10038.

THE SMURFS, THE LOUD HOUSE, THE ONLY LIVING BOY, BARBIE, TROLLS, GERONIMO STILTON, THEA STILTON, FUZZY BASEBALL, THE LUNCH WITCH, THE LITTLE MERMAID, HOTEL TRANSYLVANIA, MANOSAURS, THE RED SHOES, NANCY DREW DIARIES, ANNE OF GREEN BAGELS, and SCARLETT graphic novels are also available wherever e-books are sold.

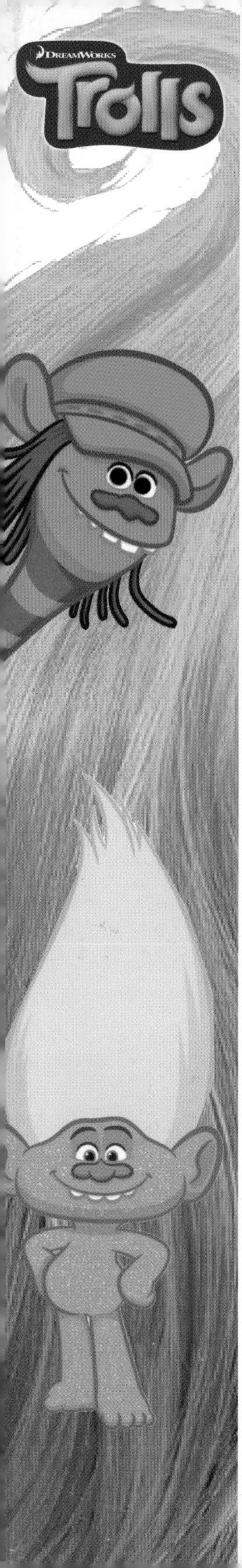
DreamWorks
Trolls

TABLE OF CONTENTS

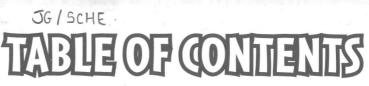

DreamWorks Trolls

3 in 1 #1

"To Eat or Not To Eat"
Script—Dave Scheidt
Art and Colors—Kathryn Hudson
Letters—Tom Orzechowski

"Bergens United"
Script—Tini Howard
Art and Colors—Kathryn Hudson
Letters—Tom Orzechowski

"Paint How You Feel"
Script—Dave Scheidt
Art and Colors—Kathryn Hudson
Letters—Tom Orzechowski

"Chefs on the Chopping Block!"
Script—Tini Howard
Art and Colors—Kathryn Hudson
Letters—Tom Orzechowski

"A Most Hairy Emergency"
Script—Dave Scheidt
Art and Colors—Kathryn Hudson
Letters—Tom Orzechowski

"Fashion Show"
Script—Dave Scheidt
Art and Colors—Kathryn Hudson
Letters—Tom Orzechowski

"Whip You Into Shape"
Script—Dave Scheidt
Art and Colors—Kathryn Hudson
Letters—Tom Orzechowski

"Bridget is on a Love Quest!"
Script—Tini Howard
Art and Colors—Kathryn Hudson
Letters—Tom Orzechowski

"The Woods"
Script—Dave Scheidt
Art and Colors—Kathryn Hudson
Letters—Tom Orzechowski

"Hide and Seek"
Script—Dave Scheidt
Art and Colors—Kathryn Hudson
Letters—Tom Orzechowski

"A Very Vanilla Nightmare"
Script—Dave Scheidt
Art and Colors—Kathryn Hudson
Letters—Tom Orzechowski

"Lost the Beat?"
Script—Dave Scheidt
Art and Colors—Kathryn Hudson
Letters—Tom Orzechowski

"Roommates"
Script—Barry Hutchinson
Art—Miguel Fernandez
Colors —GFB

"Top of the Morning (and Night) to You!"
Script—Dave Scheidt
Art and Colors—Kathryn Hudson
Letters—Tom Orzechowski

"Wakey-Wakey"
Script—Dave Scheidt
Art and Colors—Kathryn Hudson
Letters—Tom Orzechowski

"Bad Hair Day"
Script—Barry Hutchinson
Pencils—Angel Rodriguez
Inks—Ferran Rodriguez
Colors—GFB

"Surfin' Contest"
Script—Dave Scheidt
Art and Colors—Kathryn Hudson
Letters—Tom Orzechowski

"The Dinkles Drop"
Script—Barry Hutchinson
Art and Colors—Artful Doodlers!

"Class Visitors"
Script—Dave Scheidt
Art and Colors—Kathryn Hudson
Letters—Tom Orzechowski

"Pizza Party!"
Script—Dave Scheidt
Art and Colors—Kathryn Hudson
Letters—Tom Orzechowski

"To Be or Not To Be... Somebody Els
Script—Rafał Skarżycki
Art and Colors—Artful Doodlers!
Letters—Dawn Guzzo

"Rad"
Script—Dave Scheidt
Art and Colors—Kathryn Hudson
Letters—Tom Orzechowski

"Royal Portrait"
Script—Michał Gałek
Pencils and Inks—Miguel Fernandez
Colors—Artful Doodlers!
Letters—Dawn Guzzo

"Hair School"
Script—Dave Scheidt
Art and Colors—Kathryn Hudson
Letters—Tom Orzechowski

"Bridget 2.0"
Script—Dave Scheidt
Art and Colors—Kathryn Hudson
Letters—Tom Orzechowski

"Secret Messenger"
Script—Michal Galek
Pencils—Angel Rodriguez
Inks—Ferran Rodriguez
Colors—Artful Doodlers!
Letters—Dawn Guzzo

"Listen Up!"
Script—Dave Scheidt
Art and Colors—Kathryn Hudson
Letters—Tom Orzechowski

Production—Dawn Guzzo
Editor—Jeff Whitman
Original Editors—Robert V. Conte, Bethany Bryan
Special Thanks to DreamWorks Animation LLC—Corinne Combs, Lawrence Hamashima, Barbara Layman, Mike Sund, Alex Ward, John Tanzer, and Megan Startz
Editorial Intern—Spenser Nellis
Jim Salicrup
Editor-in-Chief

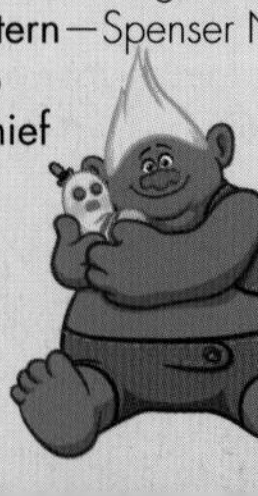

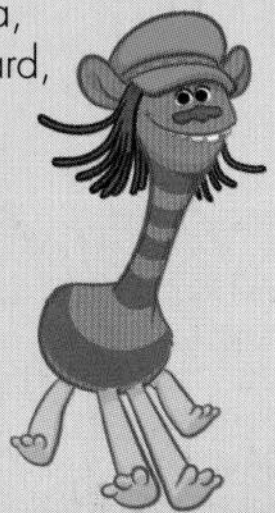

Papercutz books may be purchased for business or promotional use.For information on bulk purchases please contact Macmillan Corporate and Premium Sales Department at (800) 221-7945 x5442
PB ISBN: 978-1-54580-124-6

Printed in China
June 2018

Distributed by Macmillan
First Papercutz Printing

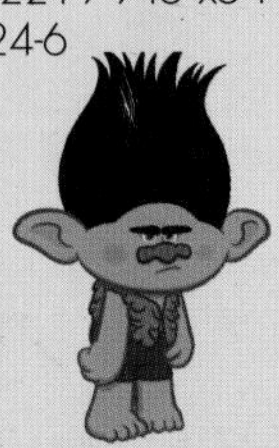

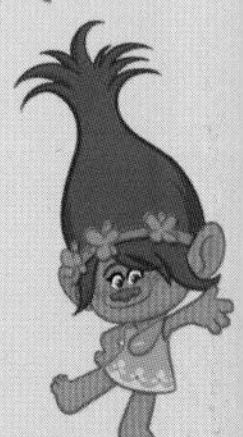

MEET THE Trolls

POPPY

Relentlessly upbeat, Poppy wields her positivity like a super-power! The heroic leader of the Trolls, Poppy always encourages her friends to believe that, with a song in your heart, you can do anything. Because when it comes to life, why say it when you can sing it?

FUN FACTS

- Loves to sing
- Eternally optimistic
- Befriends all manner of little critters
- Hugs her friends every hour, on the hour
- Cherishes scrapbooking and crafting invitations
- Knows everything sounds better with a cowbell
- Brings everyone together, Troll or otherwise

MEET THE TROLLS

BRANCH

Branch often wonders if he's the only sane individual in a town full of exuberantly happy Trolls. Reclusive and always prepared for danger, Branch must learn to embrace his inner Troll if he's ever going to let his true colors shine.

FUN FACTS

- Always prepared
- Practical
- On the lookout for danger
- Overly cautious
- Determined

MEET THE Trolls

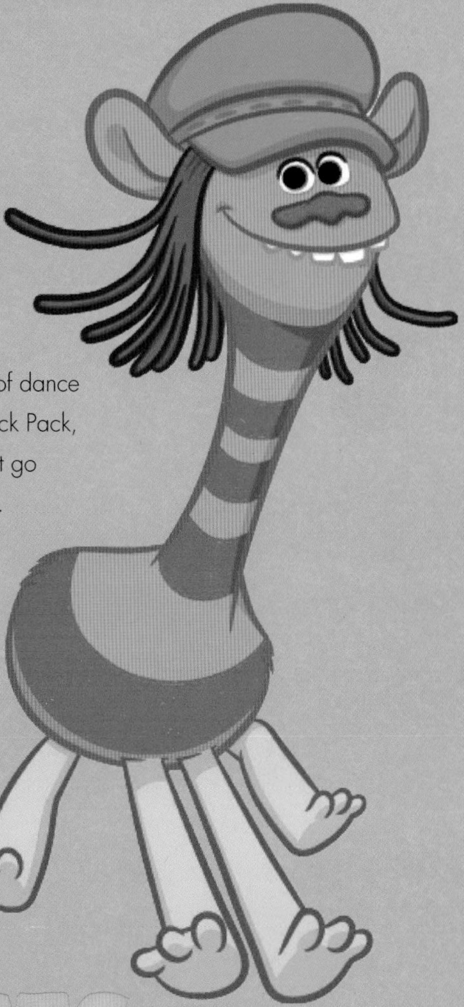

COOPER

Cooper has four feet to bust the craziest of dance moves! The friendliest member of the Snack Pack, Cooper is full of enthusiasm—and doesn't go anywhere without his signature green hat.

FUN FACTS

- Doesn't go anywhere without his signature green hat
- Always upbeat
- Full coat of Troll hair makes him especially magical

GUY DIAMOND

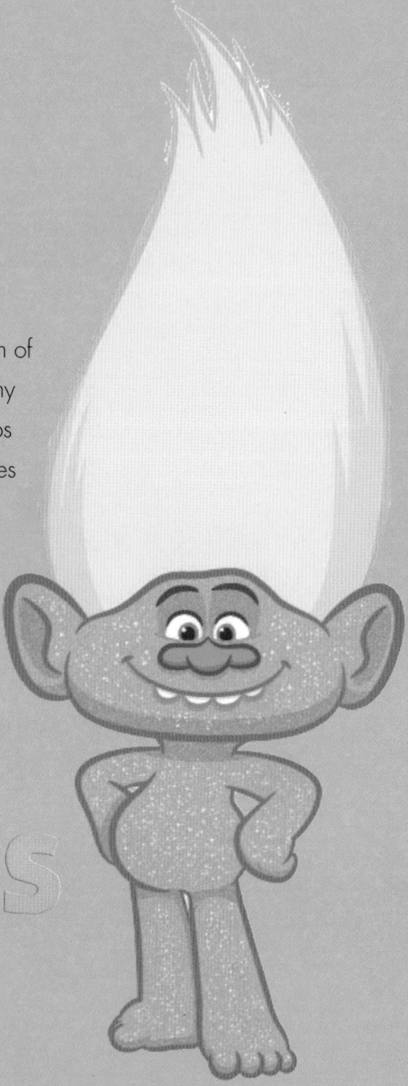

Blessed with heaps of confidence, but not a stitch of clothing, Guy Diamond knows how to kick off any party. This glitter Troll's upbeat energy always rubs off on whoever is around him, just like the sparkles covering his entire body!

FUN FACTS

- Popular, but not pompous
- Speaks in an auto-tune voice
- Is the living disco ball at any party

MEET THE Trolls

BIGGIE

Biggie is the biggest member of the Snack Pack, with the biggest heart. Underneath his imposing exterior he's actually a huge softie, constantly bursting into happy tears at touching moments, even at the sight of a particularly picturesque sunset. He carries around a pet worm, named Mr. Dinkles, everywhere he goes.

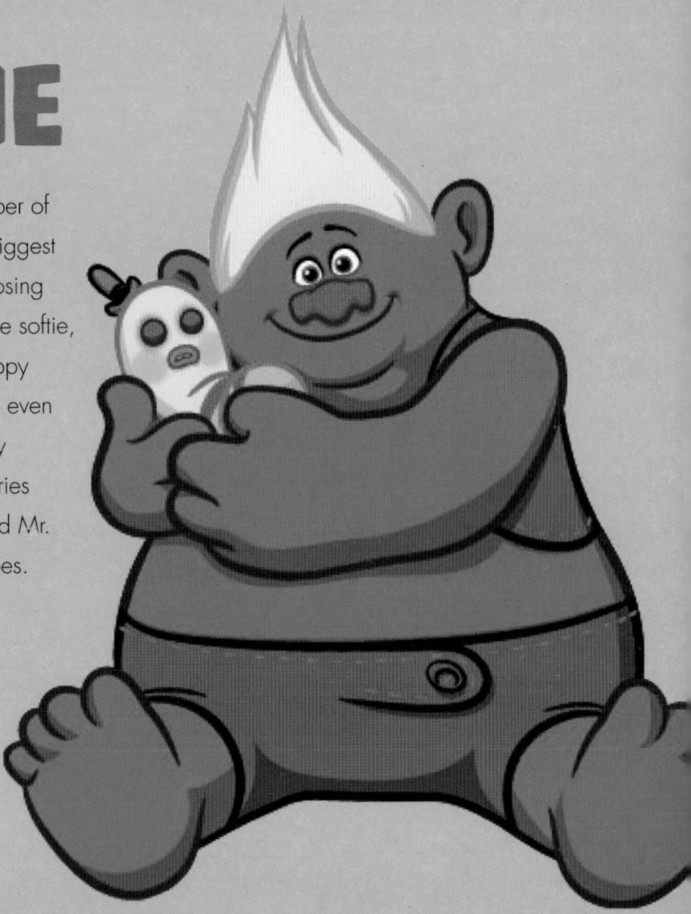

FUN FACTS

- Big advocate of the short vest/no shirt look
- Loves to dress up Mr. Dinkles in adorable little outfits for photo shoots and/or flash mob dances
- Favorite snack: the cupcakes Mr. Dinkles makes after drinking happy tears

MEET THE Trolls

SATIN & CHENILLE

Satin and Chenille are the most fashion-forward members of the Snack Pack, and their fashion knowledge is extensive, covering everything from haute couture runways to the latest street fashions. These twins are connected by a loop made of their brightly colored hair! Satin and Chenille are instrumental in putting together all of Poppy's various dresses and outfits.

FUN FACTS

- Satin is the pink one; Chenille's the blue one
- They're total BFFFs—Best Fashion Friends Forever
- Four hands means quick costume changes during big Troll Village events
- These twins are all about independence; They never ever wear the same outfit at the same time!

MEET THE Trolls

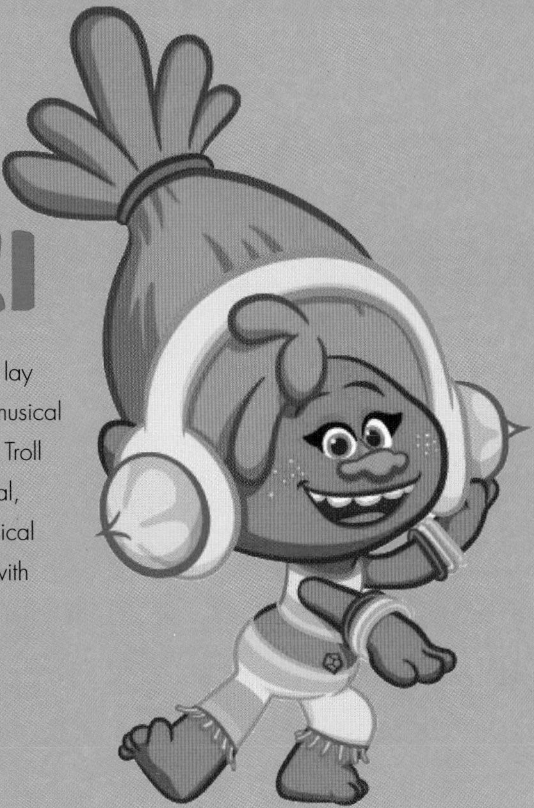

DJ SUKI

DJ Suki can always be counted on to lay down some beats for an impromptu musical moment—of which there are many in Troll Village. Her DJ equipment is all natural, consisting of various colorful and musical critters that she scratches and mixes with to create totally unique sounds.

FUN FACTS

- Troll Village's resident mash-up expert
- Wears headphones made of yarn
- Drops a needle-scratch noise during awkward moments
- Her playlist is always upbeat and up-tempo

MEET THE Trolls

HARPER

Harper believes that no canvas is too small when it comes to letting all her true colors shine! Her own hair is all Harper needs to express herself in every color imaginable. If a picture is worth a thousand words, then Harper can say...well, she can say a lot!

FUN FACTS

- Can speak, but would rather create than chat
- Uses her hair like a giant paintbrush
- Covered head-to-toe in paint...
- ...except for her smock, which stays magically spotless

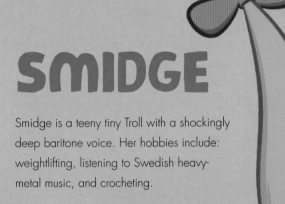

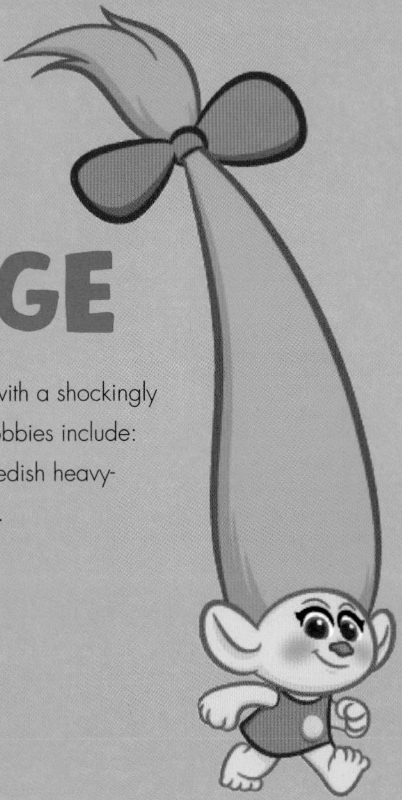

SMIDGE

Smidge is a teeny tiny Troll with a shockingly deep baritone voice. Her hobbies include: weightlifting, listening to Swedish heavy-metal music, and crocheting.

FUN FACTS

- Incredibly disciplined when it comes to fitness and nutrition
- Likes to fit in a quick workout during any dance number
- Jumps rope and lifts dumbells with her own long hair

MEET THE Trolls

CREEK

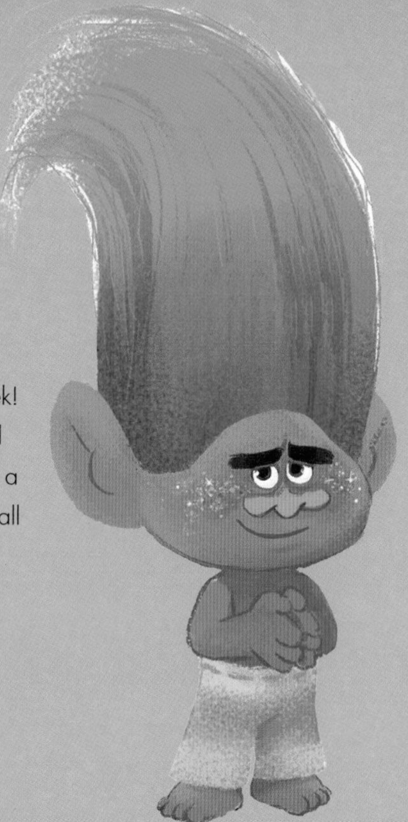

He's calm, collected and capable—he's Creek! Positive, supportive and reassuring as a friend and dance partner, Creek is what's known as a Troll's Troll—all the guys want to be him, and all the girls want to be with him!

FUN FACTS

- Always knows what to say to cheer up others
- His freckles are made of glitter
- When he sings, other Trolls listen
- Somehow always manages to steal the spotlight and be the center of attention

MEET THE Trolls

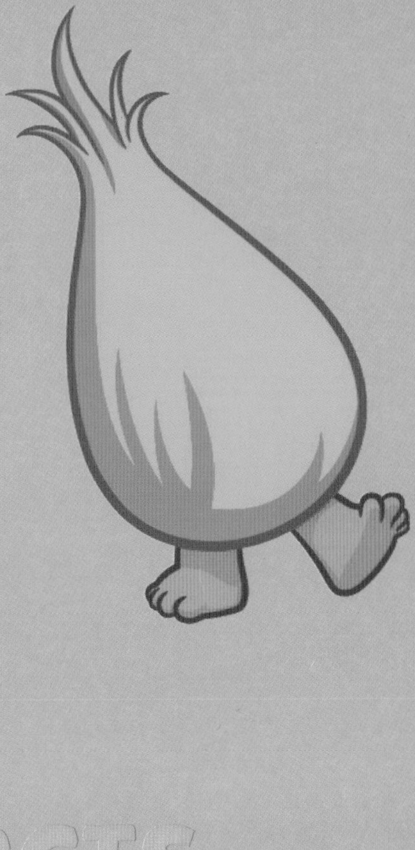

FUZZBERT

An enigma wrapped in a riddle, Fuzzbert is a Troll that's made entirely of hair—only his two feet are visible beneath a tuft of bright green Troll hair. Sort of like the "Cousin It" of Troll Village, he communicates with the other Trolls using Wookie-like guttural noises (which they all seem to be able to understand just fine).

FUN FACTS

- Really hard to hear under all of that hair
- Hair shakes when Fuzzbert laughs
- Nicknamed "Twinkle Toes" when dancing
- Uses entire body to tickle other Trolls

MEET THE TROLLS

MADDY

Maddy isn't just a hair stylist, she's a Hair Architect—a glamour designer working wonders with the Trolls' already magical hair, which she styles and shapes into amazing new creations. Maddy often teams up with the Fashion Twins, pairing her trendy 'dos with their latest couture!

FUN FACTS

- Runs Troll Village's local hair salon
- Loves to gossip
- Favorite part of her job: Helping others let their true colors shine
- Can double anyone's height with Troll hair extensions

KING GRISTLE

Following a very unhappy day in his childhood, King Gristle dedicated his rule to returning happiness to Bergen Town. Gristle is convinced that Trolls are the key to cheering up his people, and he may be right, but not in the way he expects!

FUN FACTS

- Actually pretty good at busting rhymes
- Roller-skating is his secret talent
- His idea of a fancy date is going to Bergen Town's premier all-you-can-eat pizza buffet
- Will never sit down to a meal without a freshly pressed bib

MEET THE BERGENS

BRIDGET

Sweet, sensitive, soft-spoken, and kind-hearted, Bridget is a world apart from every other Bergen. Stuck being the scullery maid and dishwasher in Bergen Town's Royal Kitchen, will Bridget ever find someone to love her inner self and let her true colors shine?

FUN FACTS

- Believes in herself, but unsure how to communicate that to others
- Treats everyone with respect, even if she doesn't get any
- Secretly romantic
- Wants to find happiness in a way that's different from other Bergens

MEET THE BERGENS

CHEF

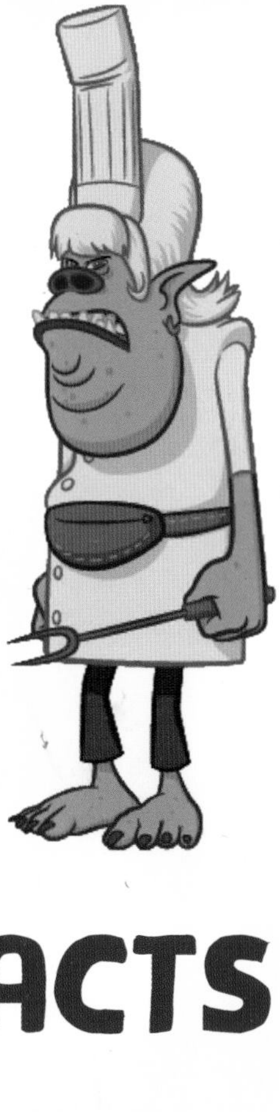

Chef likes Trolls. She likes them drenched in butter, she likes them spread on toast, and during Trollstice she makes an excellent Troll meatloaf! But all of that deflated like a bad Troll soufflé the day the Trolls escaped. Now, after wandering the forest in exile, Chef has started cooking up a new recipe to bring Trolls back to Bergen Town.

FUN FACTS

- Impatient and gruff
- Loves to whack underlings with her ladle
- Has many Troll recipes, like Troll-loaf and Egg-Trolls
- Secretly holds the power in Bergen Town

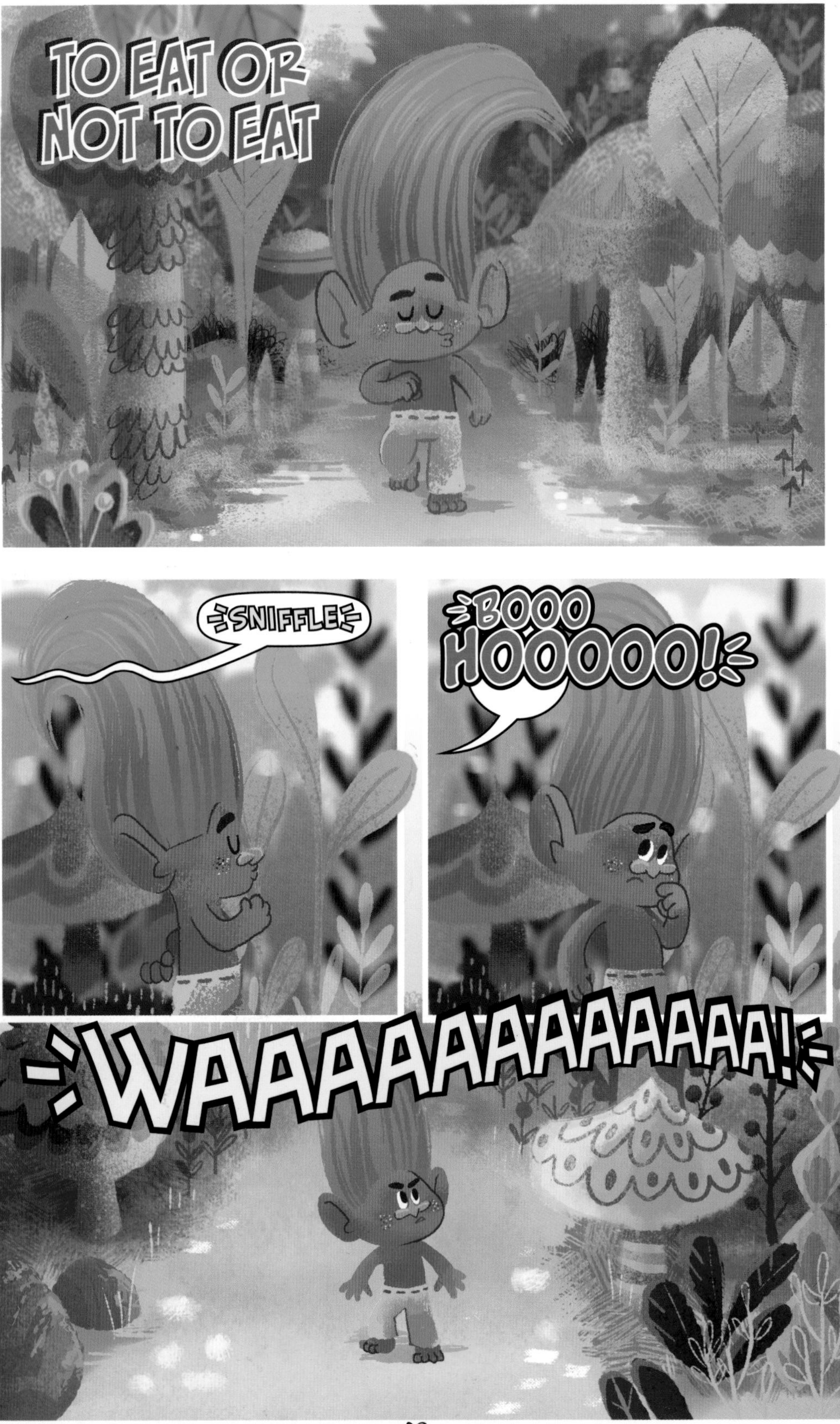
TO EAT OR NOT TO EAT
SNIFFLE
BOOO HOOOOOO!
WAAAAAAAAAAAAA!

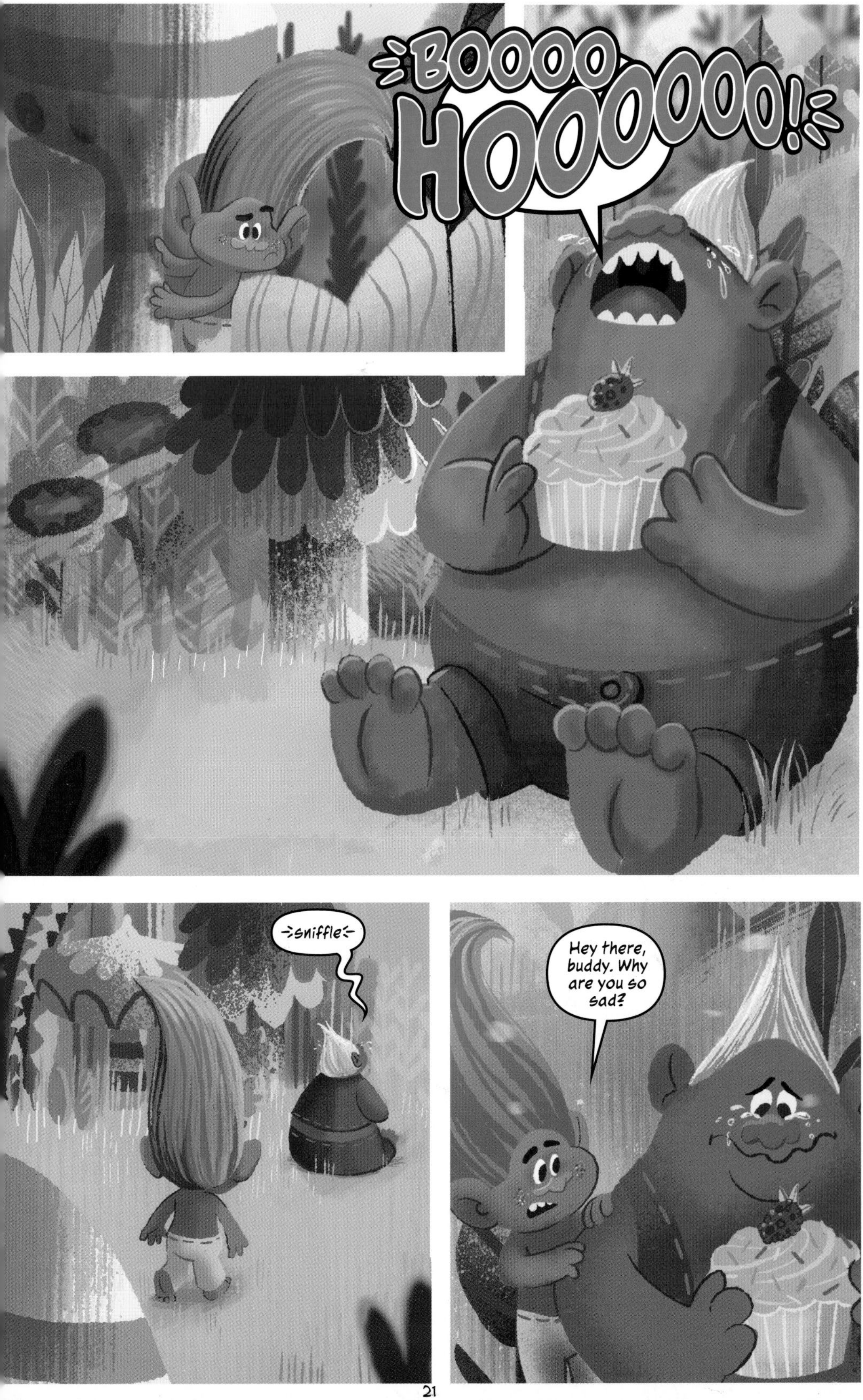
BOOOO HOOOOOOO!
sniffle
Hey there, buddy. Why are you so sad?

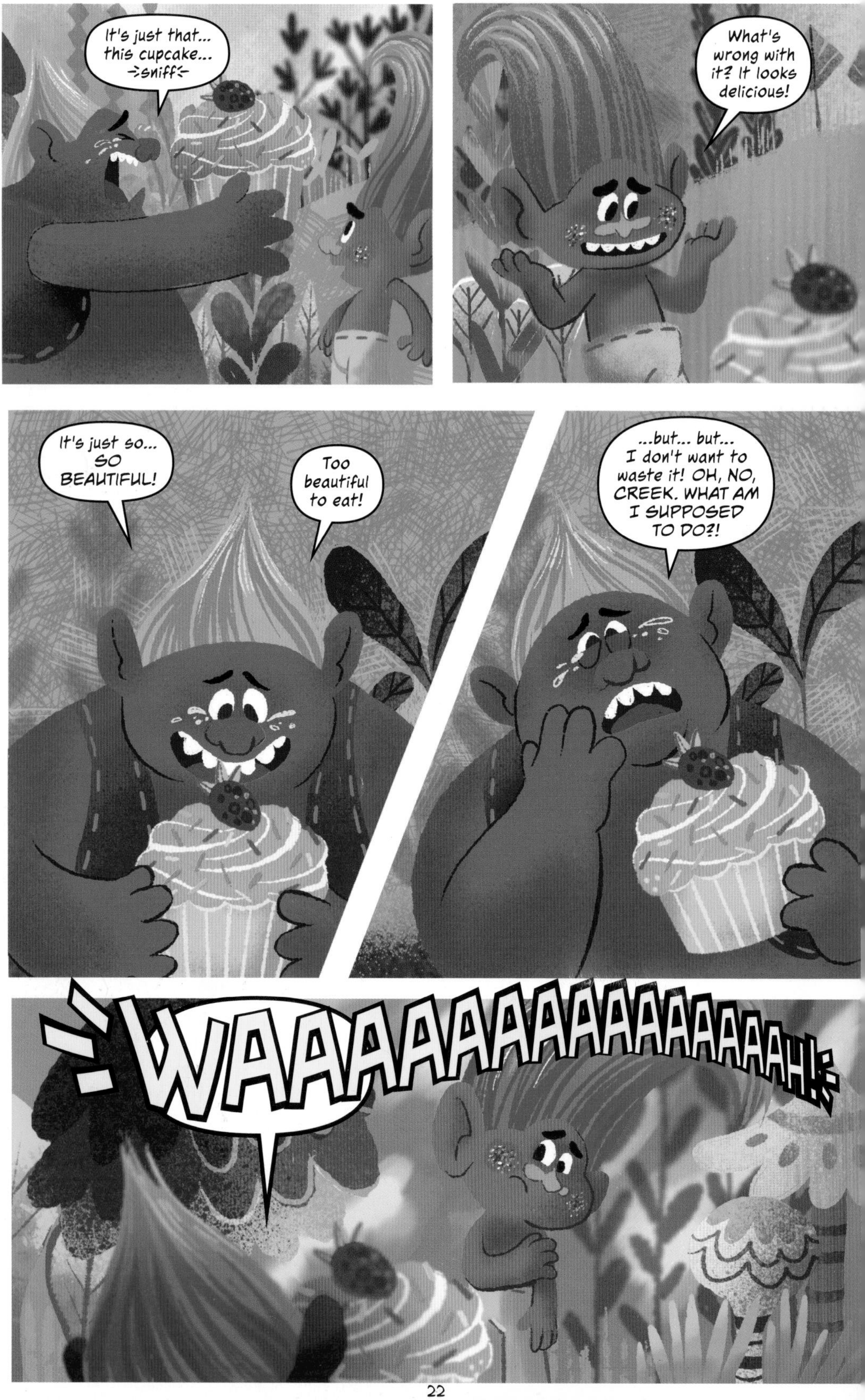
It's just that... this cupcake... ⇢sniff⇠
What's wrong with it? It looks delicious!
It's just so... SO BEAUTIFUL!
Too beautiful to eat!
...but... but... I don't want to waste it! OH, NO, CREEK. WHAT AM I SUPPOSED TO DO?!
WAAAAAAAAAAAAAAAAAH!

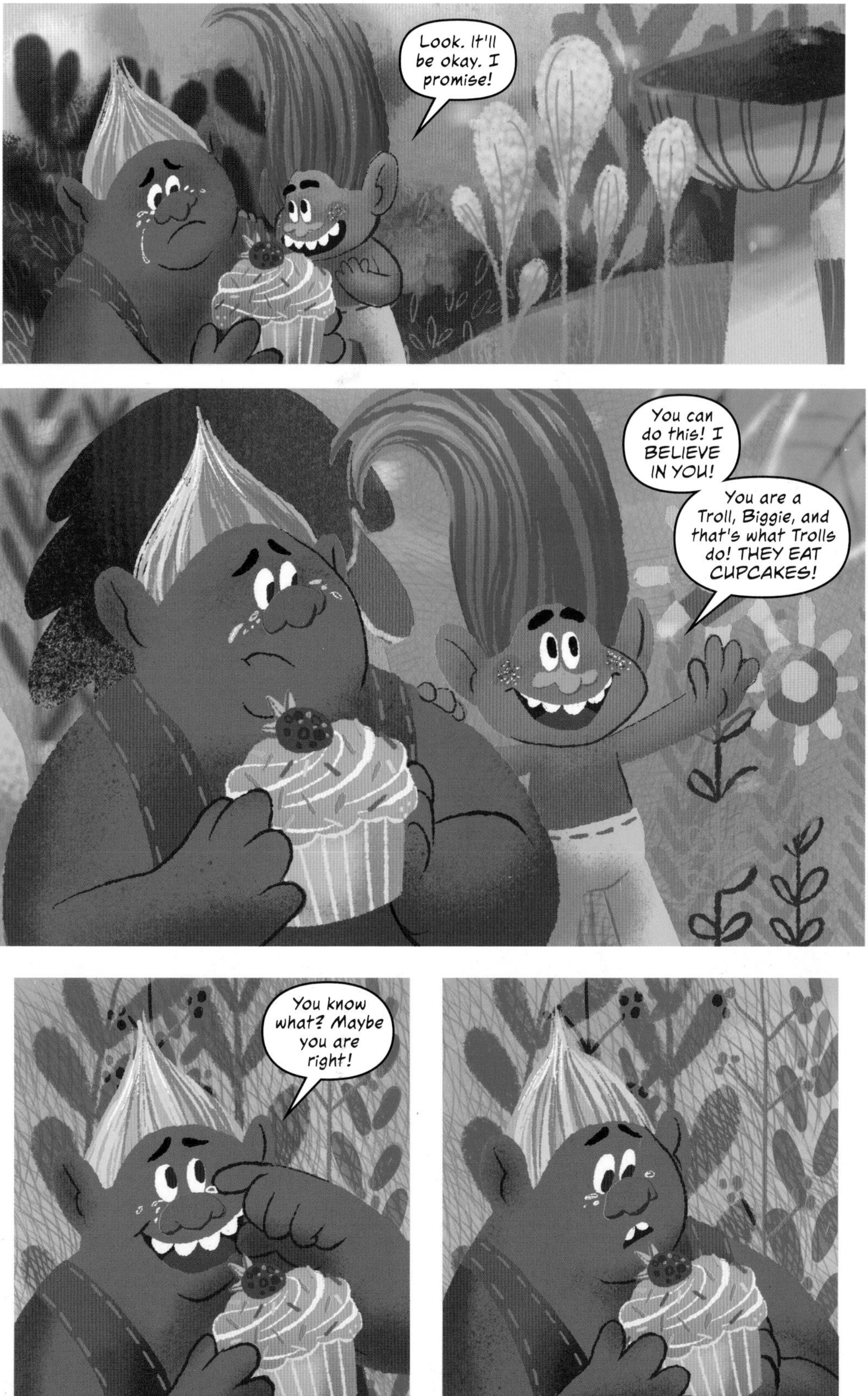
Look. It'll be okay. I promise!
You can do this! I BELIEVE IN YOU!
You are a Troll, Biggie, and that's what Trolls do! THEY EAT CUPCAKES!
You know what? Maybe you are right!

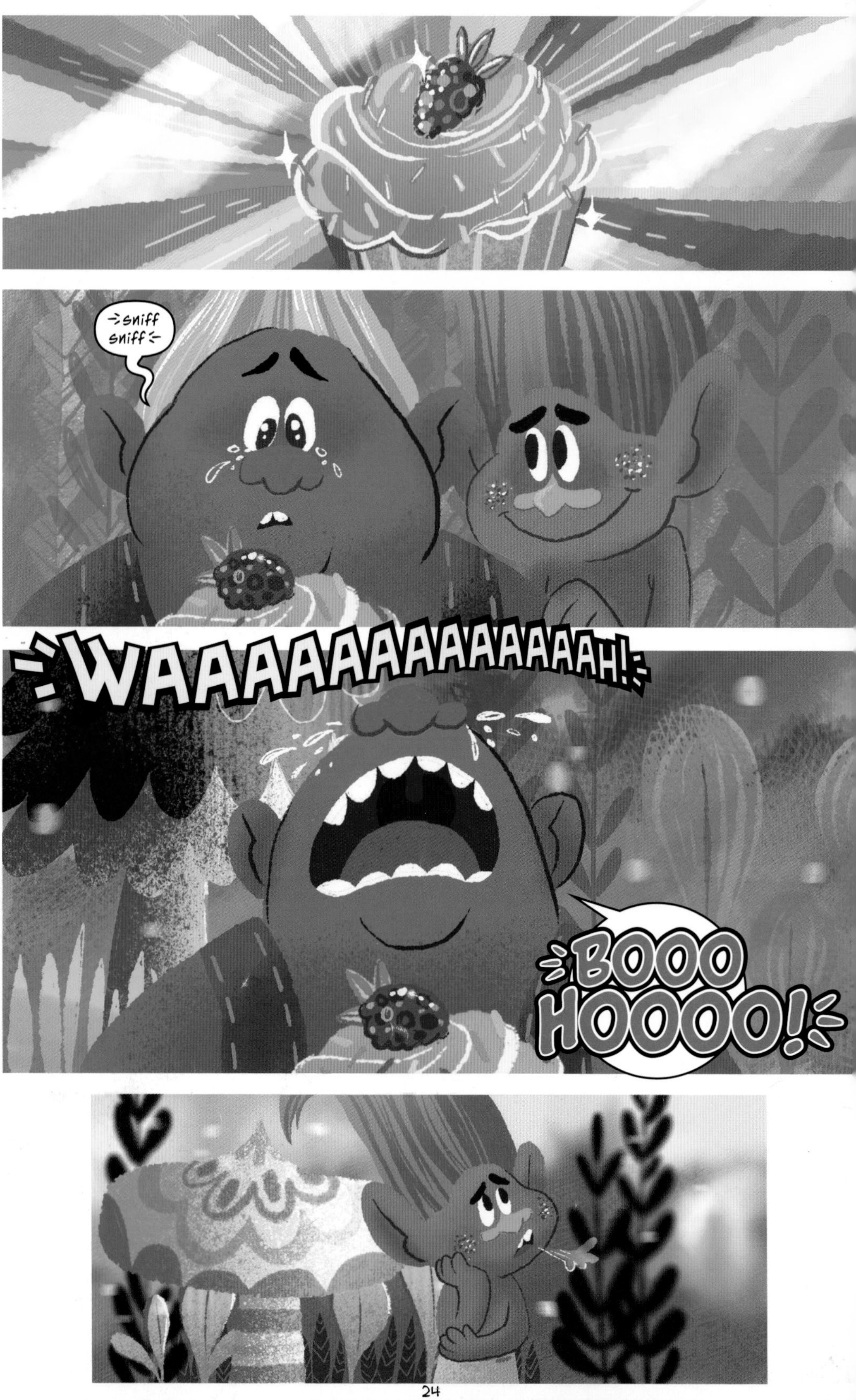
sniff sniff
WAAAAAAAAAAAAAAH!
BOOO HOOOO!

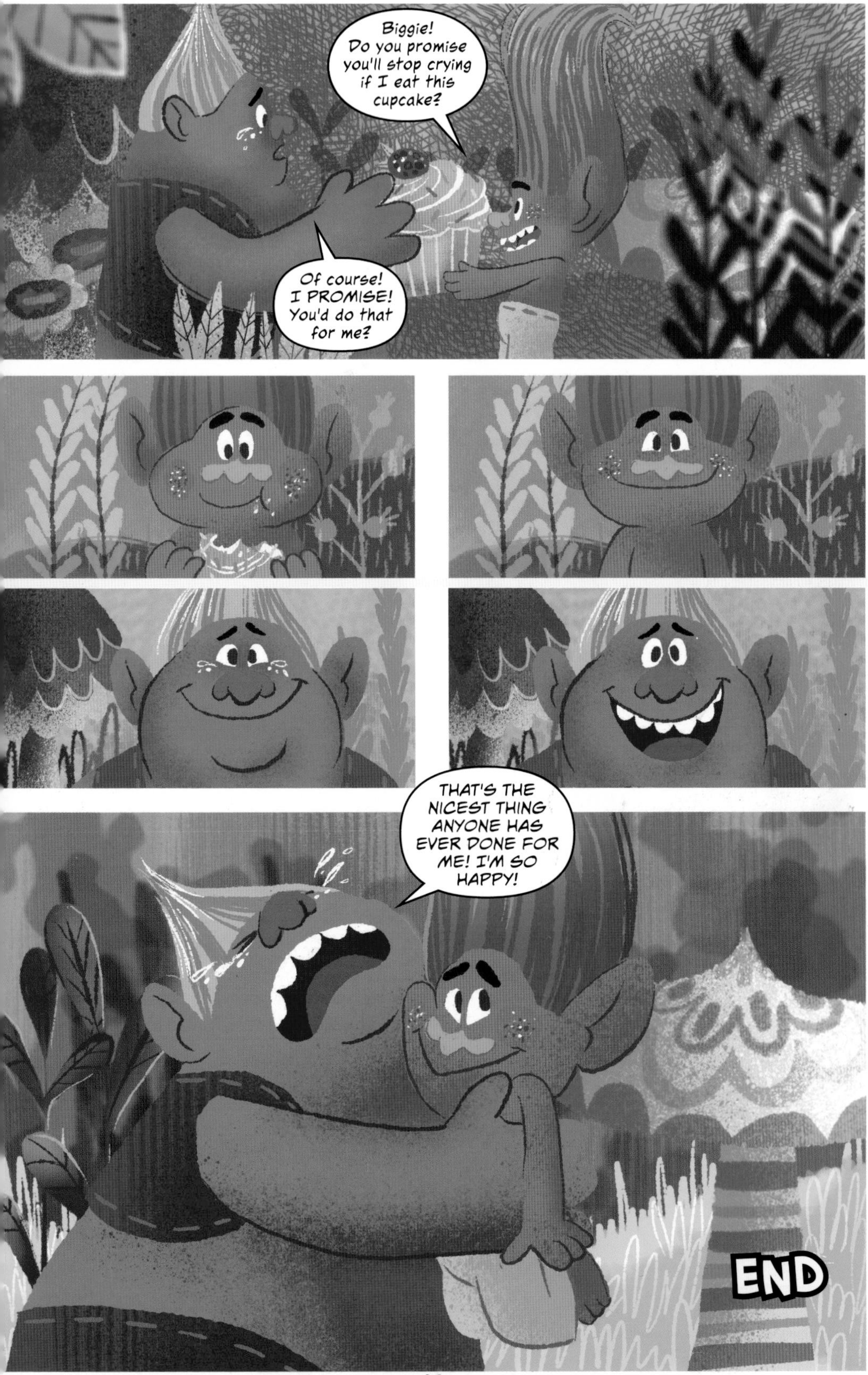
Biggie! Do you promise you'll stop crying if I eat this cupcake?
Of course! I PROMISE! You'd do that for me?
THAT'S THE NICEST THING ANYONE HAS EVER DONE FOR ME! I'M SO HAPPY!
END

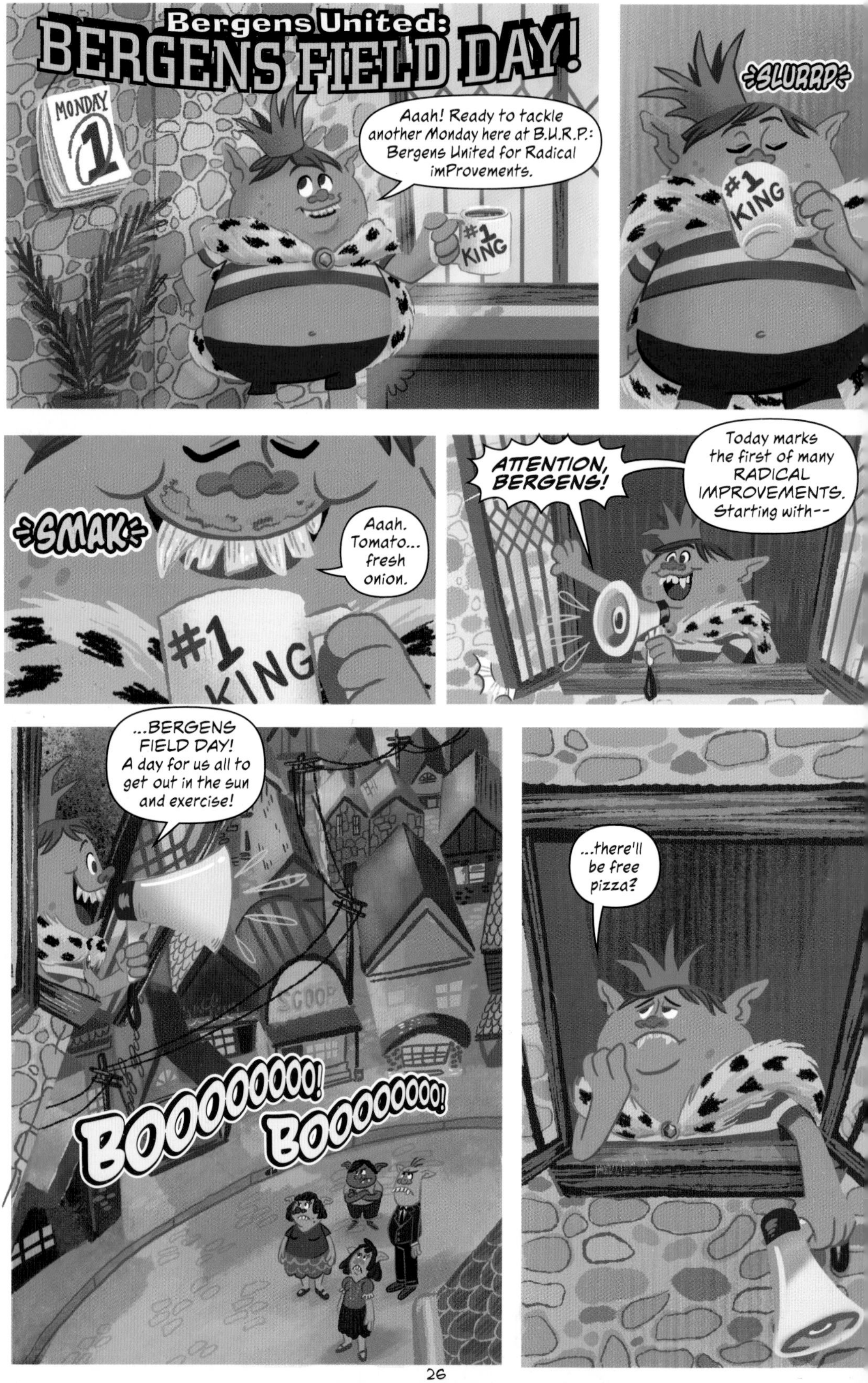
Bergens United:
BERGENS FIELD DAY!
MONDAY 1
Aaah! Ready to tackle another Monday here at B.U.R.P.: Bergens United for Radical imProvements.
#1 KING
SLURRP
#1 KING
SMAK
Aaah. Tomato... fresh onion.
#1 KING
ATTENTION, BERGENS!
Today marks the first of many RADICAL IMPROVEMENTS. Starting with--
...BERGENS FIELD DAY! A day for us all to get out in the sun and exercise!
SCOOP
BOOOOOOOO! BOOOOOOOO!
...there'll be free pizza?

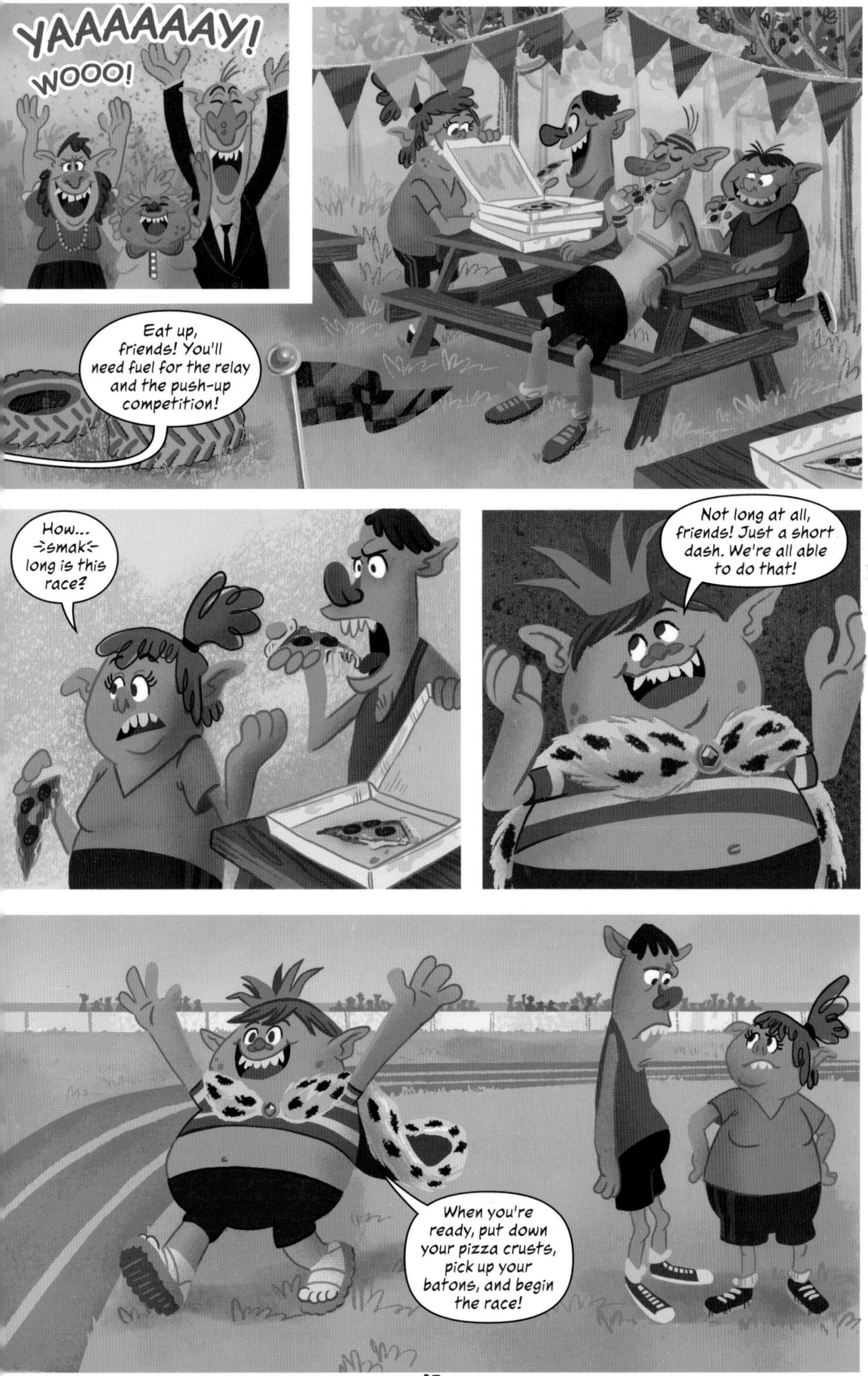
YAAAAAAY!
WOOO!
Eat up, friends! You'll need fuel for the relay and the push-up competition!
How... ⇝smak⇜ long is this race?
Not long at all, friends! Just a short dash. We're all able to do that!
When you're ready, put down your pizza crusts, pick up your batons, and begin the race!

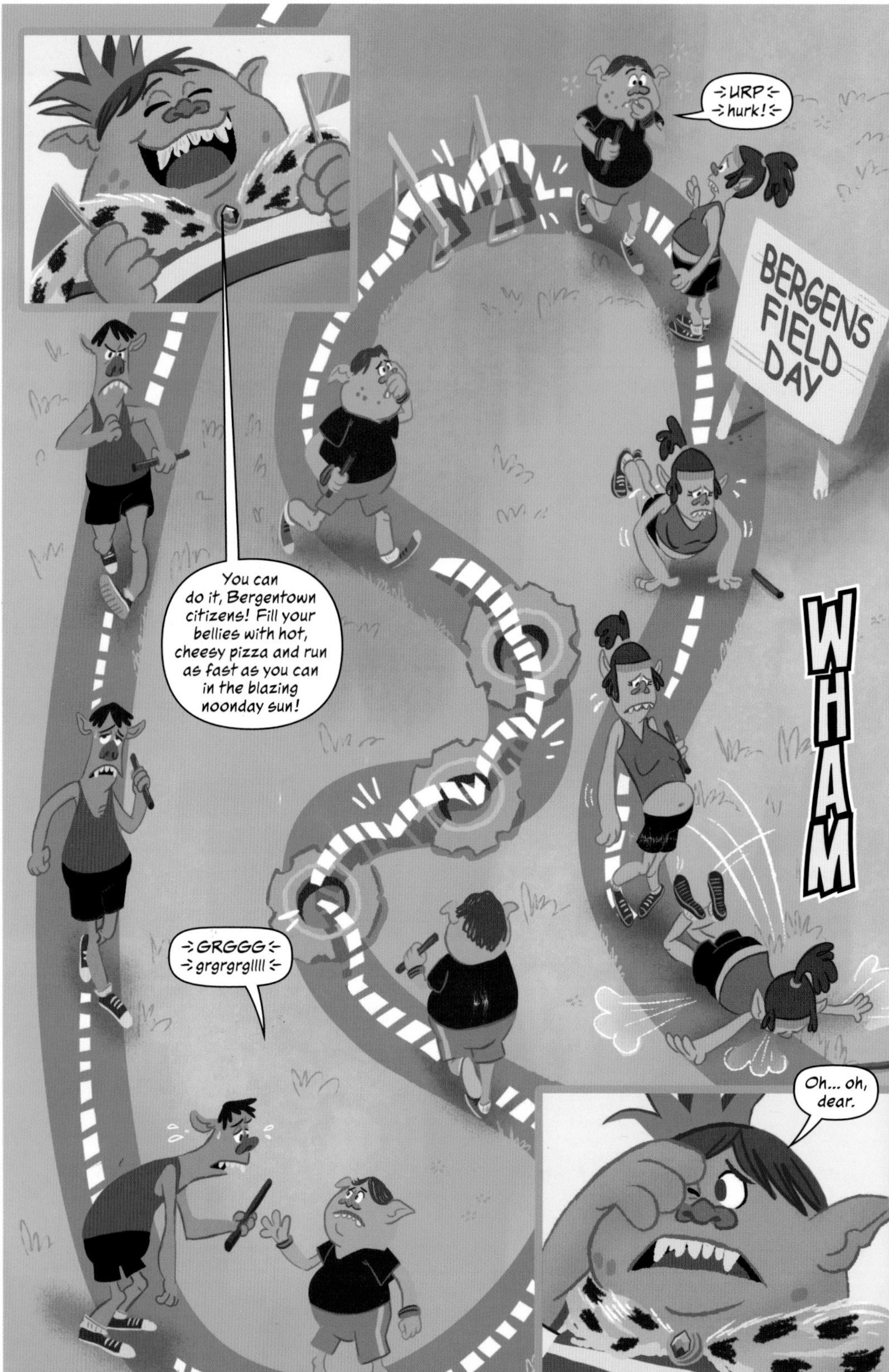
You can do it, Bergentown citizens! Fill your bellies with hot, cheesy pizza and run as fast as you can in the blazing noonday sun!
URP hurk!
BERGENS FIELD DAY
GRGGG grgrgrglll
WHAM
Oh... oh, dear.

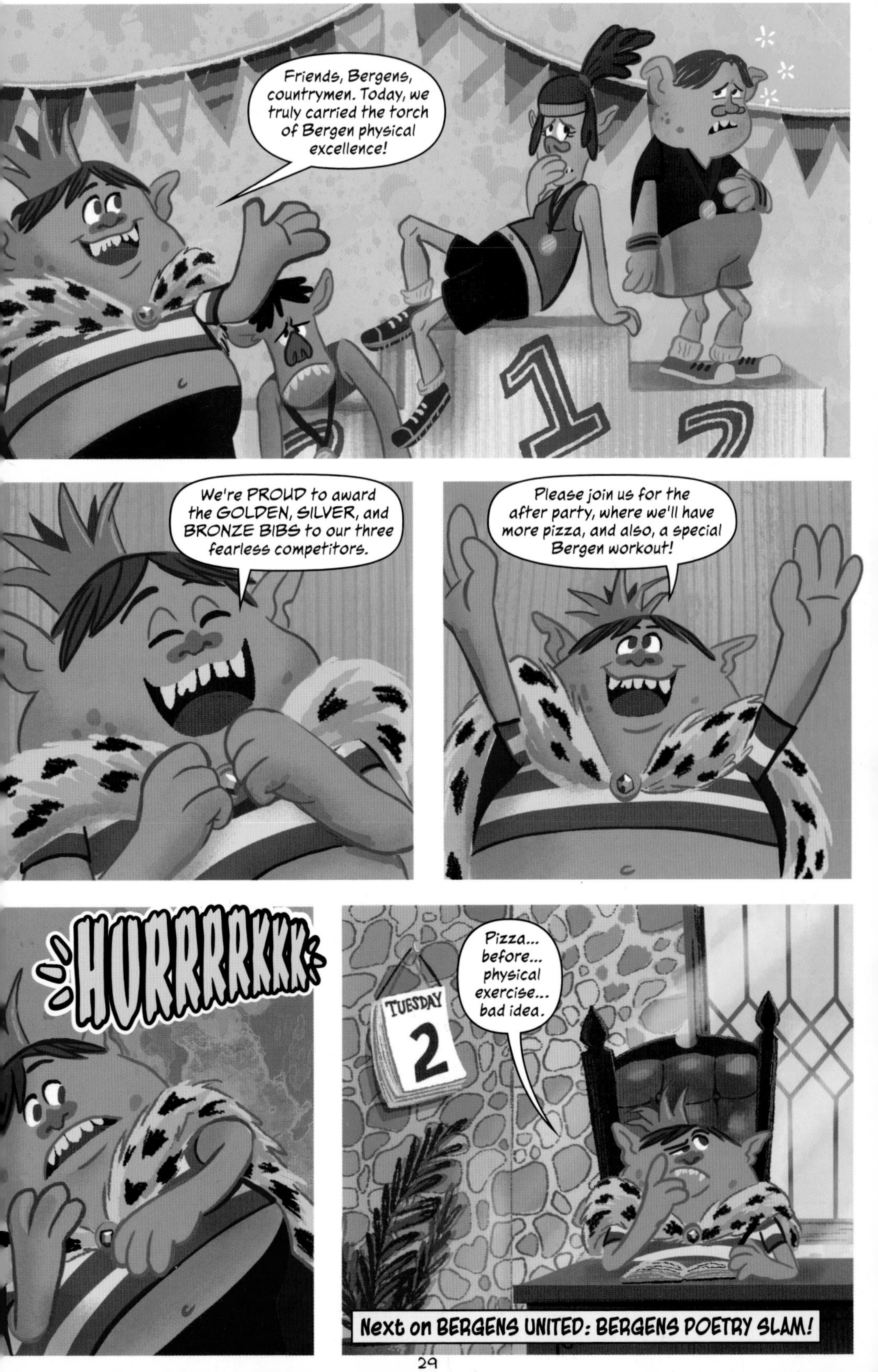
Friends, Bergens, countrymen. Today, we truly carried the torch of Bergen physical excellence!
1
2
We're PROUD to award the GOLDEN, SILVER, and BRONZE BIBS to our three fearless competitors.
Please join us for the after party, where we'll have more pizza, and also, a special Bergen workout!
HURRRRKKK
TUESDAY
2
Pizza... before... physical exercise... bad idea.
Next on BERGENS UNITED: BERGENS POETRY SLAM!

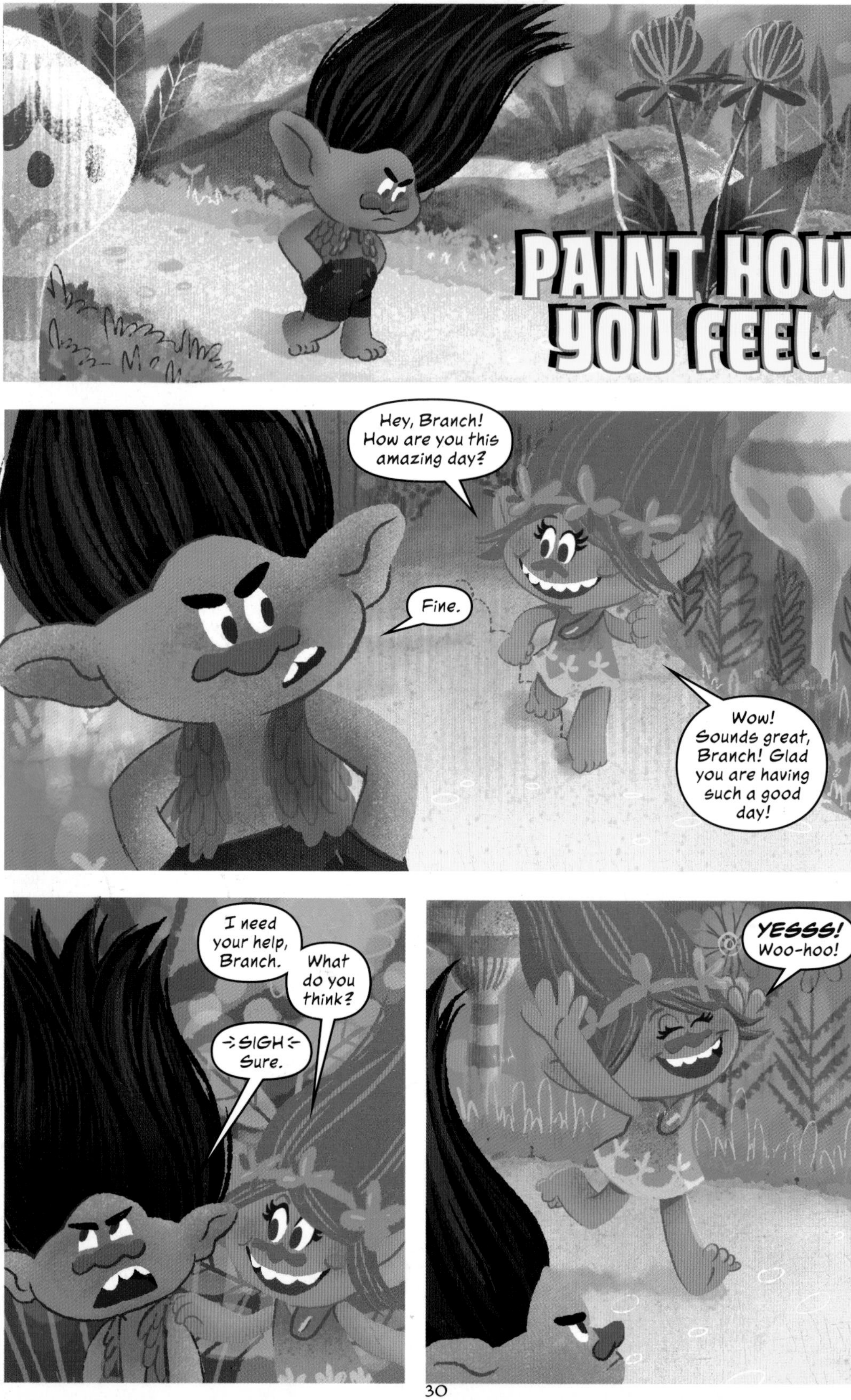
PAINT HOW YOU FEEL
Hey, Branch! How are you this amazing day?
Fine.
Wow! Sounds great, Branch! Glad you are having such a good day!
I need your help, Branch.
What do you think?
SIGH Sure.
YESSS! Woo-hoo!

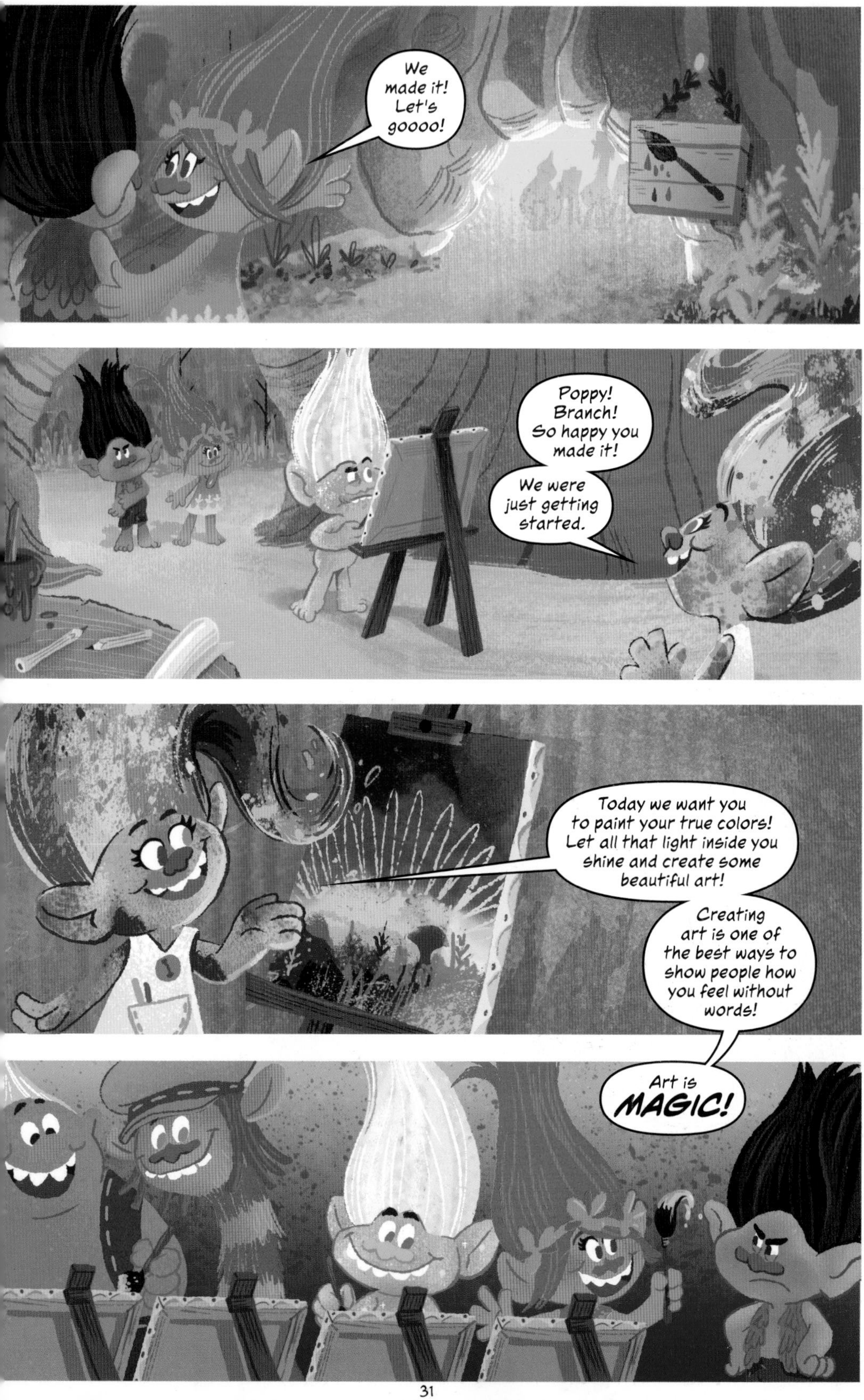
We made it! Let's goooo!
Poppy! Branch! So happy you made it!
We were just getting started.
Today we want you to paint your true colors! Let all that light inside you shine and create some beautiful art!
Creating art is one of the best ways to show people how you feel without words!
Art is MAGIC!

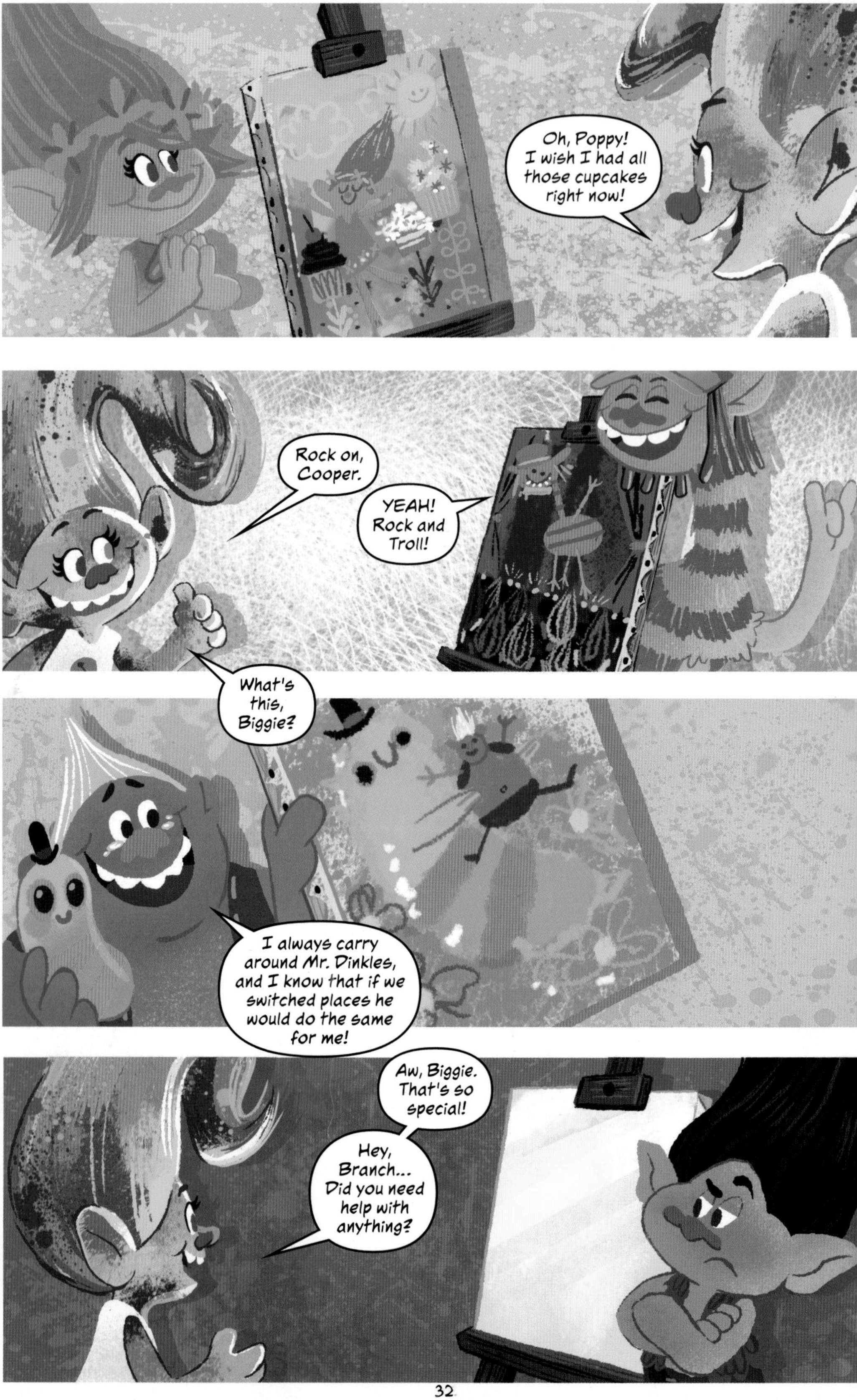

Oh, Poppy! I wish I had all those cupcakes right now!
Rock on, Cooper.
YEAH! Rock and Troll!
What's this, Biggie?
I always carry around Mr. Dinkles, and I know that if we switched places he would do the same for me!
Aw, Biggie. That's so special!
Hey, Branch... Did you need help with anything?

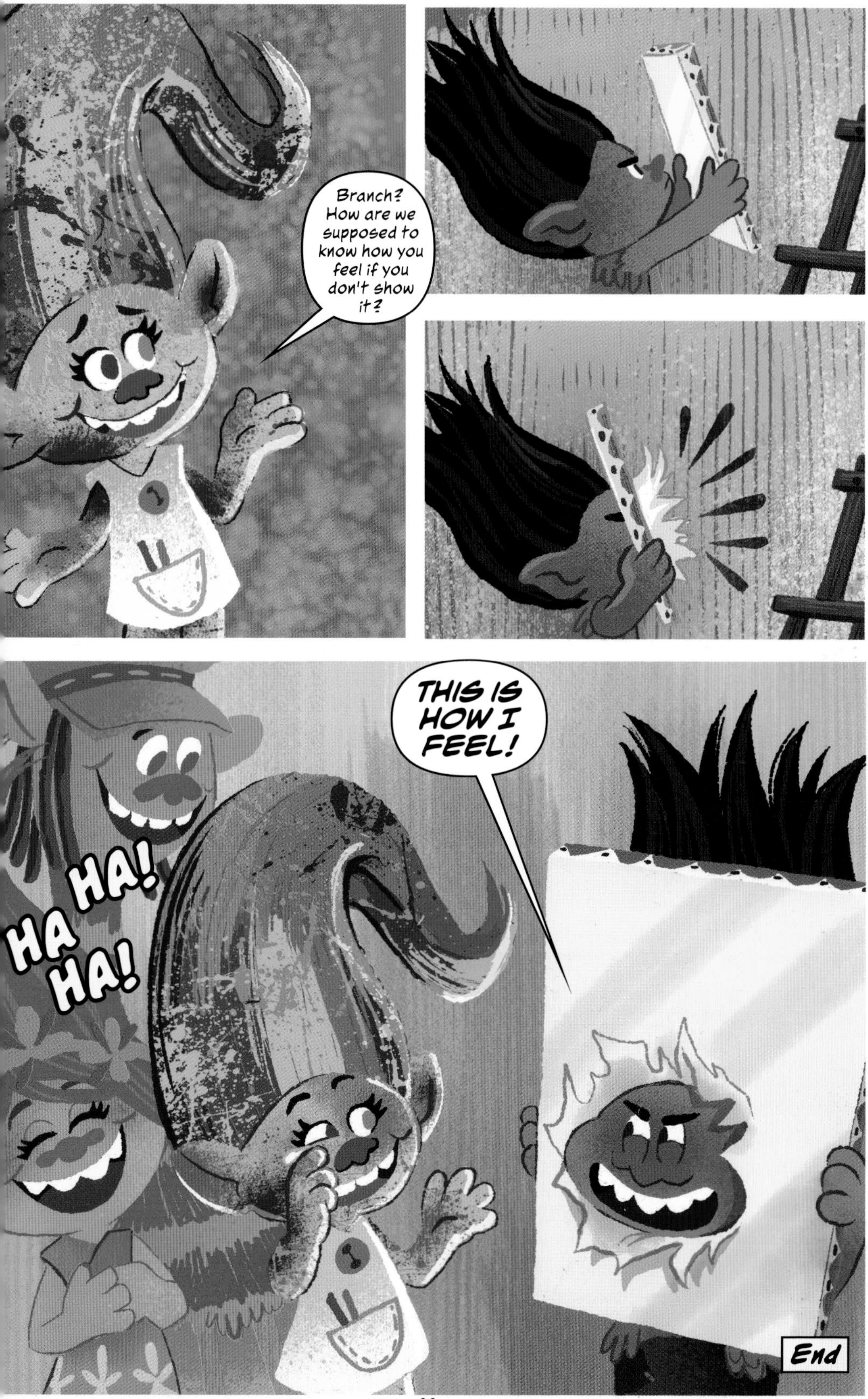

Branch? How are we supposed to know how you feel if you don't show it?
THIS IS HOW I FEEL!
HA HA! HA HA!
End

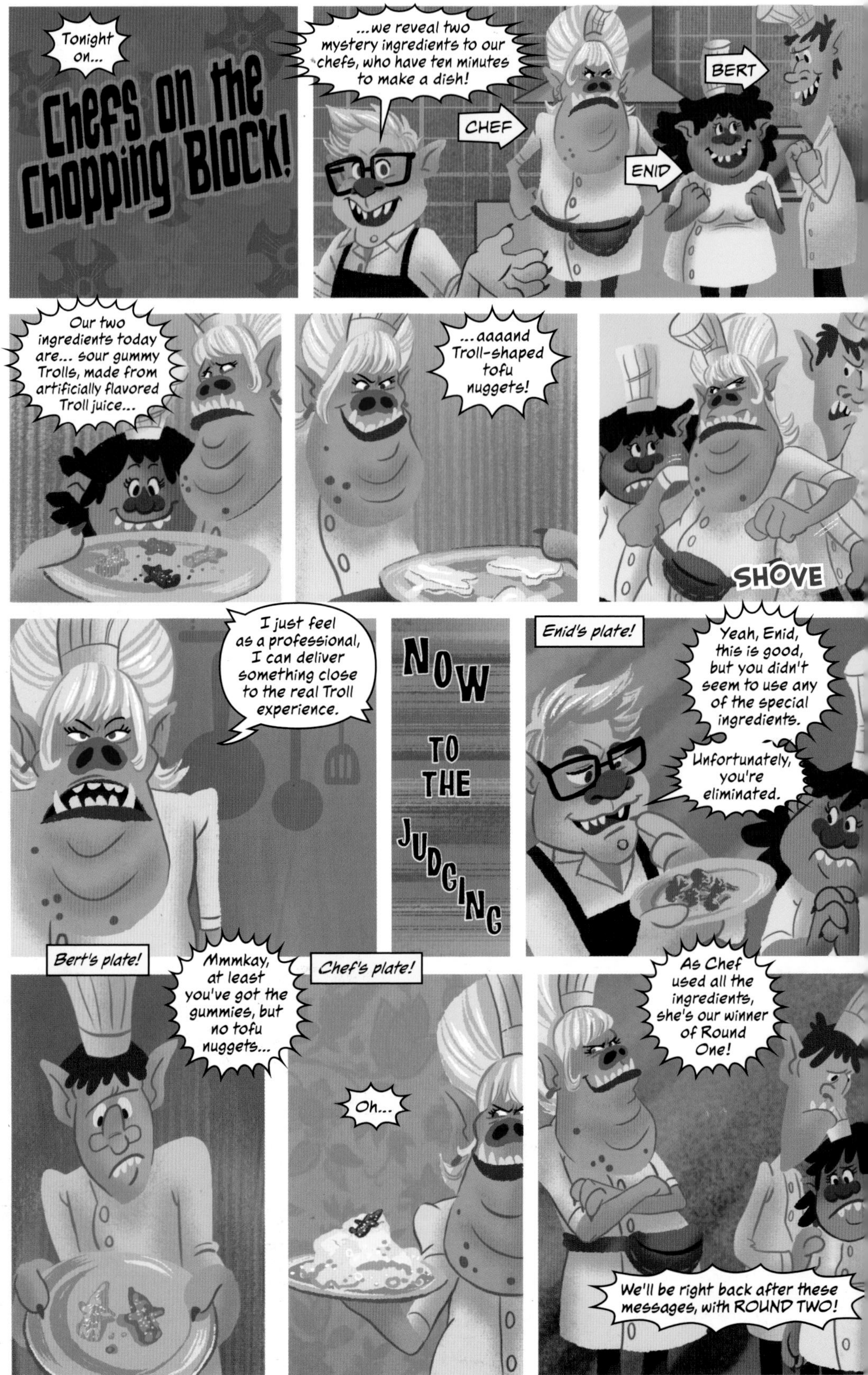

Tonight on...
Chefs on the Chopping Block!
...we reveal two mystery ingredients to our chefs, who have ten minutes to make a dish!
CHEF
BERT
ENID
Our two ingredients today are... sour gummy Trolls, made from artificially flavored Troll juice...
...aaaand Troll-shaped tofu nuggets!
SHOVE
I just feel as a professional, I can deliver something close to the real Troll experience.
NOW TO THE JUDGING
Enid's plate!
Yeah, Enid, this is good, but you didn't seem to use any of the special ingredients.
Unfortunately, you're eliminated.
Bert's plate!
Mmmkay, at least you've got the gummies, but no tofu nuggets...
Chef's plate!
Oh...
As Chef used all the ingredients, she's our winner of Round One!
We'll be right back after these messages, with ROUND TWO!

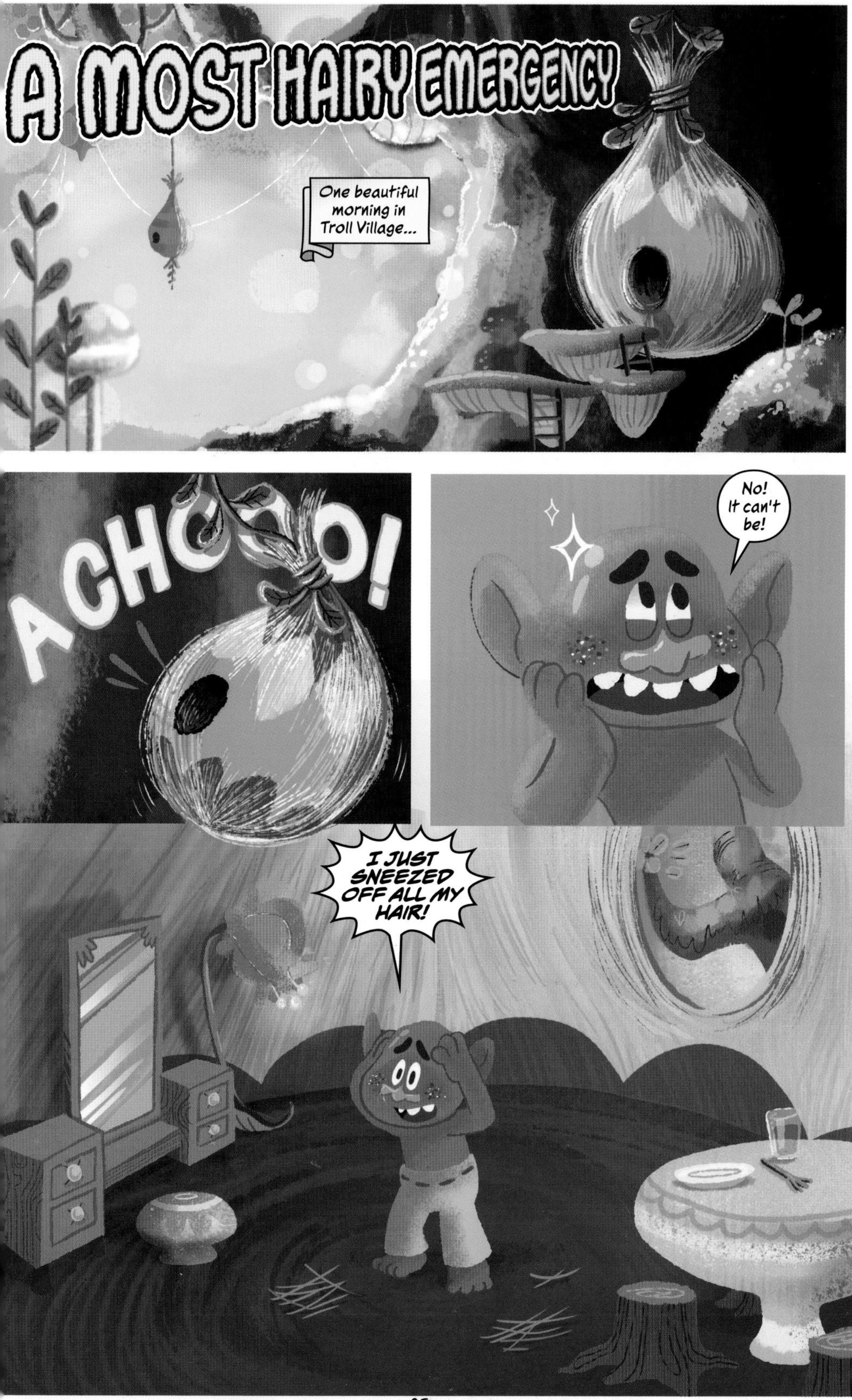
A MOST HAIRY EMERGENCY
One beautiful morning in Troll Village...
ACHOOO!
No! It can't be!
I JUST SNEEZED OFF ALL MY HAIR!

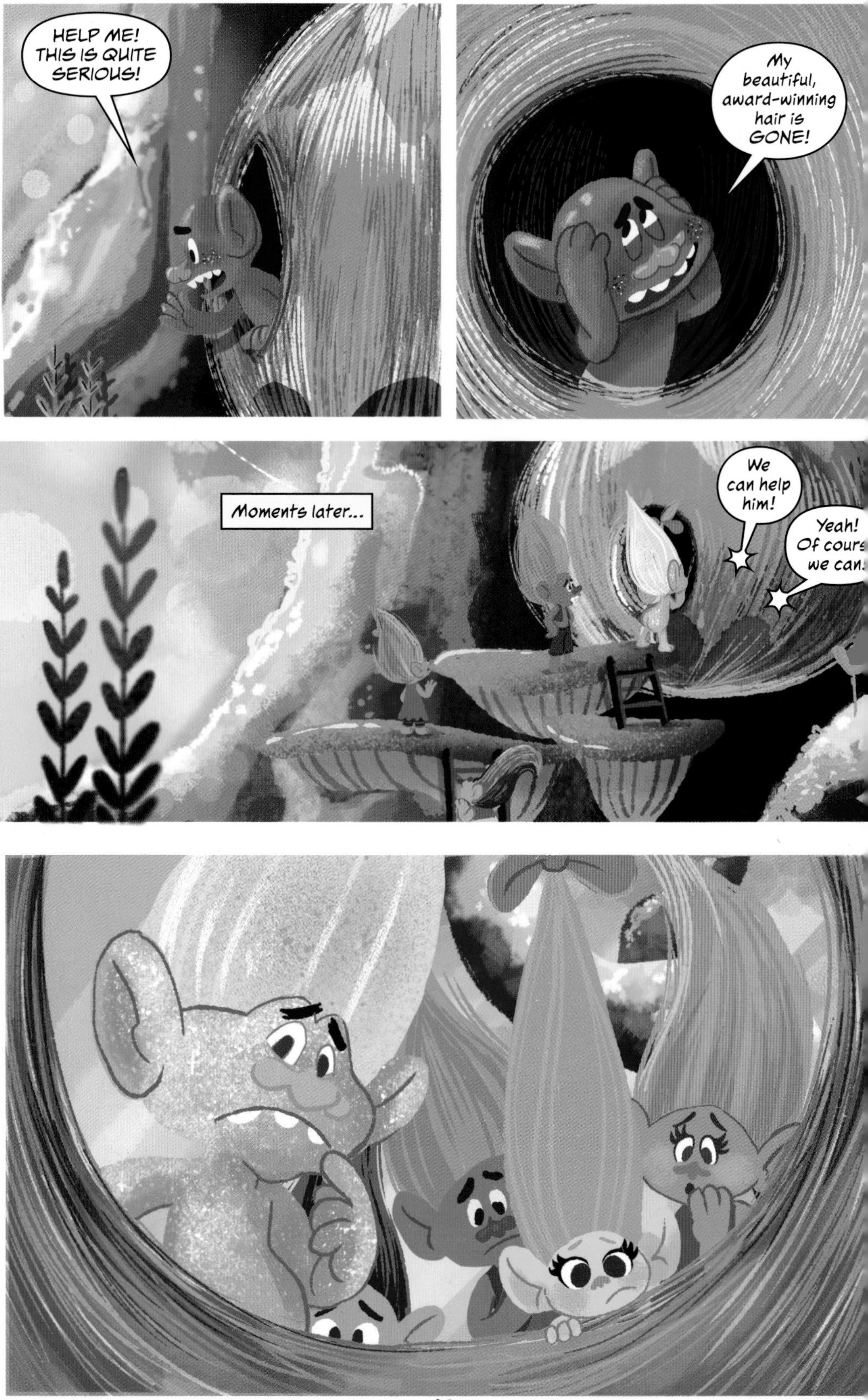
HELP ME! THIS IS QUITE SERIOUS!
My beautiful, award-winning hair is GONE!
Moments later...
We can help him!
Yeah! Of cours we can

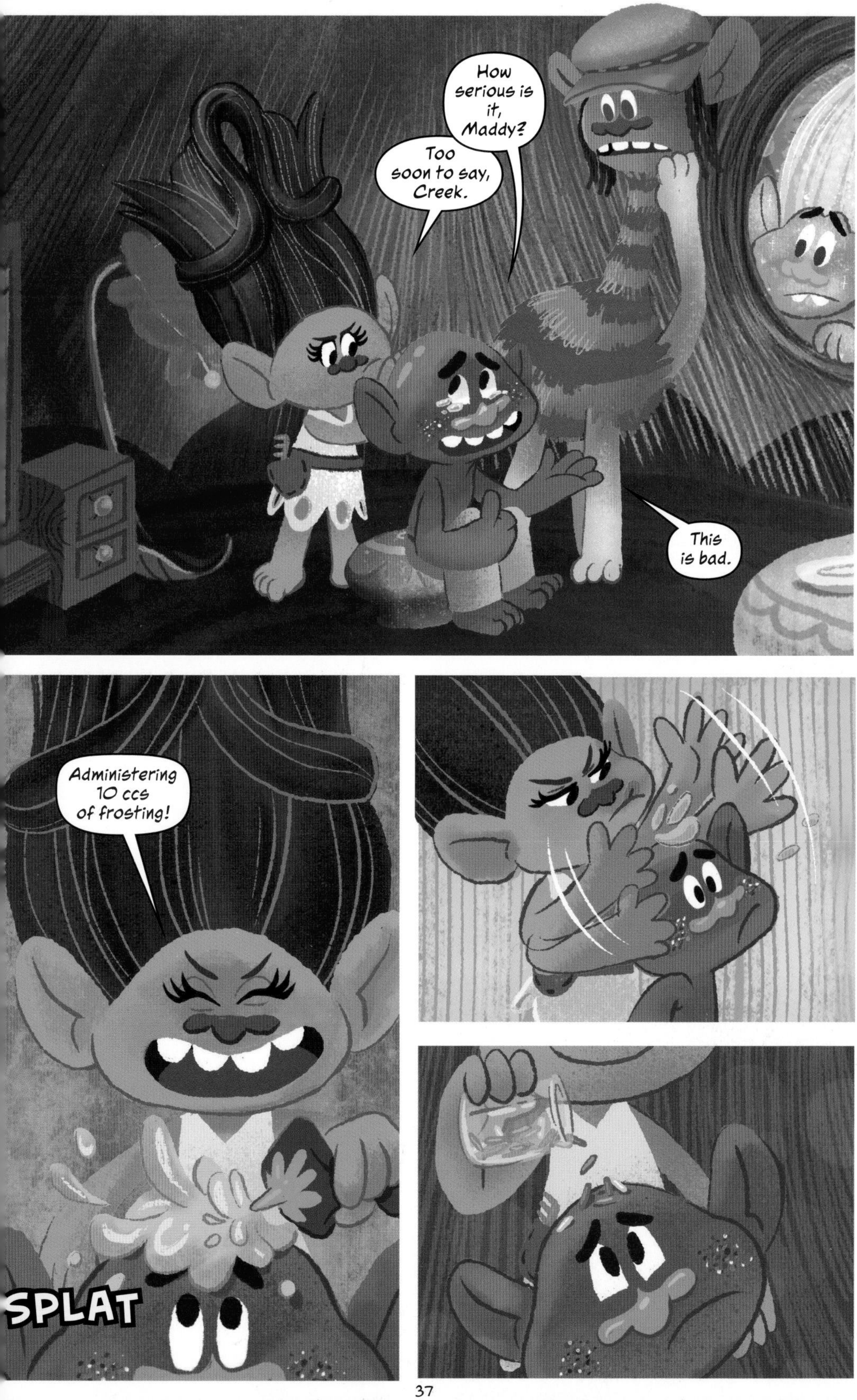
How serious is it, Maddy?
Too soon to say, Creek.
This is bad.
Administering 10 ccs of frosting!
SPLAT

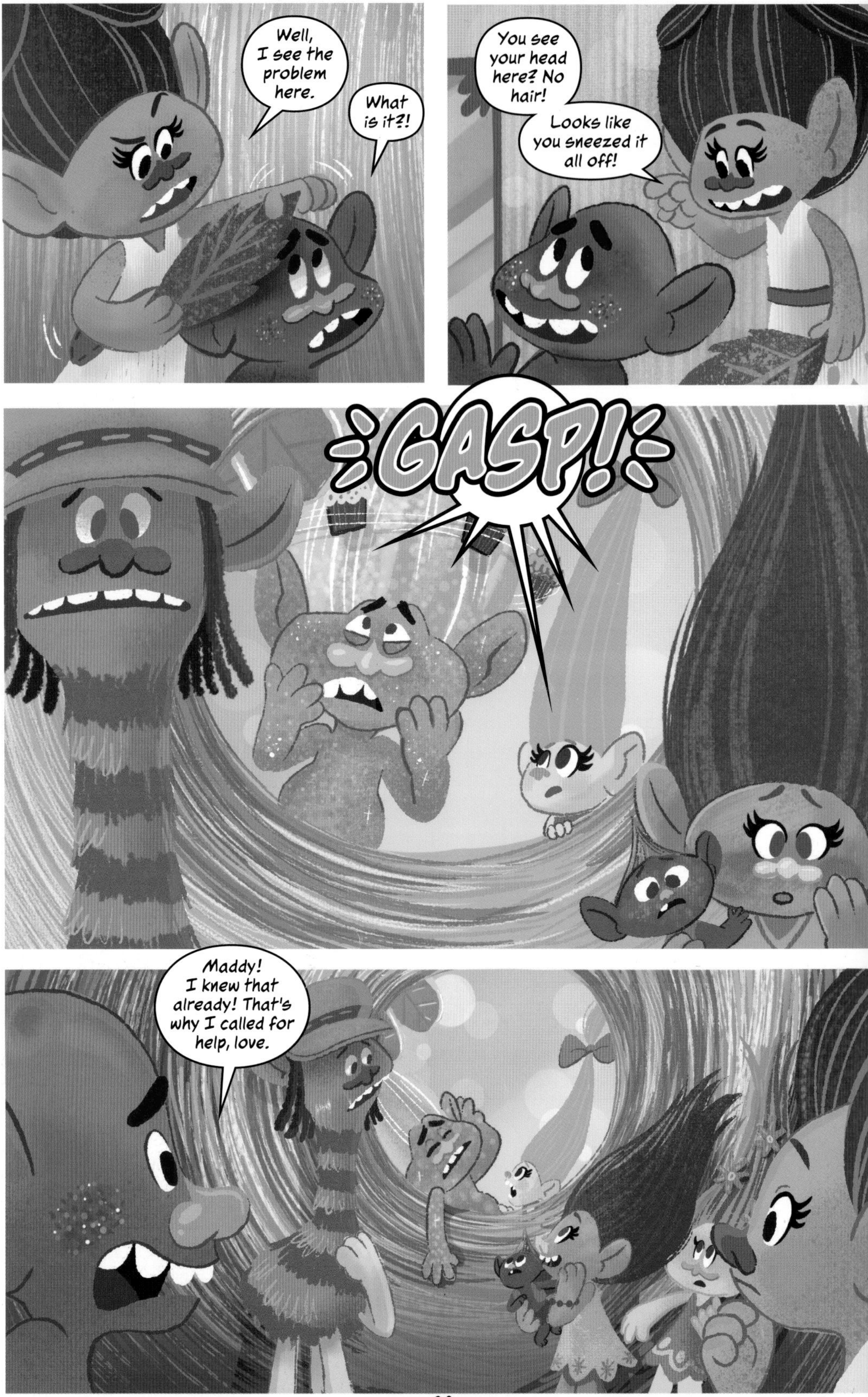
Well, I see the problem here.
What is it?!
You see your head here? No hair!
Looks like you sneezed it all off!
GASP!
Maddy! I knew that already! That's why I called for help, love.

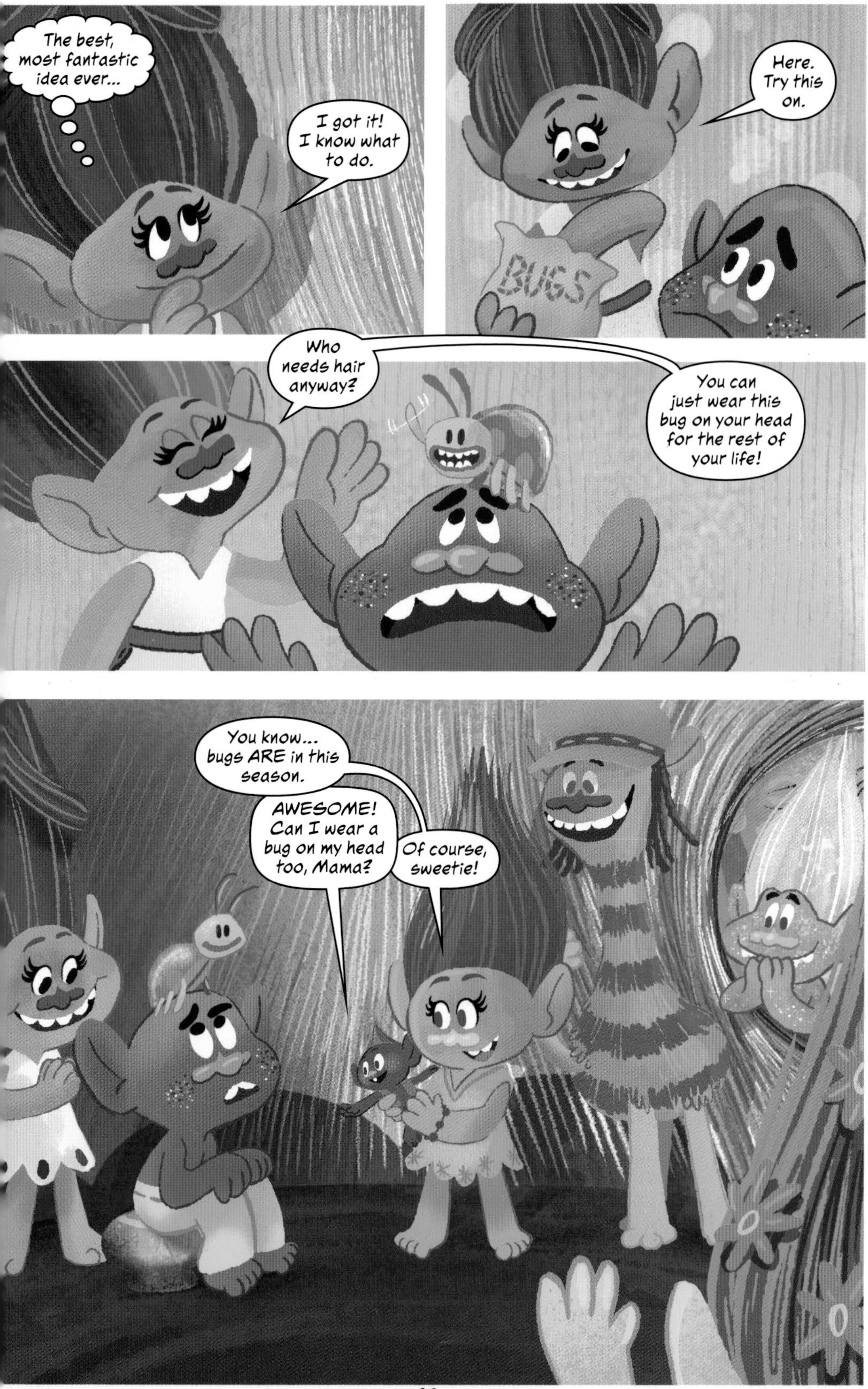
The best, most fantastic idea ever...
I got it! I know what to do.
Here. Try this on.
BUGS
Who needs hair anyway?
You can just wear this bug on your head for the rest of your life!
You know... bugs ARE in this season.
AWESOME! Can I wear a bug on my head too, Mama?
Of course, sweetie!

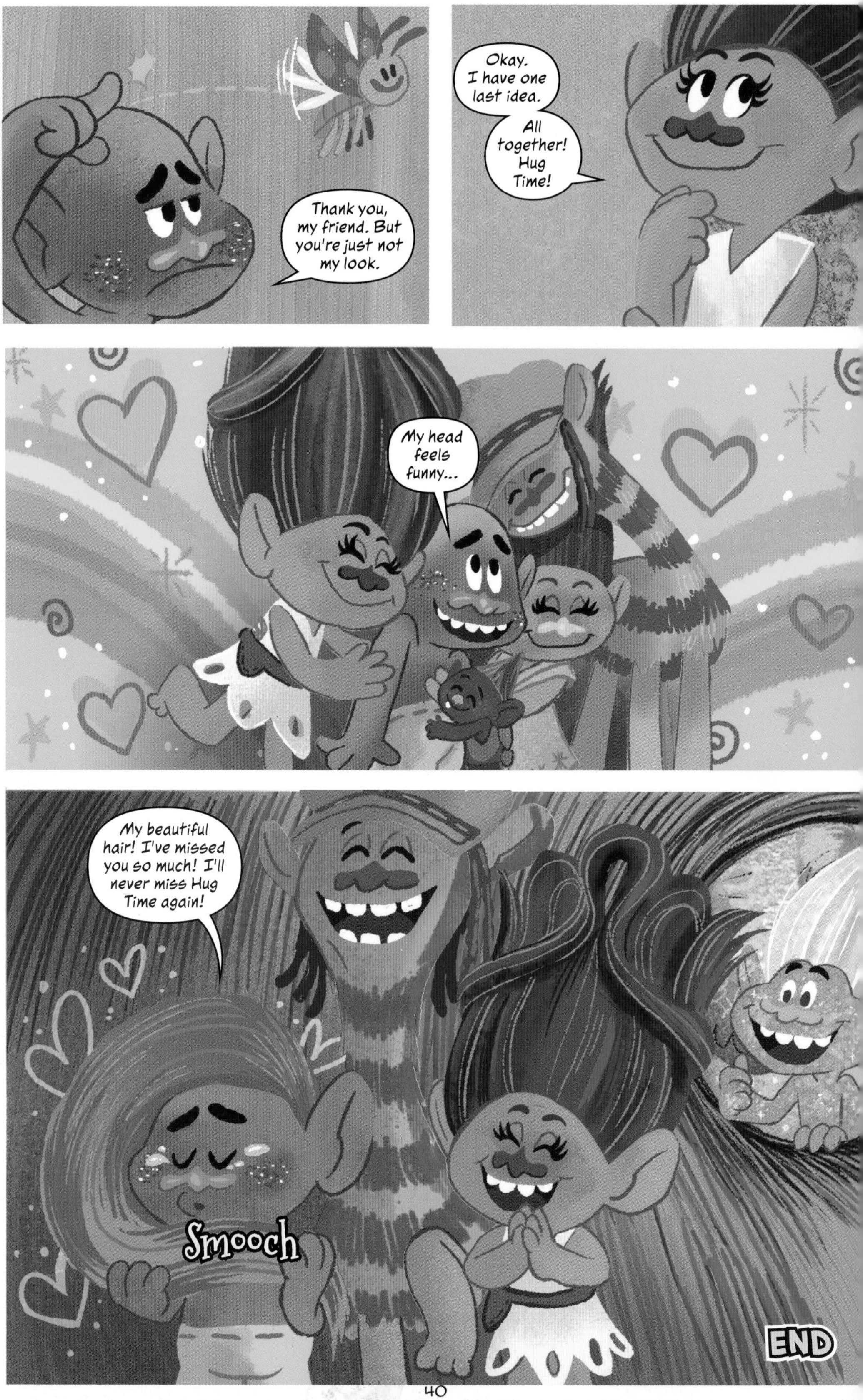
Thank you, my friend. But you're just not my look.
Okay. I have one last idea.
All together! Hug Time!
My head feels funny...
My beautiful hair! I've missed you so much! I'll never miss Hug Time again!
Smooch
END

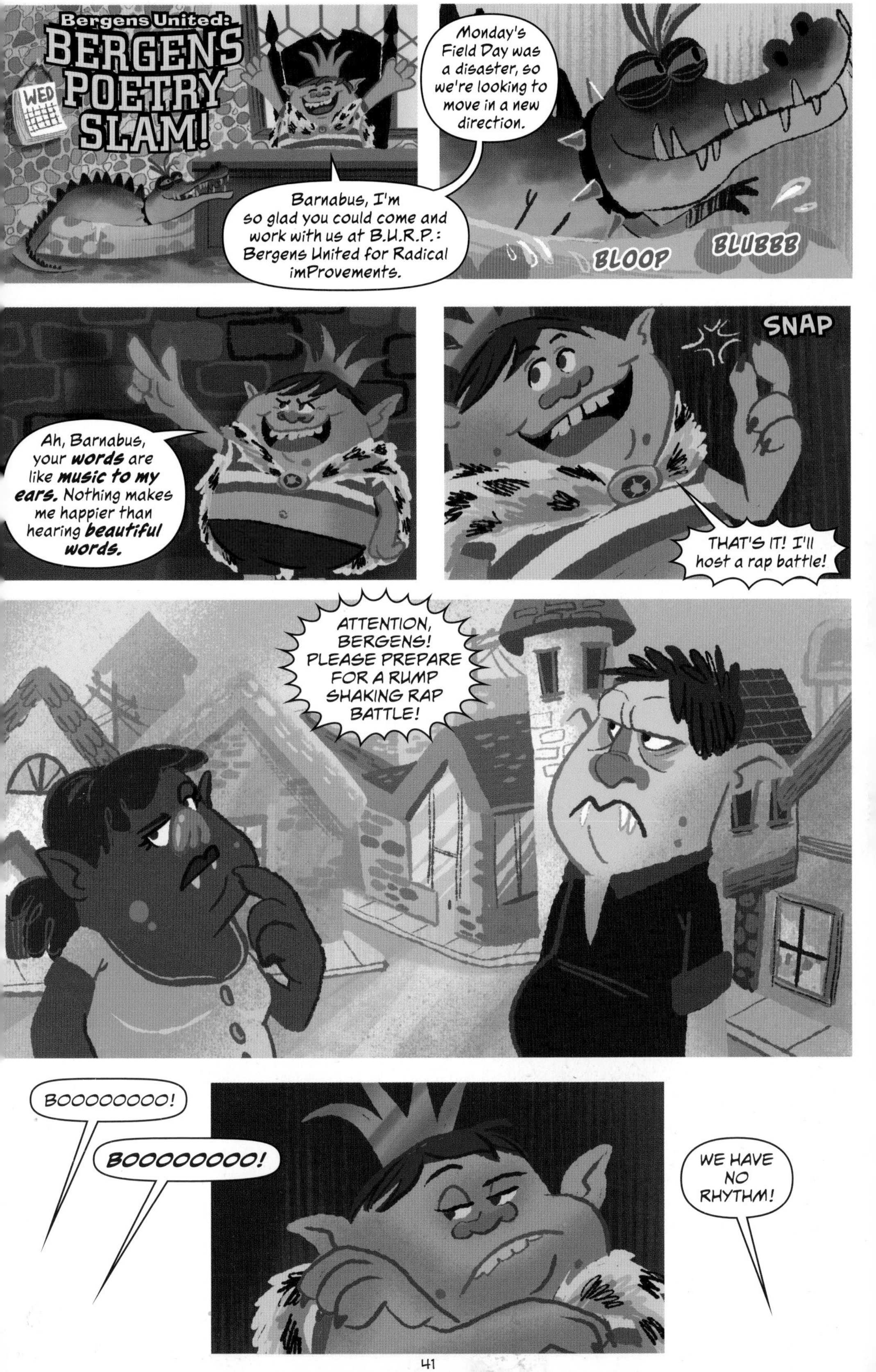
Bergens United:
BERGENS POETRY SLAM!
WED
Barnabus, I'm so glad you could come and work with us at B.U.R.P.: Bergens United for Radical imProvements.
Monday's Field Day was a disaster, so we're looking to move in a new direction.
BLOOP
BLUBBB
Ah, Barnabus, your **words** are like **music to my ears.** Nothing makes me happier than hearing **beautiful words.**
SNAP
THAT'S IT! I'll host a rap battle!
ATTENTION, BERGENS! PLEASE PREPARE FOR A RUMP SHAKING RAP BATTLE!
BOOOOOOOO!
BOOOOOOOO!
WE HAVE NO RHYTHM!

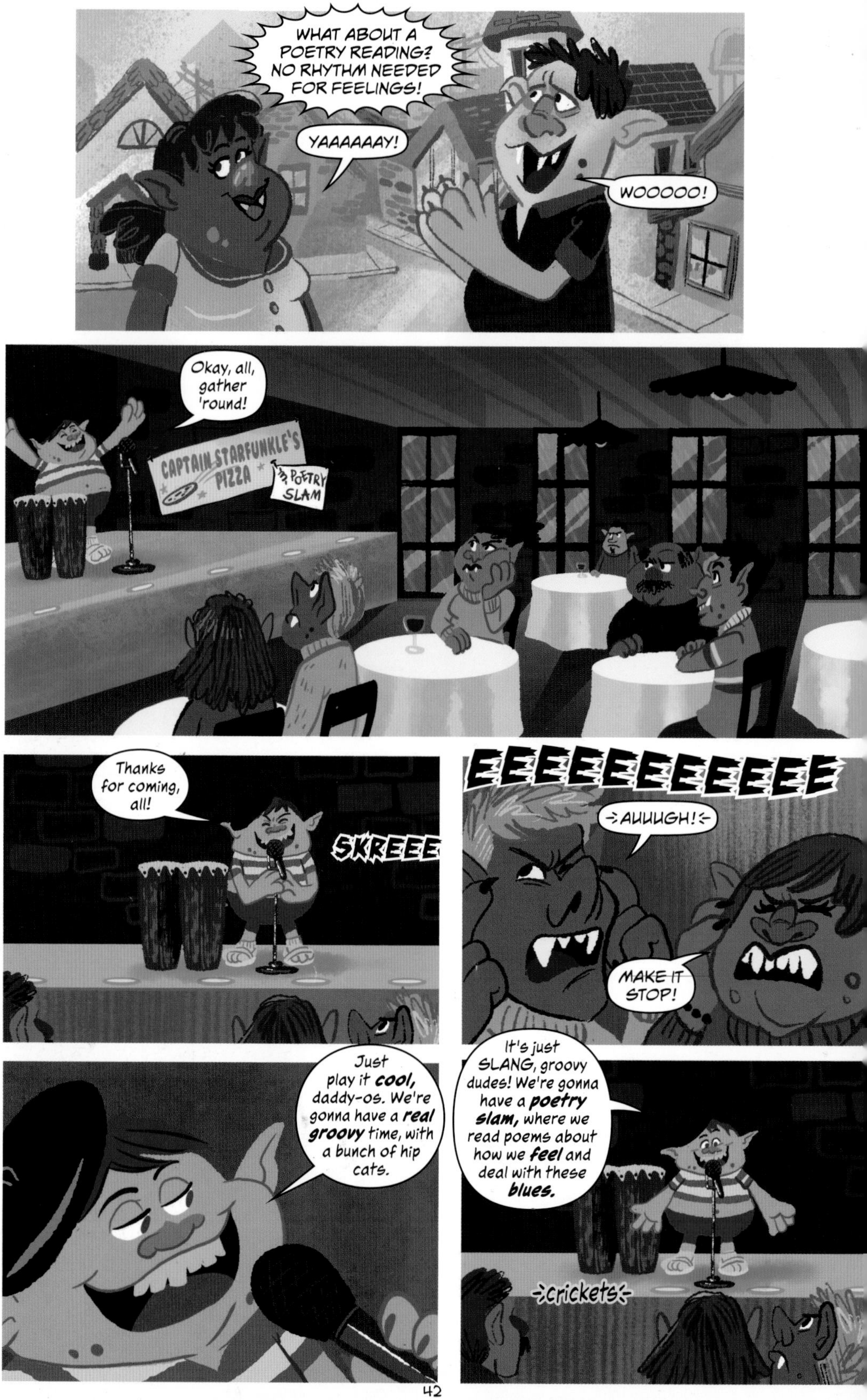
WHAT ABOUT A POETRY READING? NO RHYTHM NEEDED FOR FEELINGS!
YAAAAAAY!
WOOOOO!
Okay, all, gather 'round!
CAPTAIN STARFUNKLE'S PIZZA
POETRY SLAM
Thanks for coming, all!
SKREEE
EEEEEEEEEEEE
AUUUGH!
MAKE IT STOP!
Just play it **cool,** daddy-os. We're gonna have a **real groovy** time, with a bunch of hip cats.
It's just SLANG, groovy dudes! We're gonna have a **poetry slam,** where we read poems about how we **feel** and deal with these **blues.**
crickets

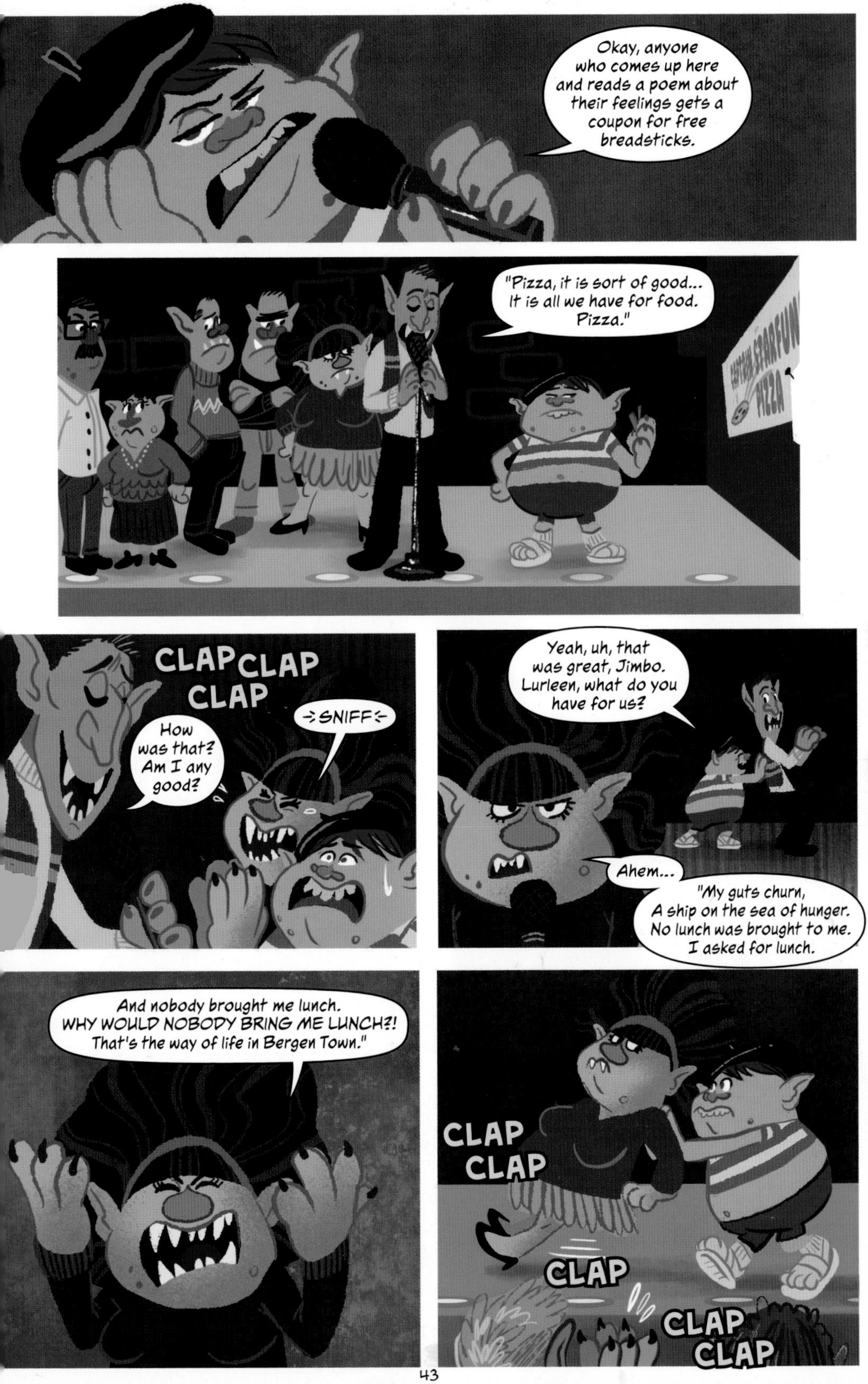

Okay, anyone who comes up here and reads a poem about their feelings gets a coupon for free breadsticks.
"Pizza, it is sort of good... It is all we have for food. Pizza."
CLAP CLAP CLAP
How was that? Am I any good?
SNIFF
Yeah, uh, that was great, Jimbo. Lurleen, what do you have for us?
Ahem...
"My guts churn, A ship on the sea of hunger. No lunch was brought to me. I asked for lunch.
And nobody brought me lunch. WHY WOULD NOBODY BRING ME LUNCH?! That's the way of life in Bergen Town."
CLAP CLAP
CLAP
CLAP CLAP

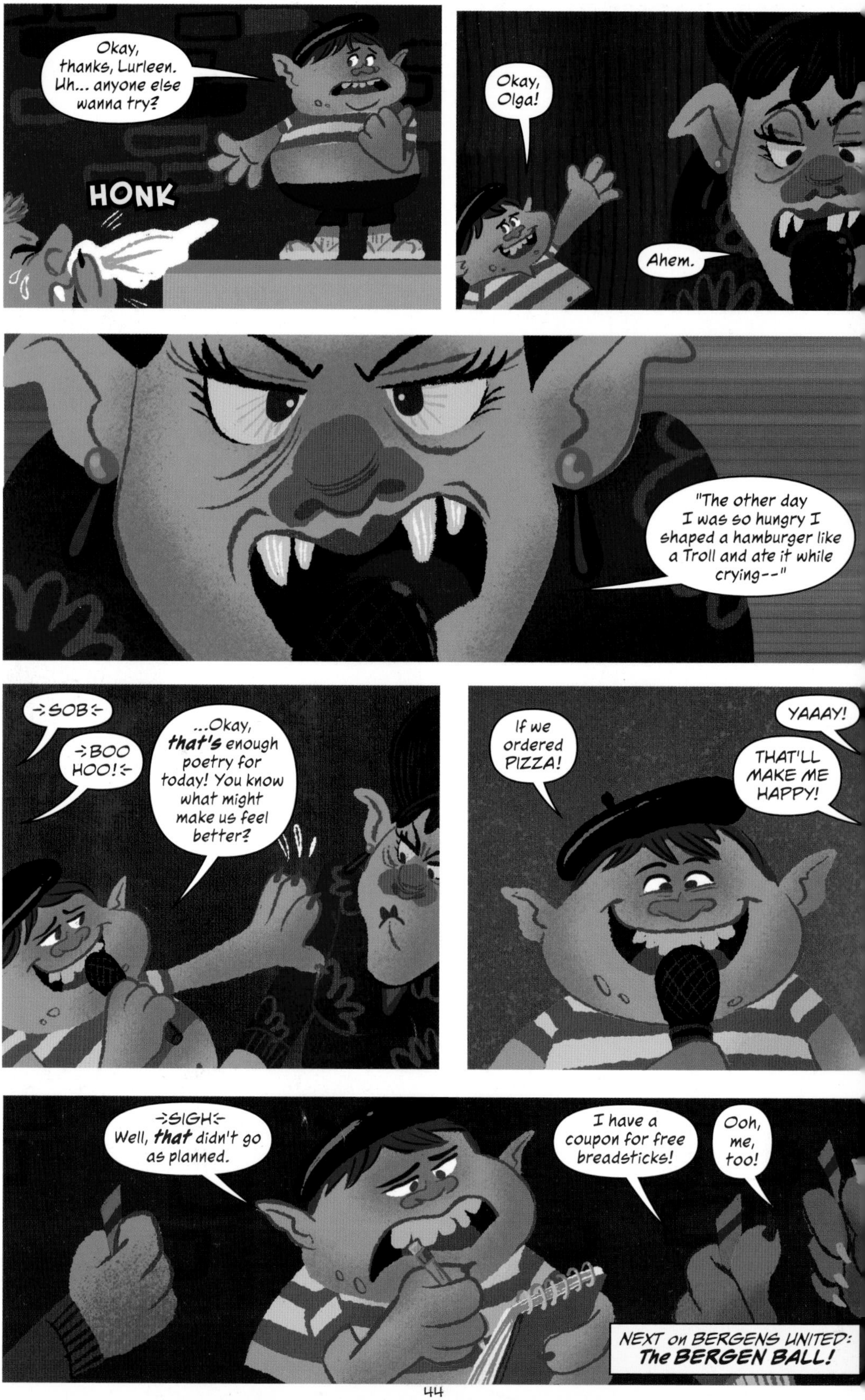
Okay, thanks, Lurleen. Uh... anyone else wanna try?
HONK
Okay, Olga!
Ahem.
"The other day I was so hungry I shaped a hamburger like a Troll and ate it while crying--"
SOB
BOO HOO!
...Okay, that's enough poetry for today! You know what might make us feel better?
If we ordered PIZZA!
YAAAY!
THAT'LL MAKE ME HAPPY!
SIGH
Well, that didn't go as planned.
I have a coupon for free breadsticks!
Ooh, me, too!
NEXT on BERGENS UNITED: The BERGEN BALL!

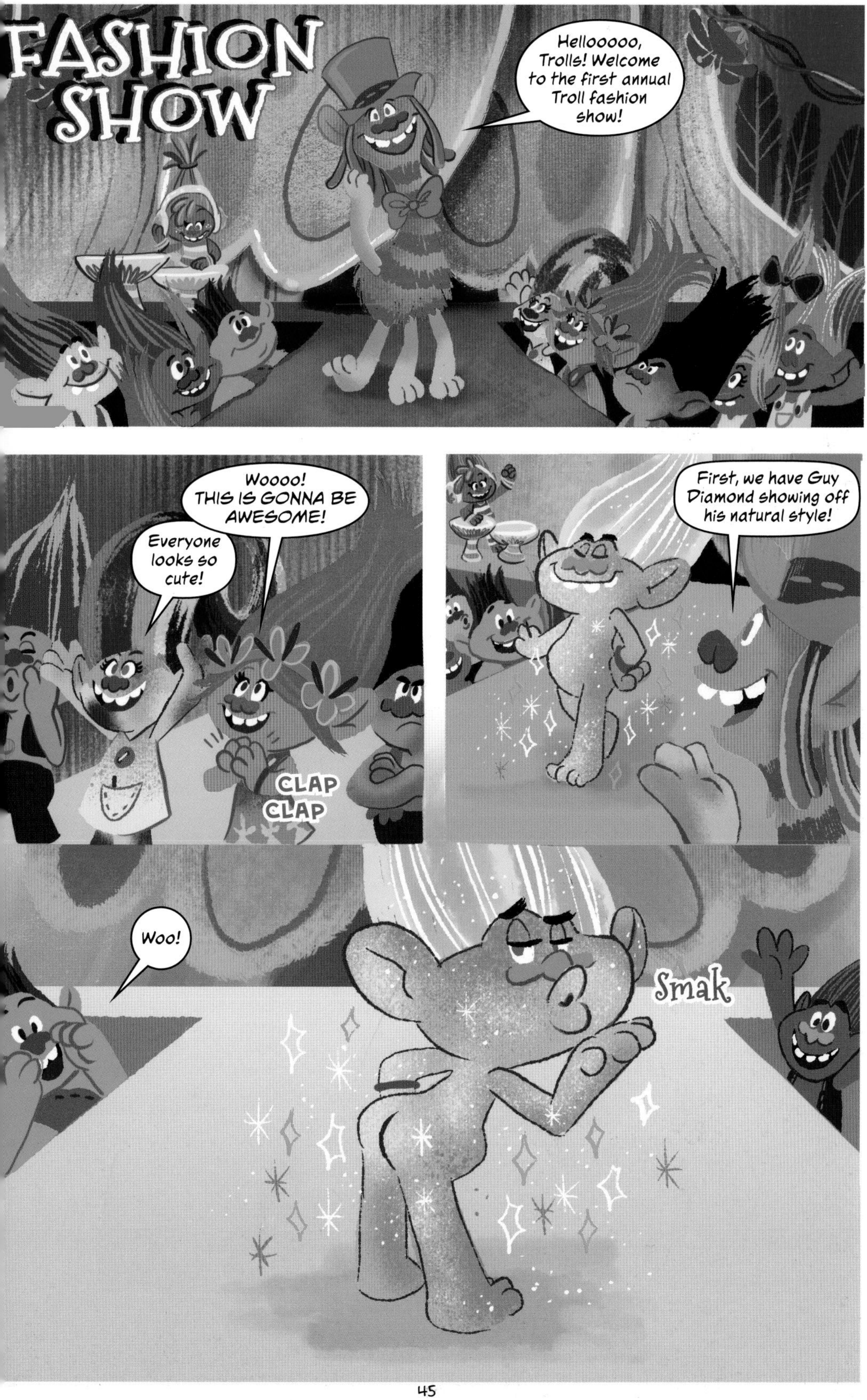
FASHION SHOW
Hellooooo, Trolls! Welcome to the first annual Troll fashion show!
Woooo! THIS IS GONNA BE AWESOME!
Everyone looks so cute!
CLAP CLAP
First, we have Guy Diamond showing off his natural style!
Woo!
Smak

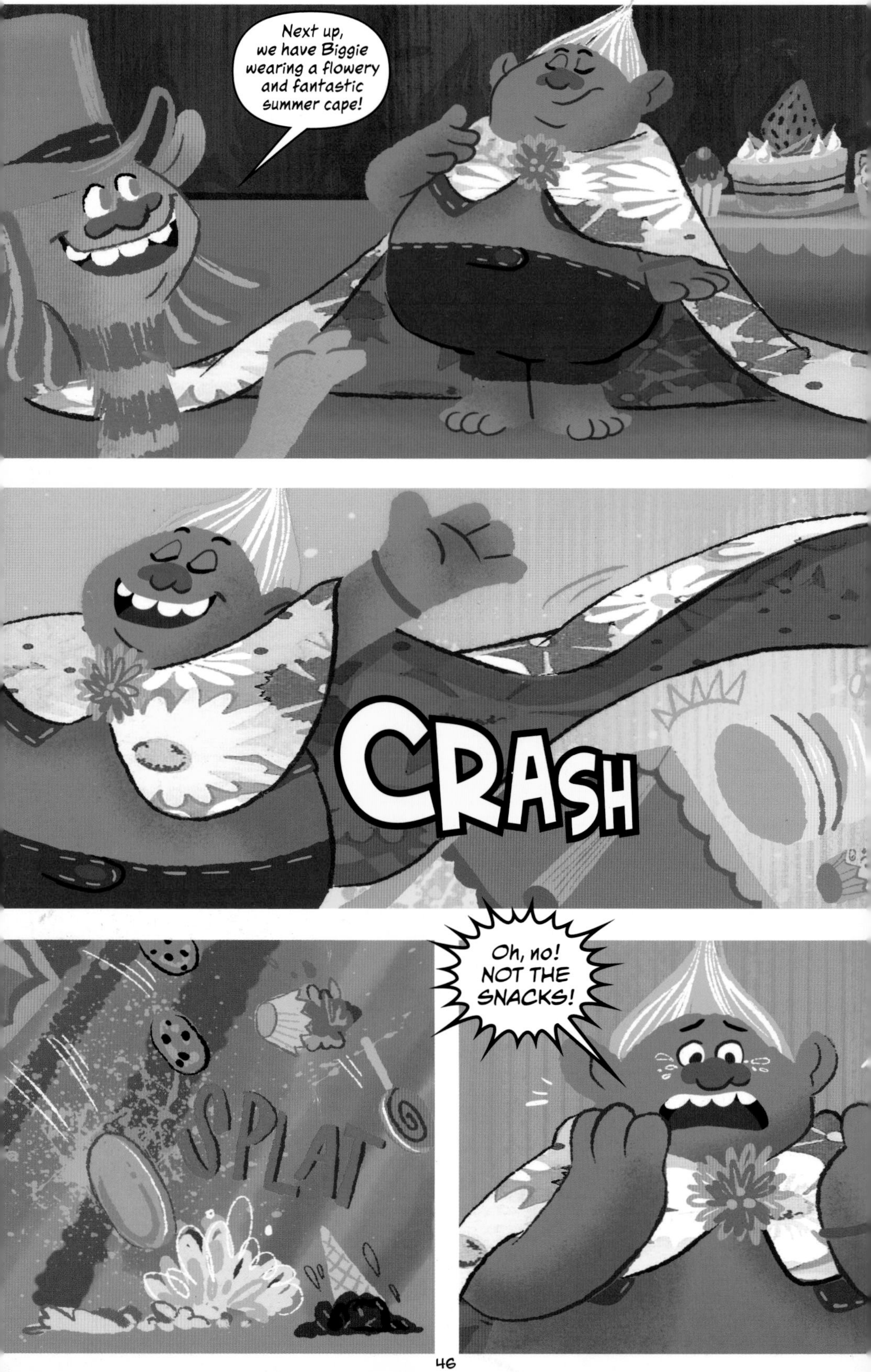
Next up, we have Biggie wearing a flowery and fantastic summer cape!
CRASH
SPLAT
Oh, no! NOT THE SNACKS!

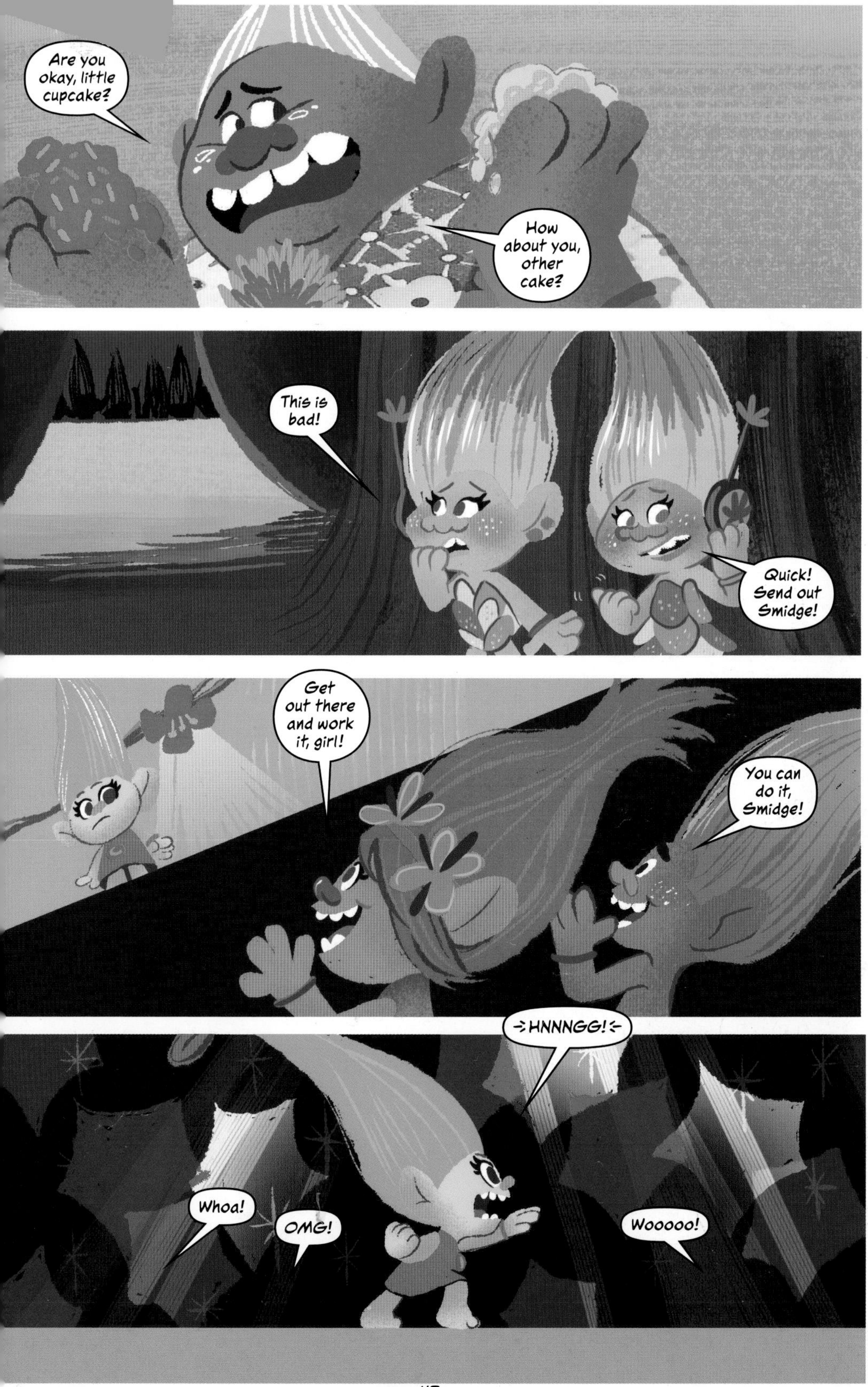
Are you okay, little cupcake?
How about you, other cake?
This is bad!
Quick! Send out Smidge!
Get out there and work it, girl!
You can do it, Smidge!
HNNNGG!
Whoa!
OMG!
Wooooo!

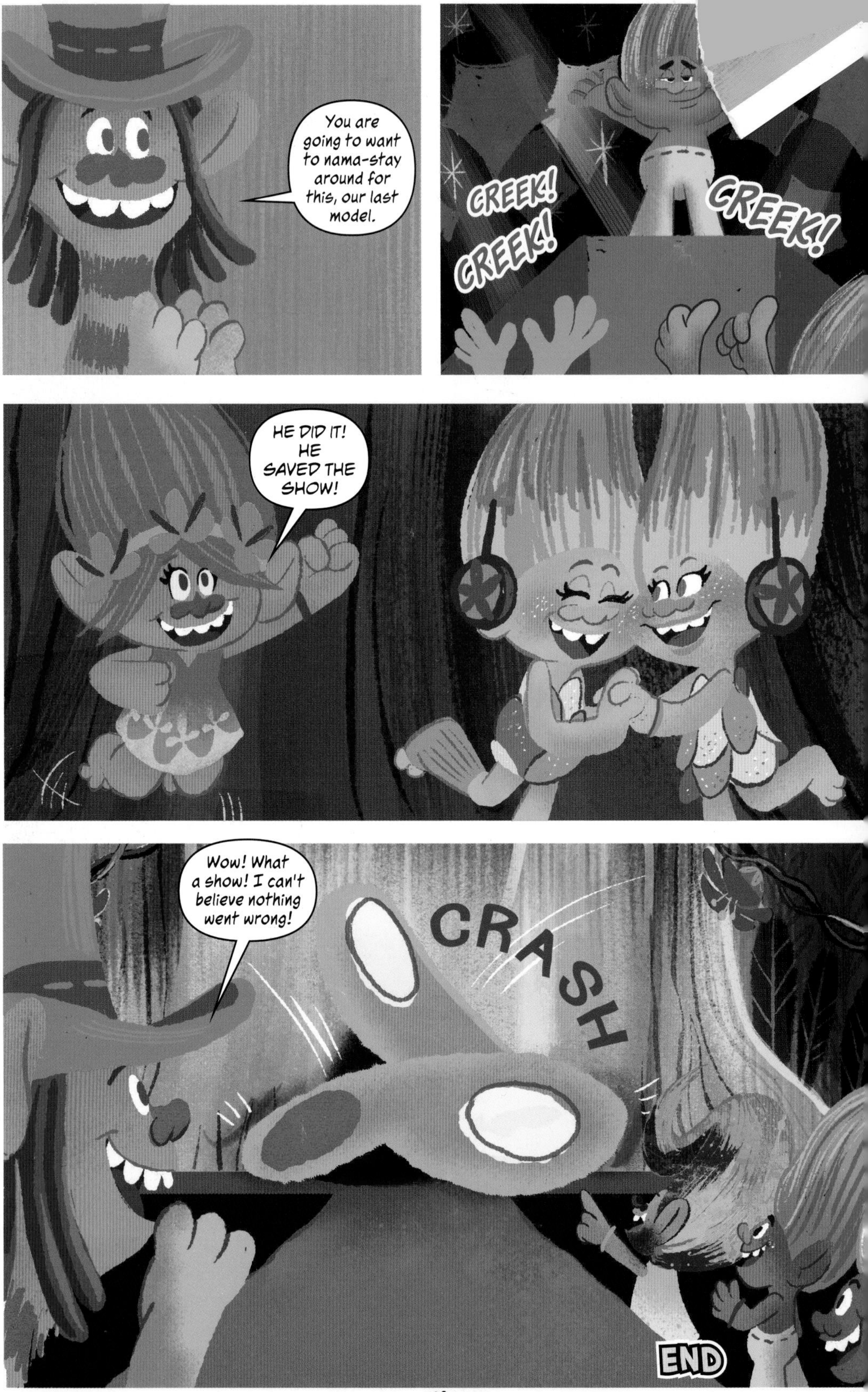
You are going to want to nama-stay around for this, our last model.
CREEK!
CREEK!
CREEK!
HE DID IT! HE SAVED THE SHOW!
Wow! What a show! I can't believe nothing went wrong!
CRASH
END

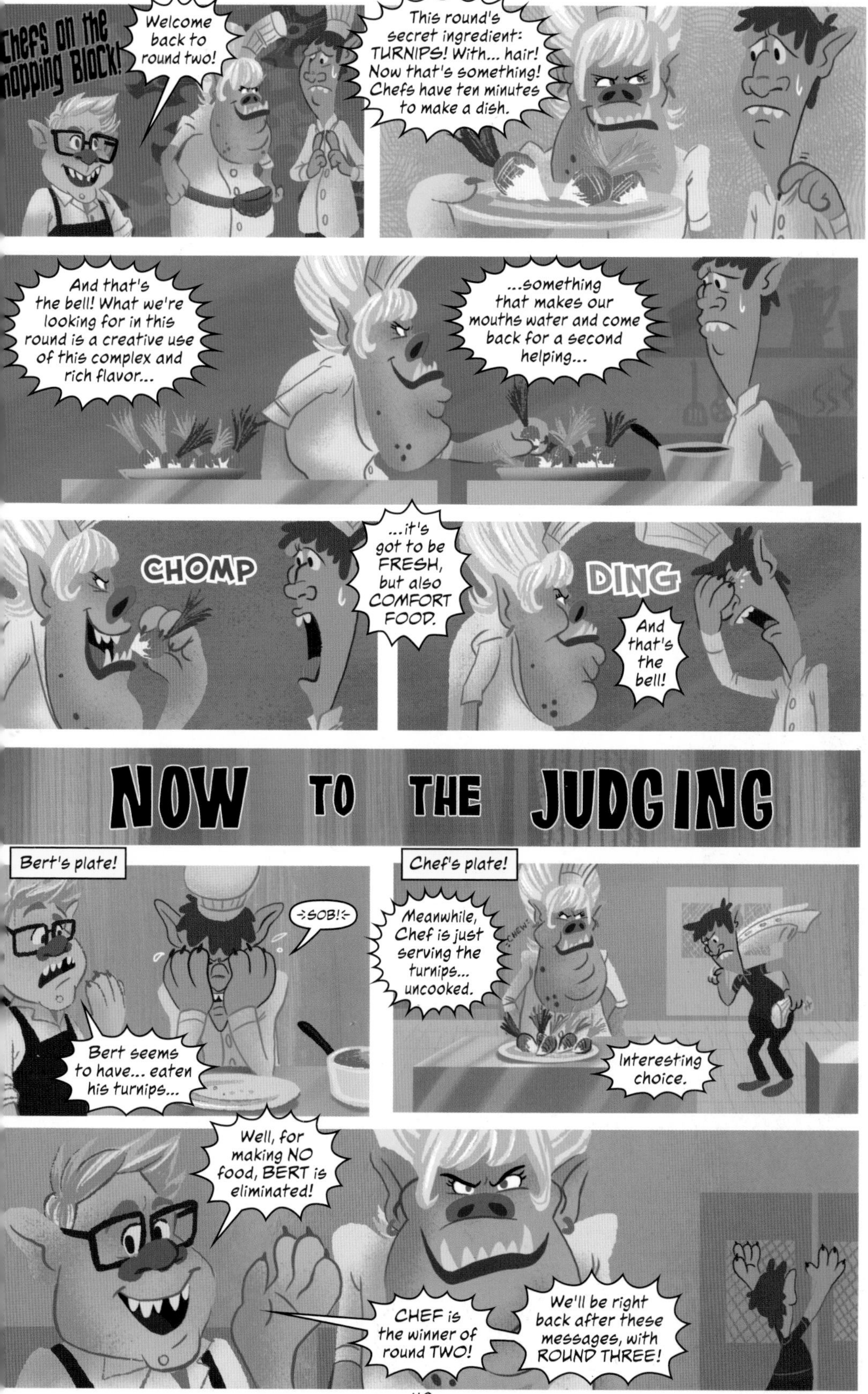
Chefs on the
hopping Block!
Welcome back to round two!
This round's secret ingredient: TURNIPS! With... hair! Now that's something! Chefs have ten minutes to make a dish.
And that's the bell! What we're looking for in this round is a creative use of this complex and rich flavor...
...something that makes our mouths water and come back for a second helping...
CHOMP
...it's got to be FRESH, but also COMFORT FOOD.
DING
And that's the bell!
NOW TO THE JUDGING
Bert's plate!
SOB!
Bert seems to have... eaten his turnips...
Chef's plate!
Meanwhile, Chef is just serving the turnips... uncooked.
Interesting choice.
Well, for making NO food, BERT is eliminated!
CHEF is the winner of round TWO!
We'll be right back after these messages, with ROUND THREE!

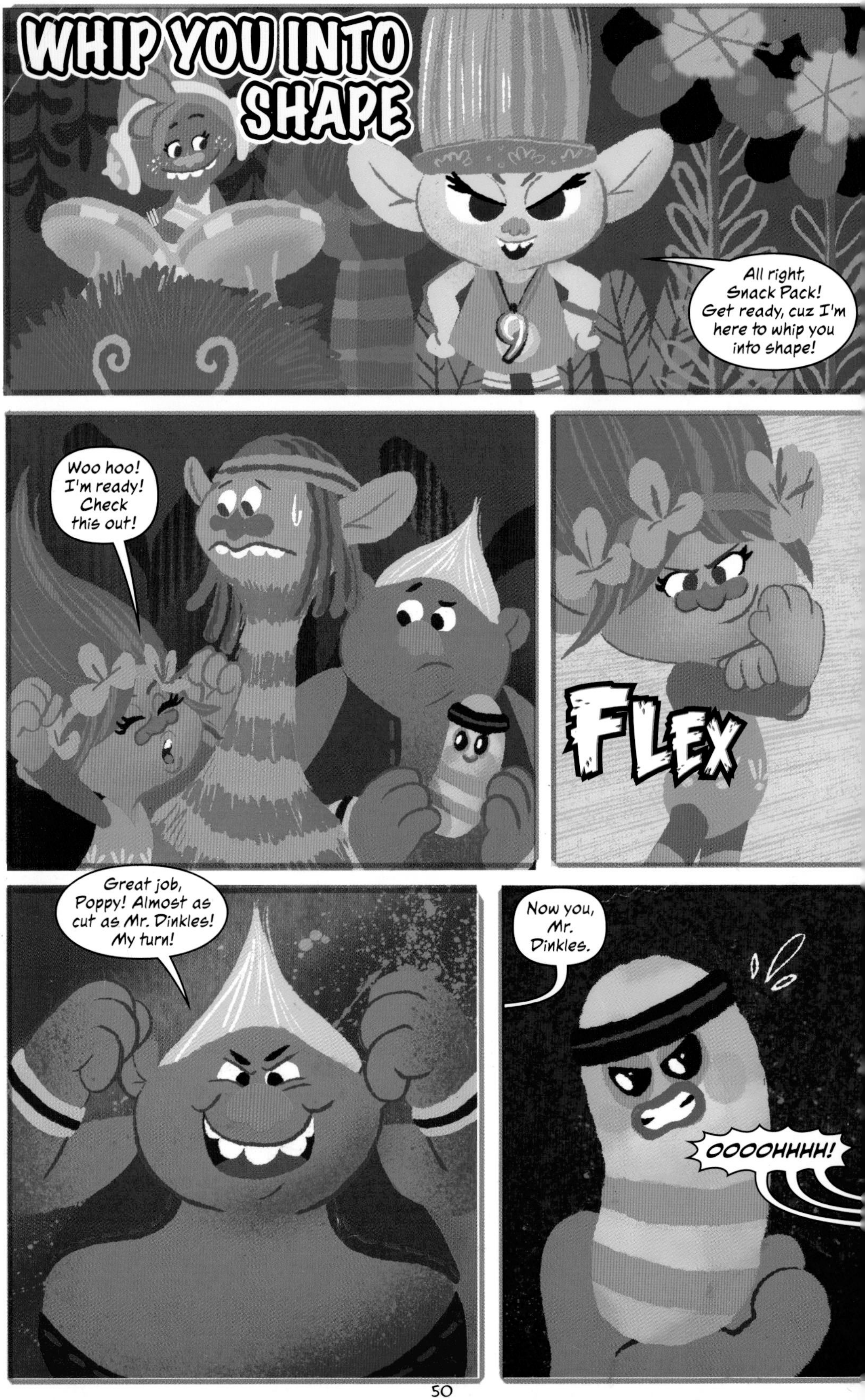
WHIP YOU INTO SHAPE
All right, Snack Pack! Get ready, cuz I'm here to whip you into shape!
Woo hoo! I'm ready! Check this out!
FLEX
Great job, Poppy! Almost as cut as Mr. Dinkles! My turn!
Now you, Mr. Dinkles.
OOOOHHHH!

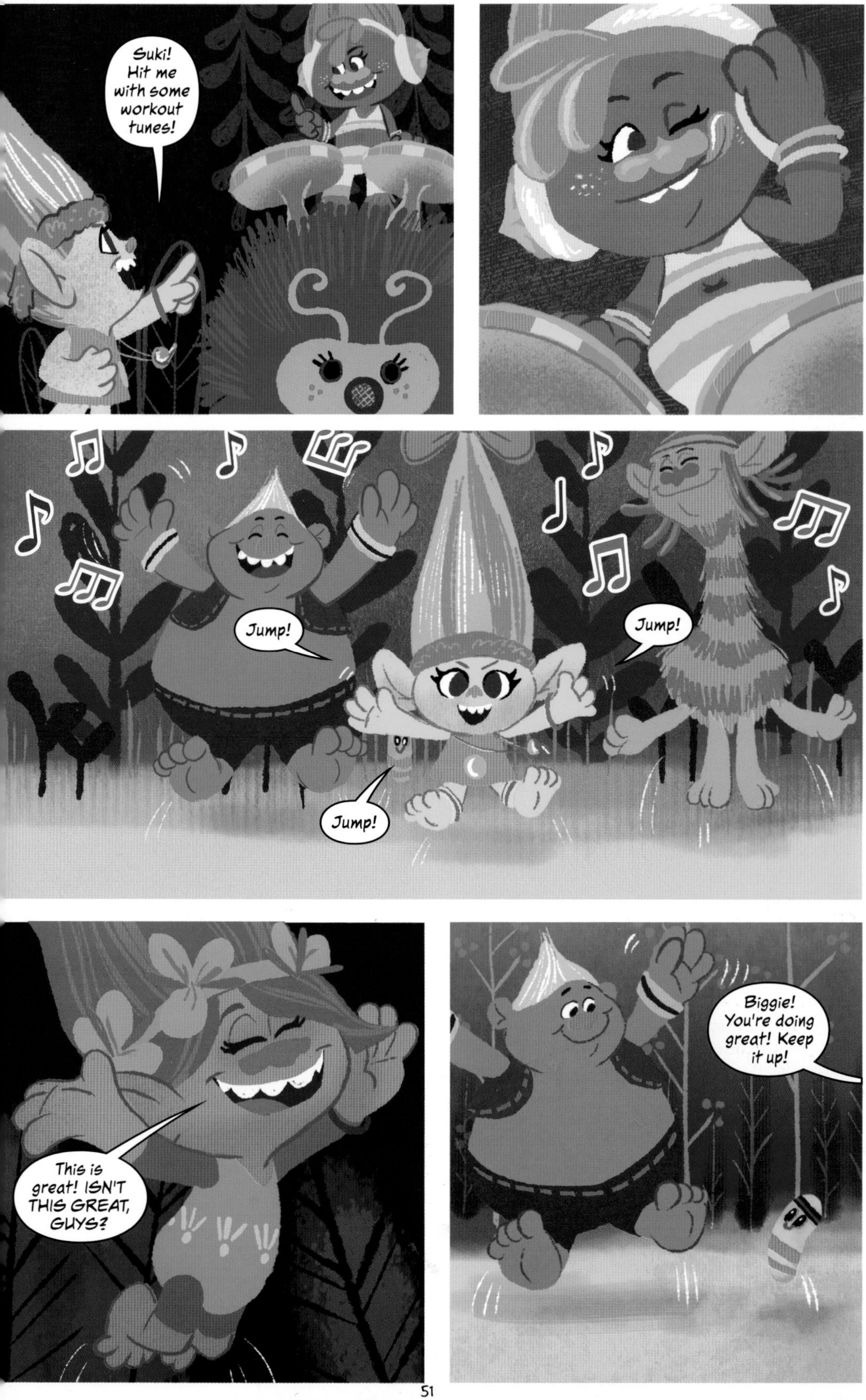
Suki! Hit me with some workout tunes!
Jump!
Jump!
Jump!
This is great! ISN'T THIS GREAT, GUYS?
Biggie! You're doing great! Keep it up!

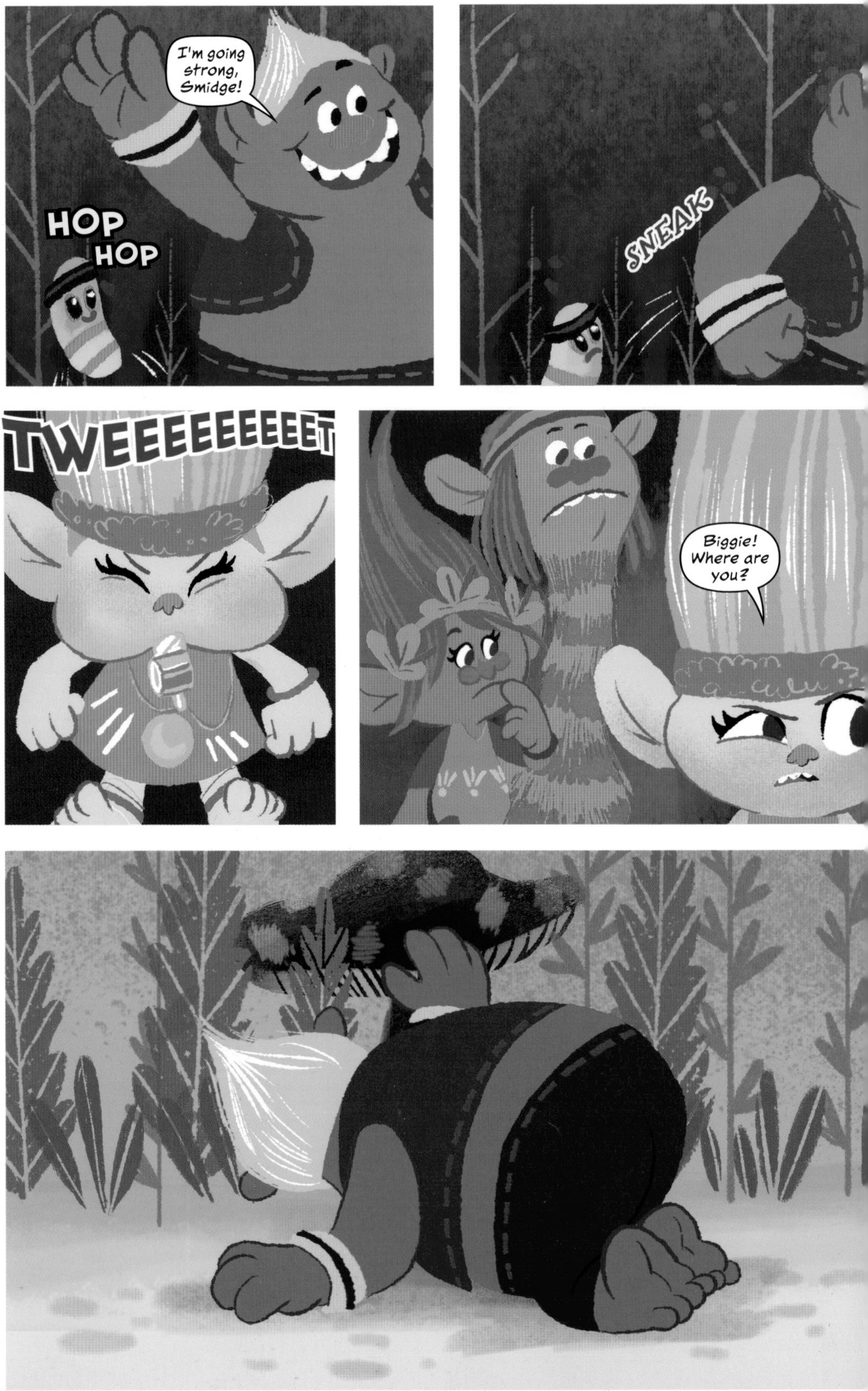
I'm going strong, Smidge!
HOP HOP
SNEAK
TWEEEEEEEEET
Biggie! Where are you?

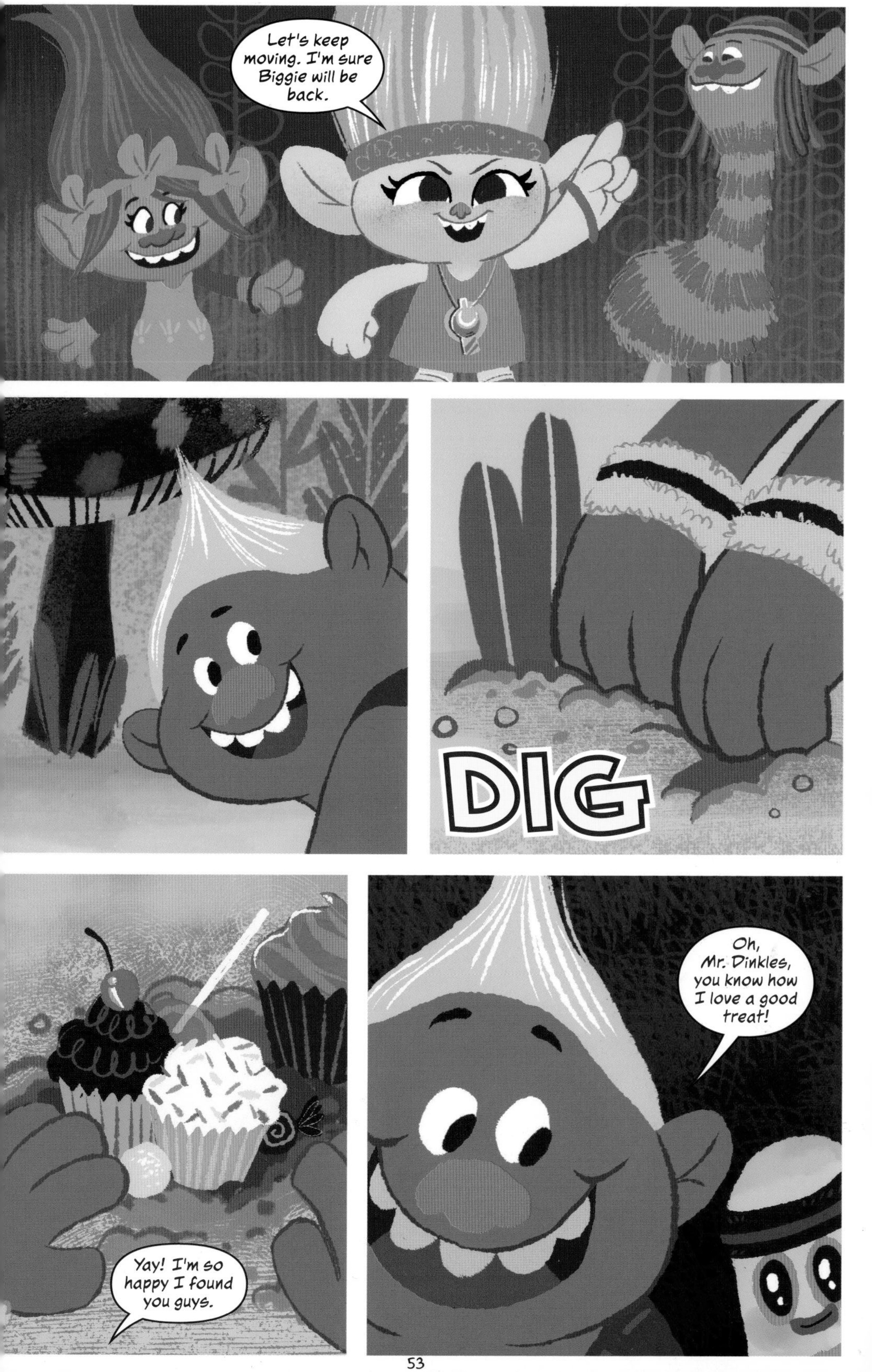
Let's keep moving. I'm sure Biggie will be back.
DIG
Yay! I'm so happy I found you guys.
Oh, Mr. Dinkles, you know how I love a good treat!

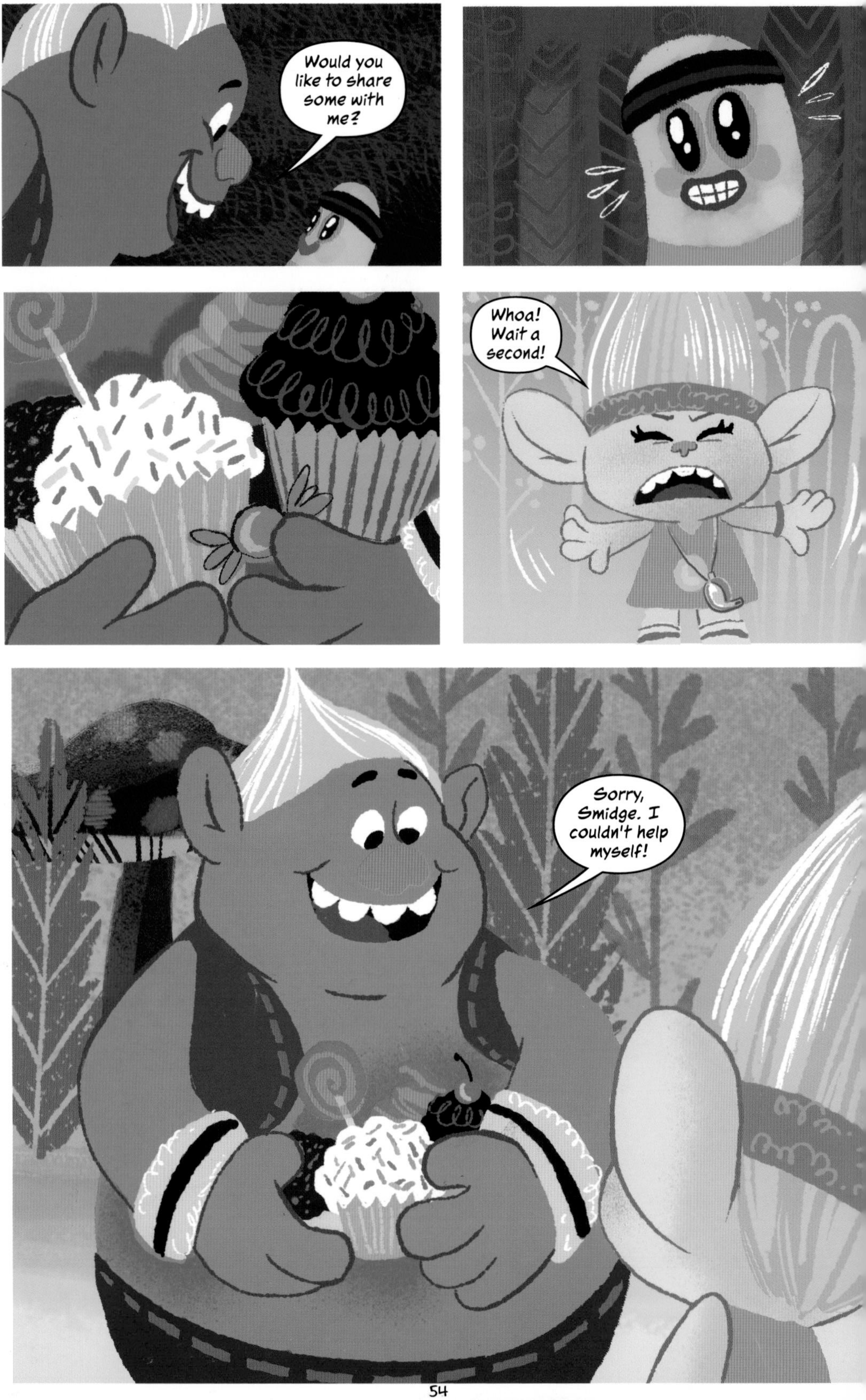
Would you like to share some with me?
Whoa! Wait a second!
Sorry, Smidge. I couldn't help myself!

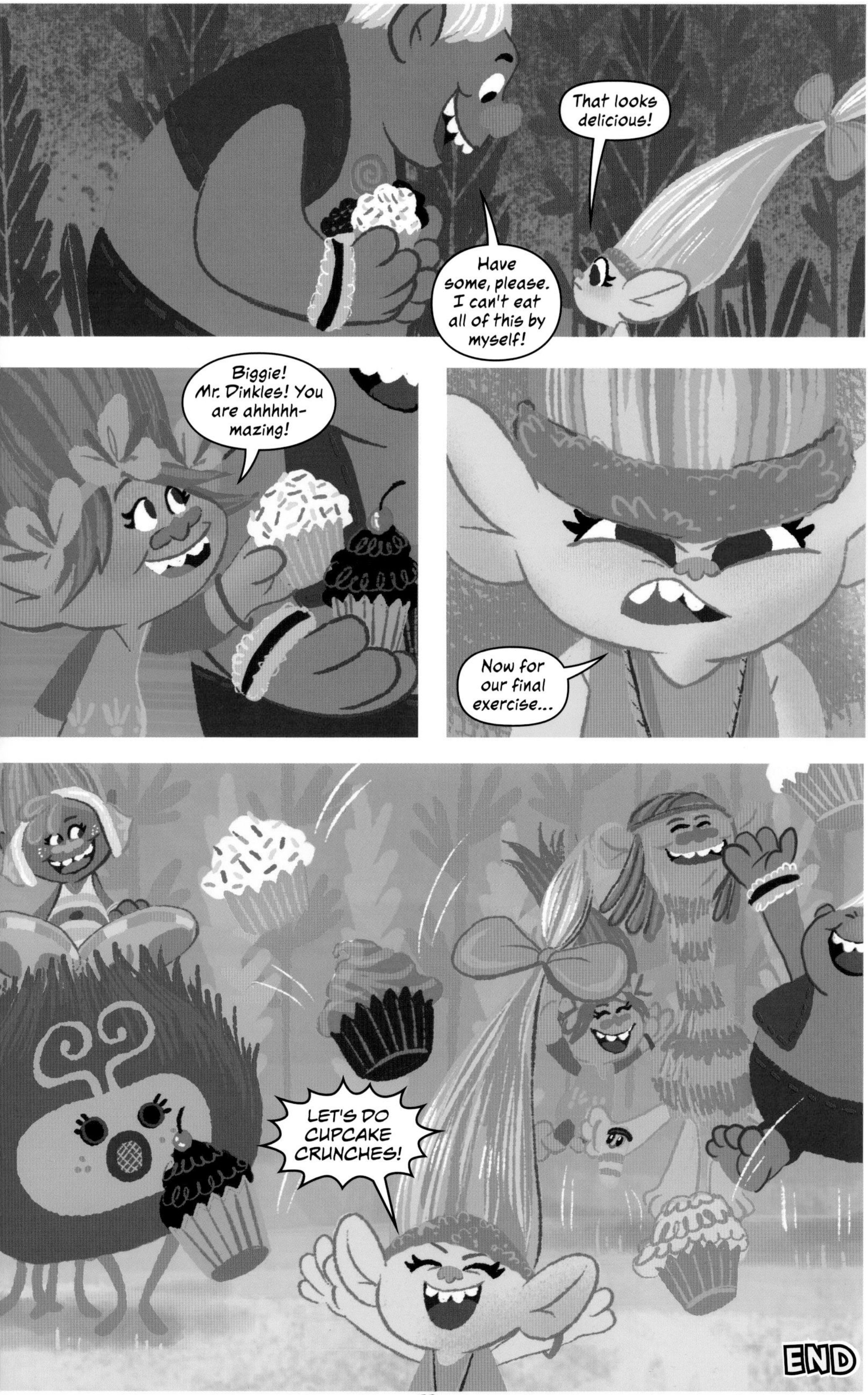
That looks delicious!
Have some, please. I can't eat all of this by myself!
Biggie! Mr. Dinkles! You are ahhhhh-mazing!
Now for our final exercise...
LET'S DO CUPCAKE CRUNCHES!
END

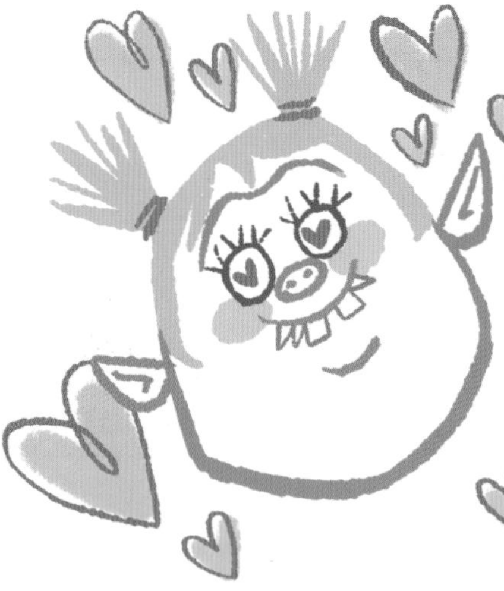

BRIDGET is on... ...a *LOVE QUEST!*

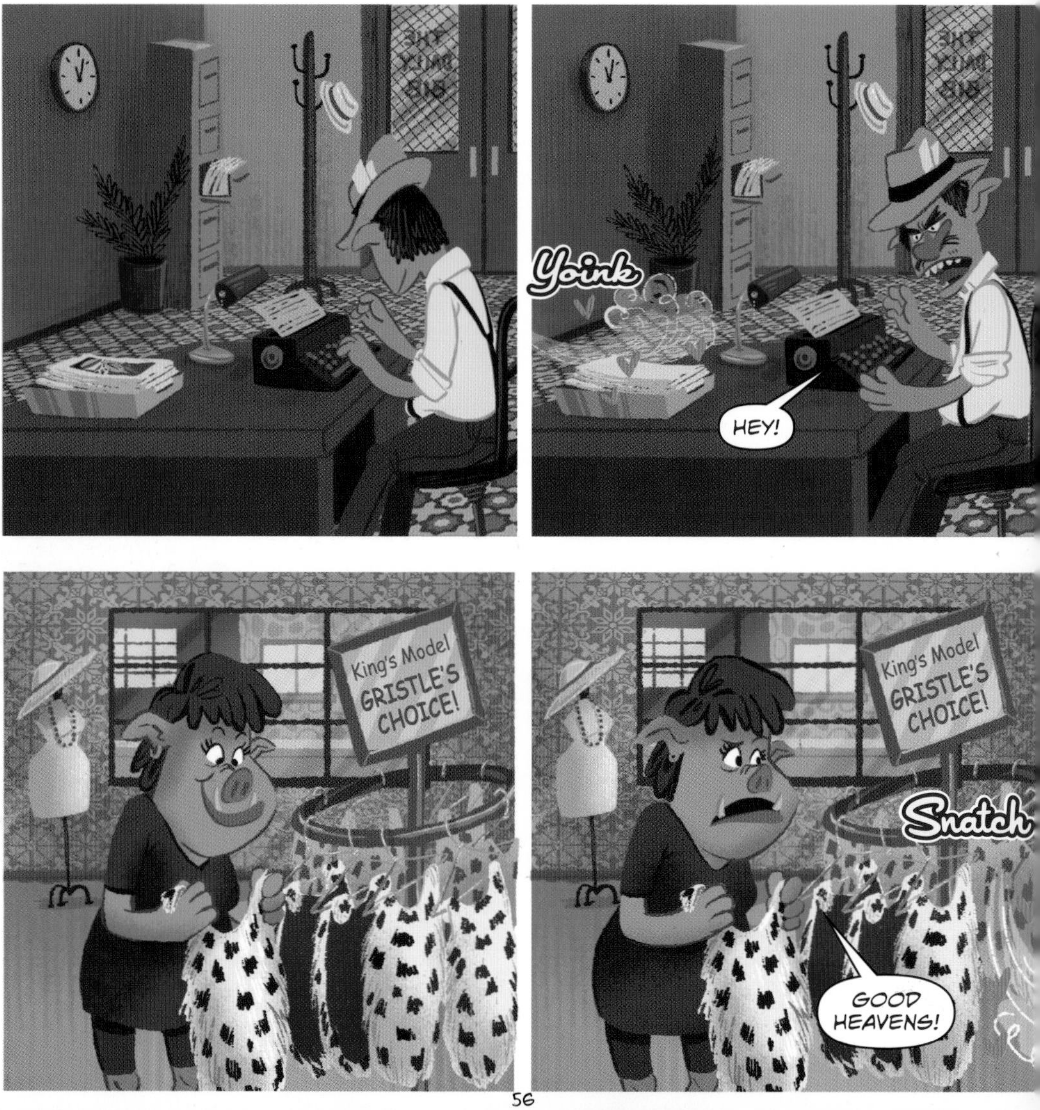
Yoink
HEY!
King's Model GRISTLE'S CHOICE!
King's Model GRISTLE'S CHOICE!
Snatch
GOOD HEAVENS!

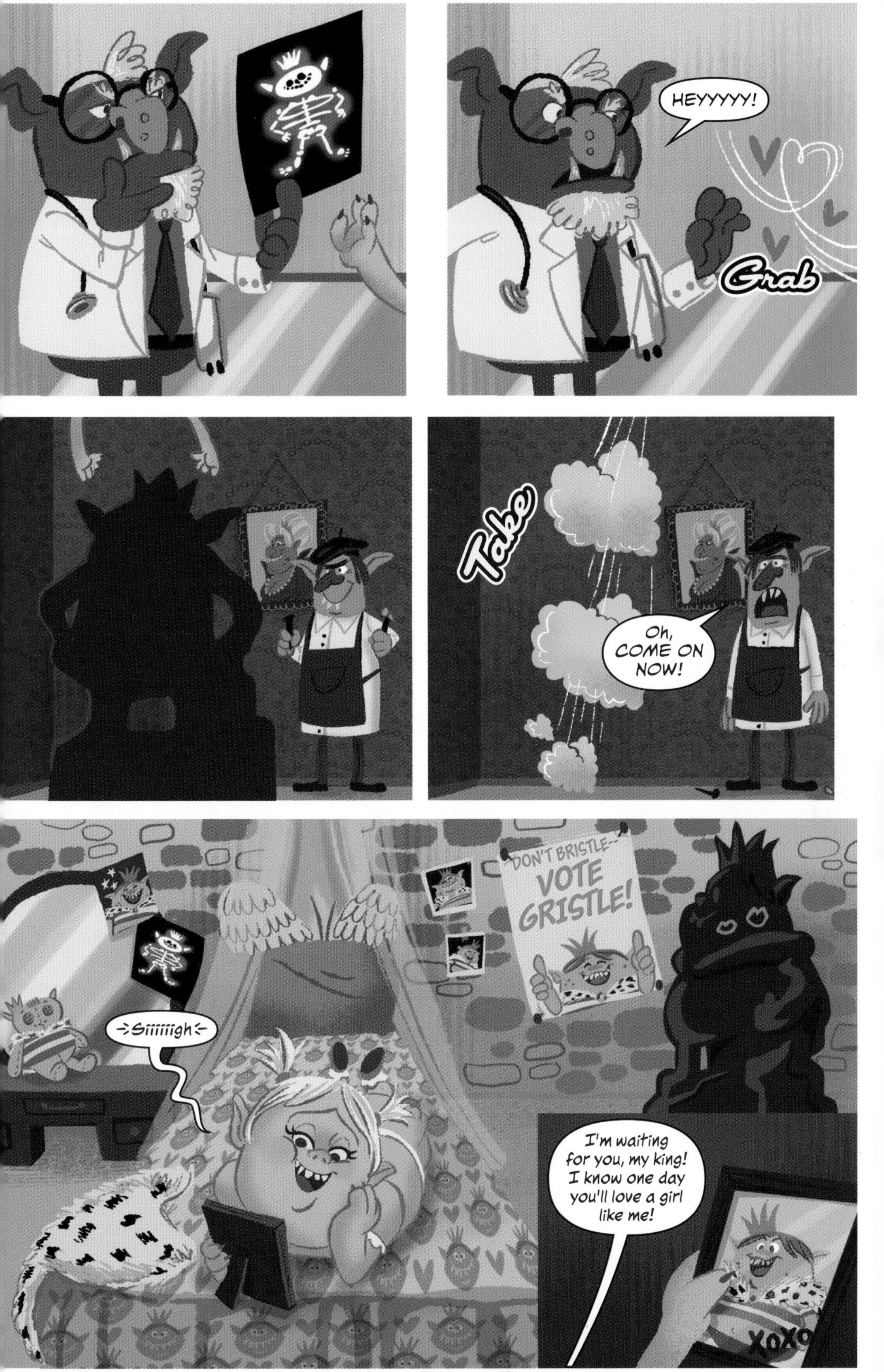
HEYYYYY!
Grab
Take
Oh, COME ON NOW!
DON'T BRISTLE--
VOTE GRISTLE!
Siiiiiigh
I'm waiting for you, my king! I know one day you'll love a girl like me!
XOXO

THE WOODS

THERE'S NO SUCH THING AS GHOSTS!

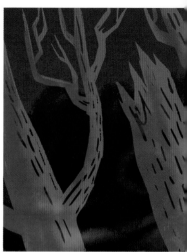

Oh! Oh, they are real!

They are really real!

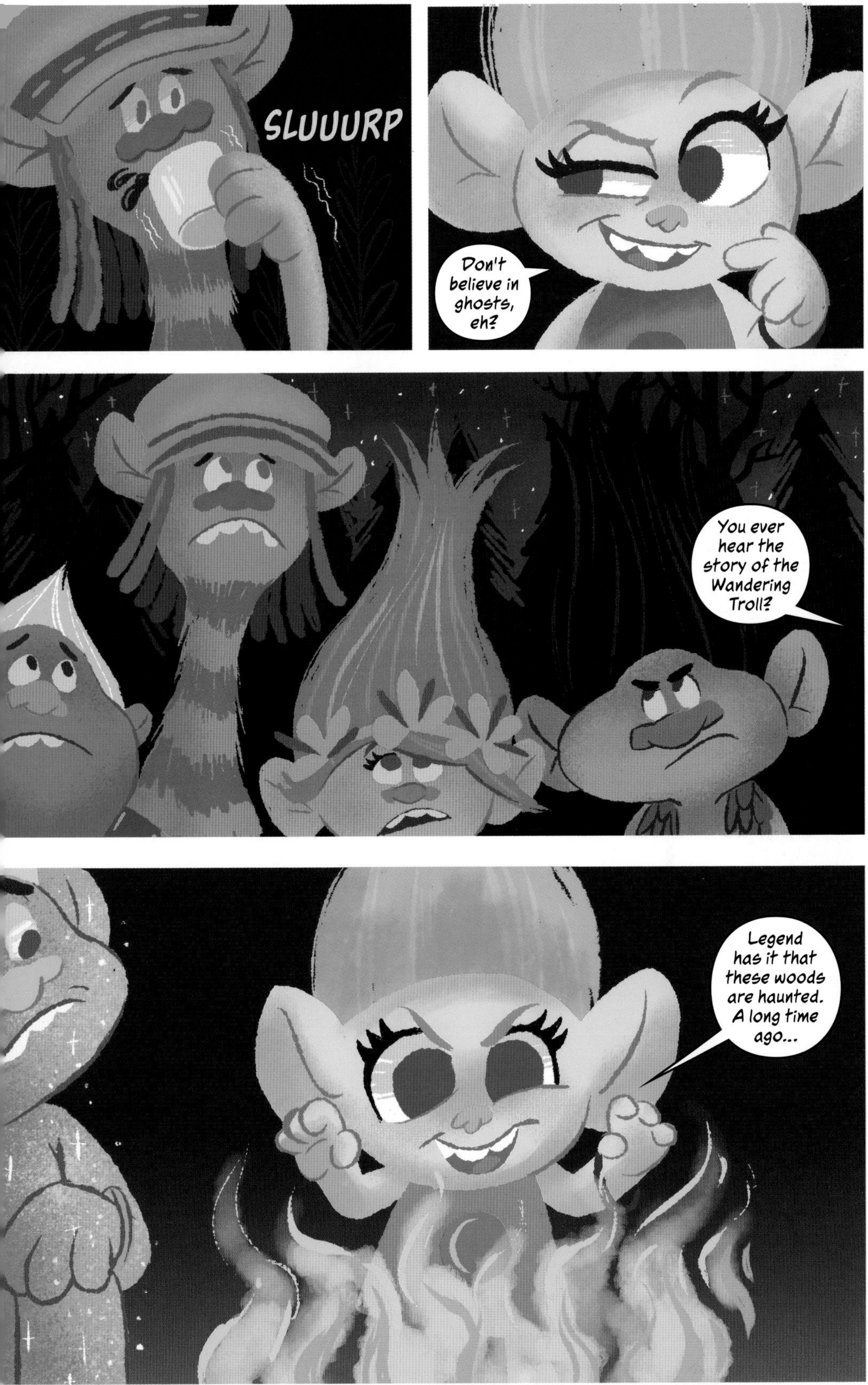

SLUUURP
Don't believe in ghosts, eh?
You ever hear the story of the Wandering Troll?
Legend has it that these woods are haunted. A long time ago...

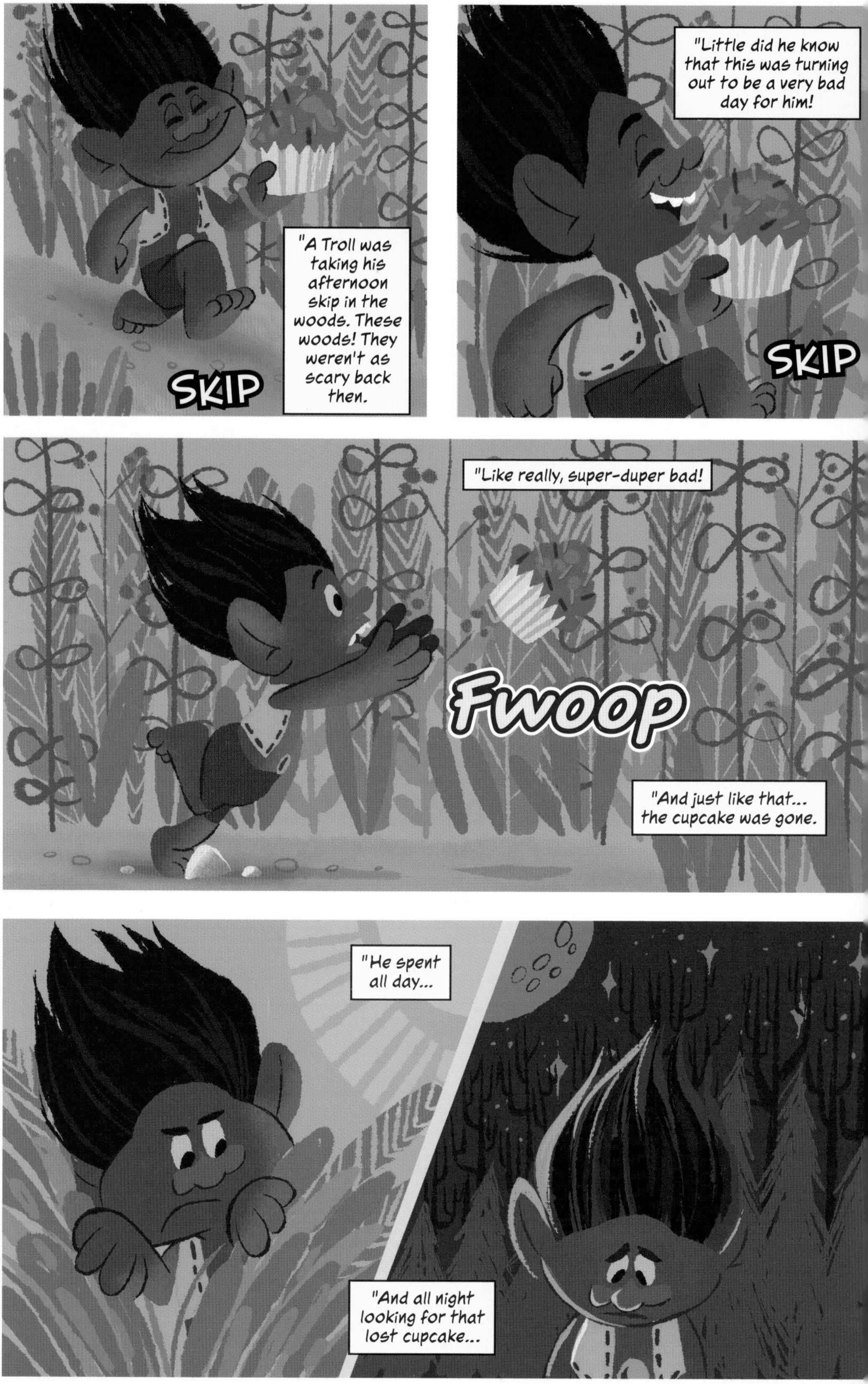
"A Troll was taking his afternoon skip in the woods. These woods! They weren't as scary back then.
SKIP
"Little did he know that this was turning out to be a very bad day for him!
SKIP
"Like really, super-duper bad!
Fwoop
"And just like that... the cupcake was gone.
"He spent all day...
"And all night looking for that lost cupcake...

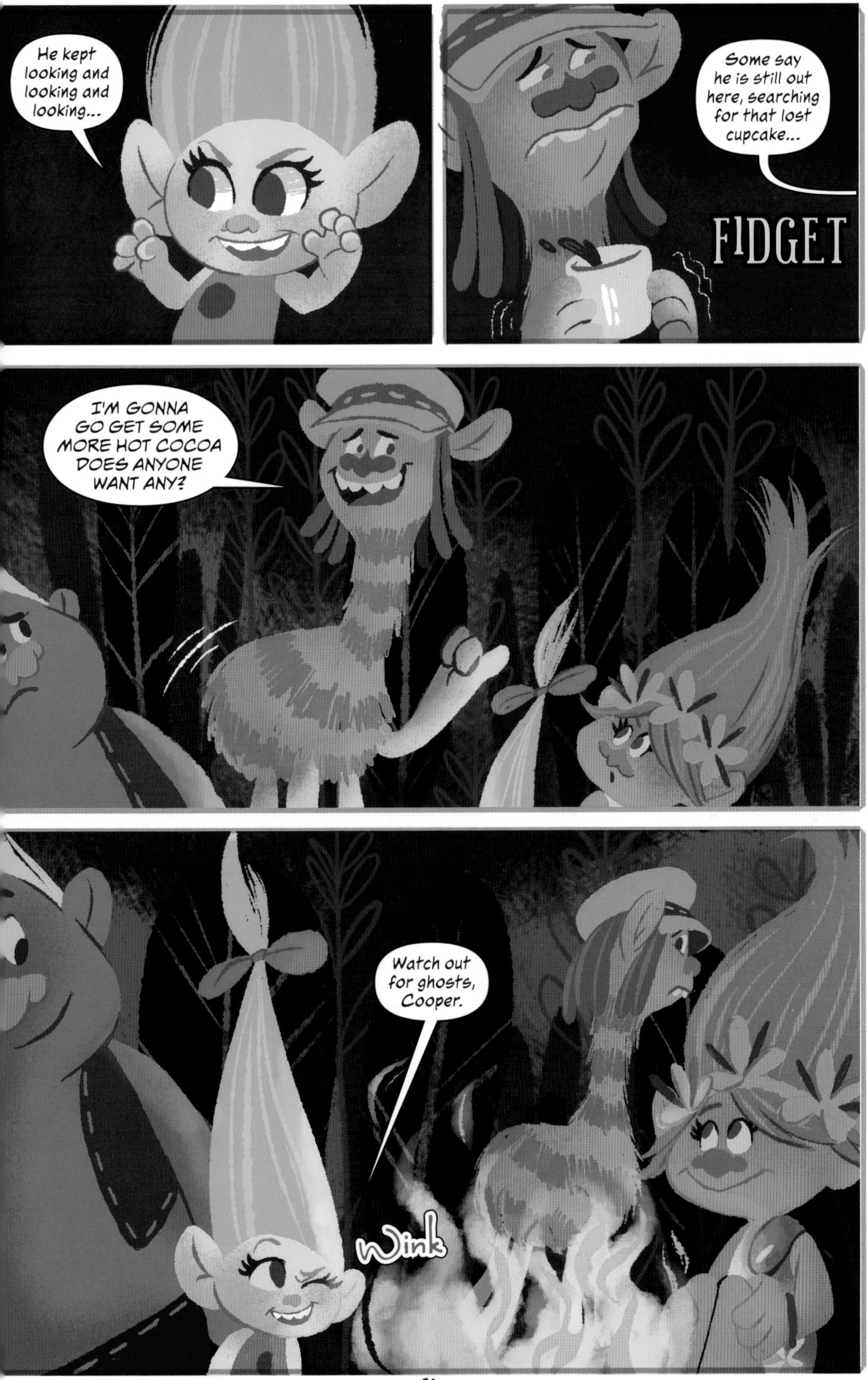
He kept looking and looking and looking...
Some say he is still out here, searching for that lost cupcake...
FIDGET
I'M GONNA GO GET SOME MORE HOT COCOA DOES ANYONE WANT ANY?
Watch out for ghosts, Cooper.
Wink

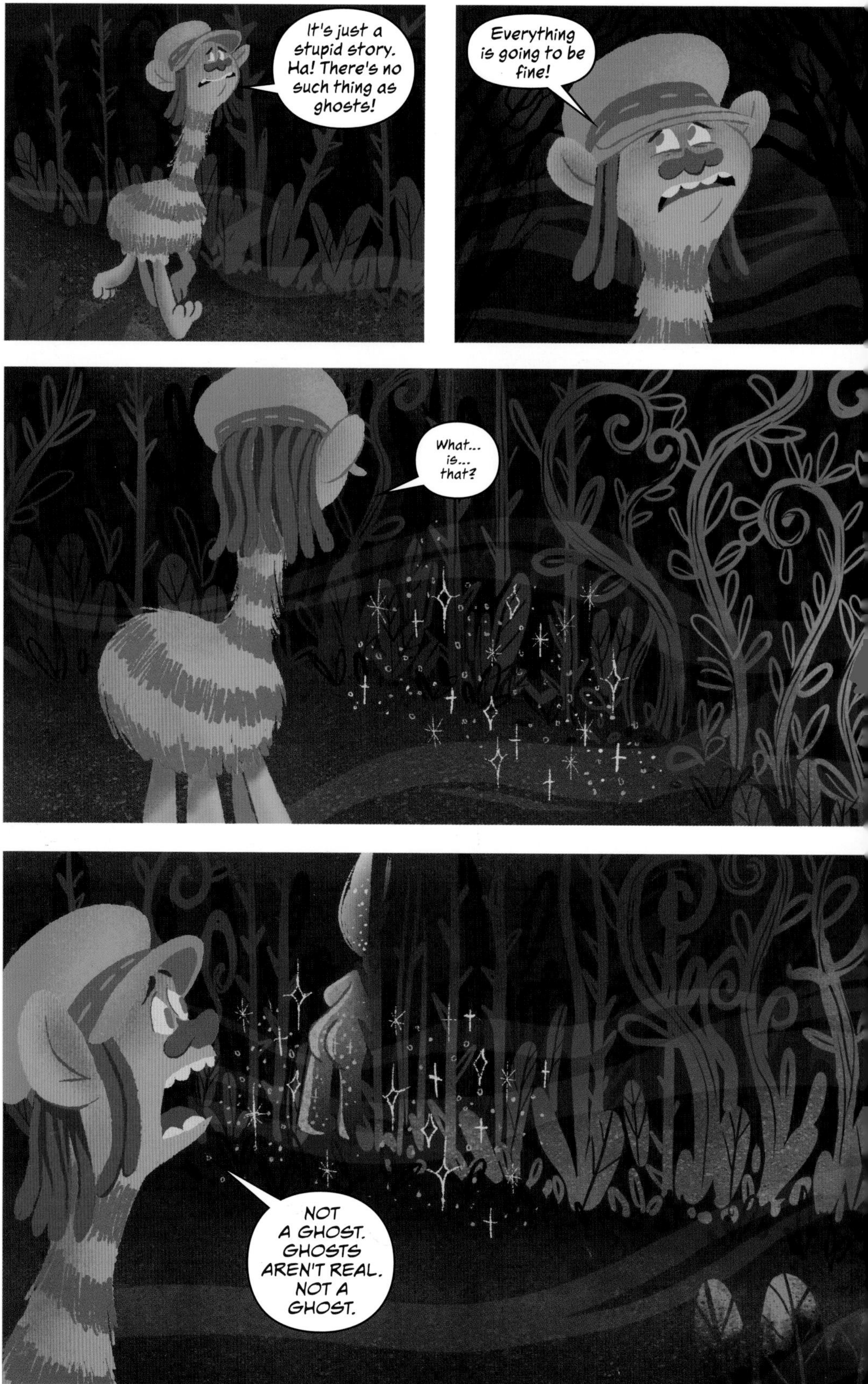
It's just a stupid story. Ha! There's no such thing as ghosts!
Everything is going to be fine!
What... is... that?
NOT A GHOST. GHOSTS AREN'T REAL. NOT A GHOST.

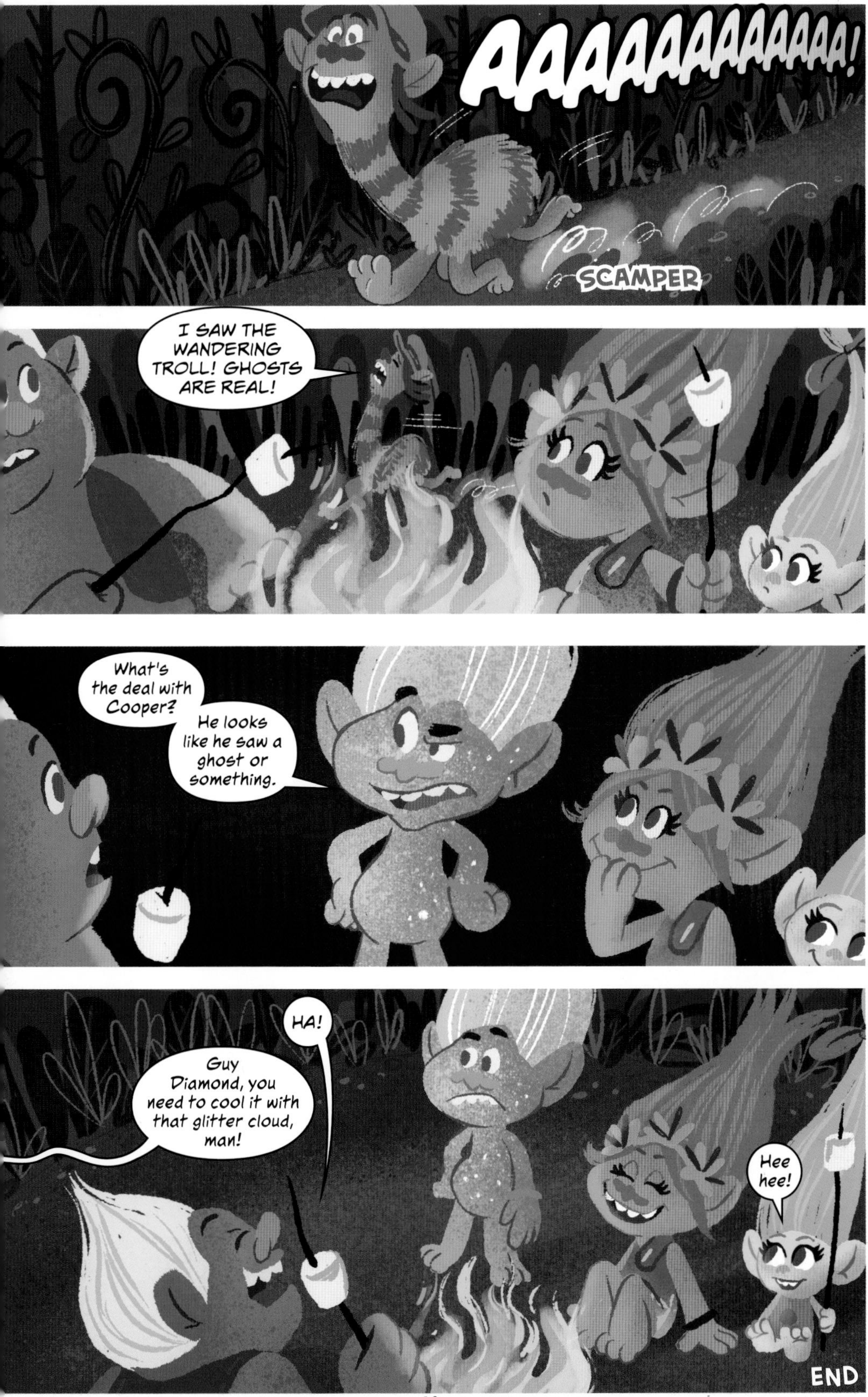
AAAAAAAAAAAA!
SCAMPER
I SAW THE WANDERING TROLL! GHOSTS ARE REAL!
What's the deal with Cooper?
He looks like he saw a ghost or something.
HA!
Guy Diamond, you need to cool it with that glitter cloud, man!
Hee hee!
END

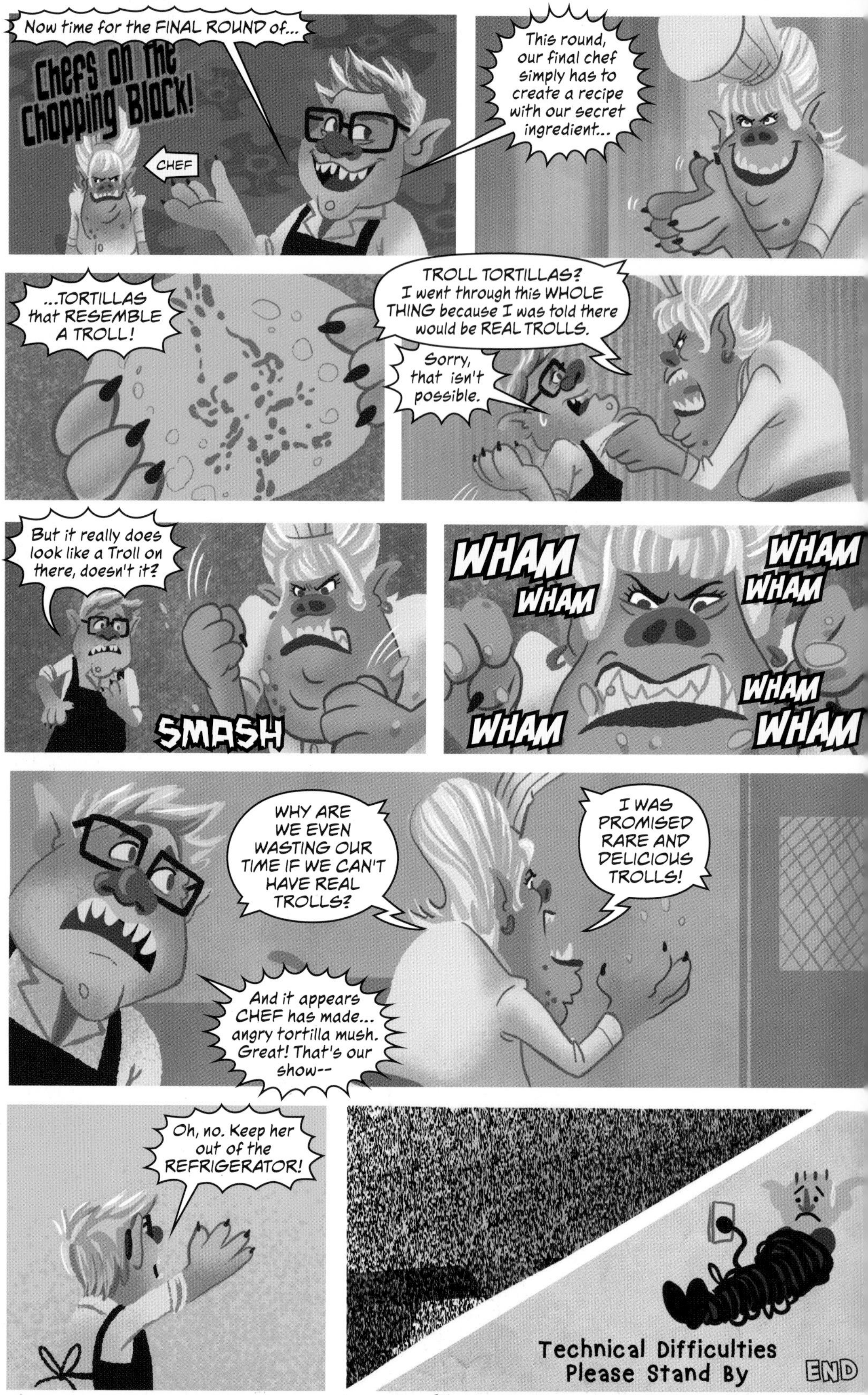

Now time for the FINAL ROUND of...
Chefs on the Chopping Block!
CHEF
This round, our final chef simply has to create a recipe with our secret ingredient...
...TORTILLAS that RESEMBLE A TROLL!
TROLL TORTILLAS? I went through this WHOLE THING because I was told there would be REAL TROLLS.
Sorry, that isn't possible.
But it really does look like a Troll on there, doesn't it?
SMASH
WHAM
WHAM
WHAM
WHAM
WHAM
WHAM
WHAM
WHY ARE WE EVEN WASTING OUR TIME IF WE CAN'T HAVE REAL TROLLS?
I WAS PROMISED RARE AND DELICIOUS TROLLS!
And it appears CHEF has made... angry tortilla mush. Great! That's our show--
Oh, no. Keep her out of the REFRIGERATOR!
Technical Difficulties Please Stand By
END

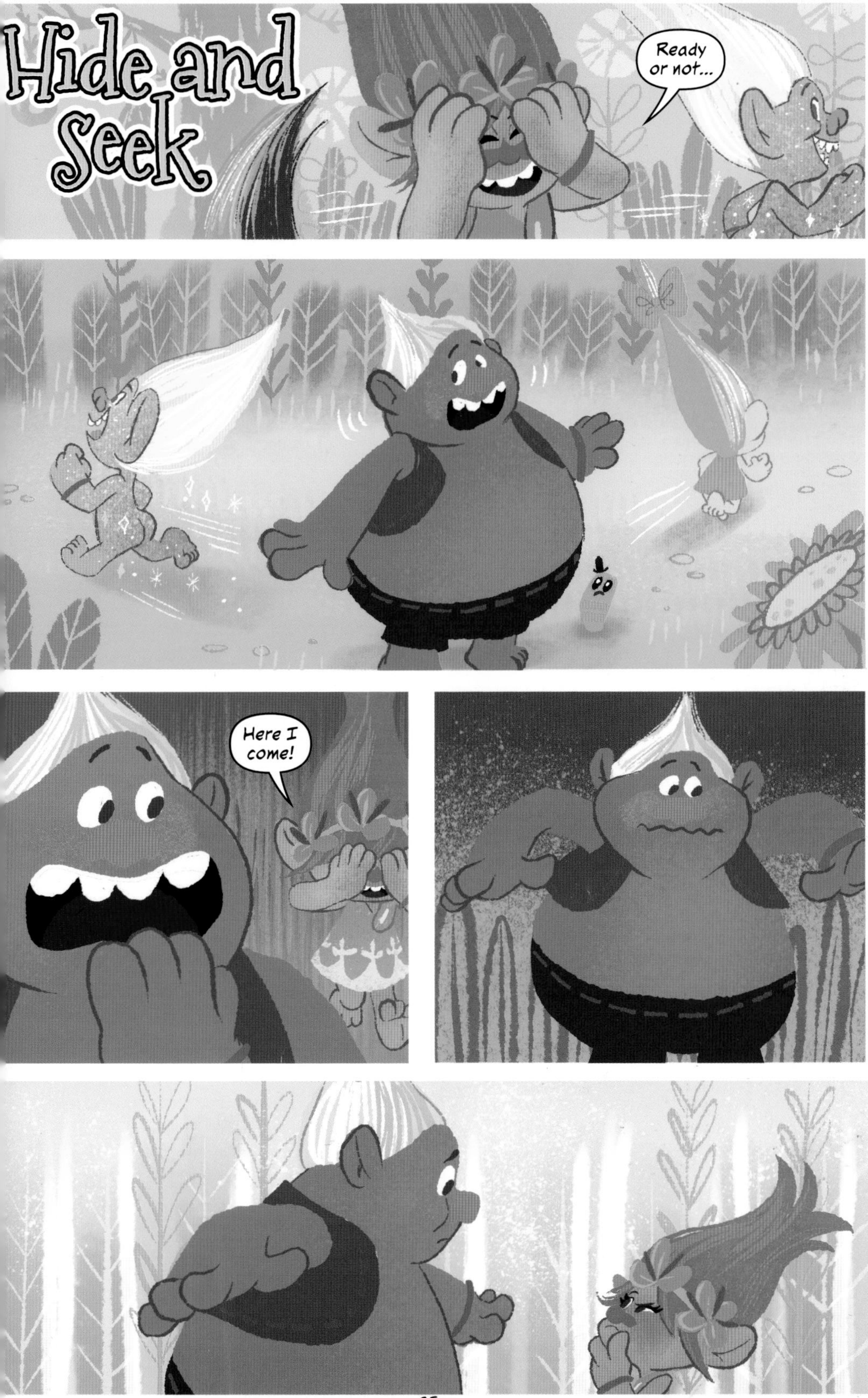
Hide and Seek
Ready or not...
Here I come!

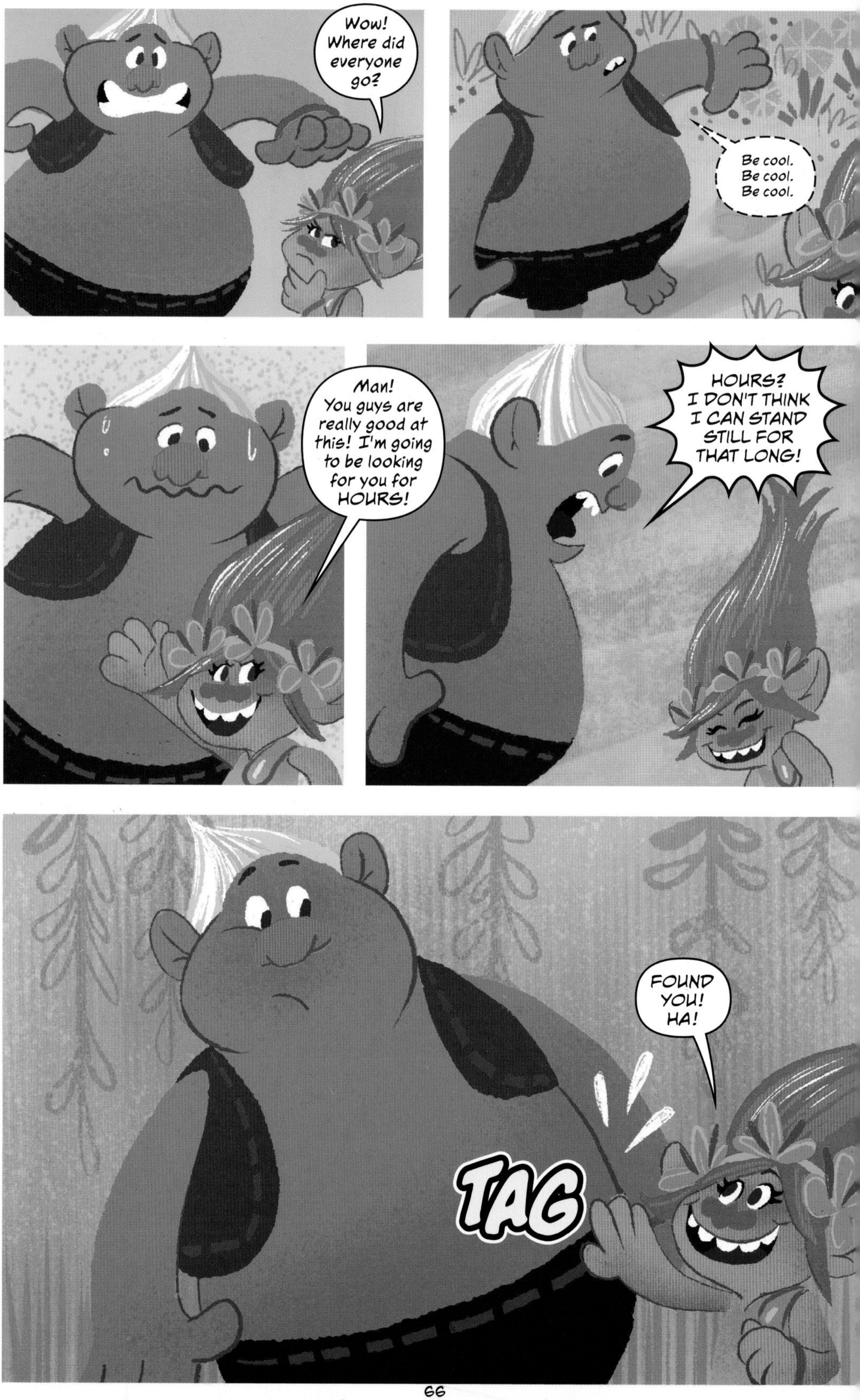
Wow! Where did everyone go?
Be cool. Be cool. Be cool.
Man! You guys are really good at this! I'm going to be looking for you for HOURS!
HOURS? I DON'T THINK I CAN STAND STILL FOR THAT LONG!
FOUND YOU! HA!
TAG

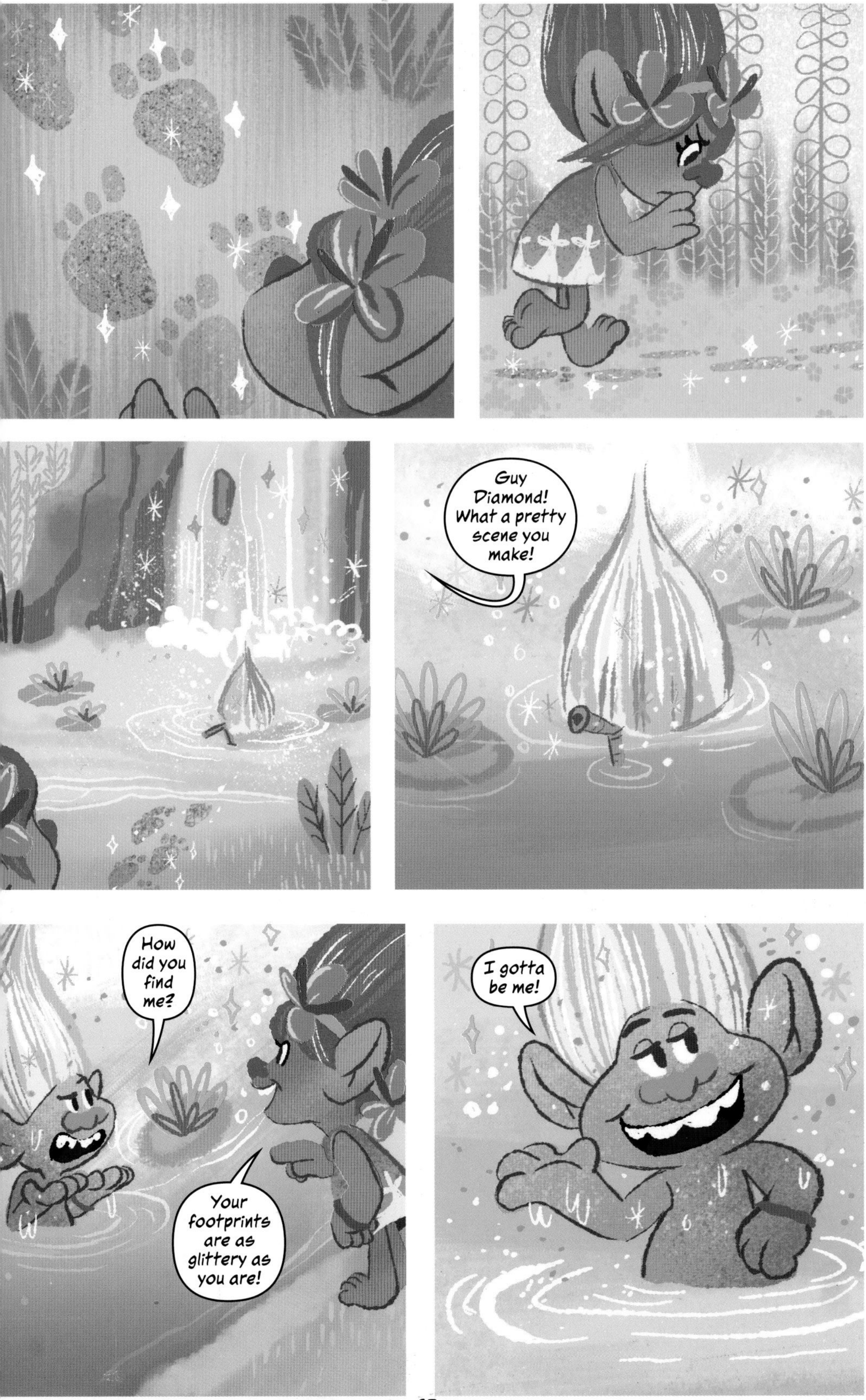
Guy Diamond! What a pretty scene you make!
How did you find me?
Your footprints are as glittery as you are!
I gotta be me!

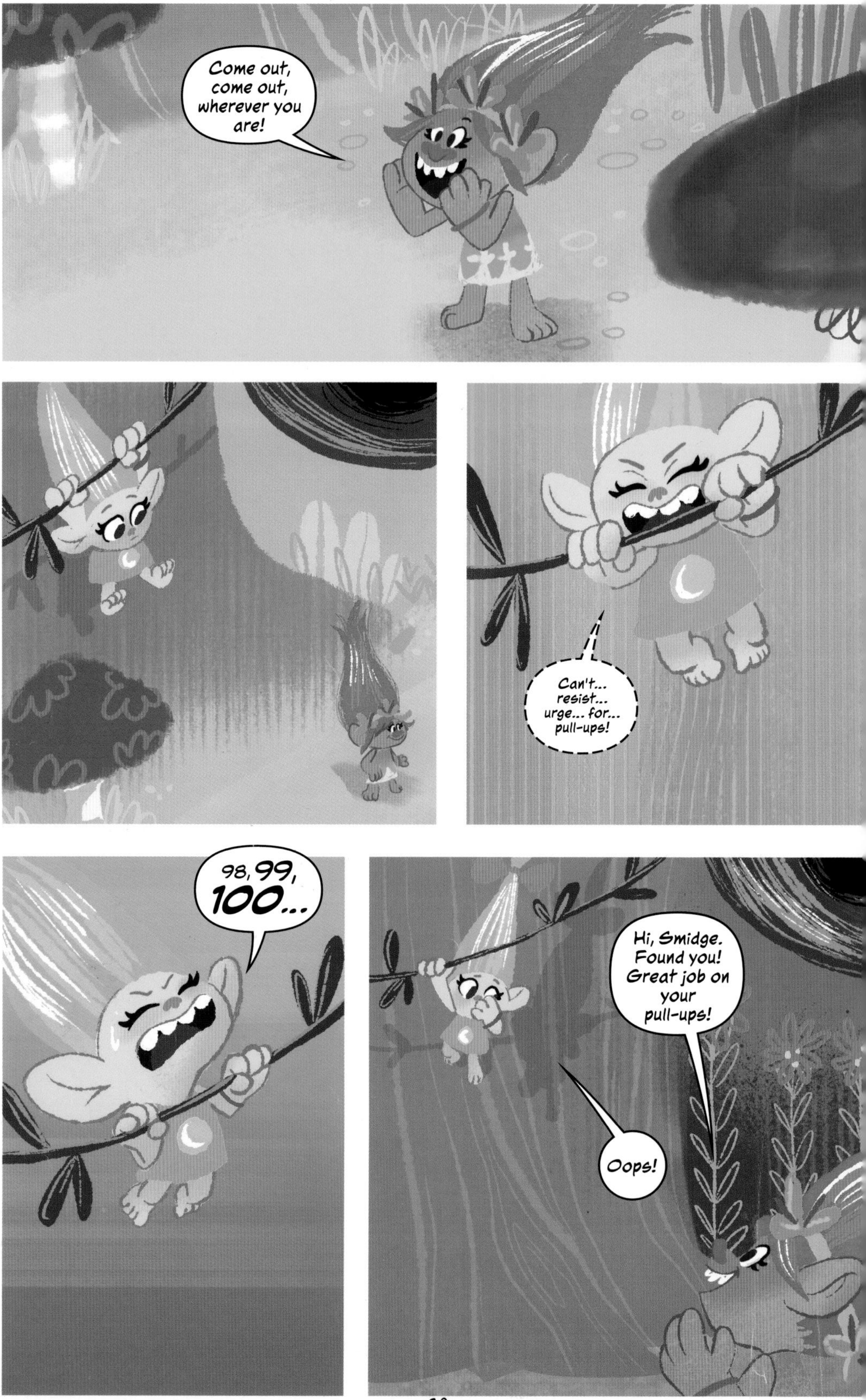
Come out, come out, wherever you are!
Can't... resist... urge... for... pull-ups!
98, 99, 100...
Hi, Smidge. Found you! Great job on your pull-ups!
Oops!

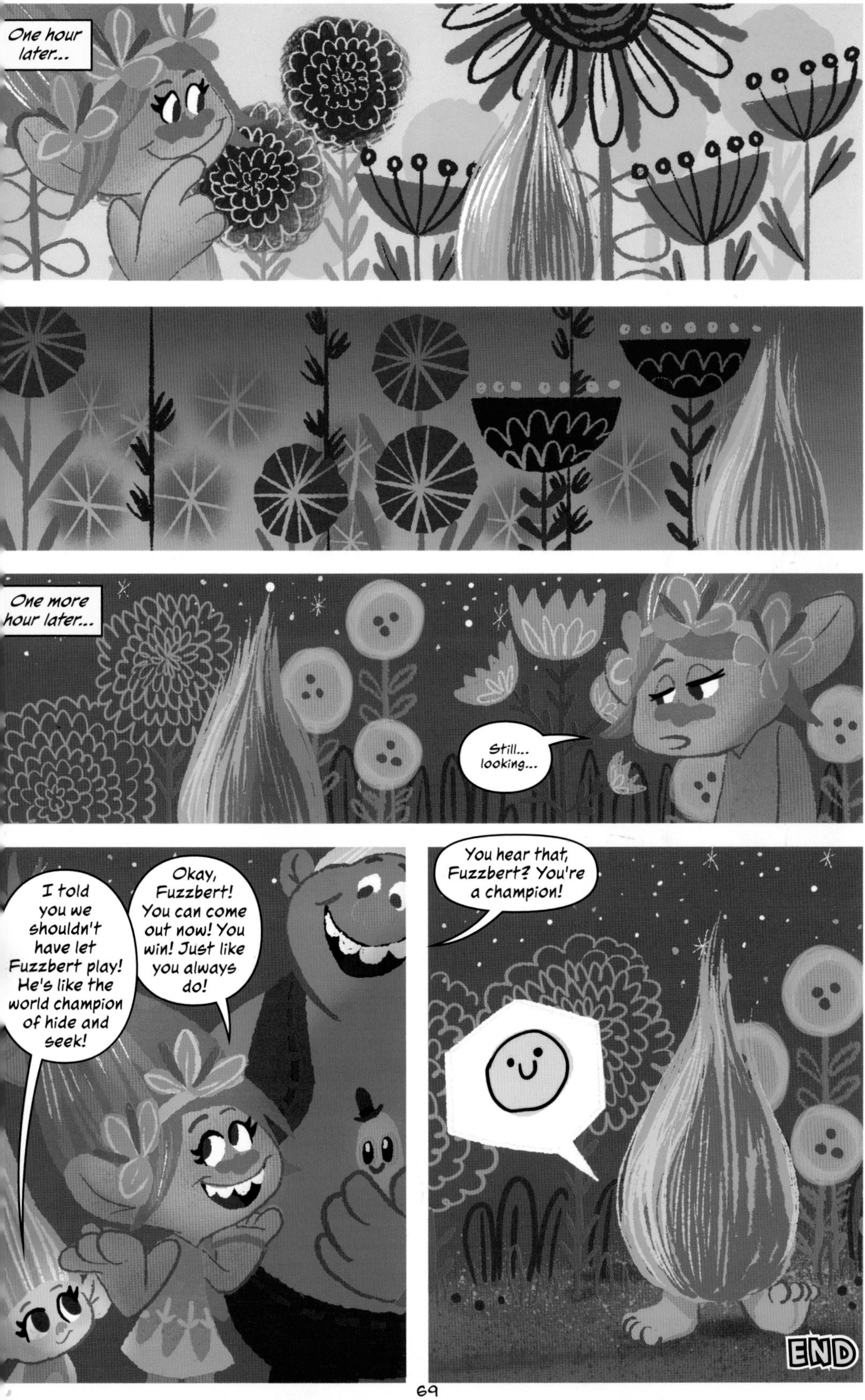

One hour later...
One more hour later...
Still... looking...
I told you we shouldn't have let Fuzzbert play! He's like the world champion of hide and seek!
Okay, Fuzzbert! You can come out now! You win! Just like you always do!
You hear that, Fuzzbert? You're a champion!
END

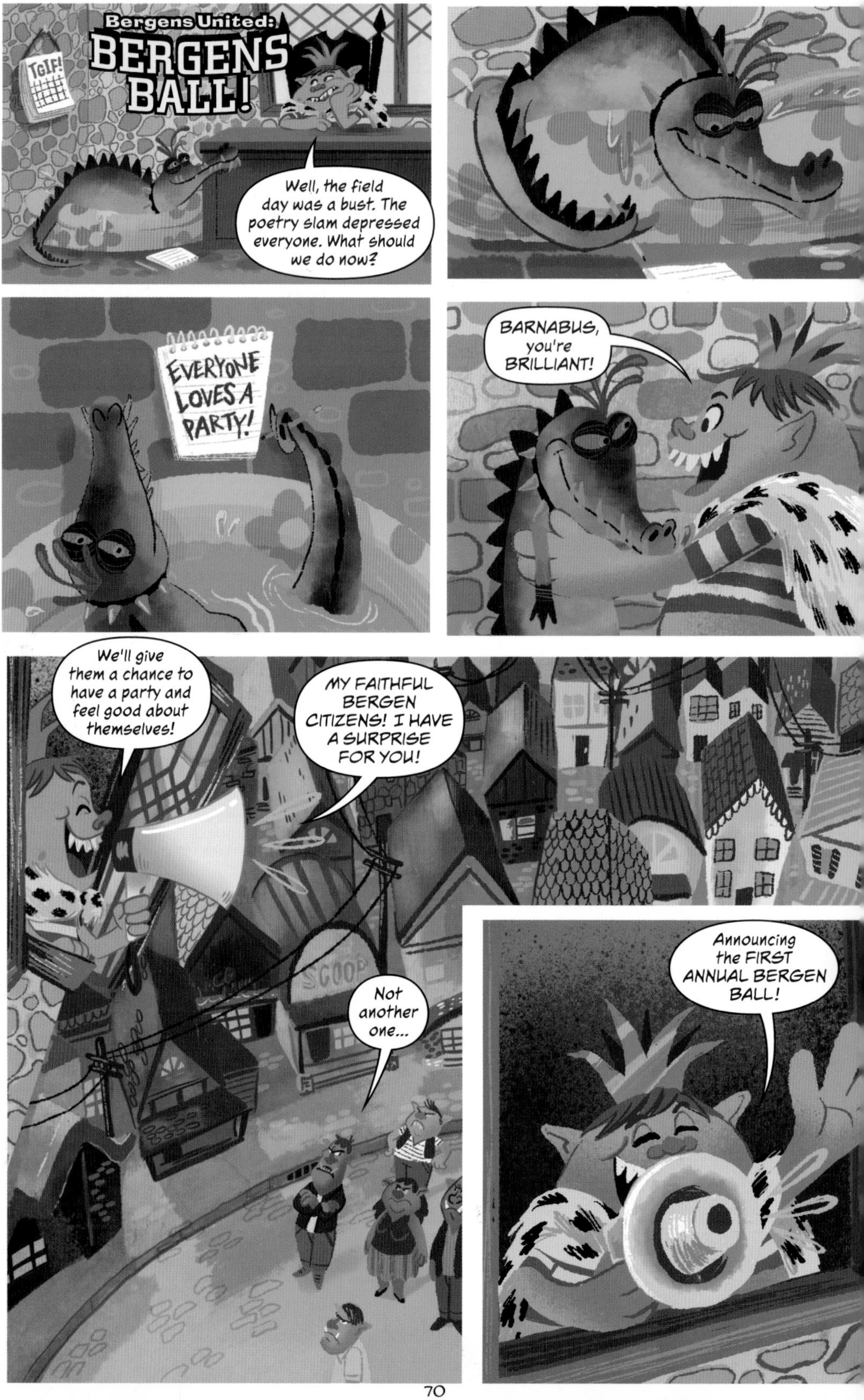
Bergens United:
BERGENS BALL!
TGIF!
Well, the field day was a bust. The poetry slam depressed everyone. What should we do now?
EVERYONE LOVES A PARTY!
BARNABUS, you're BRILLIANT!
We'll give them a chance to have a party and feel good about themselves!
MY FAITHFUL BERGEN CITIZENS! I HAVE A SURPRISE FOR YOU!
SCOOP
Not another one...
Announcing the FIRST ANNUAL BERGEN BALL!

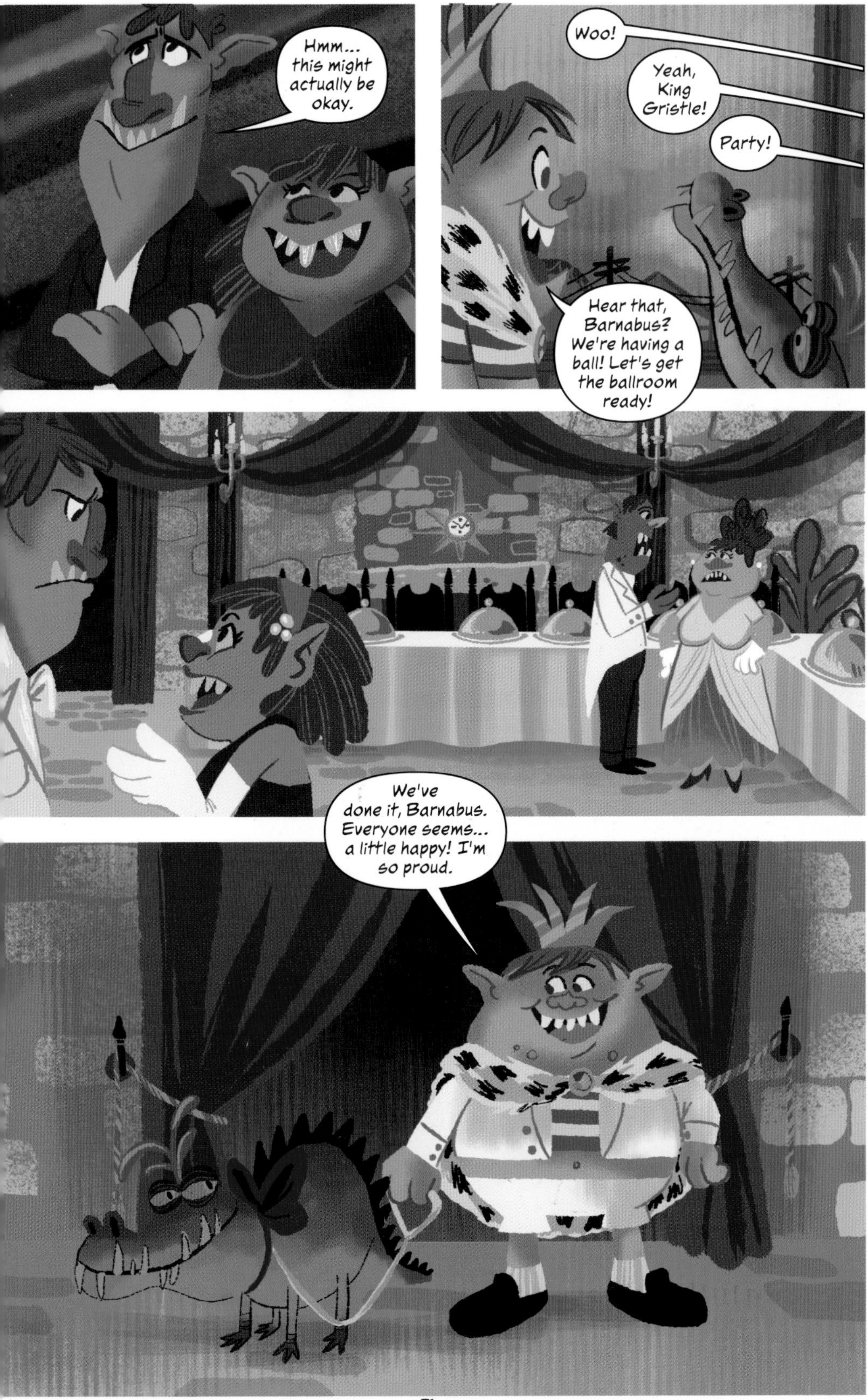
Hmm... this might actually be okay.
Woo!
Yeah, King Gristle!
Party!
Hear that, Barnabus? We're having a ball! Let's get the ballroom ready!
We've done it, Barnabus. Everyone seems... a little happy! I'm so proud.

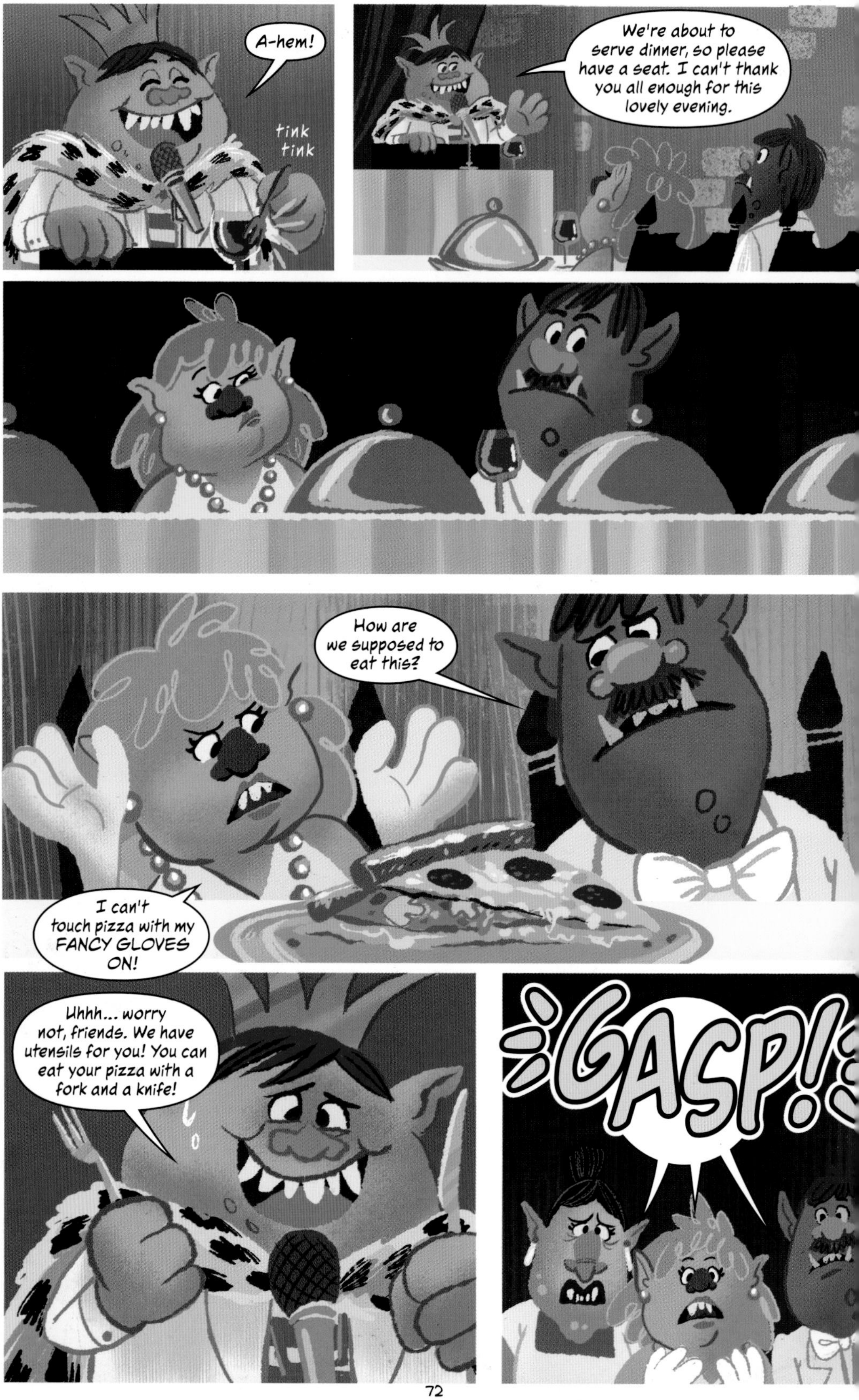
A-hem!
tink tink
We're about to serve dinner, so please have a seat. I can't thank you all enough for this lovely evening.
How are we supposed to eat this?
I can't touch pizza with my FANCY GLOVES ON!
Uhhh... worry not, friends. We have utensils for you! You can eat your pizza with a fork and a knife!
GASP!

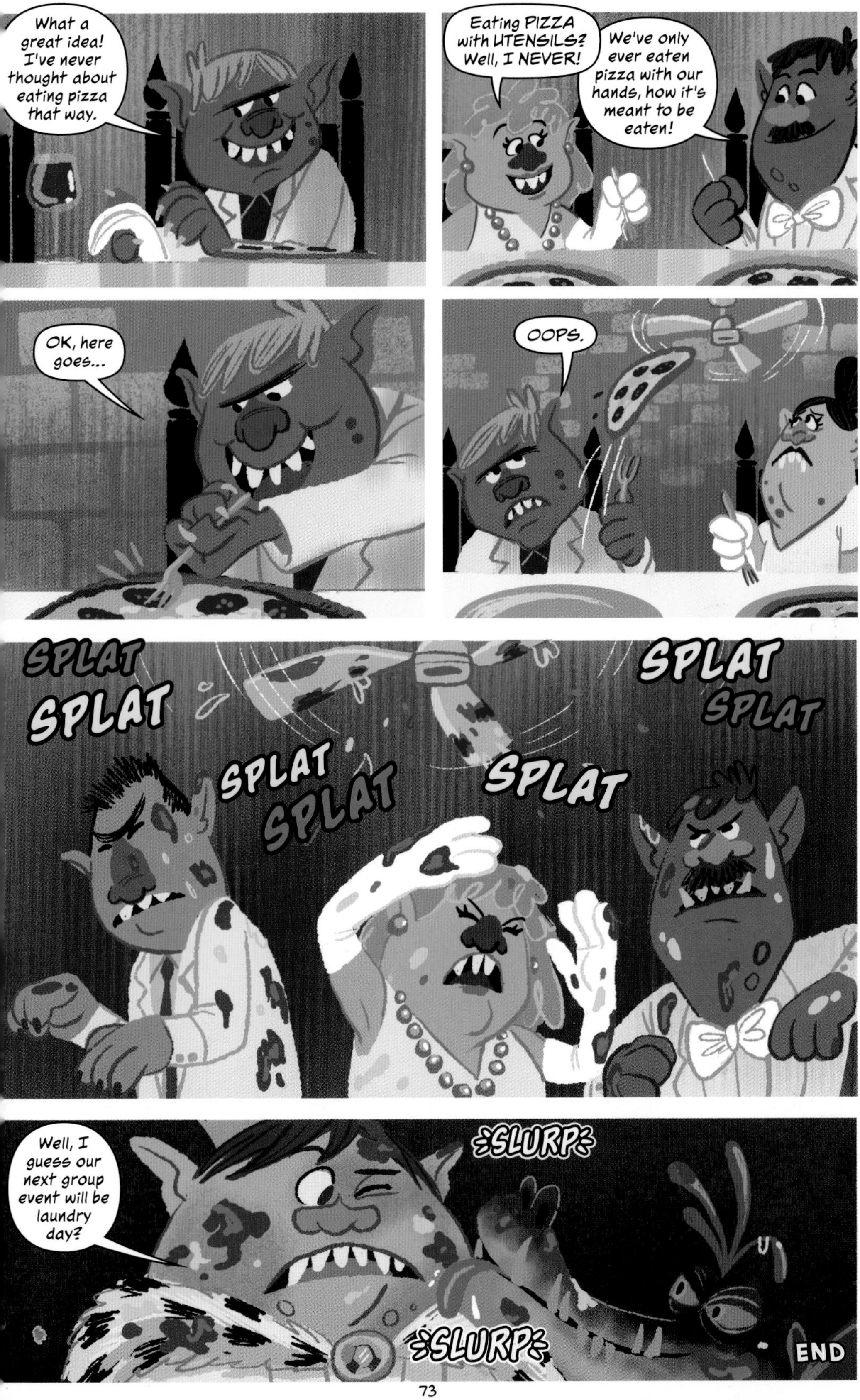
What a great idea! I've never thought about eating pizza that way.
Eating PIZZA with UTENSILS? Well, I NEVER!
We've only ever eaten pizza with our hands, how it's meant to be eaten!
OK, here goes...
OOPS.
SPLAT
SPLAT
SPLAT
SPLAT
SPLAT
SPLAT
SPLAT
SPLAT
Well, I guess our next group event will be laundry day?
SLURP
SLURP
END

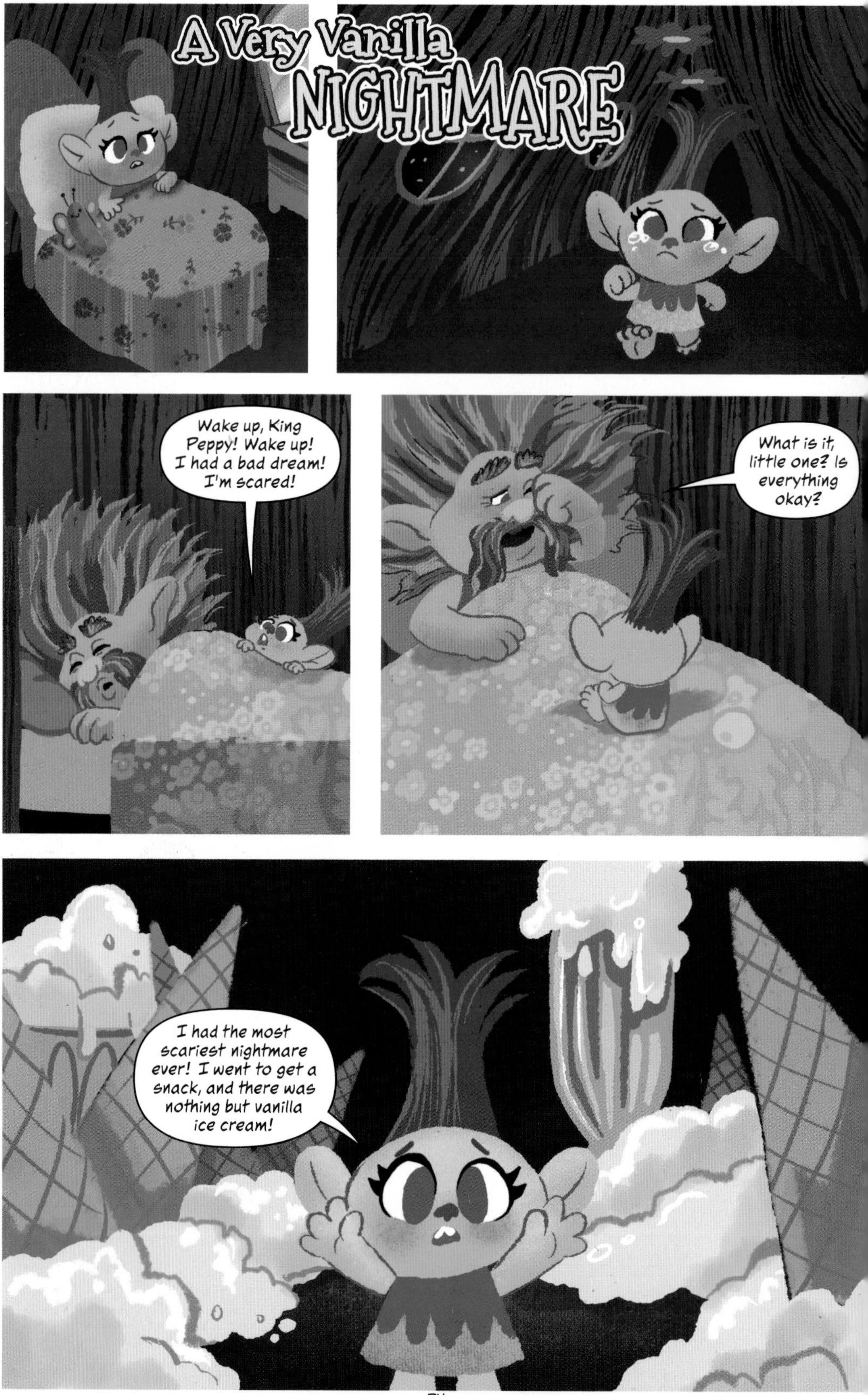
A Very Vanilla NIGHTMARE
Wake up, King Peppy! Wake up! I had a bad dream! I'm scared!
What is it, little one? Is everything okay?
I had the most scariest nightmare ever! I went to get a snack, and there was nothing but vanilla ice cream!

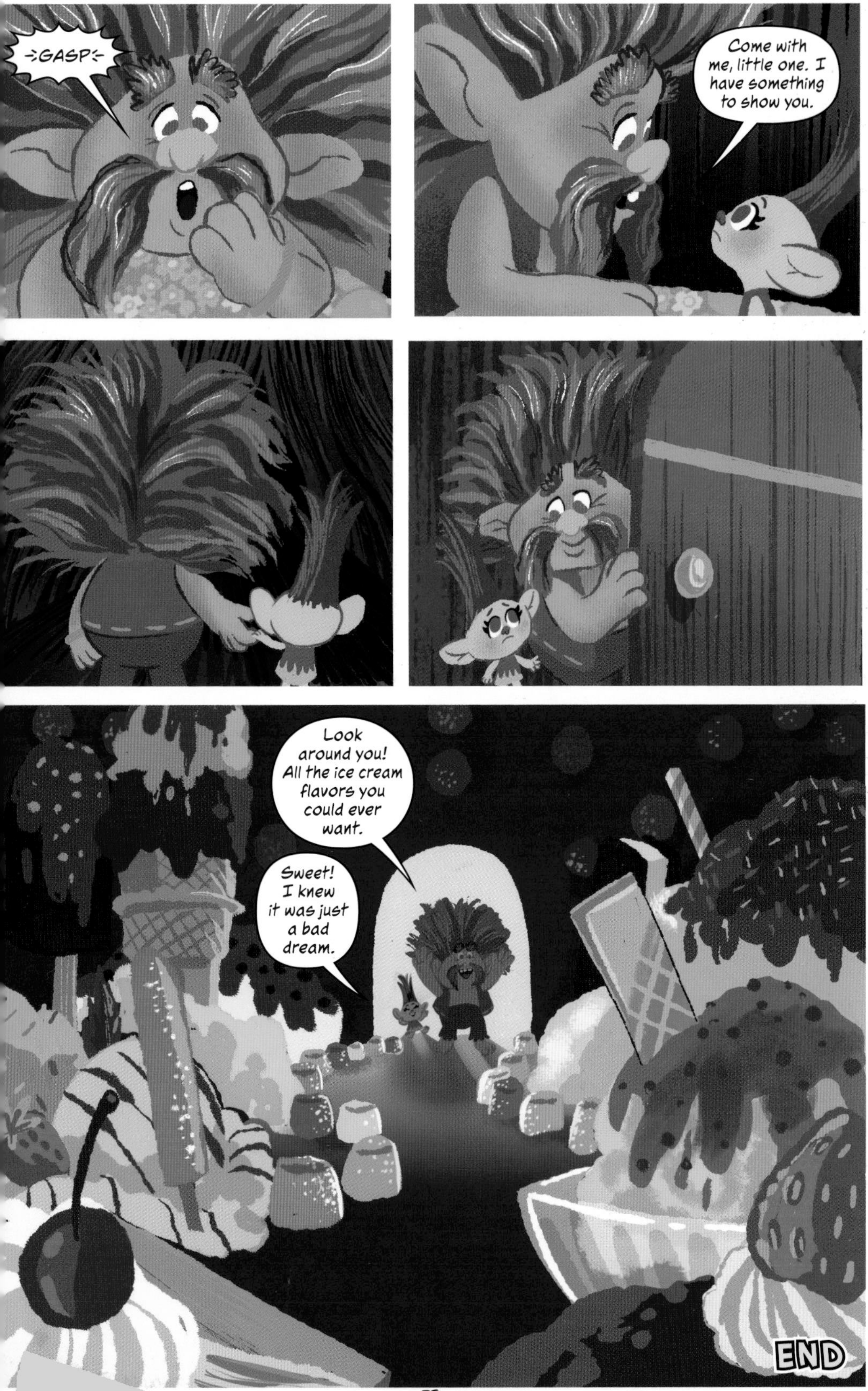

GASP
Come with me, little one. I have something to show you.
Look around you! All the ice cream flavors you could ever want.
Sweet! I knew it was just a bad dream.
END

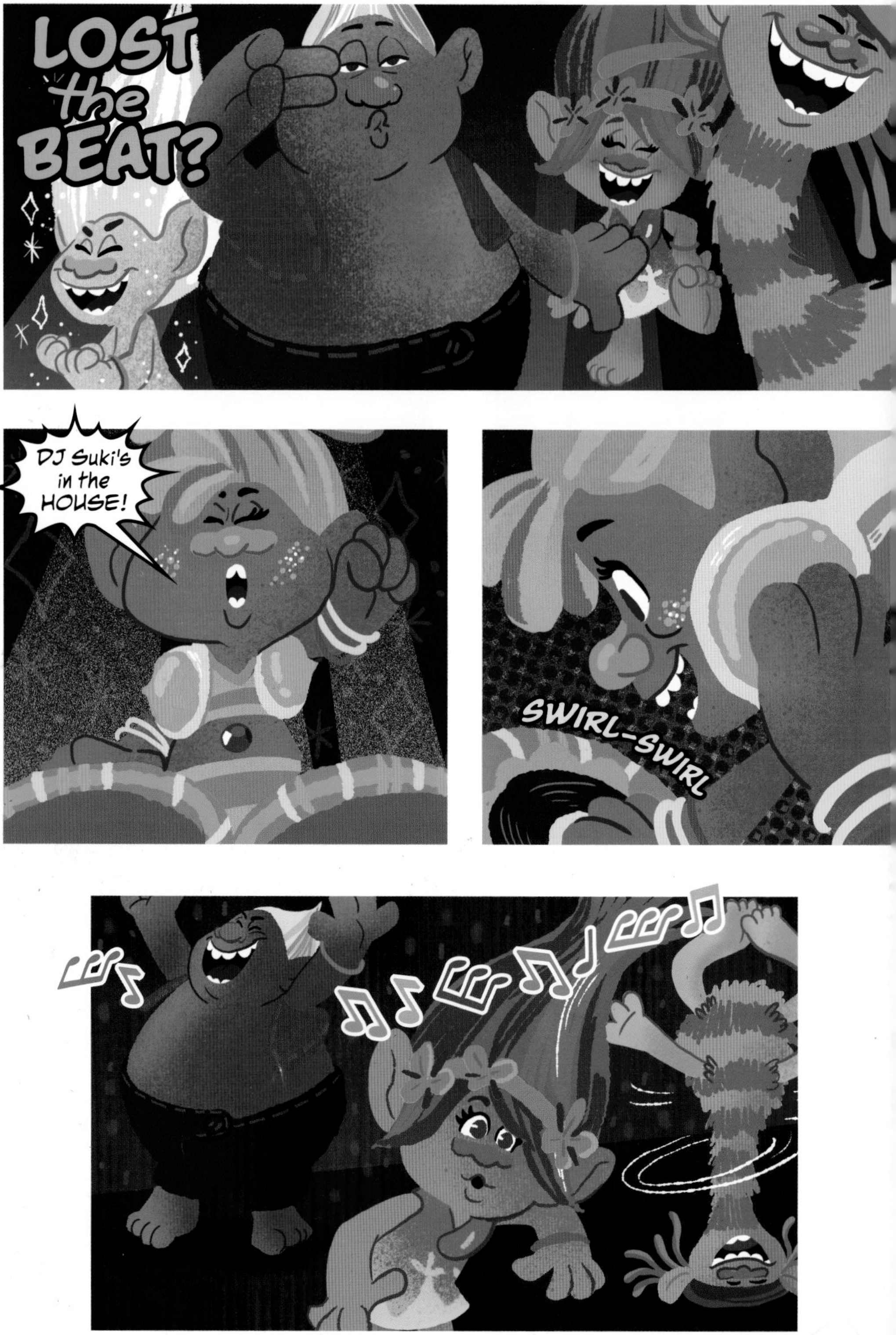
LOST the BEAT?
DJ Suki's in the HOUSE!
SWIRL-SWIRL

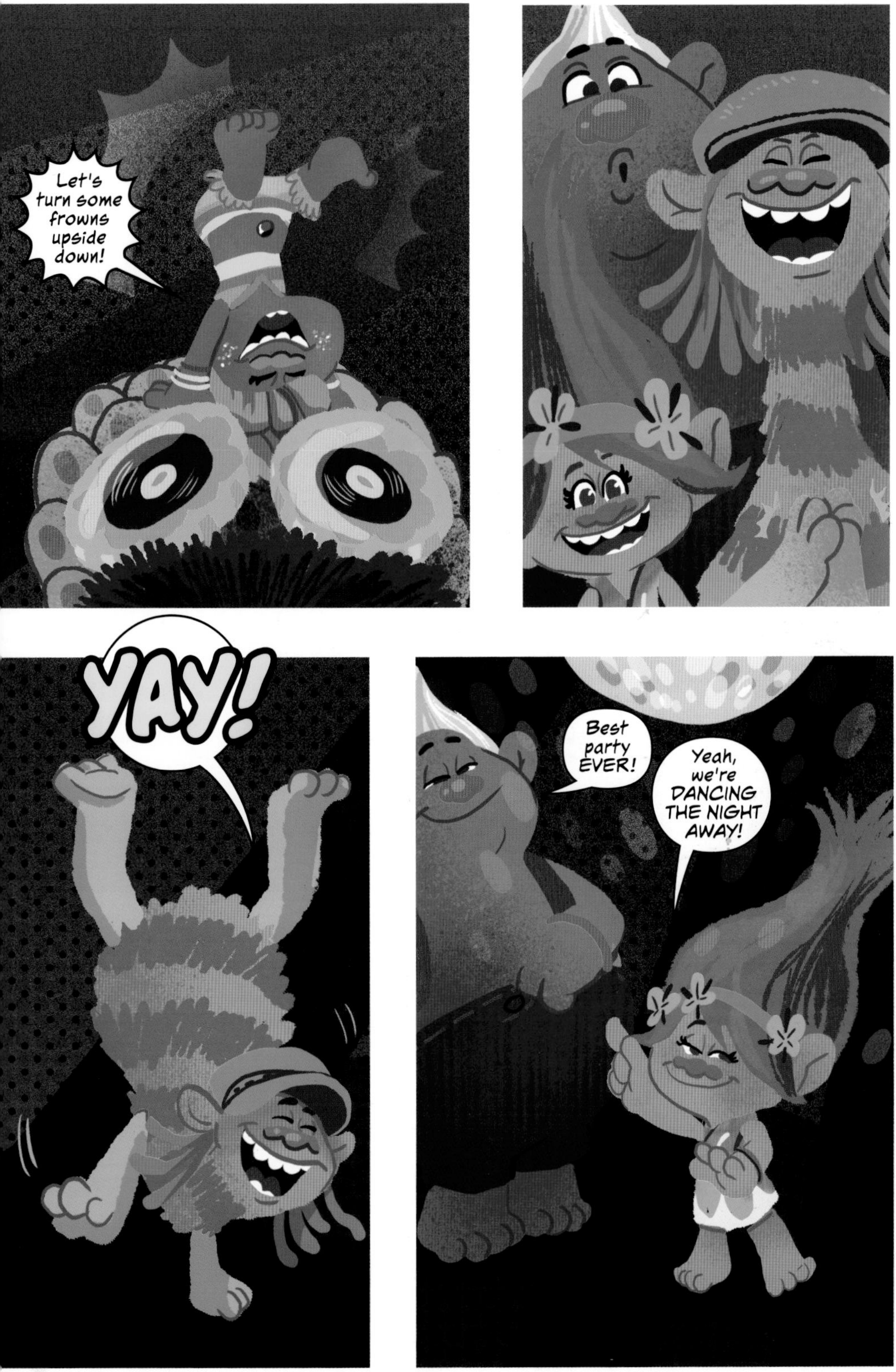
Let's turn some frowns upside down!
YAY!
Best party EVER!
Yeah, we're DANCING THE NIGHT AWAY!

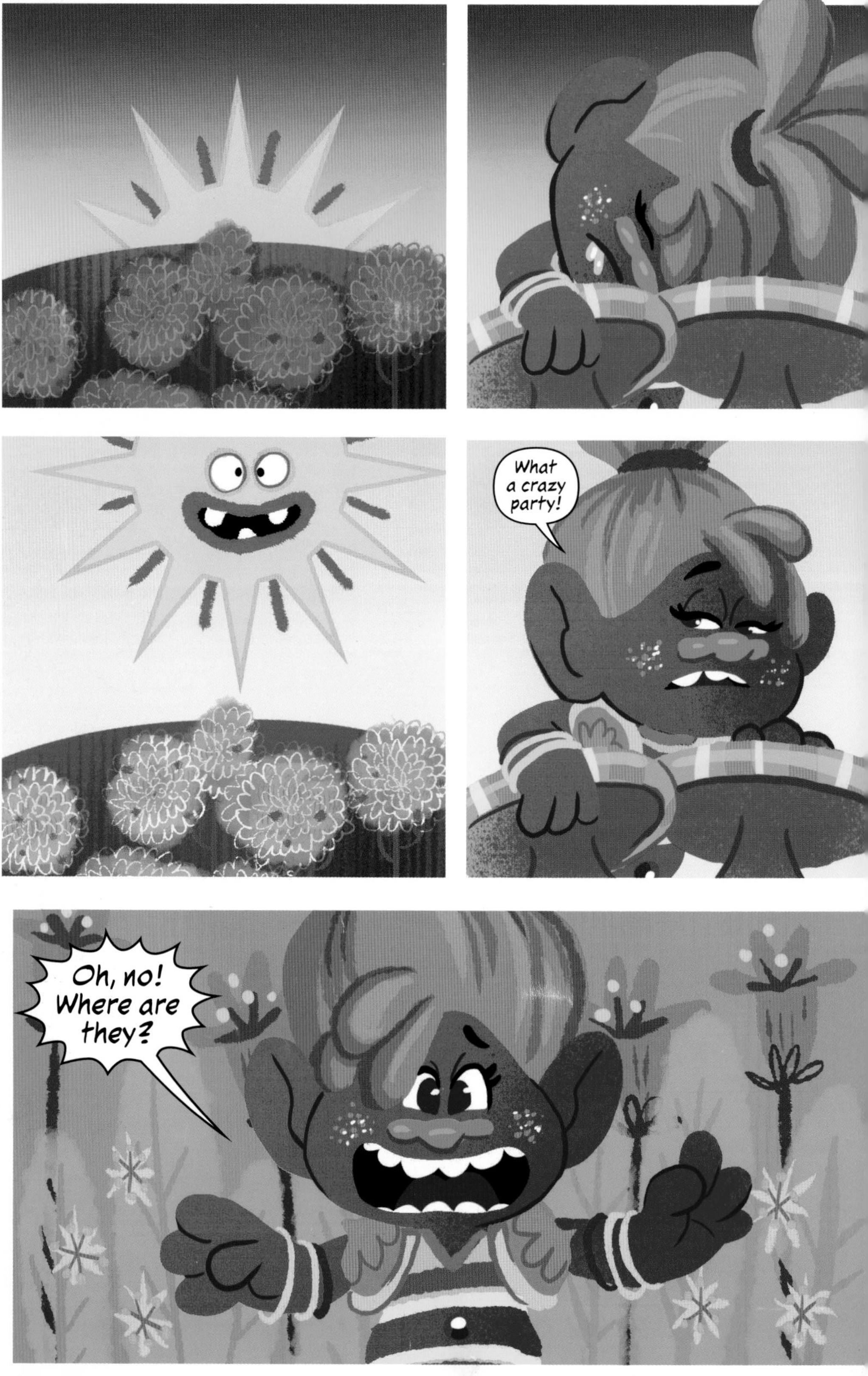
What a crazy party!
Oh, no! Where are they?

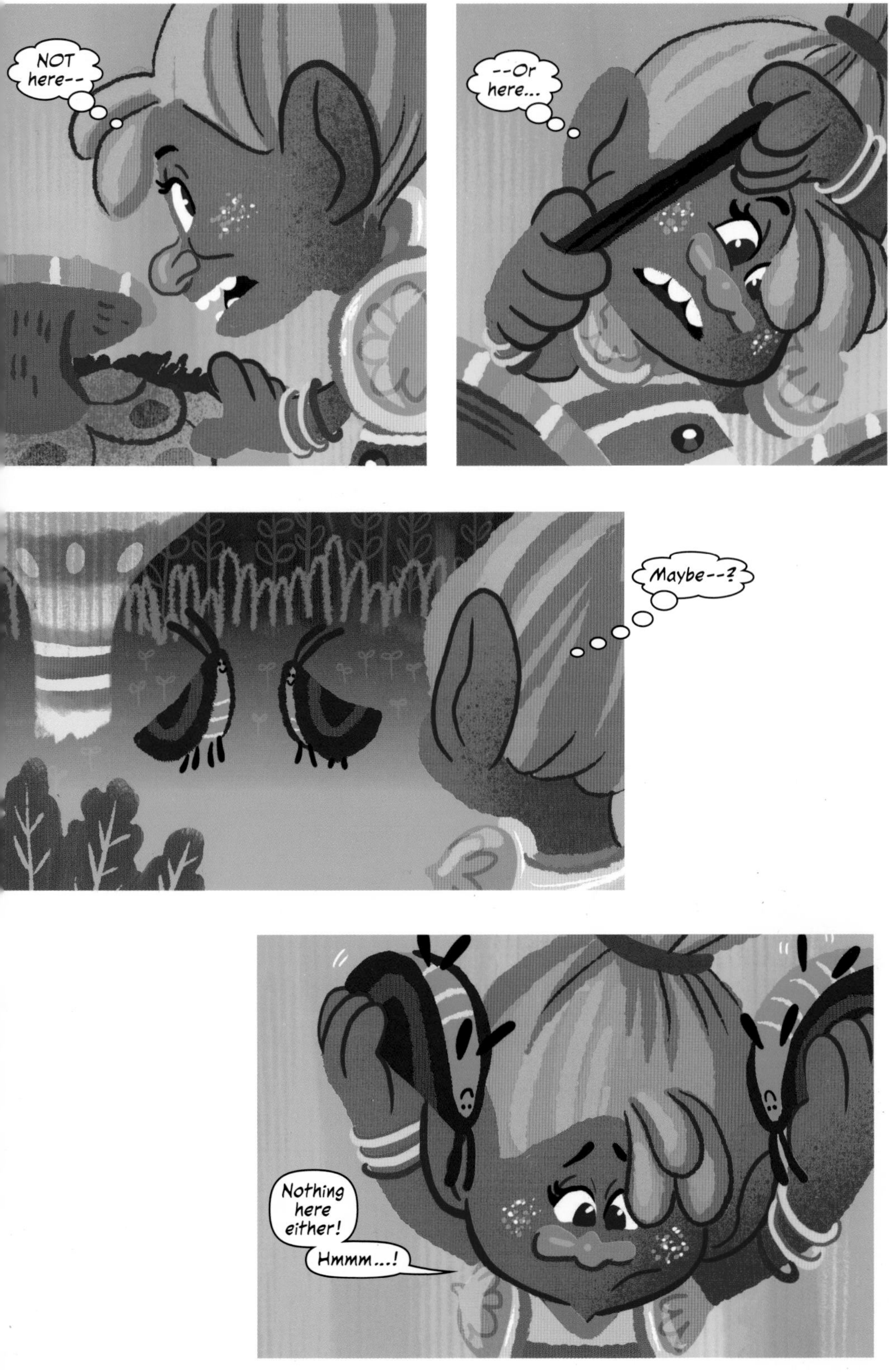
NOT here--
--Or here...
Maybe--?
Nothing here either!
Hmmm...!

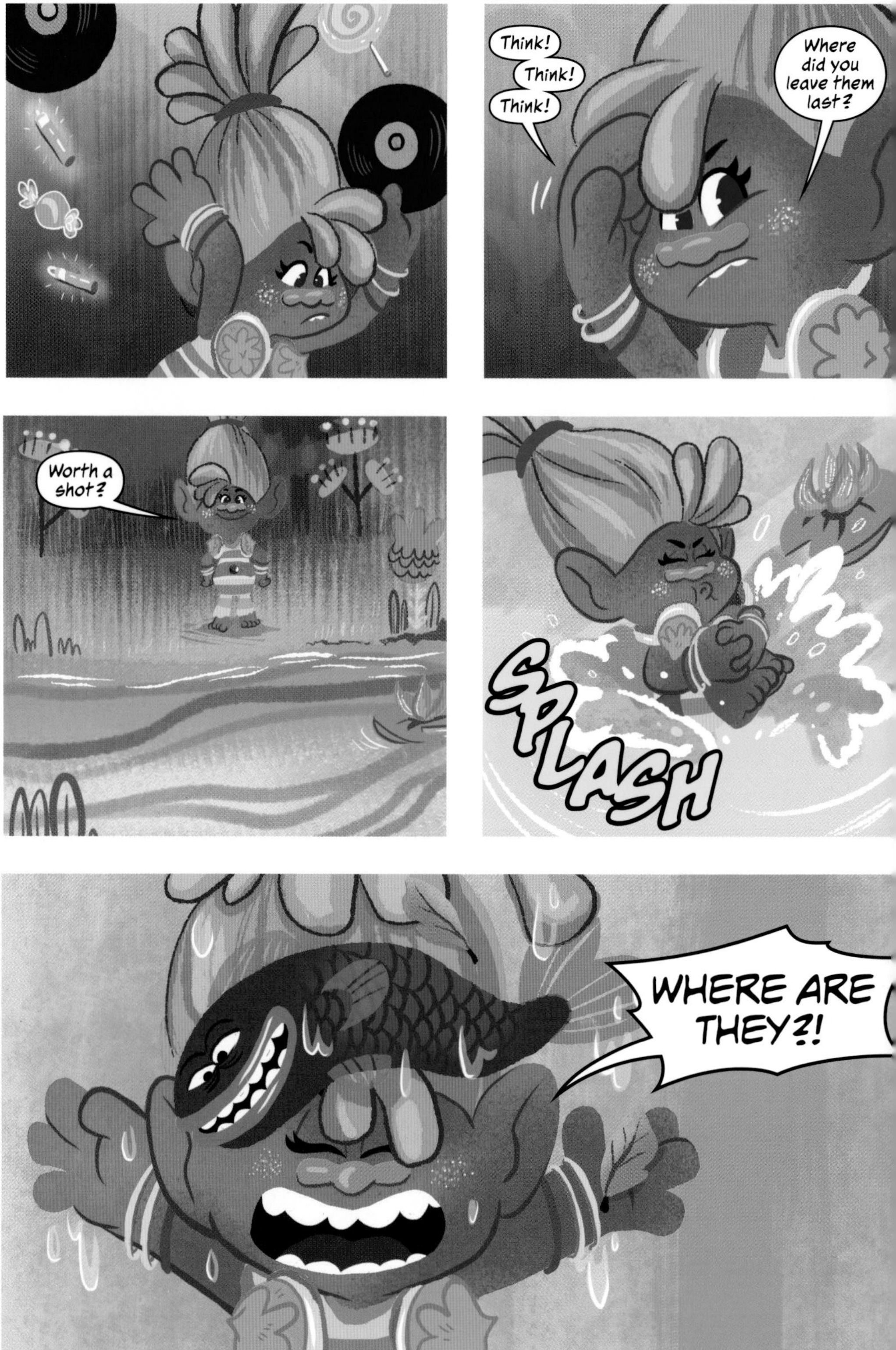
Think!
Think!
Think!
Where did you leave them last?
Worth a shot?
SPLASH
WHERE ARE THEY?!

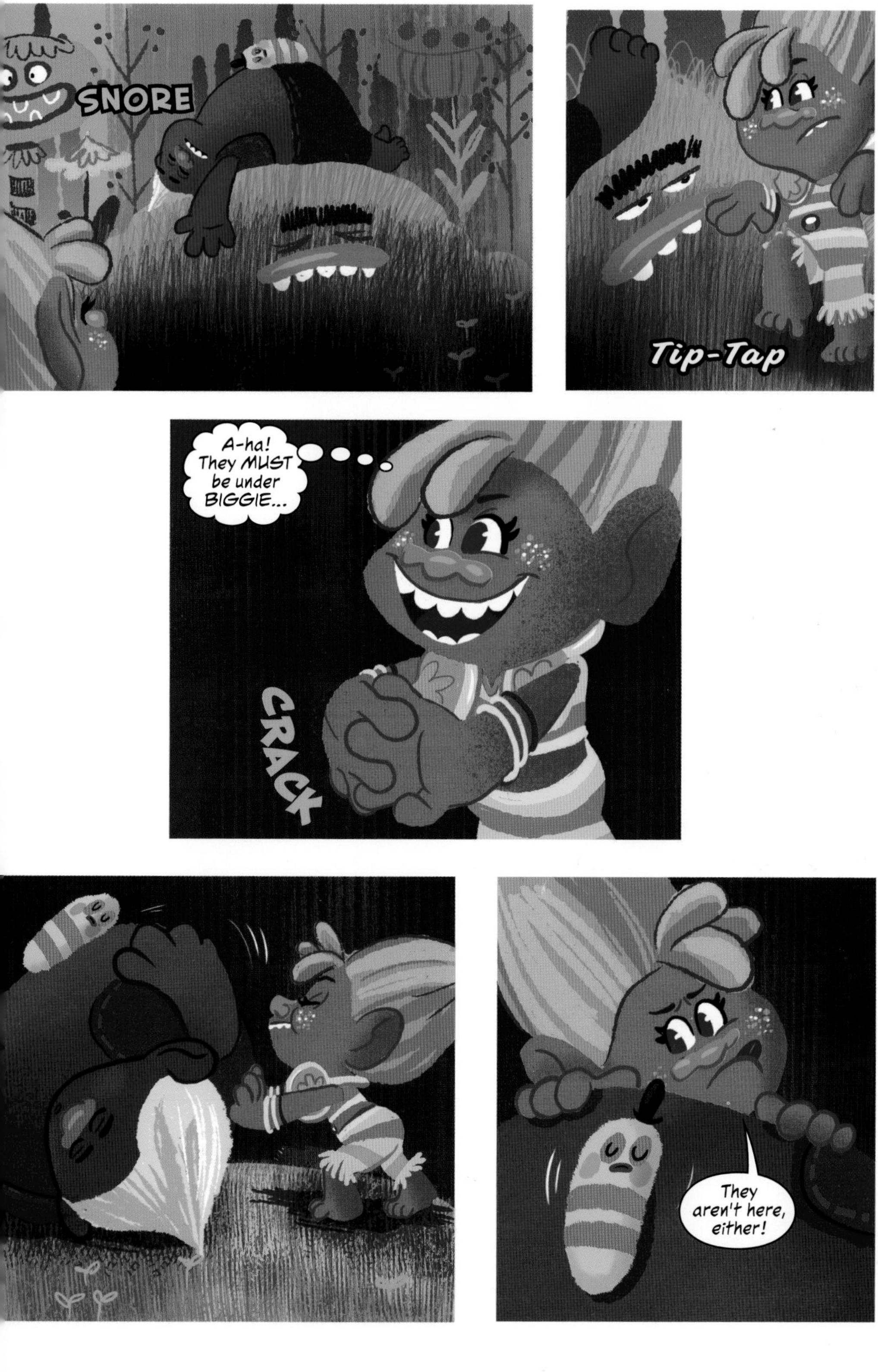
SNORE
Tip-Tap
A-ha! They MUST be under BIGGIE...
CRACK
They aren't here, either!

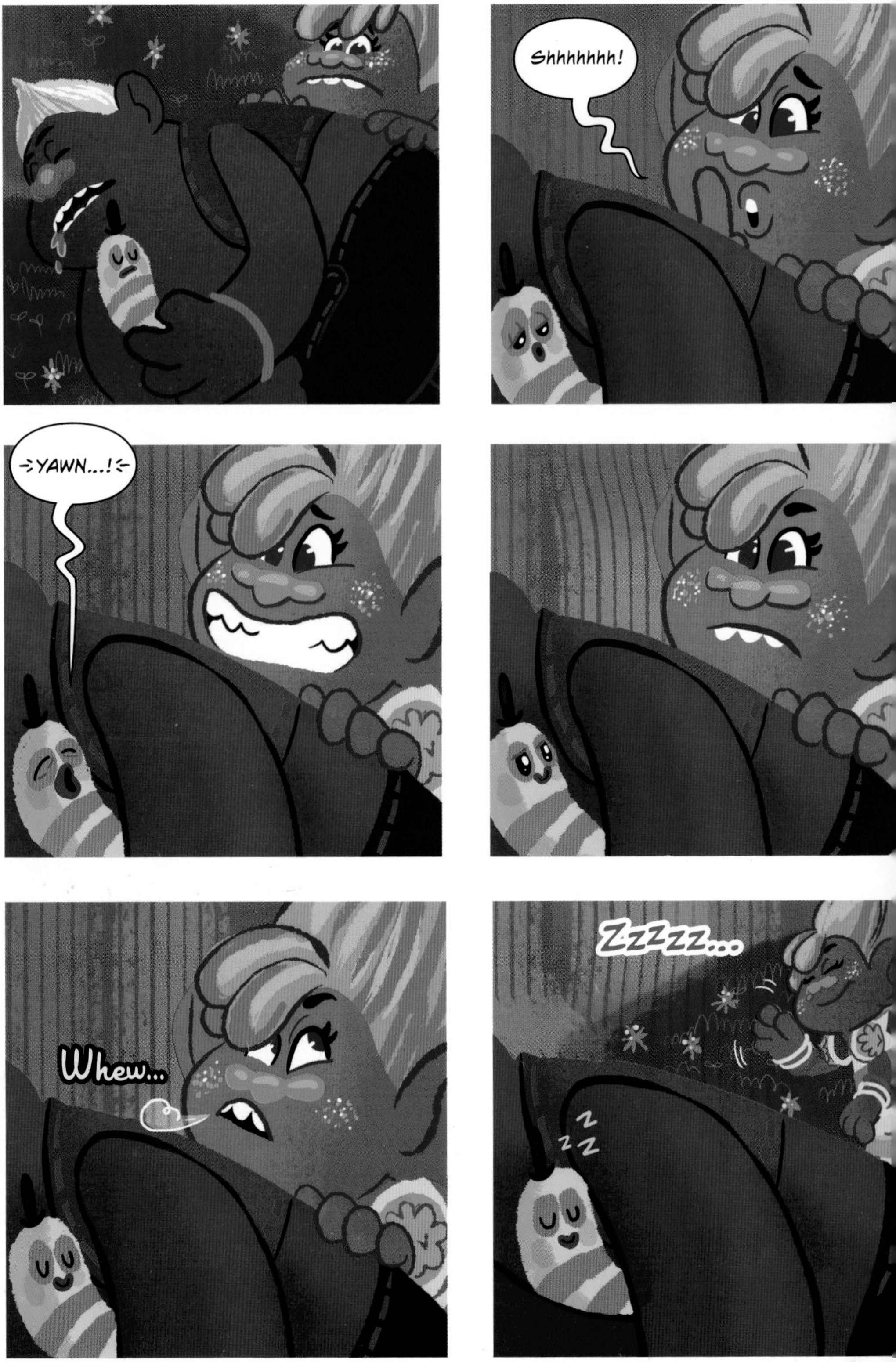
Shhhhhhh!
YAWN...!
Whew...
Zzzzz...
Z
Z Z

LA-LA-LA...

Oh, Poppy! Poppy! Poppy! Poppy!

DJ Suki! Is everything okay?

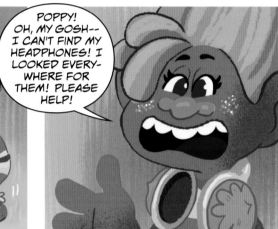

POPPY! OH, MY GOSH-- I CAN'T FIND MY HEADPHONES! I LOOKED EVERY-WHERE FOR THEM! PLEASE HELP!

I know where your head-phones are!

WHERE?!

Around your neck, silly!

That was the only place I didn't look...!

HA HA HA HA!

End

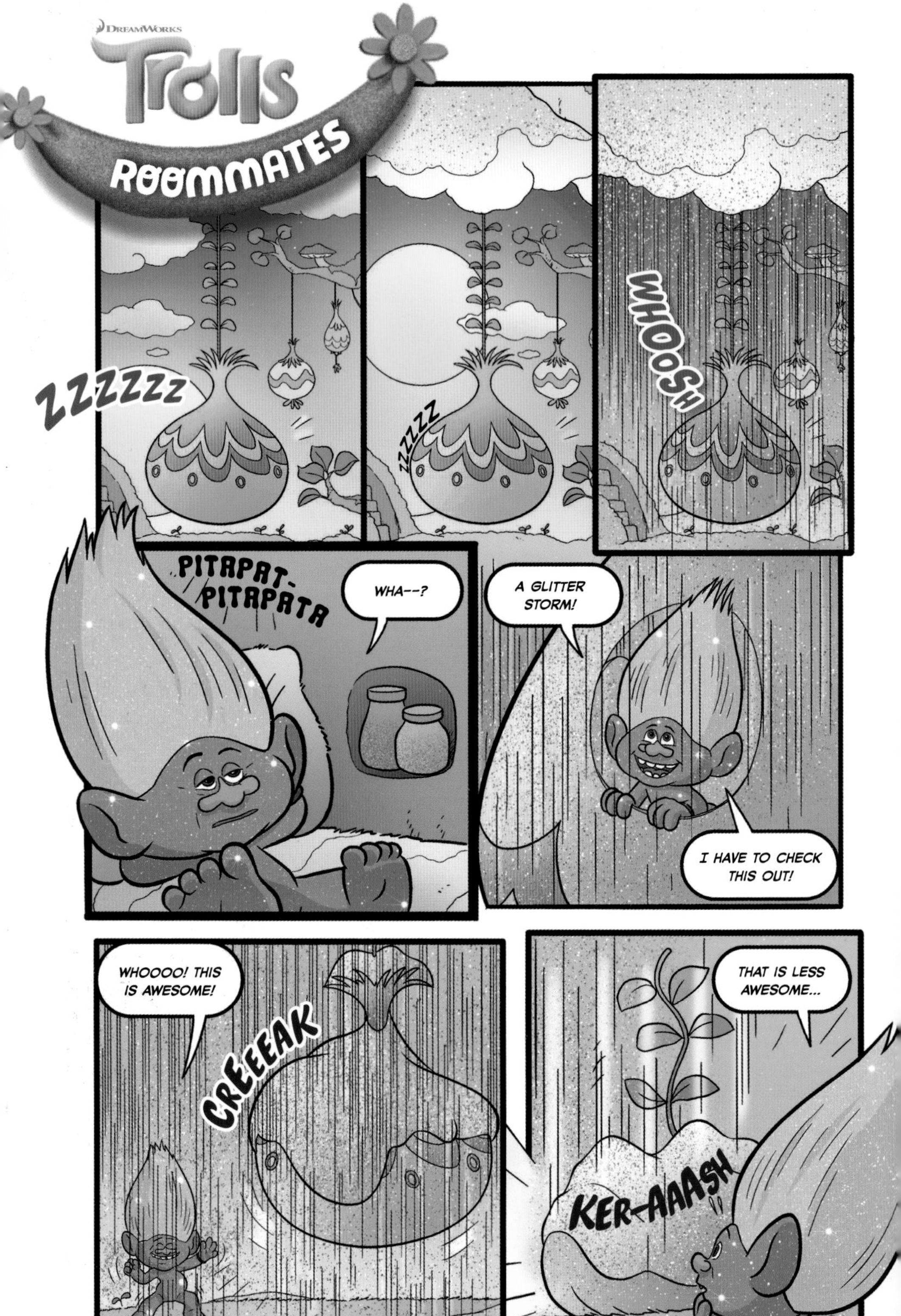
DreamWorks
Trolls
ROOMMATES
ZZZZZZ
ZZZZZ
WHOOSH
PITAPAT-PITAPATA
WHA--?
A GLITTER STORM!
I HAVE TO CHECK THIS OUT!
WHOOOO! THIS IS AWESOME!
CREEEAK
THAT IS LESS AWESOME...
KER-AAASH

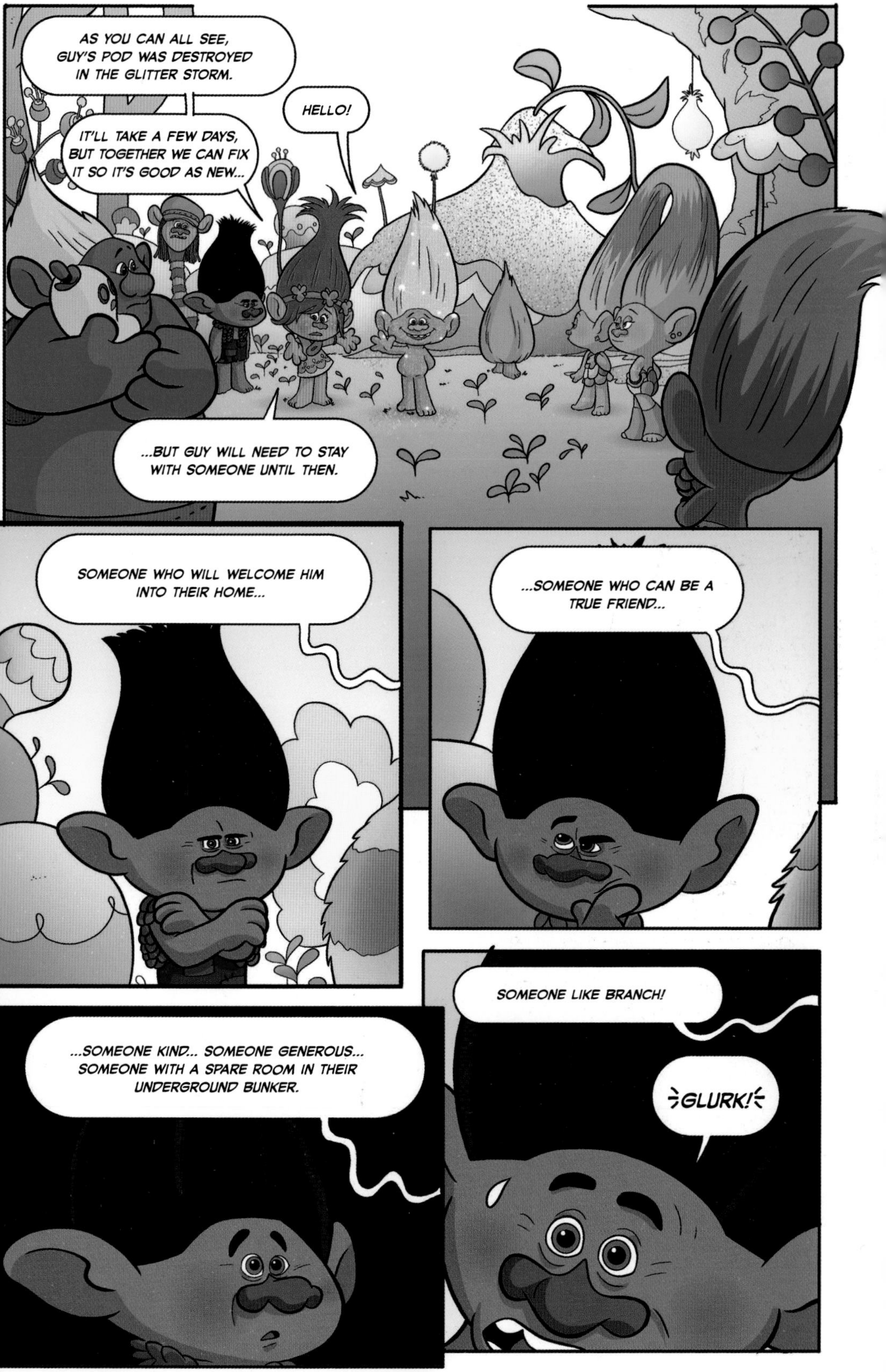
AS YOU CAN ALL SEE, GUY'S POD WAS DESTROYED IN THE GLITTER STORM.
HELLO!
IT'LL TAKE A FEW DAYS, BUT TOGETHER WE CAN FIX IT SO IT'S GOOD AS NEW...
...BUT GUY WILL NEED TO STAY WITH SOMEONE UNTIL THEN.
SOMEONE WHO WILL WELCOME HIM INTO THEIR HOME...
...SOMEONE WHO CAN BE A TRUE FRIEND...
...SOMEONE KIND... SOMEONE GENEROUS... SOMEONE WITH A SPARE ROOM IN THEIR UNDERGROUND BUNKER.
SOMEONE LIKE BRANCH!
GLURK!

GIMME A HUG, ROOMIE!

NO! GET OFF! NO HUGGING!

THERE MUST BE SOMEWHERE ELSE HE CAN GO.

I'M AFRAID NOT. YOU'RE THE ONLY ONE WITH SPACE.

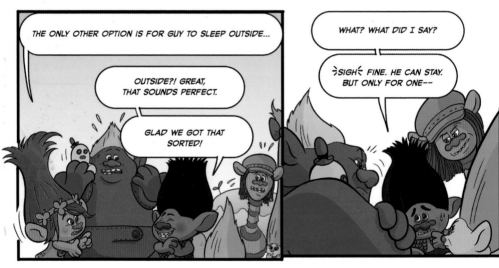

THE ONLY OTHER OPTION IS FOR GUY TO SLEEP OUTSIDE...

OUTSIDE?! GREAT, THAT SOUNDS PERFECT.

GLAD WE GOT THAT SORTED!

WHAT? WHAT DID I SAY?

⟩SIGH⟨ FINE. HE CAN STAY. BUT ONLY FOR ONE--

HOORAY! WE'RE GOING TO BE BFFs!

ARE TOO!

TOTALLY ARE!

NO, WE AREN'T.

NO!

GET OFF!

IF YOU'RE STAYING HERE, THE FIRST RULE IS--NO HUGGING!

NO HUGGING, EH?

HOW ABOUT...

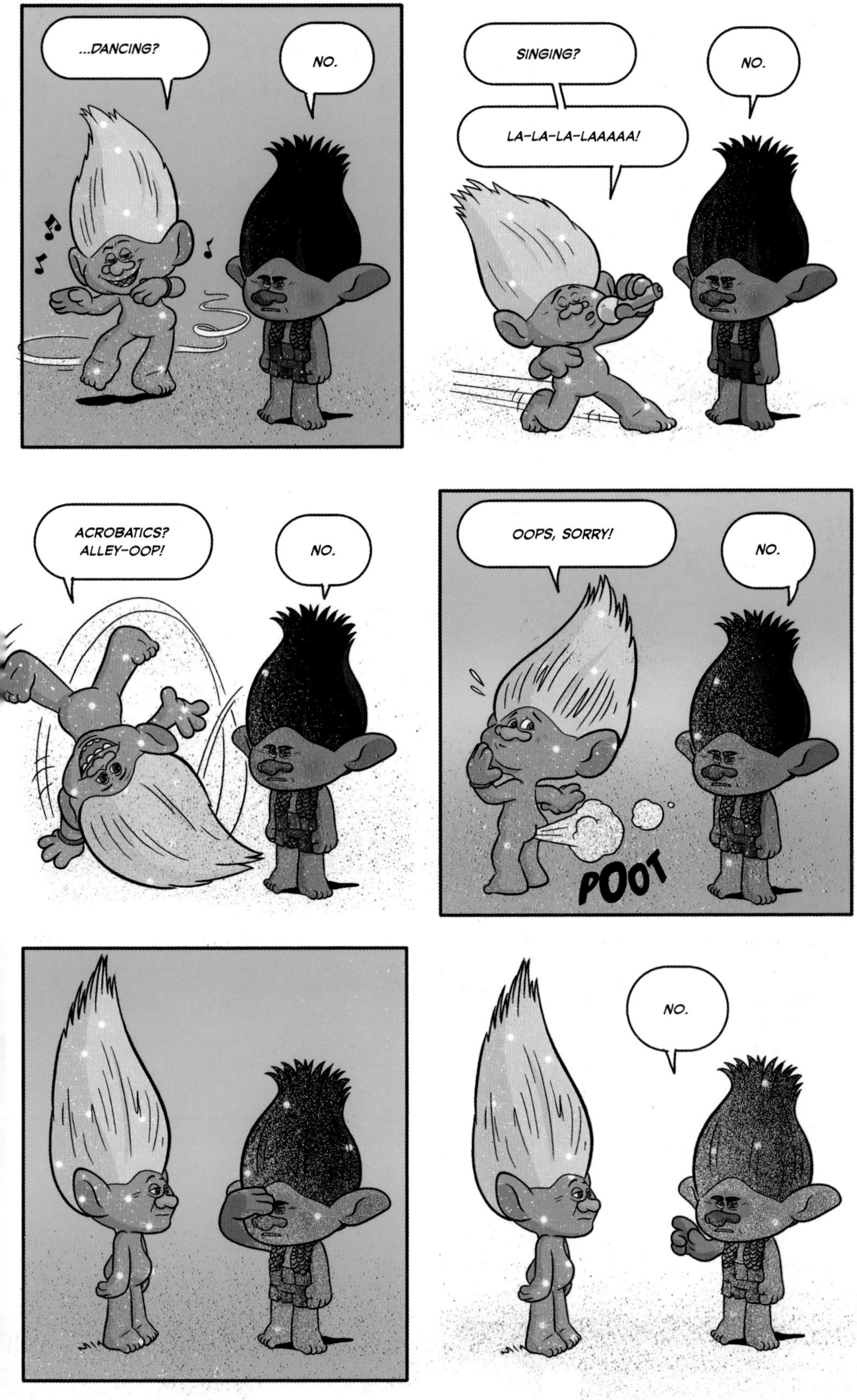
...DANCING?
NO.
SINGING?
LA-LA-LA-LAAAAA!
NO.
ACROBATICS? ALLEY-OOP!
NO.
OOPS, SORRY!
NO.
POOT
NO.

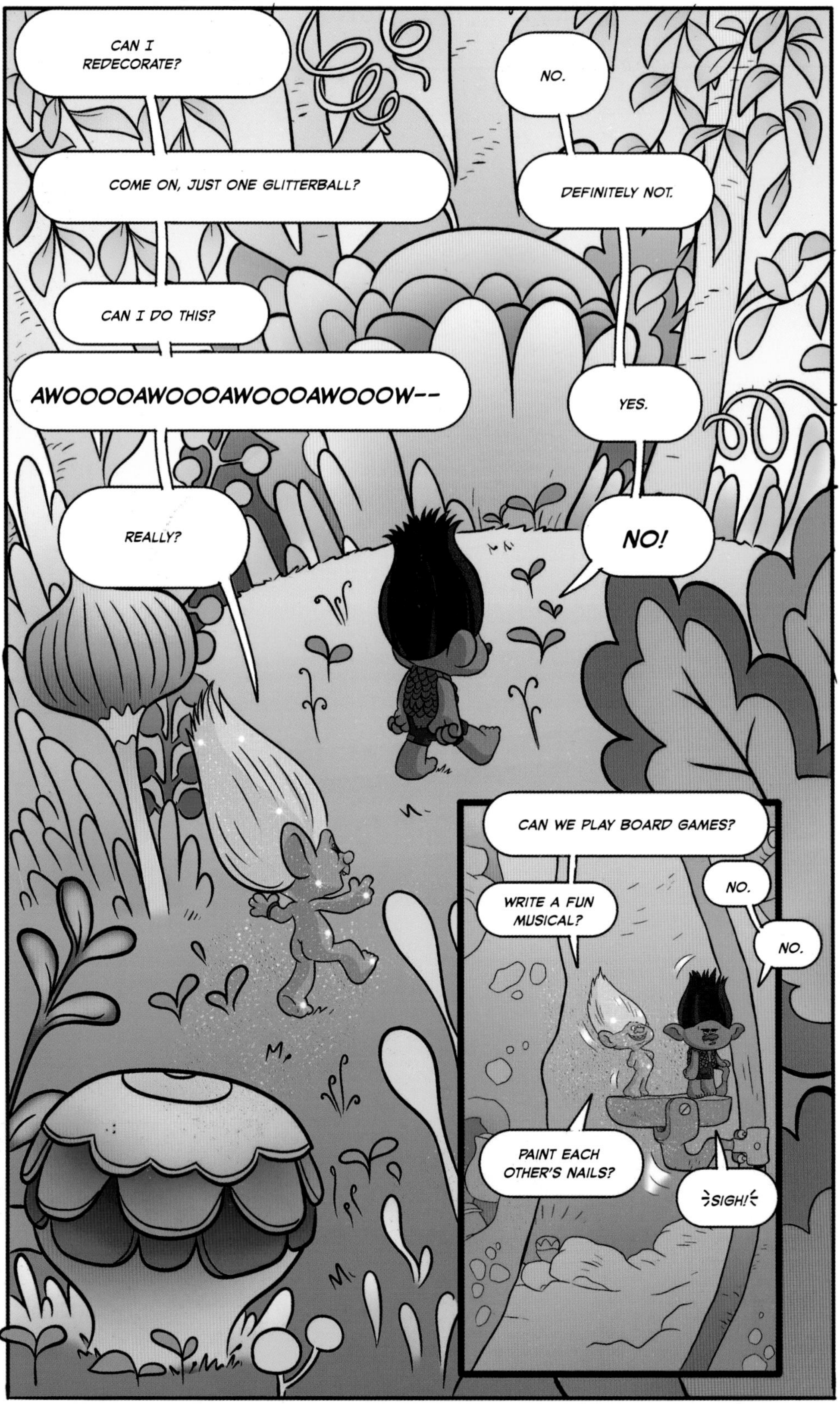
CAN I REDECORATE?
NO.
COME ON, JUST ONE GLITTERBALL?
DEFINITELY NOT.
CAN I DO THIS?
AWOOOOAWOOOAWOOOAWOOOW--
YES.
REALLY?
NO!
CAN WE PLAY BOARD GAMES?
NO.
WRITE A FUN MUSICAL?
NO.
PAINT EACH OTHER'S NAILS?
SIGH!

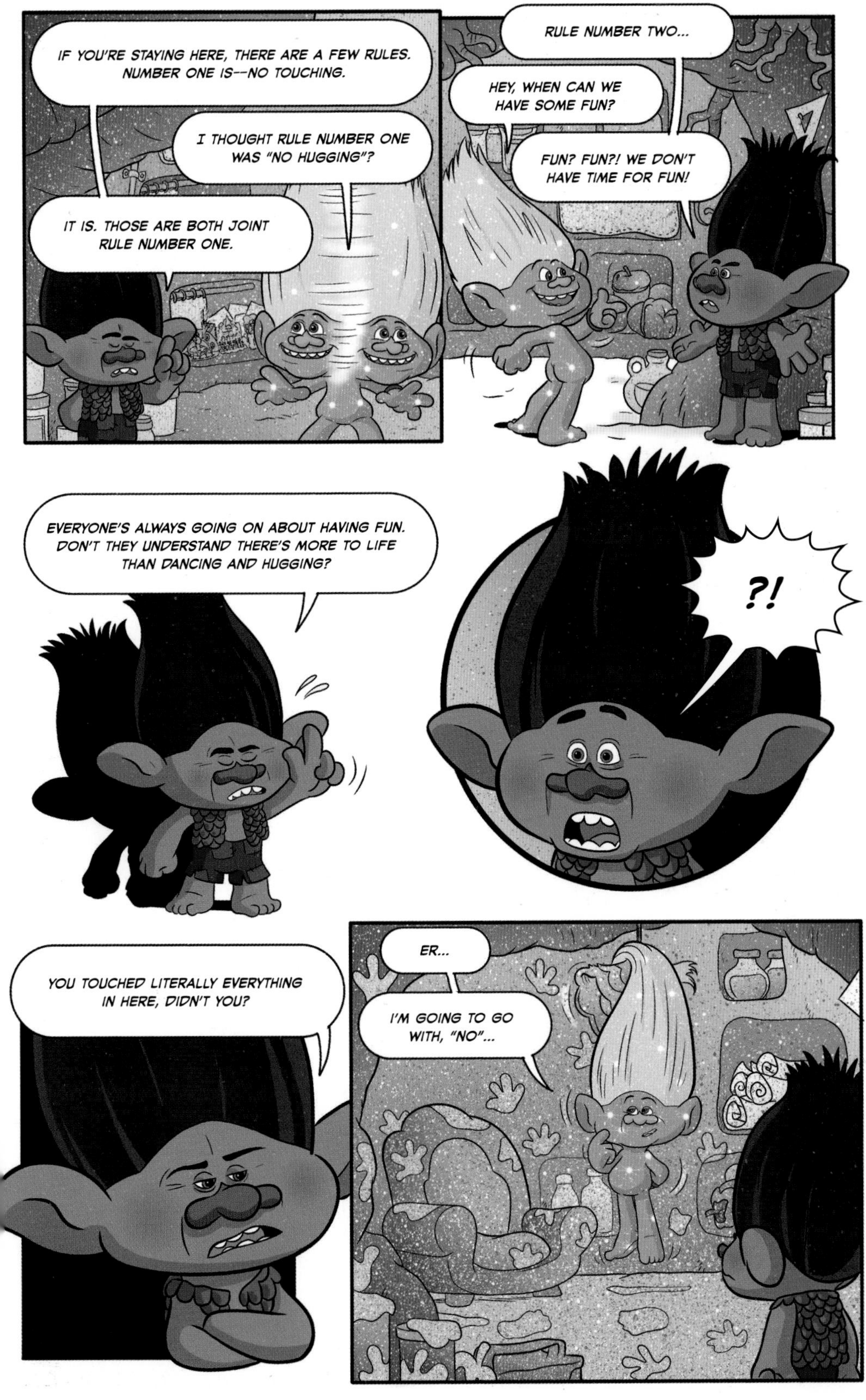
IF YOU'RE STAYING HERE, THERE ARE A FEW RULES. NUMBER ONE IS--NO TOUCHING.
I THOUGHT RULE NUMBER ONE WAS "NO HUGGING"?
IT IS. THOSE ARE BOTH JOINT RULE NUMBER ONE.
RULE NUMBER TWO...
HEY, WHEN CAN WE HAVE SOME FUN?
FUN? FUN?! WE DON'T HAVE TIME FOR FUN!
EVERYONE'S ALWAYS GOING ON ABOUT HAVING FUN. DON'T THEY UNDERSTAND THERE'S MORE TO LIFE THAN DANCING AND HUGGING?
?!
YOU TOUCHED LITERALLY EVERYTHING IN HERE, DIDN'T YOU?
ER...
I'M GOING TO GO WITH, "NO"...

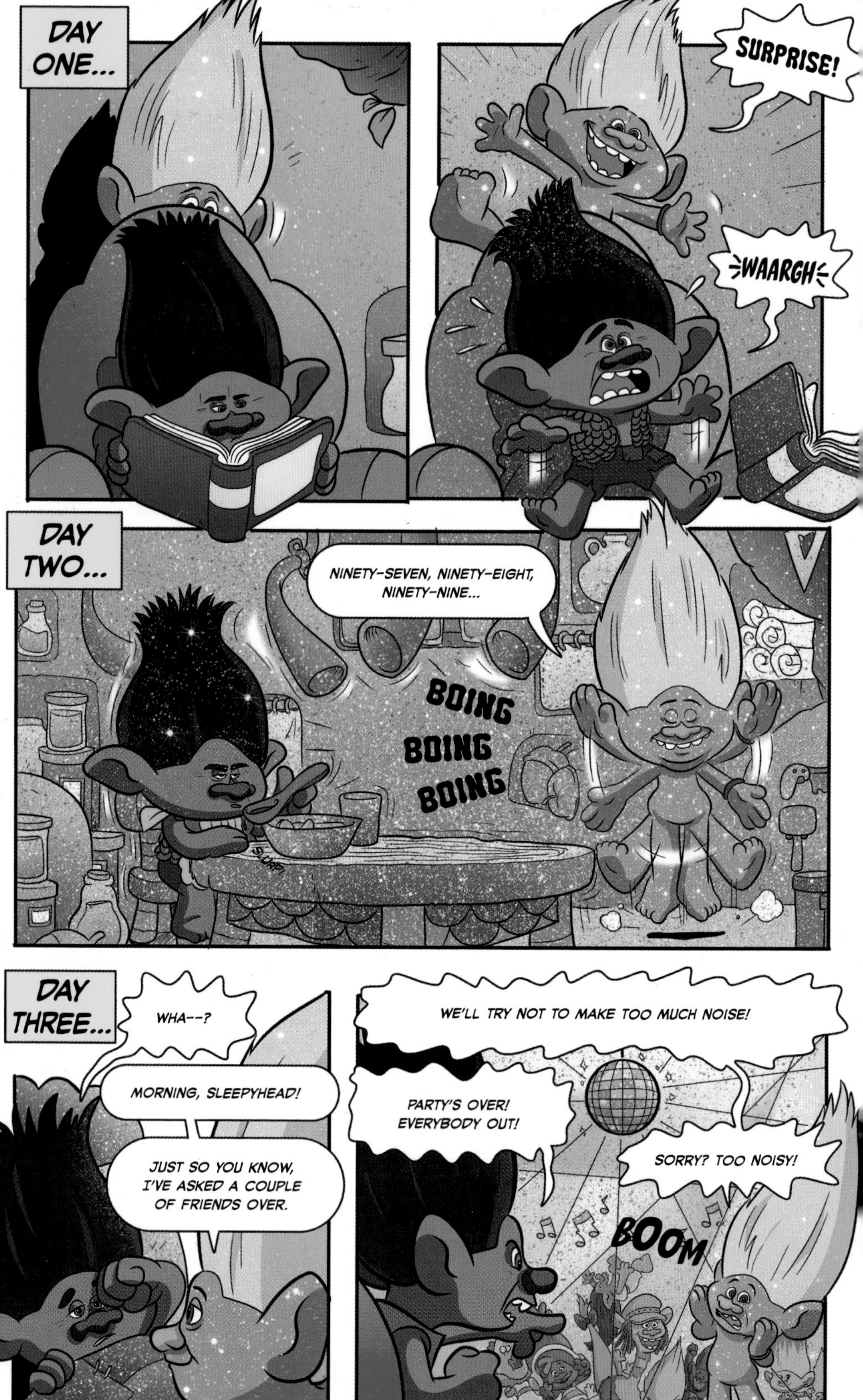
DAY ONE...
SURPRISE!
WAARGH
DAY TWO...
NINETY-SEVEN, NINETY-EIGHT, NINETY-NINE...
BOING
BOING
BOING
DAY THREE...
WHA--?
MORNING, SLEEPYHEAD!
JUST SO YOU KNOW, I'VE ASKED A COUPLE OF FRIENDS OVER.
WE'LL TRY NOT TO MAKE TOO MUCH NOISE!
PARTY'S OVER! EVERYBODY OUT!
SORRY? TOO NOISY!
BOOM

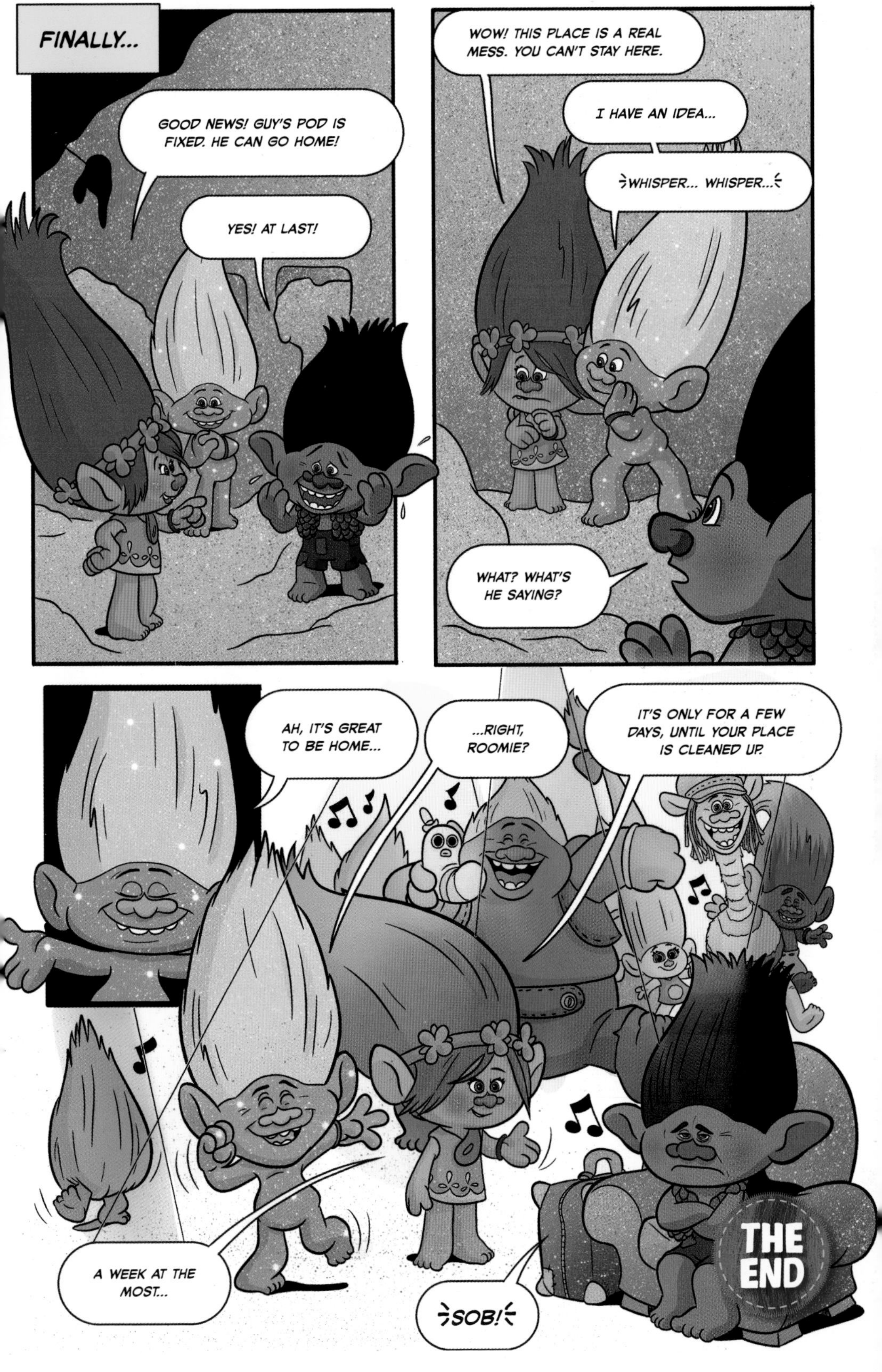
FINALLY...
GOOD NEWS! GUY'S POD IS FIXED. HE CAN GO HOME!
YES! AT LAST!
WOW! THIS PLACE IS A REAL MESS. YOU CAN'T STAY HERE.
I HAVE AN IDEA...
WHISPER... WHISPER...
WHAT? WHAT'S HE SAYING?
AH, IT'S GREAT TO BE HOME...
...RIGHT, ROOMIE?
IT'S ONLY FOR A FEW DAYS, UNTIL YOUR PLACE IS CLEANED UP.
A WEEK AT THE MOST...
SOB!
THE END

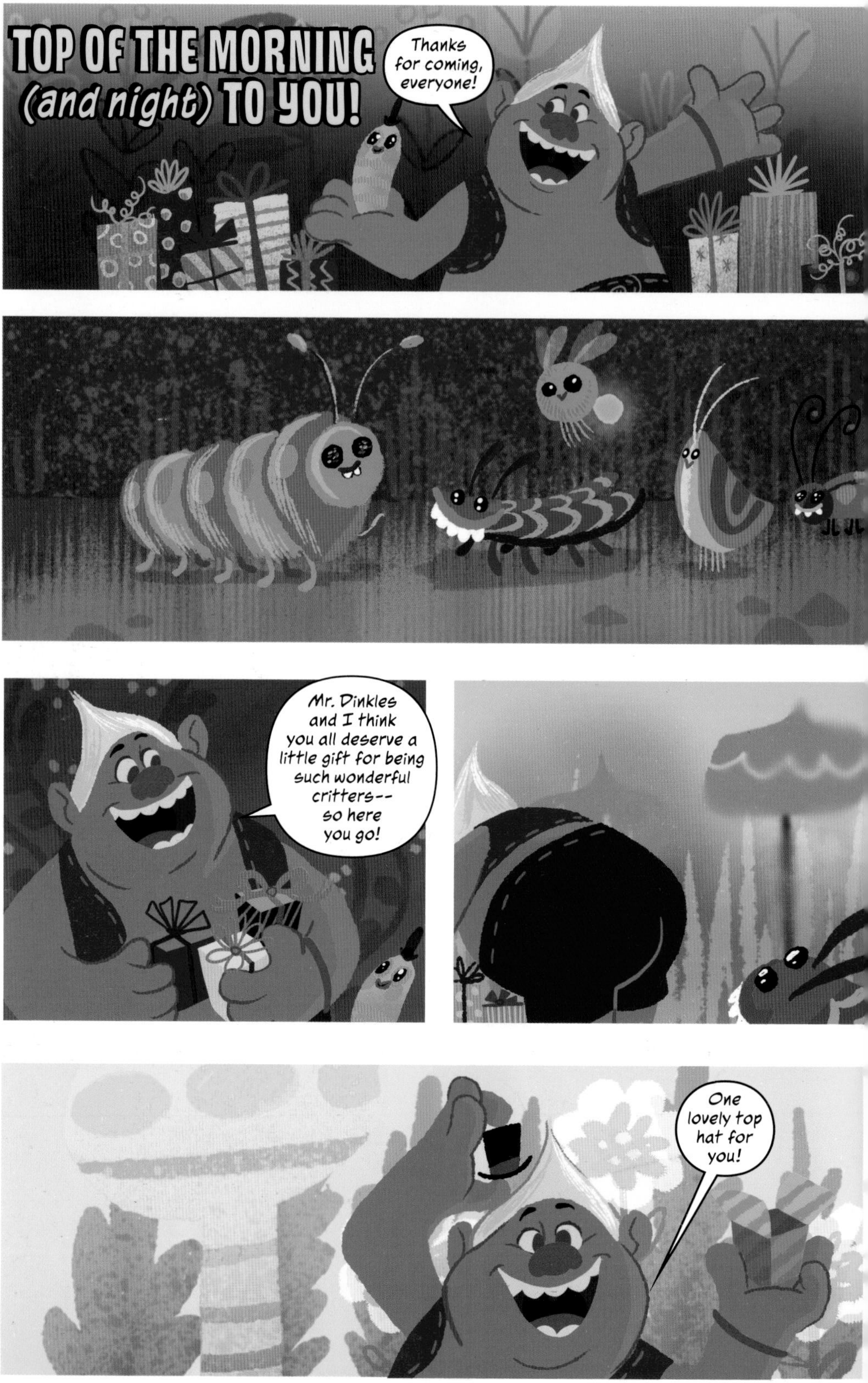
TOP OF THE MORNING (and night) TO YOU!
Thanks for coming, everyone!
Mr. Dinkles and I think you all deserve a little gift for being such wonderful critters-- so here you go!
One lovely top hat for you!

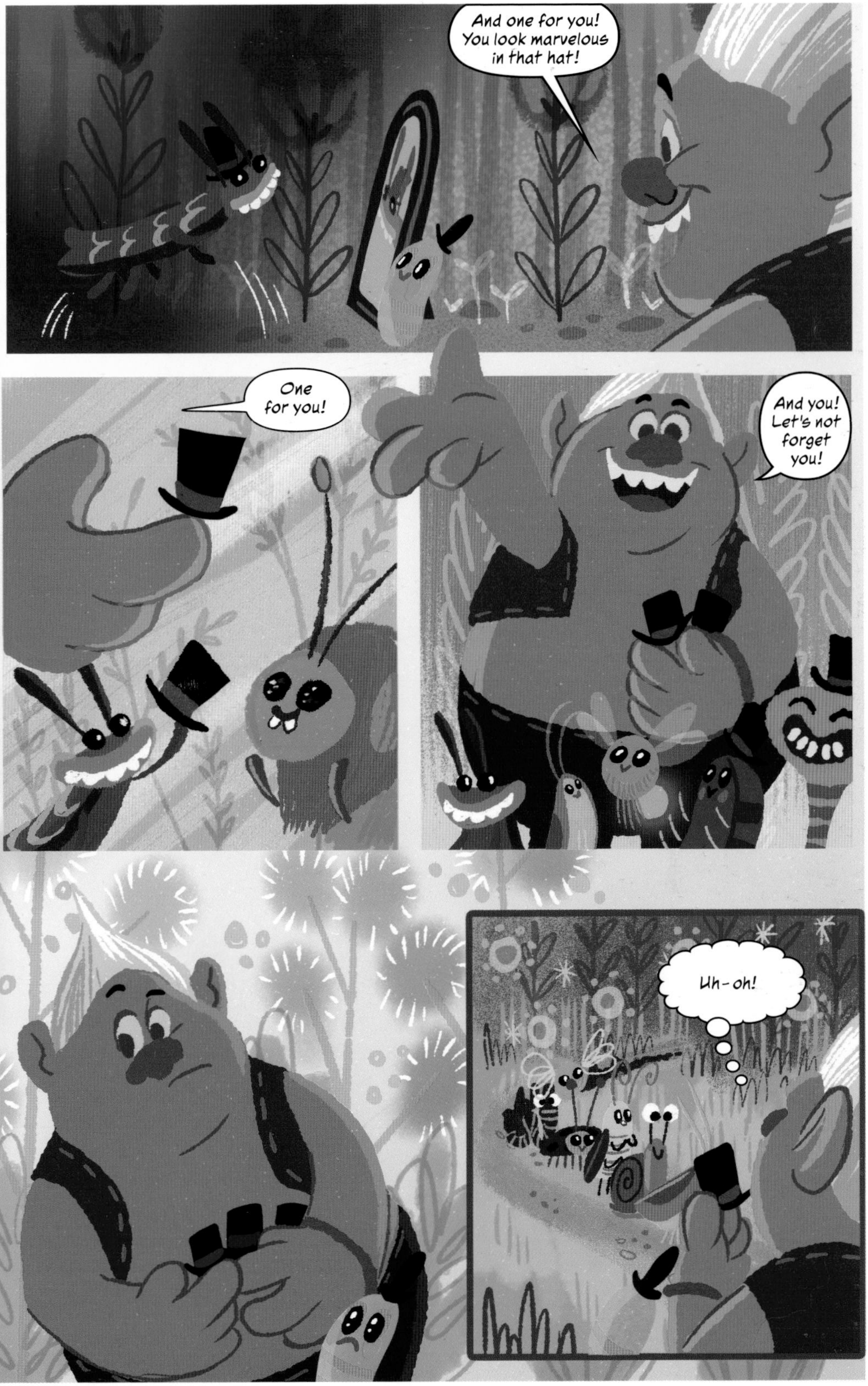
And one for you! You look marvelous in that hat!
One for you!
And you! Let's not forget you!
Uh-oh!

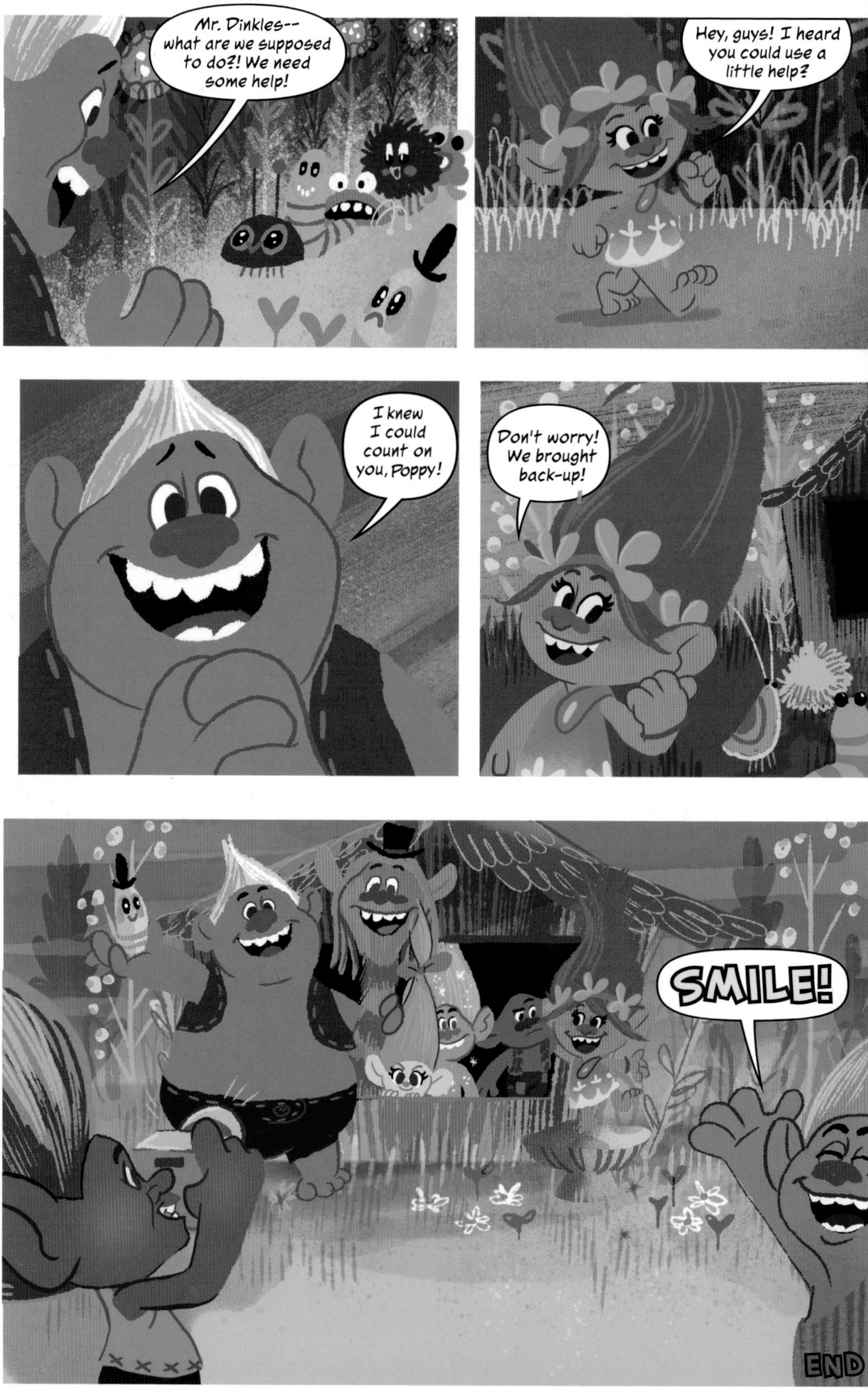
Mr. Dinkles--
what are we supposed to do?! We need some help!
Hey, guys! I heard you could use a little help?
I knew I could count on you, Poppy!
Don't worry! We brought back-up!
SMILE!
END

Wakey-Wakey

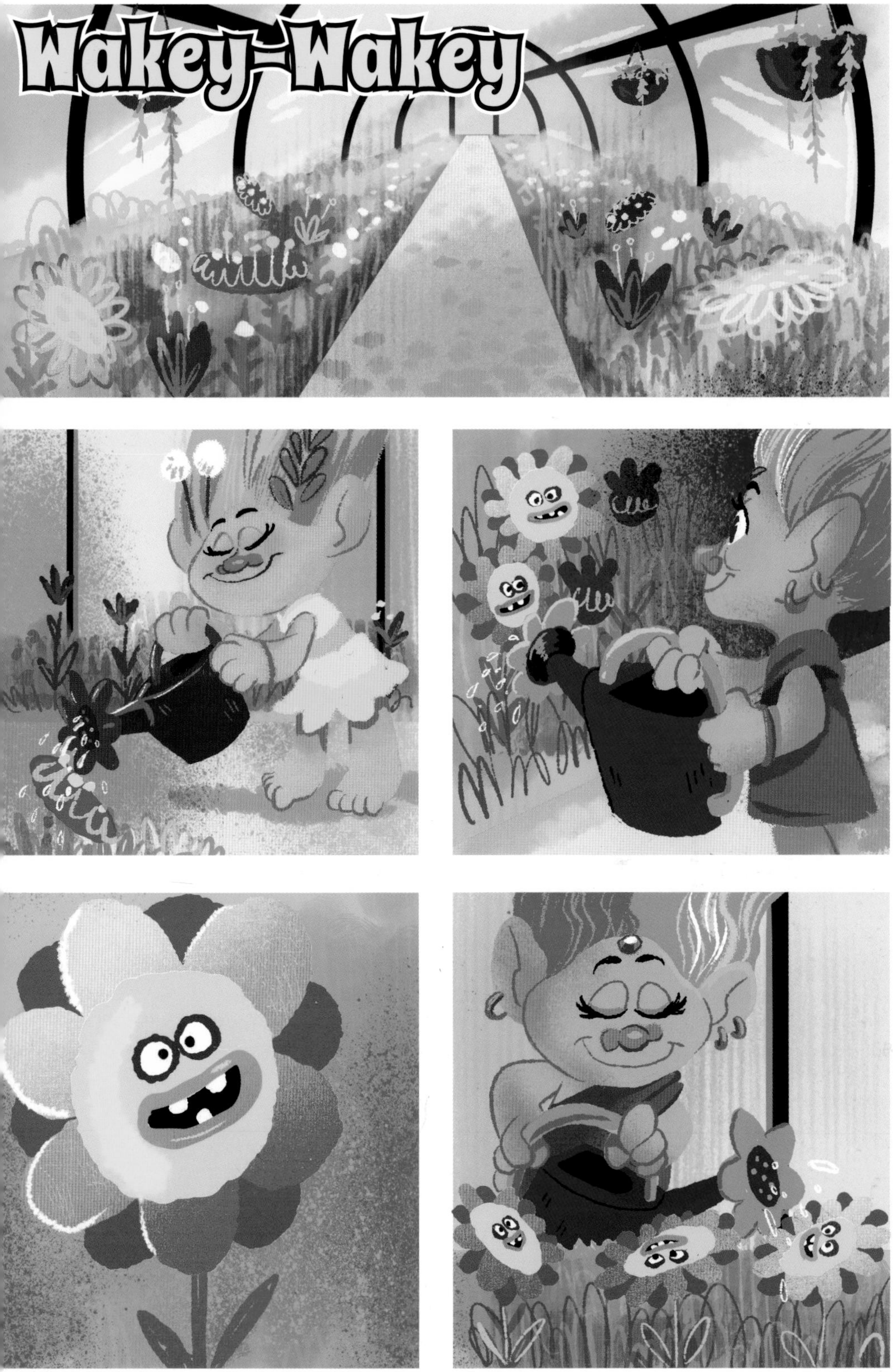

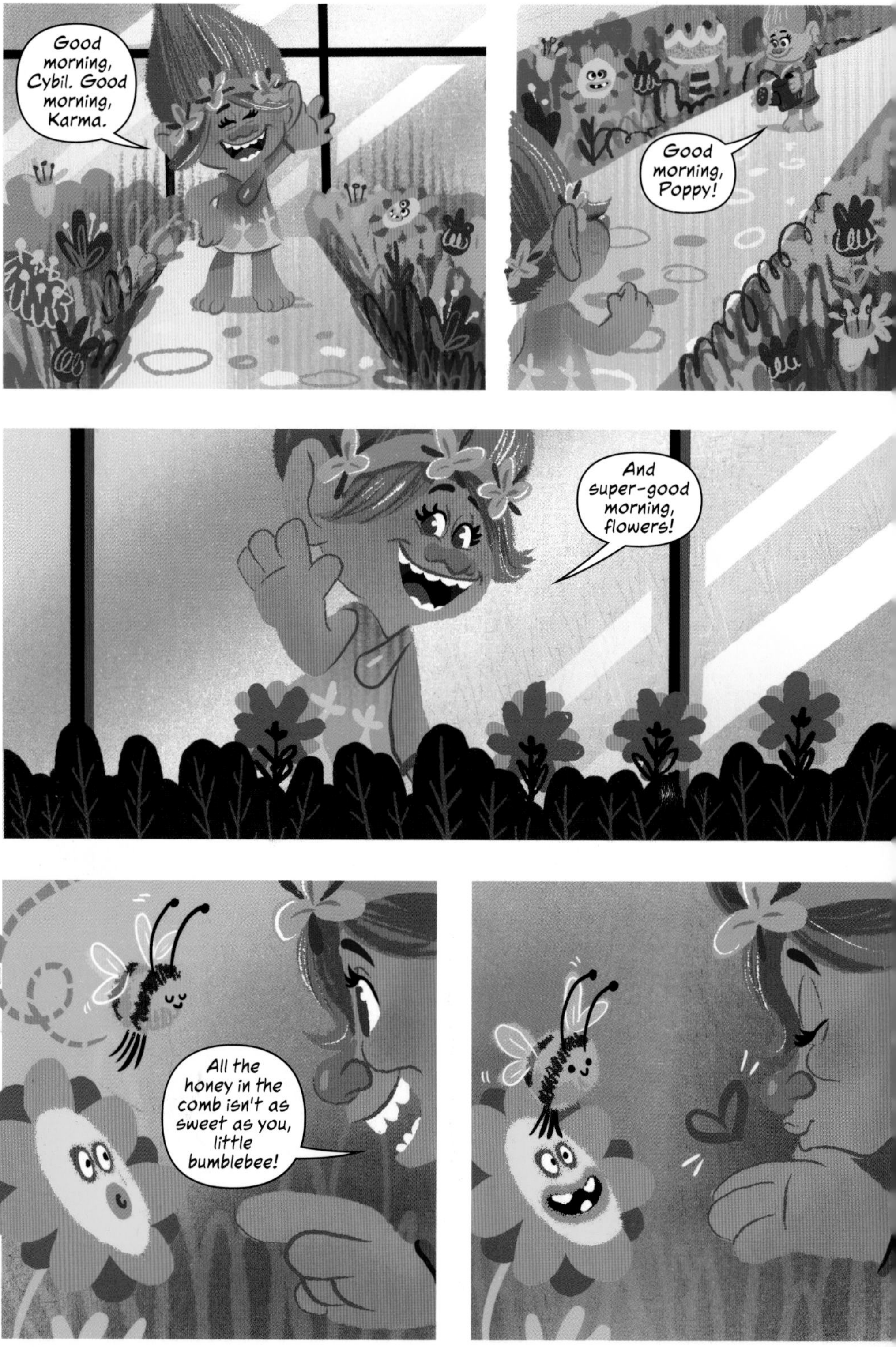
Good morning, Cybil. Good morning, Karma.
Good morning, Poppy!
And super-good morning, flowers!
All the honey in the comb isn't as sweet as you, little bumblebee!

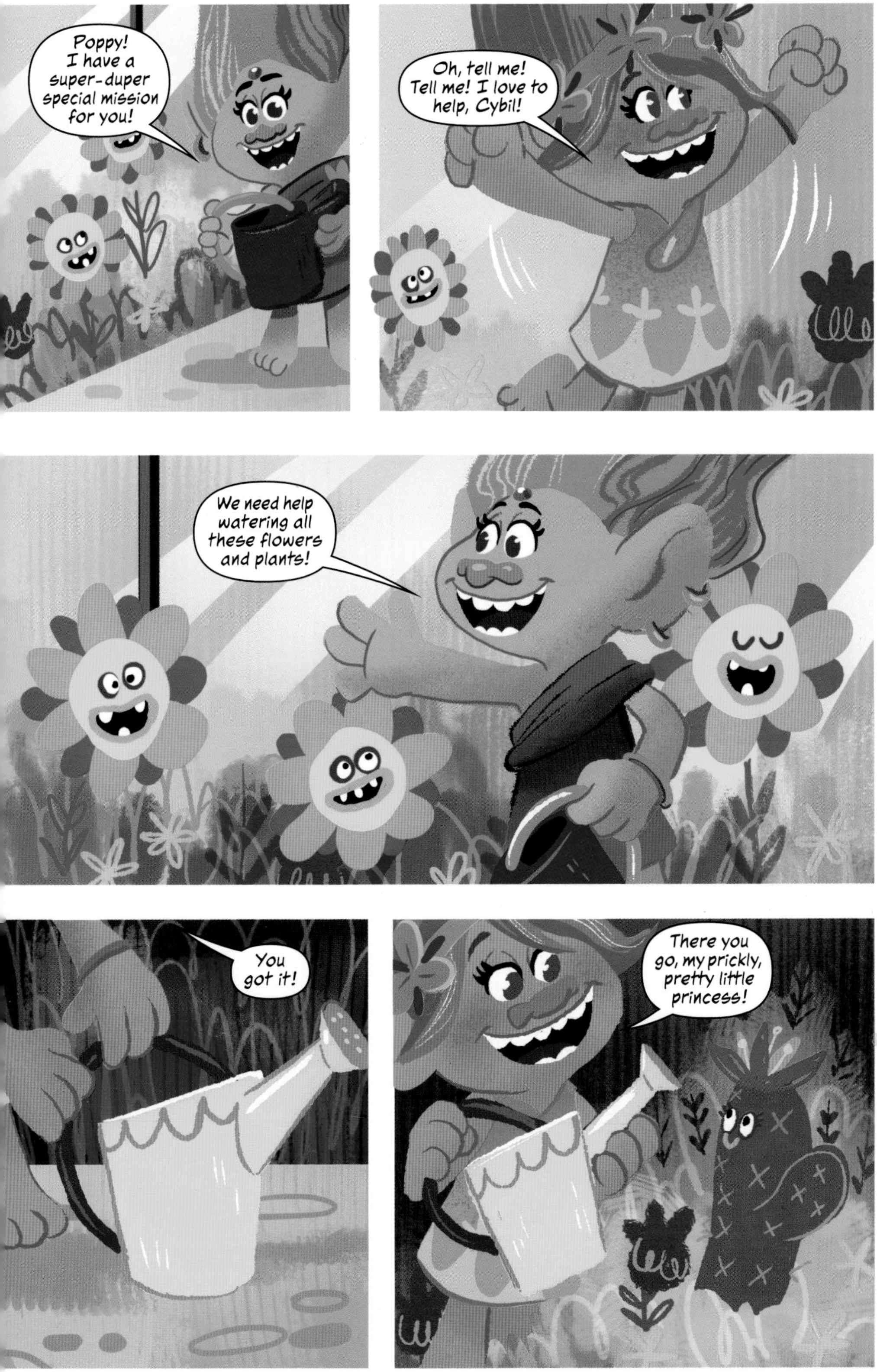
Poppy! I have a super-duper special mission for you!
Oh, tell me! Tell me! I love to help, Cybil!
We need help watering all these flowers and plants!
You got it!
There you go, my prickly, pretty little princess!

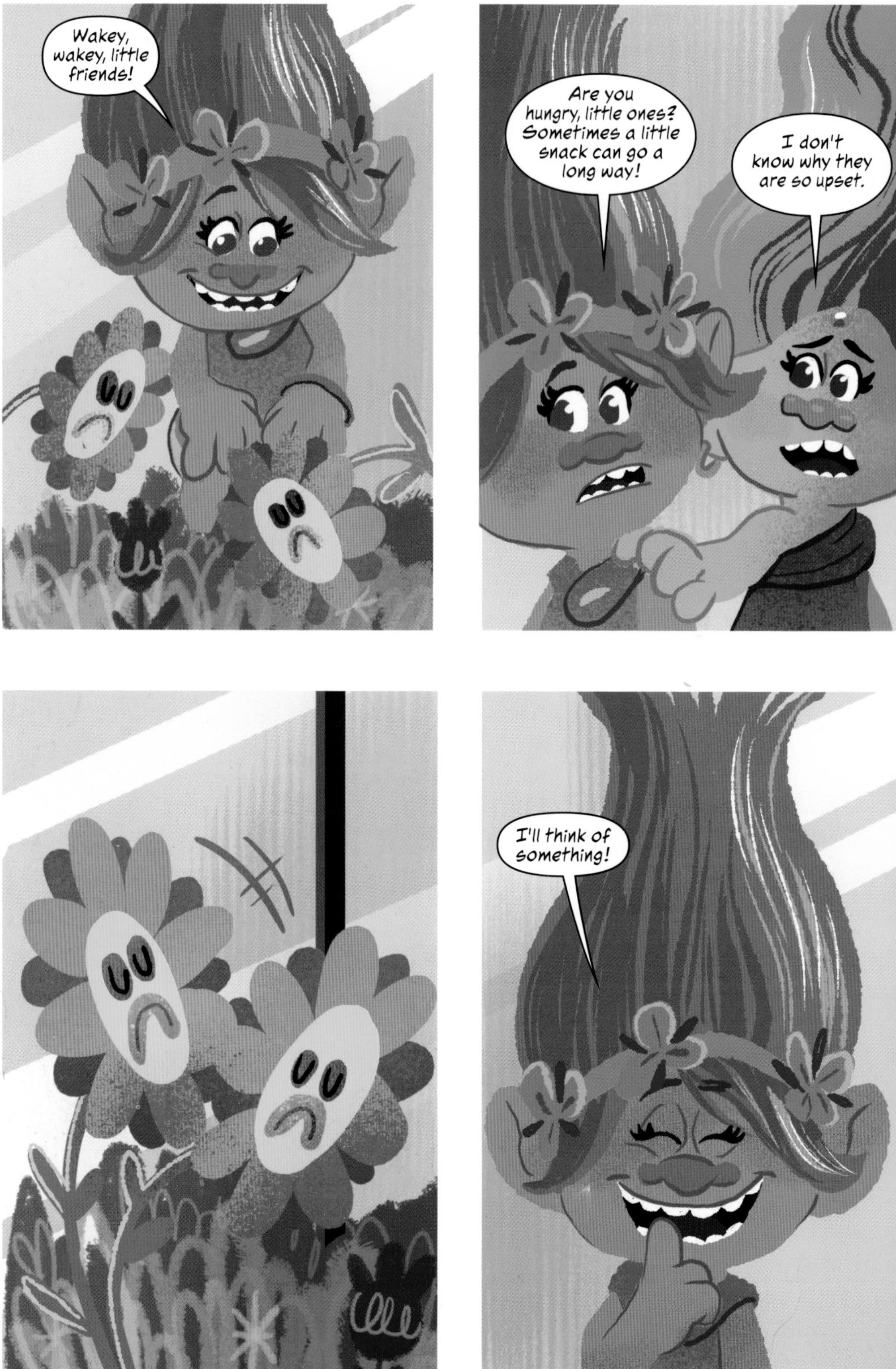
Wakey, wakey, little friends!
Are you hungry, little ones? Sometimes a little snack can go a long way!
I don't know why they are so upset.
I'll think of something!

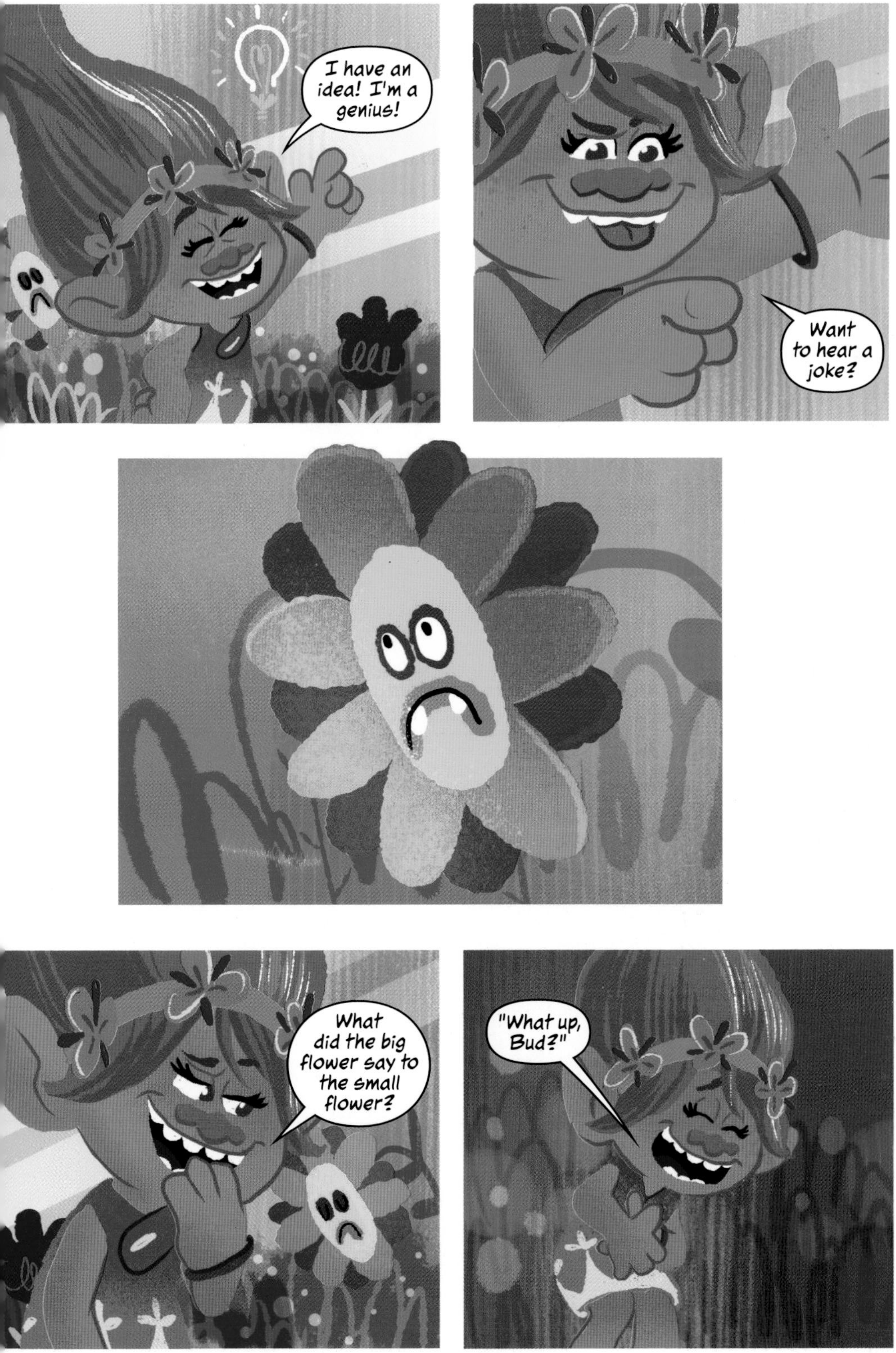
I have an idea! I'm a genius!
Want to hear a joke?
What did the big flower say to the small flower?
"What up, Bud?"

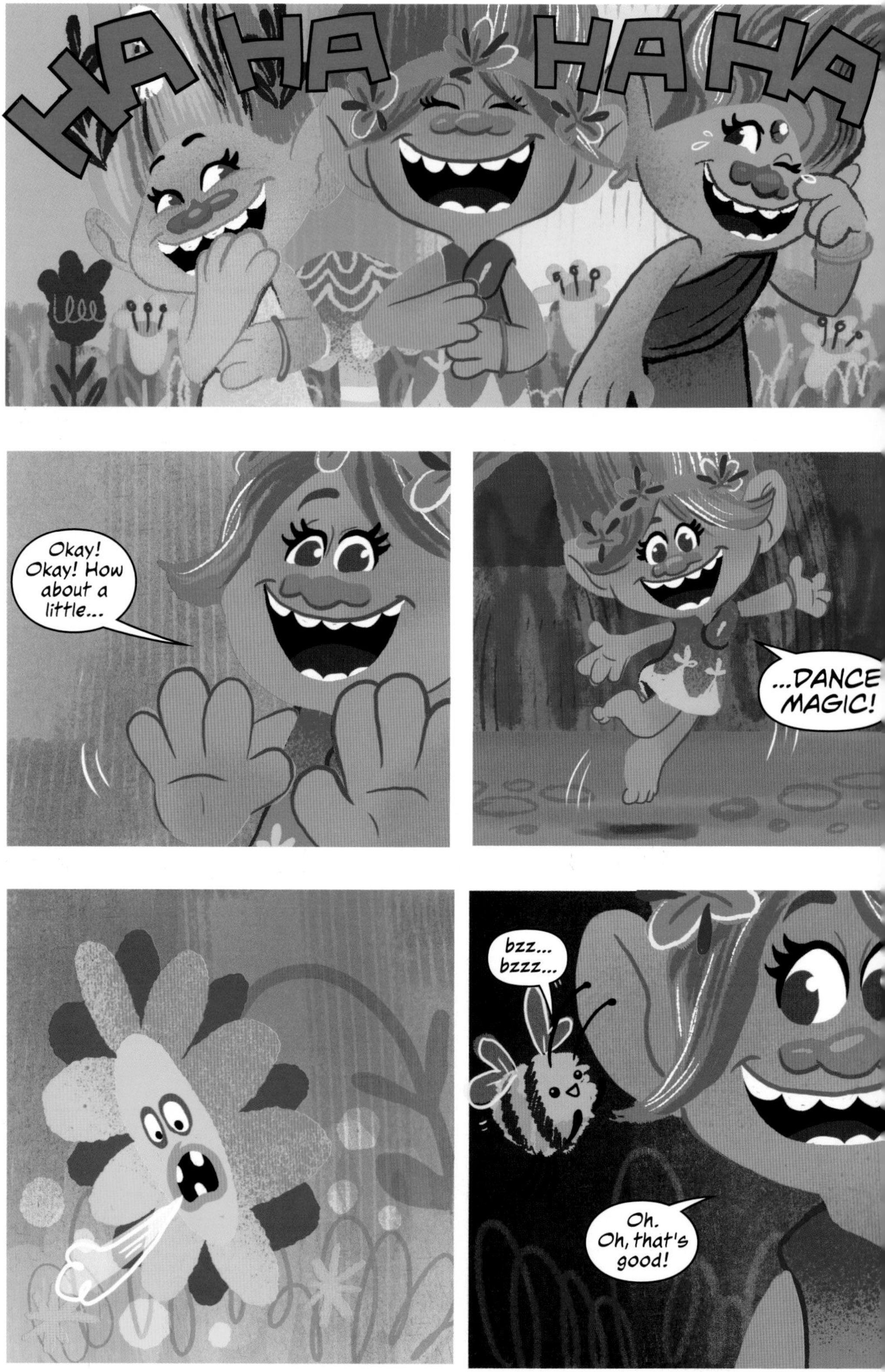
HA HA HA HA
Okay! Okay! How about a little...
...DANCE MAGIC!
bzz... bzzz...
Oh. Oh, that's good!

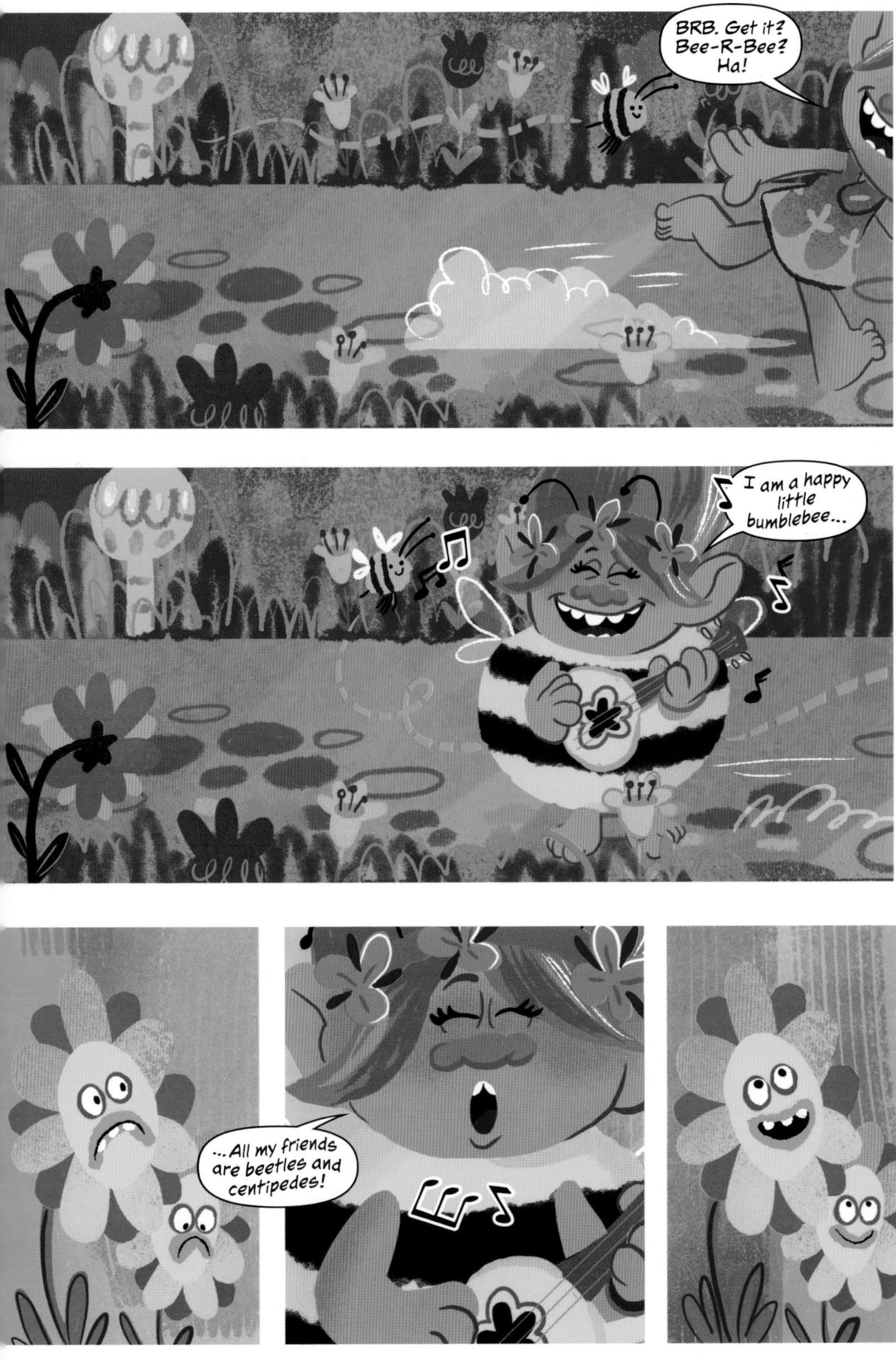
BRB. Get it? Bee-R-Bee? Ha!
I am a happy little bumblebee...
...All my friends are beetles and centipedes!

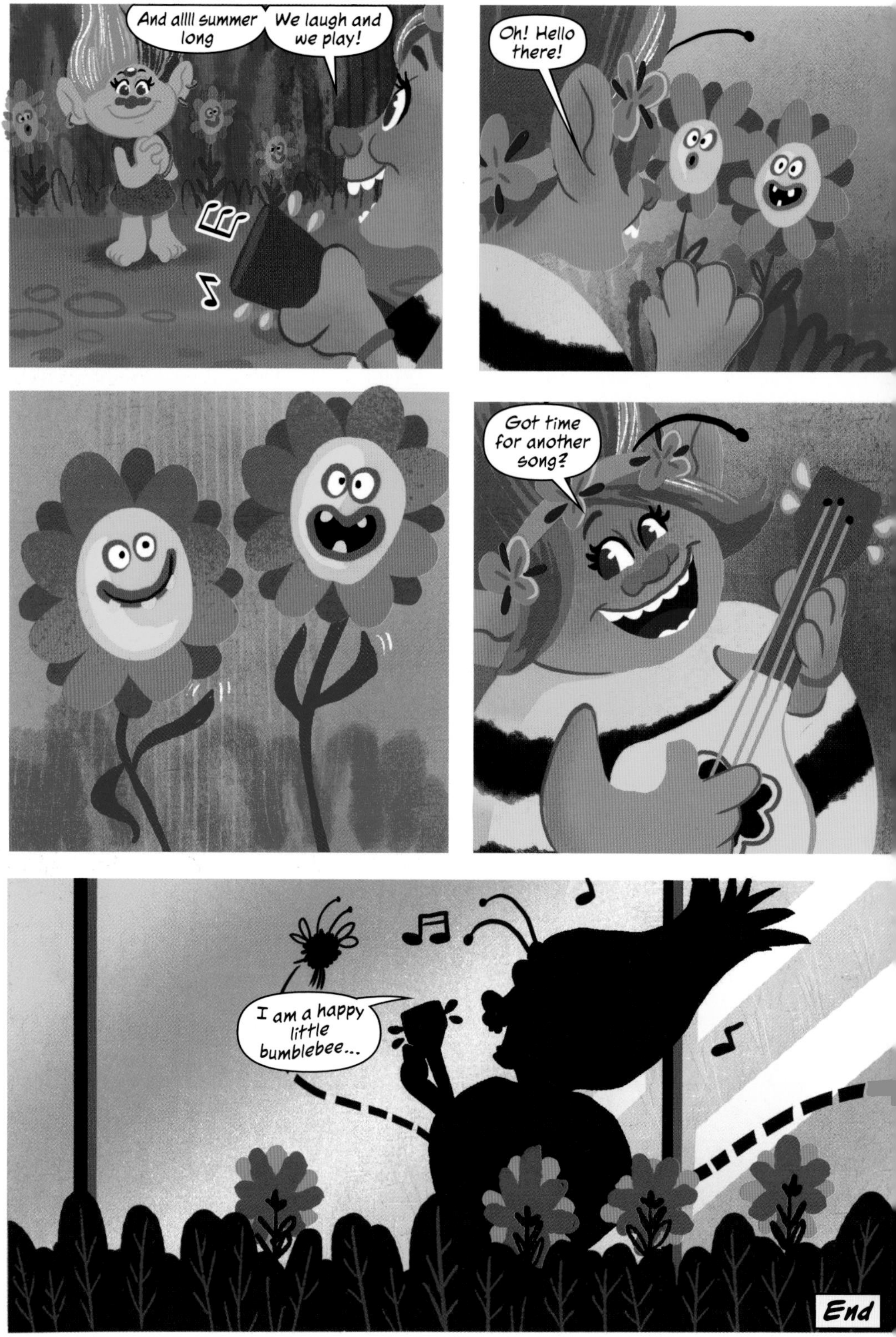
And allll summer long
We laugh and we play!
Oh! Hello there!
Got time for another song?
I am a happy little bumblebee...
End

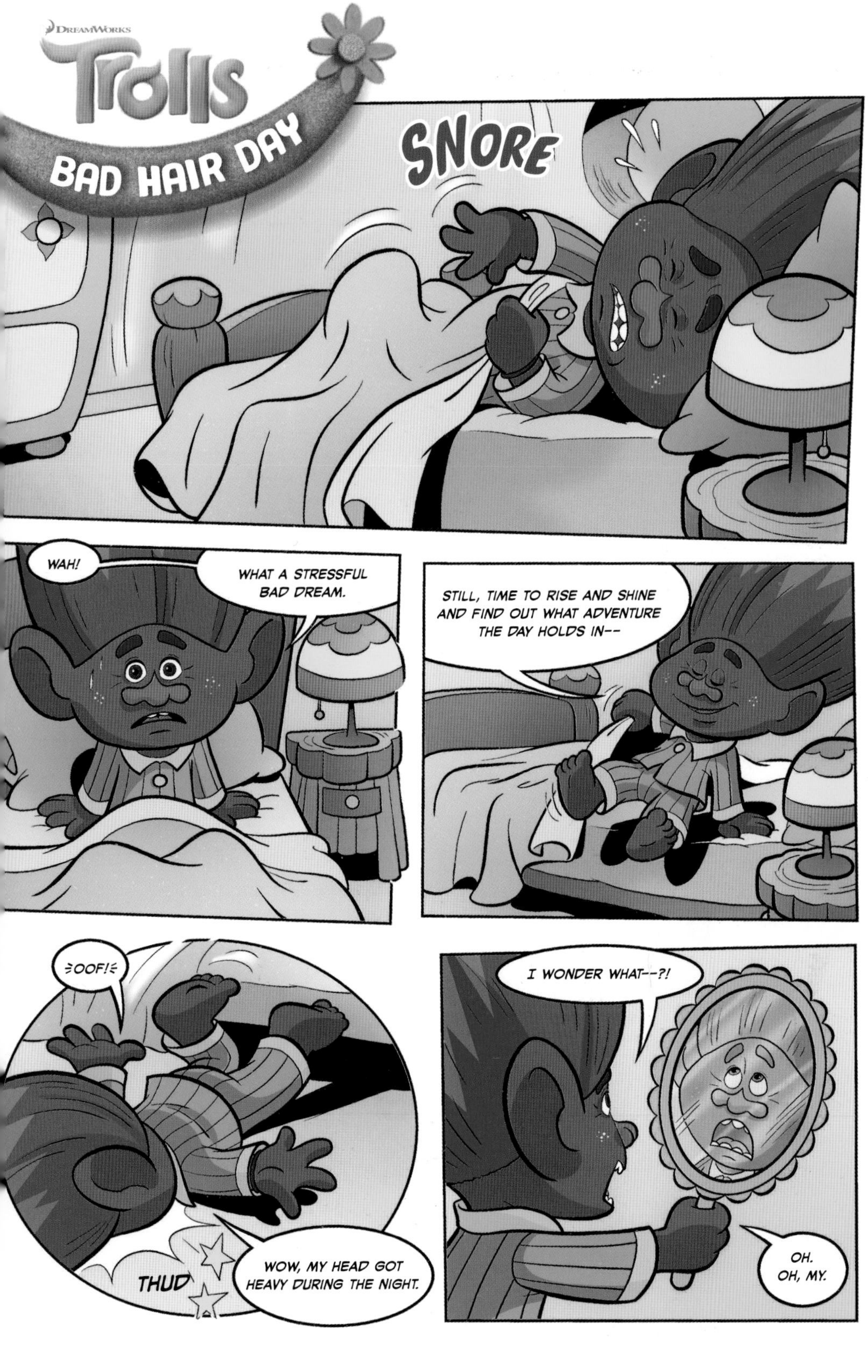
DreamWorks
Trolls
BAD HAIR DAY
SNORE
WAH!
WHAT A STRESSFUL BAD DREAM.
STILL, TIME TO RISE AND SHINE AND FIND OUT WHAT ADVENTURE THE DAY HOLDS IN--
OOF!
THUD
WOW, MY HEAD GOT HEAVY DURING THE NIGHT.
I WONDER WHAT--?!
OH. OH, MY.

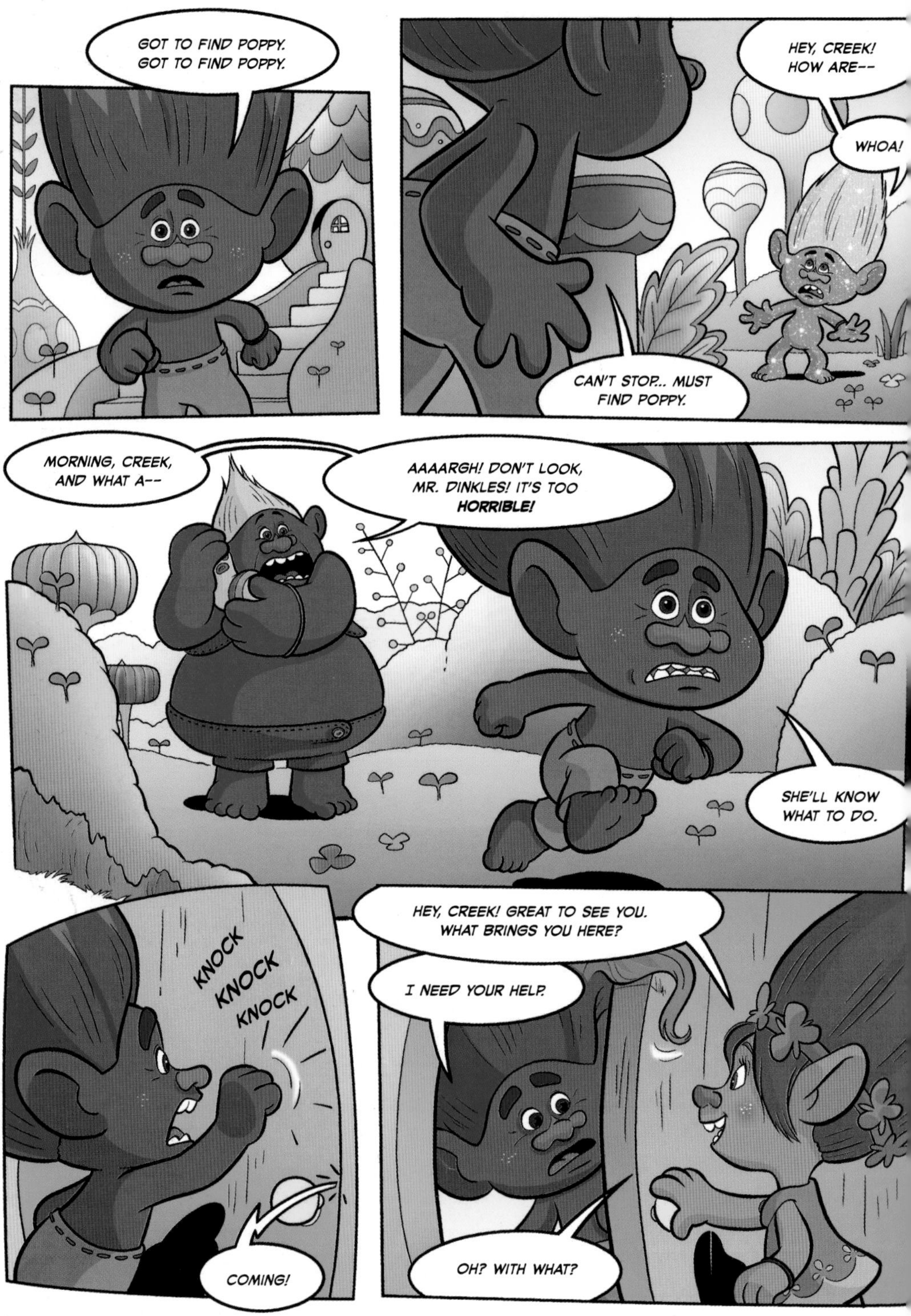
GOT TO FIND POPPY. GOT TO FIND POPPY.
HEY, CREEK! HOW ARE--
WHOA!
CAN'T STOP... MUST FIND POPPY.
MORNING, CREEK, AND WHAT A--
AAAARGH! DON'T LOOK, MR. DINKLES! IT'S TOO HORRIBLE!
SHE'LL KNOW WHAT TO DO.
KNOCK KNOCK KNOCK
COMING!
HEY, CREEK! GREAT TO SEE YOU. WHAT BRINGS YOU HERE?
I NEED YOUR HELP.
OH? WITH WHAT?

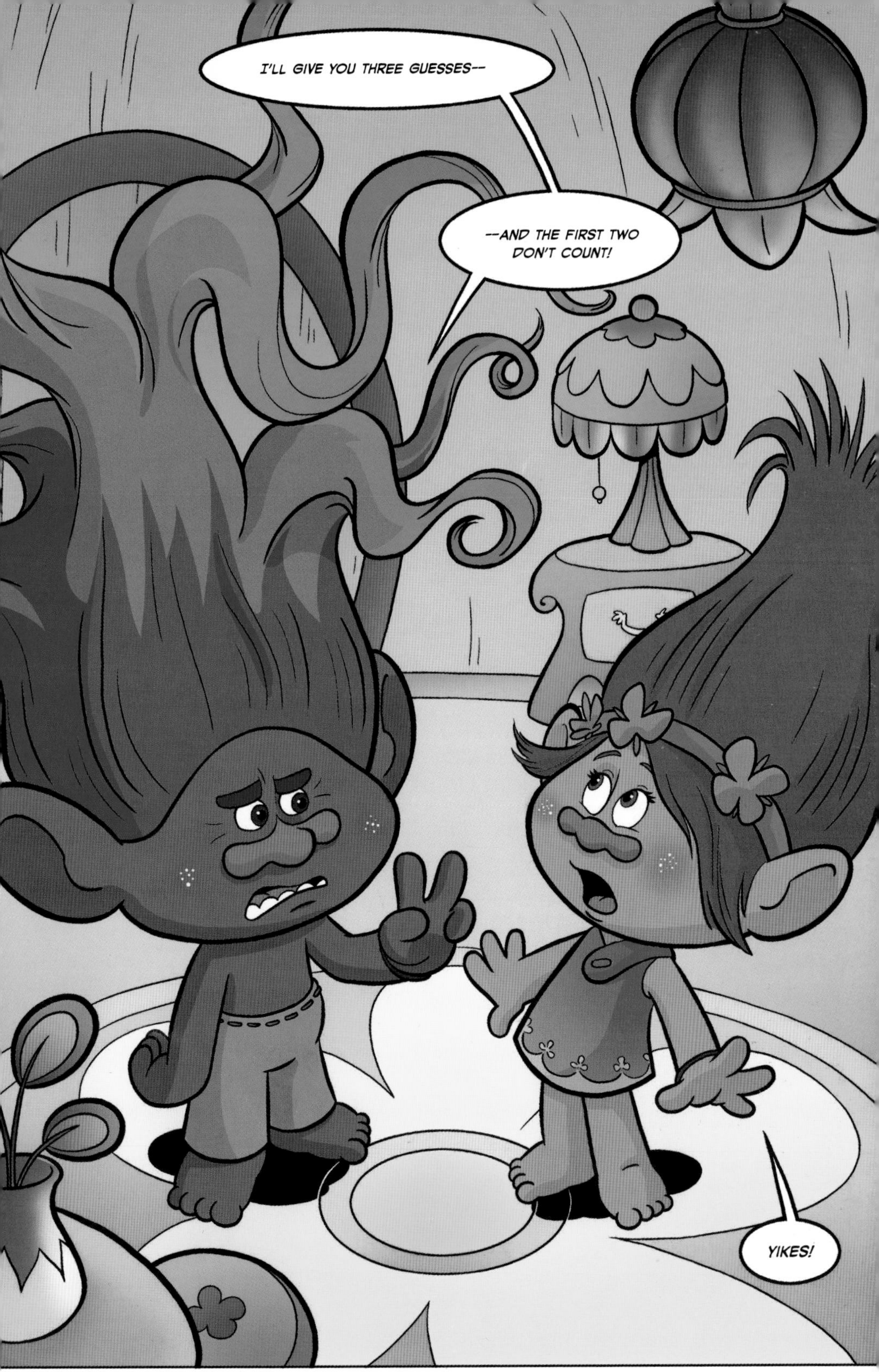
I'LL GIVE YOU THREE GUESSES--
--AND THE FIRST TWO DON'T COUNT!
YIKES!

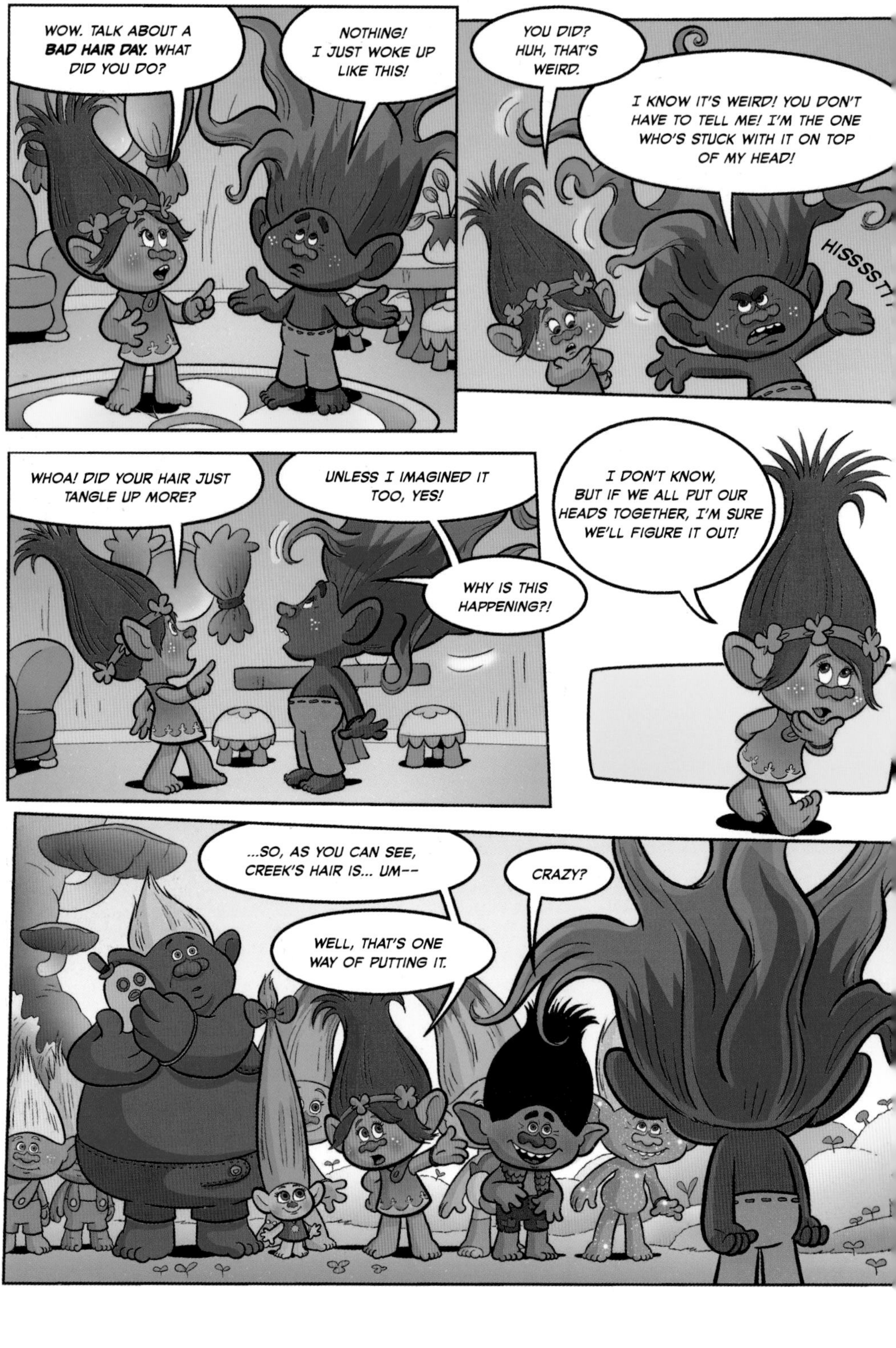
WOW. TALK ABOUT A **BAD HAIR DAY.** WHAT DID YOU DO?
NOTHING! I JUST WOKE UP LIKE THIS!
YOU DID? HUH, THAT'S WEIRD.
I KNOW IT'S WEIRD! YOU DON'T HAVE TO TELL ME! I'M THE ONE WHO'S STUCK WITH IT ON TOP OF MY HEAD!
HISSSSST!
WHOA! DID YOUR HAIR JUST TANGLE UP MORE?
UNLESS I IMAGINED IT TOO, YES!
WHY IS THIS HAPPENING?!
I DON'T KNOW, BUT IF WE ALL PUT OUR HEADS TOGETHER, I'M SURE WE'LL FIGURE IT OUT!
...SO, AS YOU CAN SEE, CREEK'S HAIR IS... UM--
CRAZY?
WELL, THAT'S ONE WAY OF PUTTING IT.

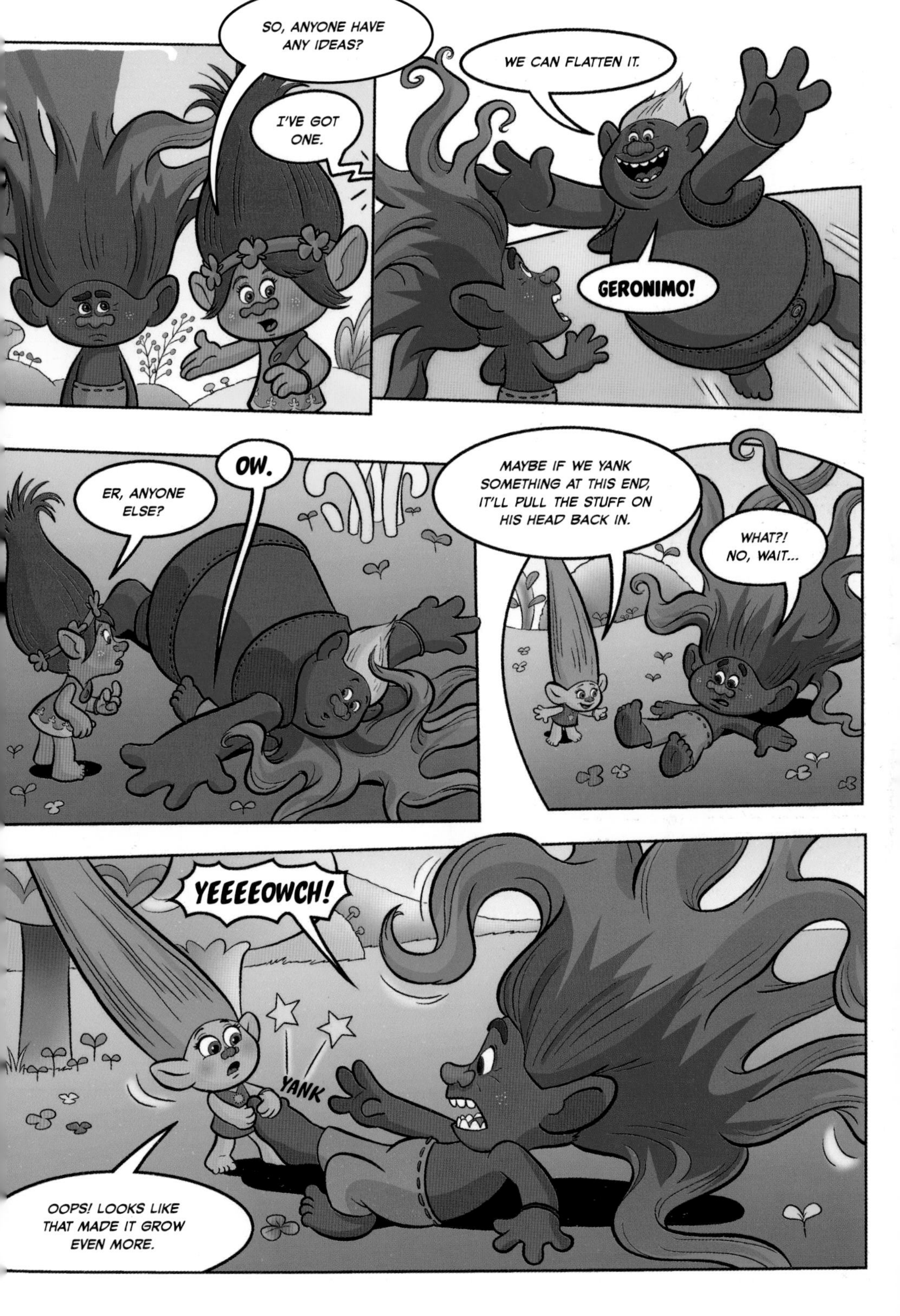
SO, ANYONE HAVE ANY IDEAS?
I'VE GOT ONE.
WE CAN FLATTEN IT.
GERONIMO!
ER, ANYONE ELSE?
OW.
MAYBE IF WE YANK SOMETHING AT THIS END, IT'LL PULL THE STUFF ON HIS HEAD BACK IN.
WHAT?! NO, WAIT...
YEEEEOWCH!
YANK
OOPS! LOOKS LIKE THAT MADE IT GROW EVEN MORE.

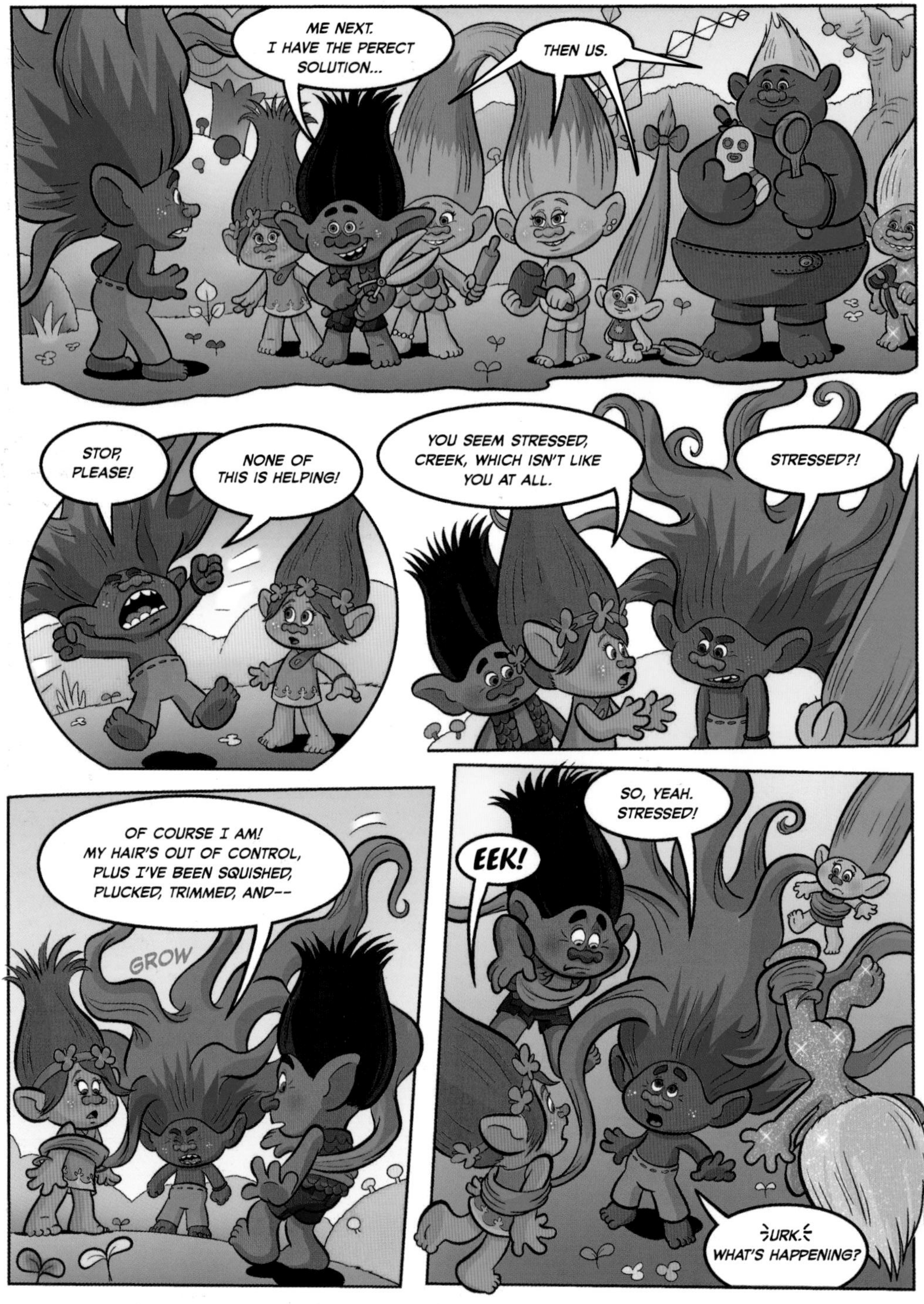

ME NEXT. I HAVE THE PERECT SOLUTION...
THEN US.
STOP, PLEASE!
NONE OF THIS IS HELPING!
YOU SEEM STRESSED, CREEK, WHICH ISN'T LIKE YOU AT ALL.
STRESSED?!
OF COURSE I AM! MY HAIR'S OUT OF CONTROL, PLUS I'VE BEEN SQUISHED, PLUCKED, TRIMMED, AND--
GROW
EEK!
SO, YEAH. STRESSED!
URK.
WHAT'S HAPPENING?

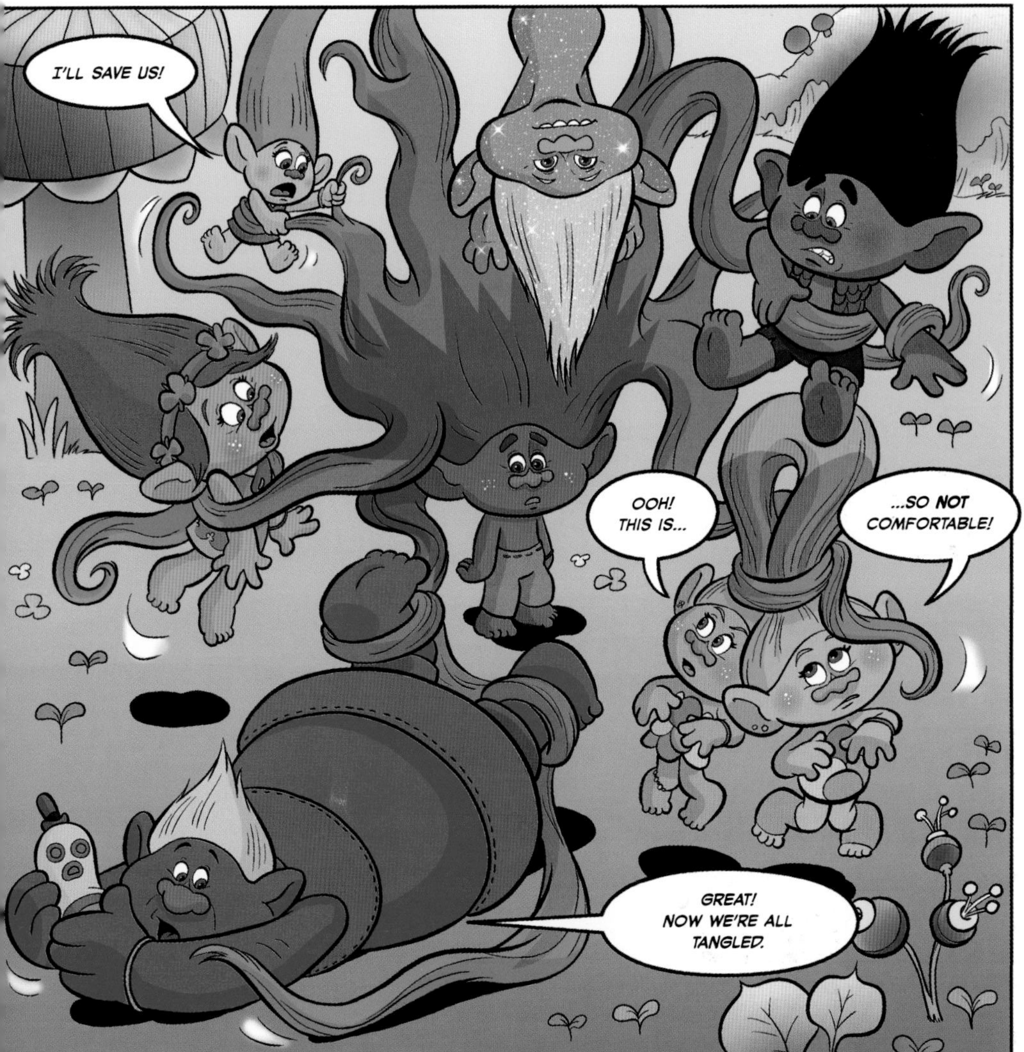
I'LL SAVE US!
OOH! THIS IS...
...SO NOT COMFORTABLE!
GREAT! NOW WE'RE ALL TANGLED.

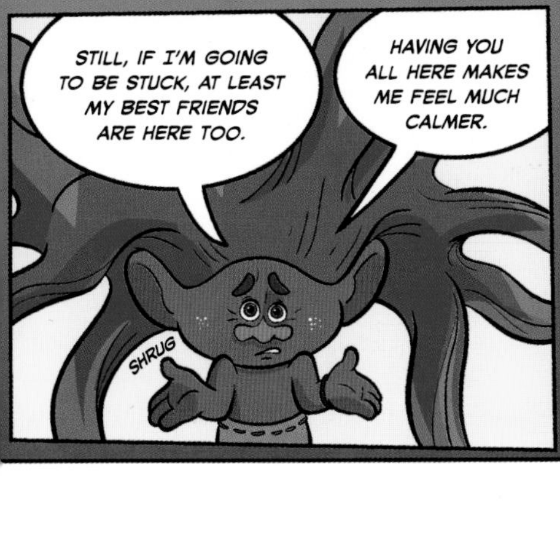
STILL, IF I'M GOING TO BE STUCK, AT LEAST MY BEST FRIENDS ARE HERE TOO.
HAVING YOU ALL HERE MAKES ME FEEL MUCH CALMER.
SHRUG

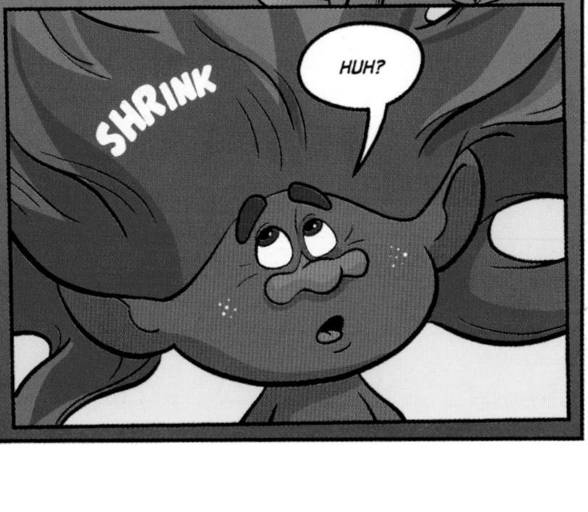
SHRINK
HUH?

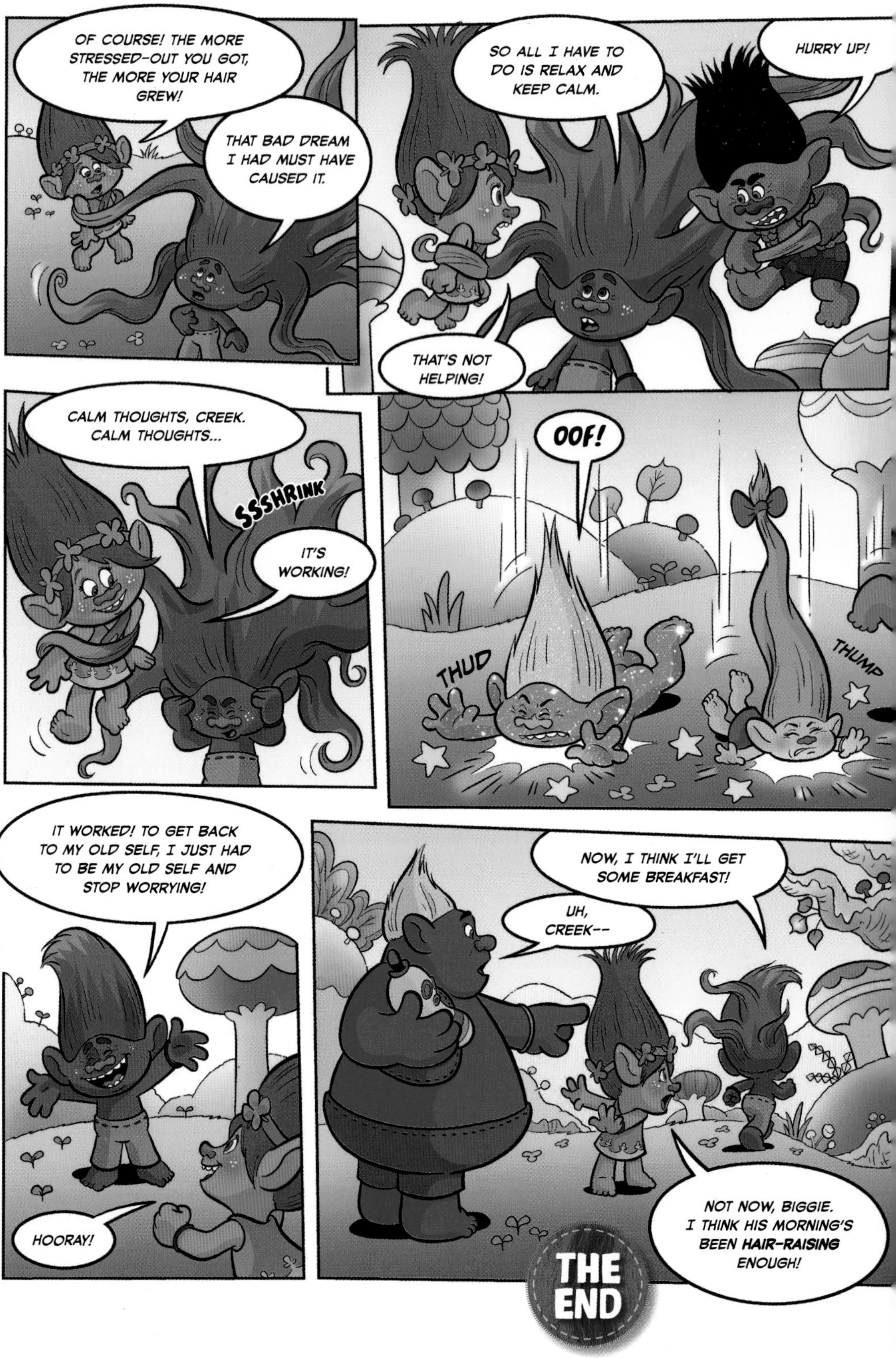
OF COURSE! THE MORE STRESSED-OUT YOU GOT, THE MORE YOUR HAIR GREW!
THAT BAD DREAM I HAD MUST HAVE CAUSED IT.
SO ALL I HAVE TO DO IS RELAX AND KEEP CALM.
HURRY UP!
THAT'S NOT HELPING!
CALM THOUGHTS, CREEK. CALM THOUGHTS...
SSSHRINK
IT'S WORKING!
OOF!
THUD
THUMP
IT WORKED! TO GET BACK TO MY OLD SELF, I JUST HAD TO BE MY OLD SELF AND STOP WORRYING!
HOORAY!
NOW, I THINK I'LL GET SOME BREAKFAST!
UH, CREEK--
NOT NOW, BIGGIE. I THINK HIS MORNING'S BEEN **HAIR-RAISING** ENOUGH!
THE END

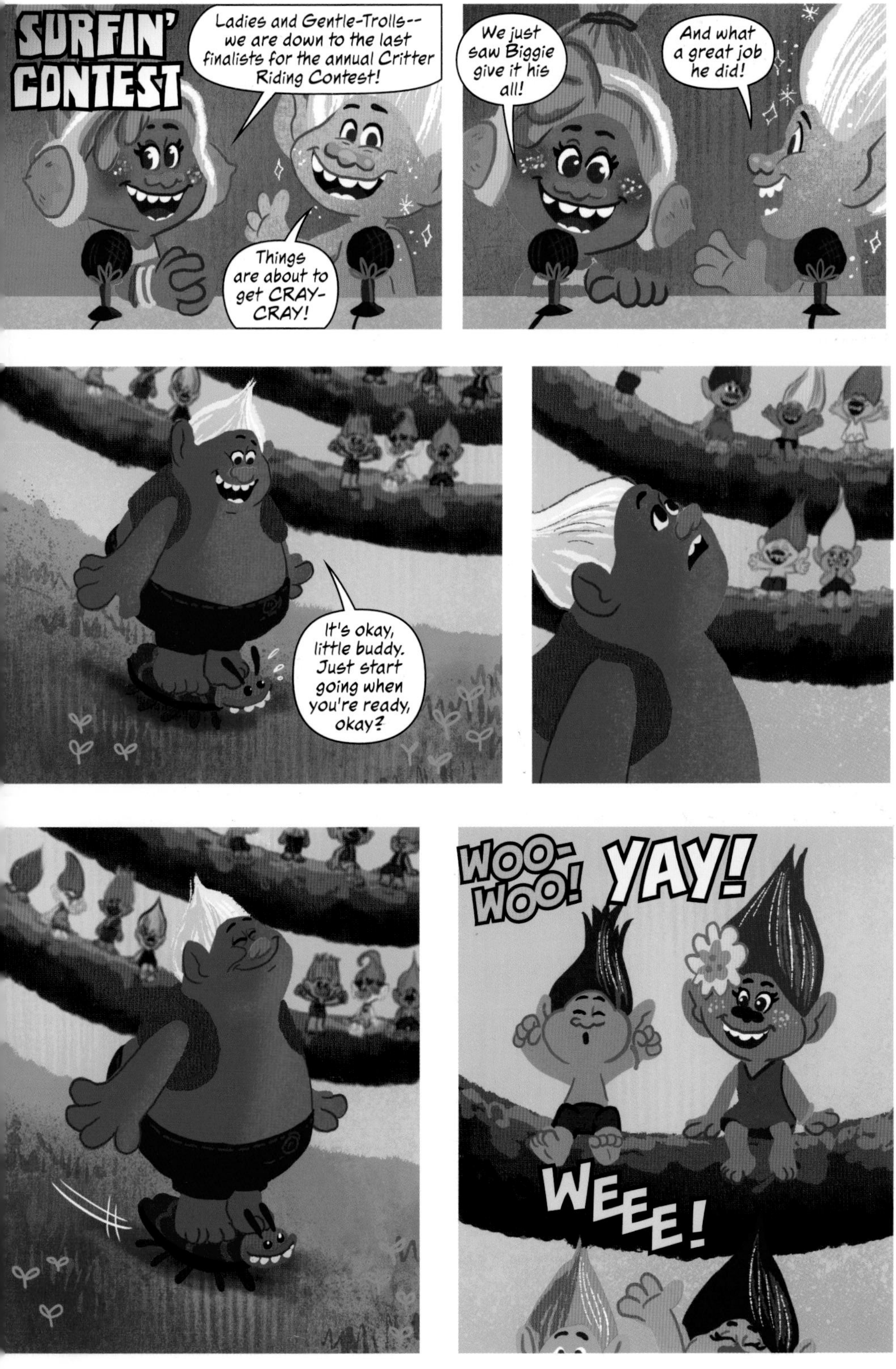
SURFIN' CONTEST
Ladies and Gentle-Trolls-- we are down to the last finalists for the annual Critter Riding Contest!
Things are about to get CRAY-CRAY!
We just saw Biggie give it his all!
And what a great job he did!
It's okay, little buddy. Just start going when you're ready, okay?
WOO-WOO!
YAY!
WEEE!

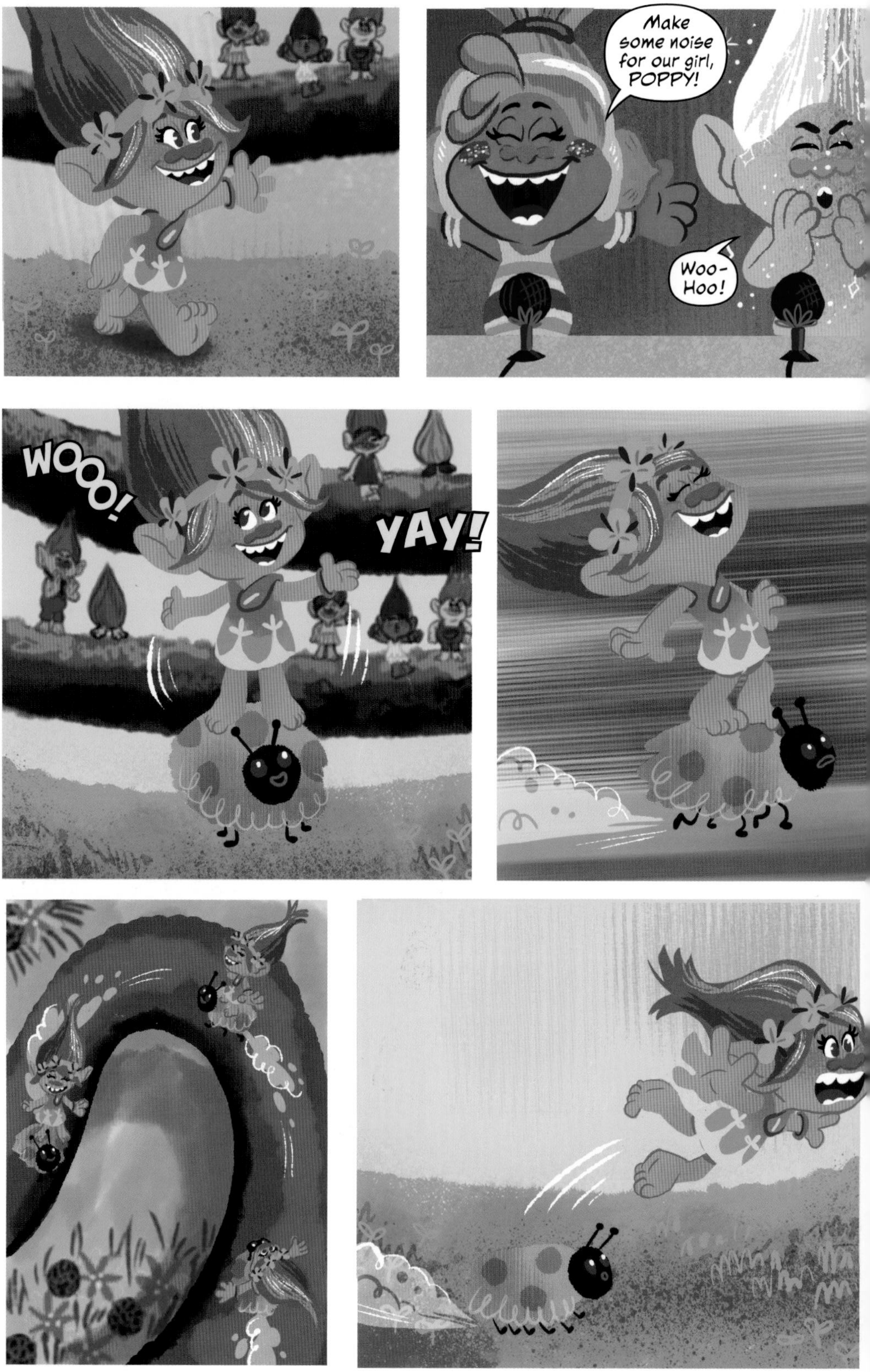
Make some noise for our girl, POPPY!
Woo-Hoo!
WOOO!
YAY!

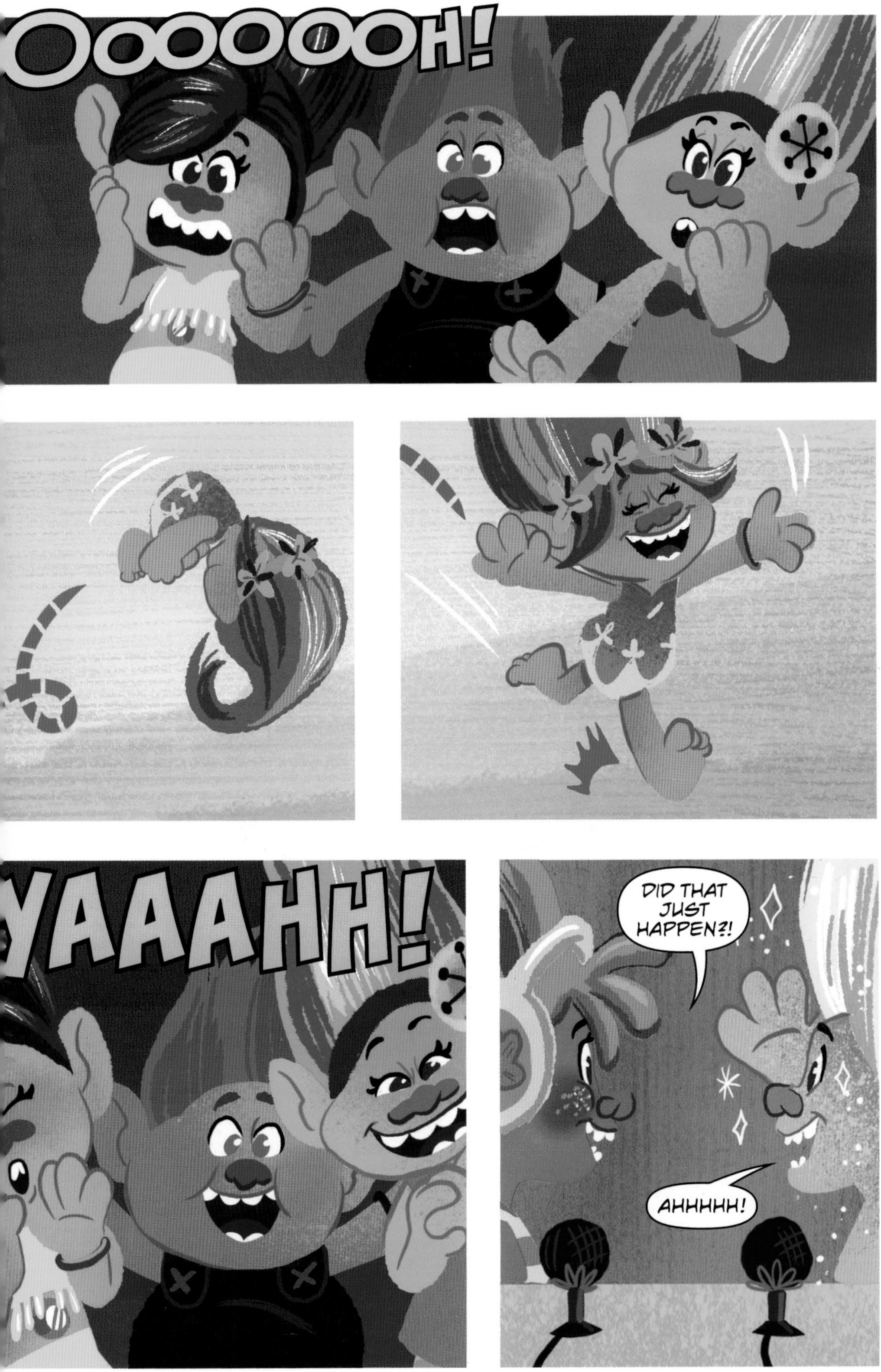
OOOOOOOH!
YAAAHH!
DID THAT JUST HAPPEN?!
AHHHHH!

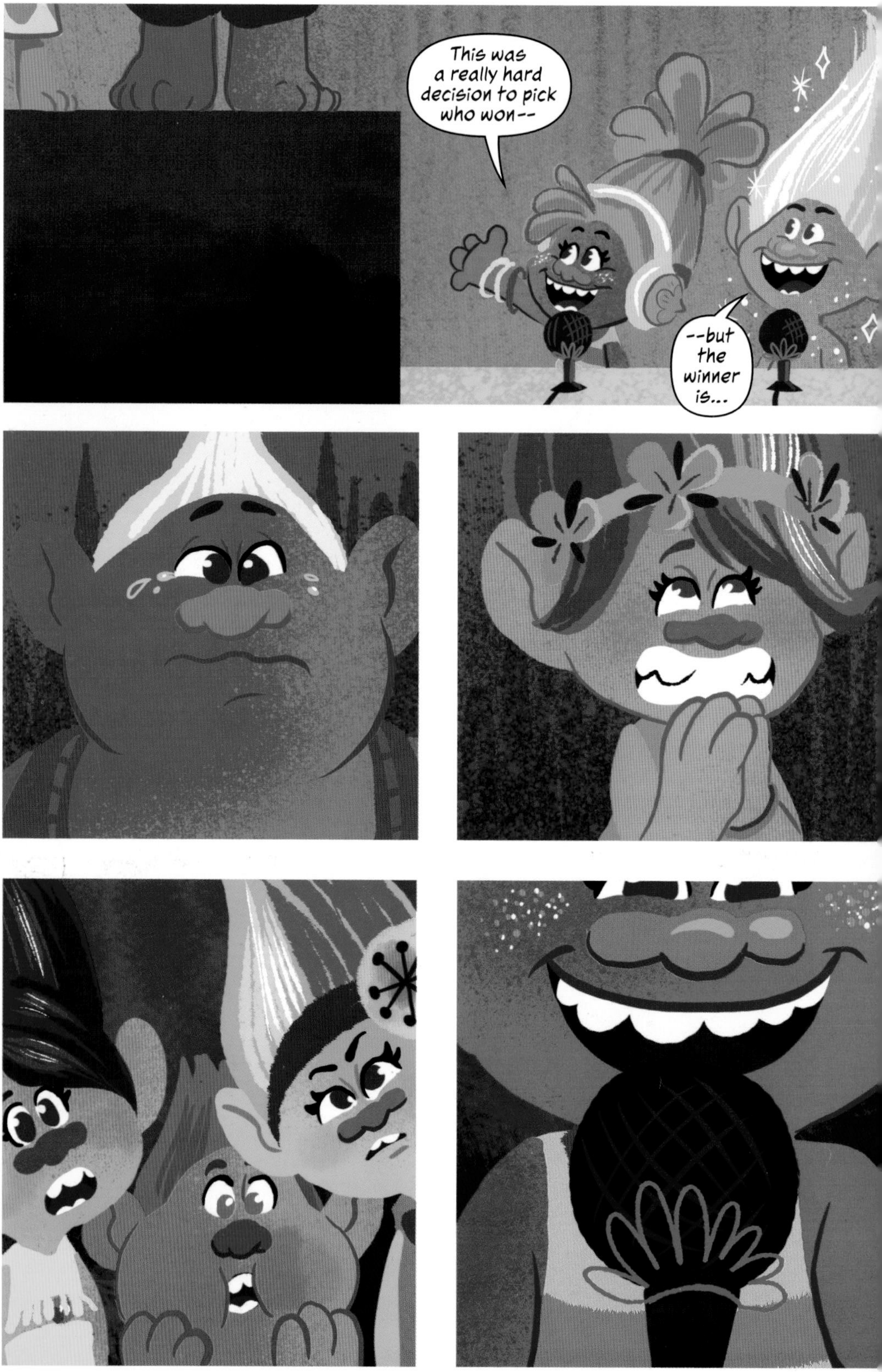
This was a really hard decision to pick who won--
--but the winner is...

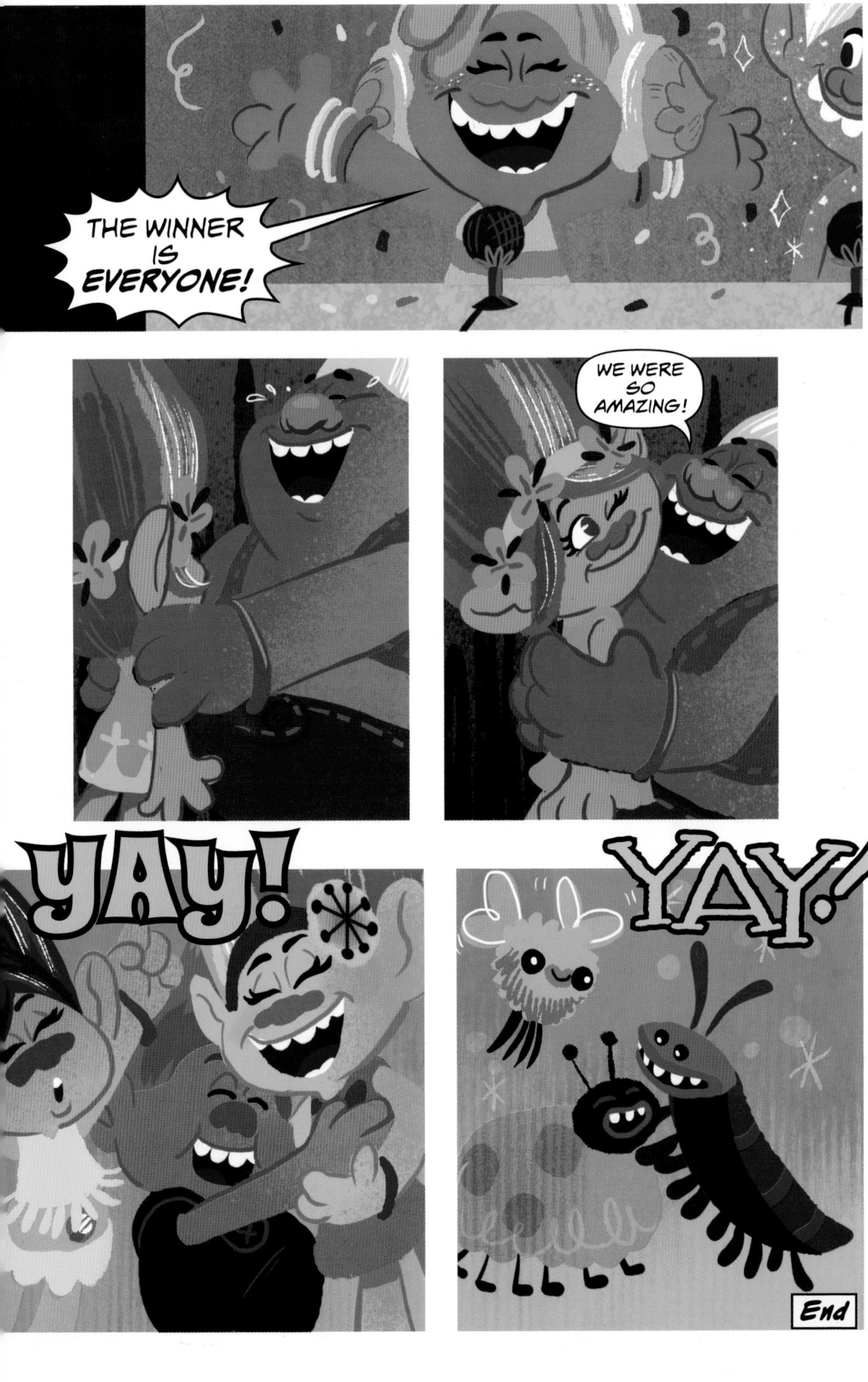
THE WINNER IS EVERYONE!
WE WERE SO AMAZING!
YAY!
YAY!
End

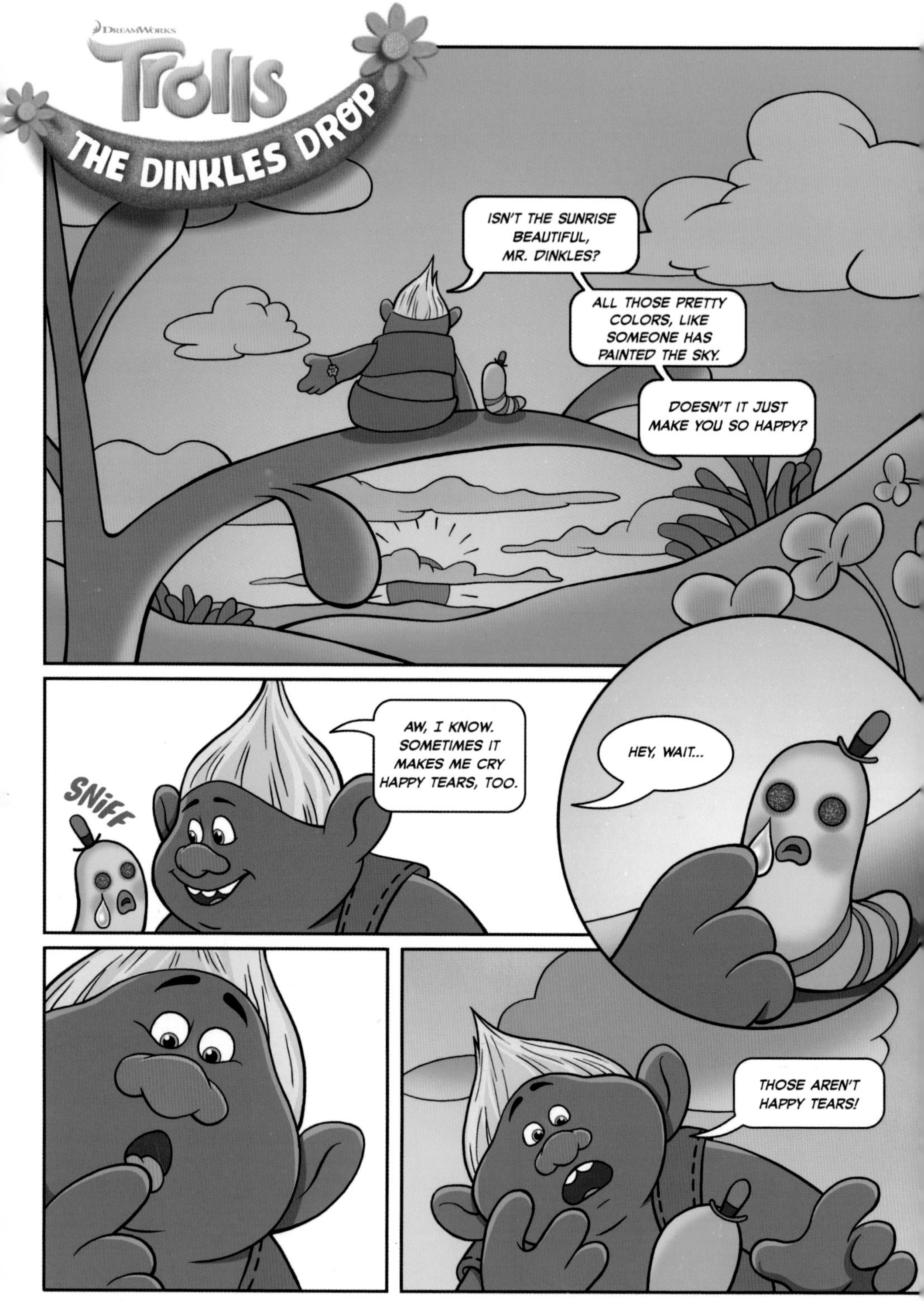
DreamWorks
Trolls
THE DINKLES DROP
ISN'T THE SUNRISE BEAUTIFUL, MR. DINKLES?
ALL THOSE PRETTY COLORS, LIKE SOMEONE HAS PAINTED THE SKY.
DOESN'T IT JUST MAKE YOU SO HAPPY?
SNIFF
AW, I KNOW. SOMETIMES IT MAKES ME CRY HAPPY TEARS, TOO.
HEY, WAIT...
THOSE AREN'T HAPPY TEARS!

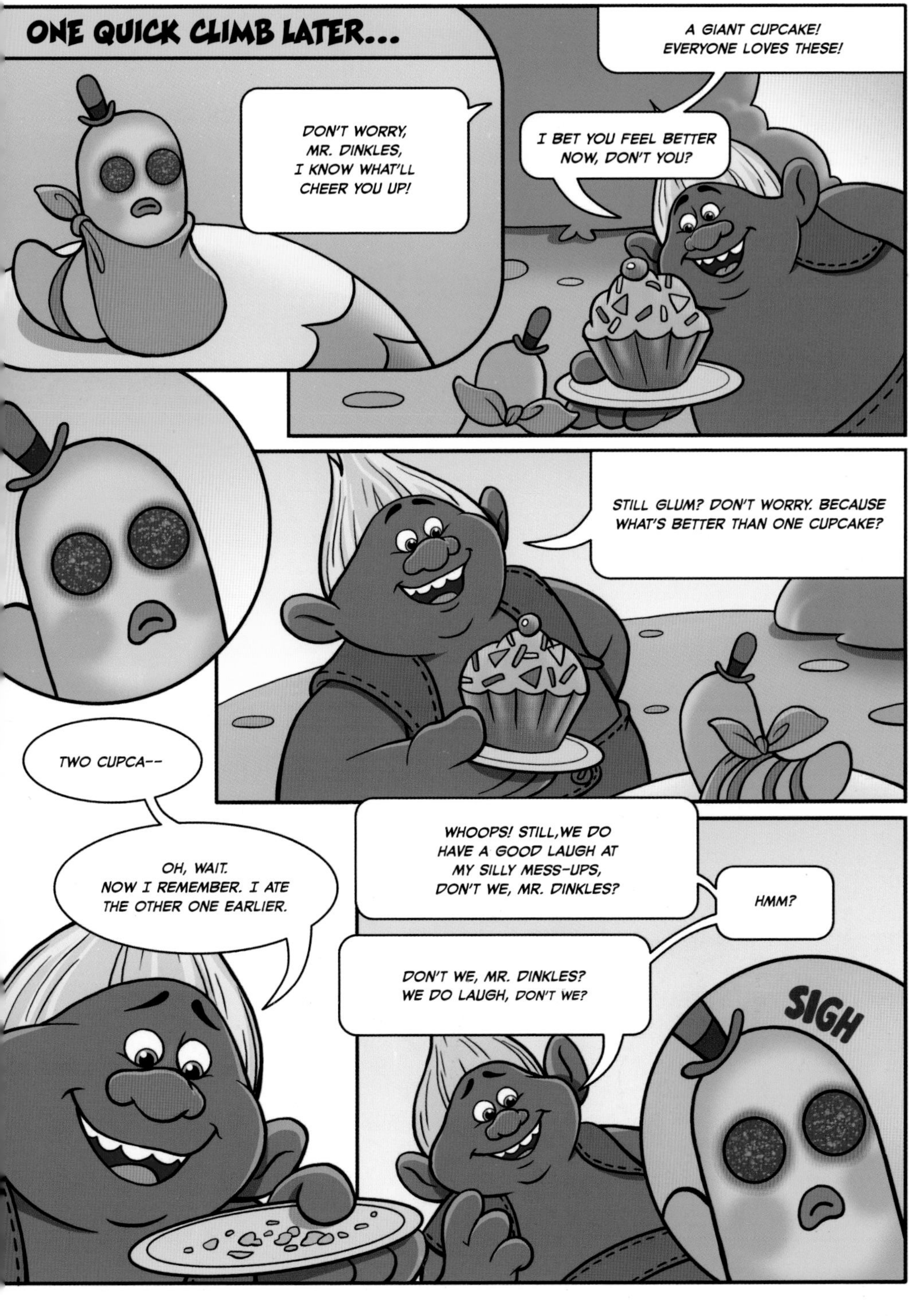
ONE QUICK CLIMB LATER...
DON'T WORRY, MR. DINKLES, I KNOW WHAT'LL CHEER YOU UP!
A GIANT CUPCAKE! EVERYONE LOVES THESE!
I BET YOU FEEL BETTER NOW, DON'T YOU?
STILL GLUM? DON'T WORRY. BECAUSE WHAT'S BETTER THAN ONE CUPCAKE?
TWO CUPCA--
OH, WAIT. NOW I REMEMBER. I ATE THE OTHER ONE EARLIER.
WHOOPS! STILL,WE DO HAVE A GOOD LAUGH AT MY SILLY MESS-UPS, DON'T WE, MR. DINKLES?
HMM?
DON'T WE, MR. DINKLES? WE DO LAUGH, DON'T WE?
SIGH

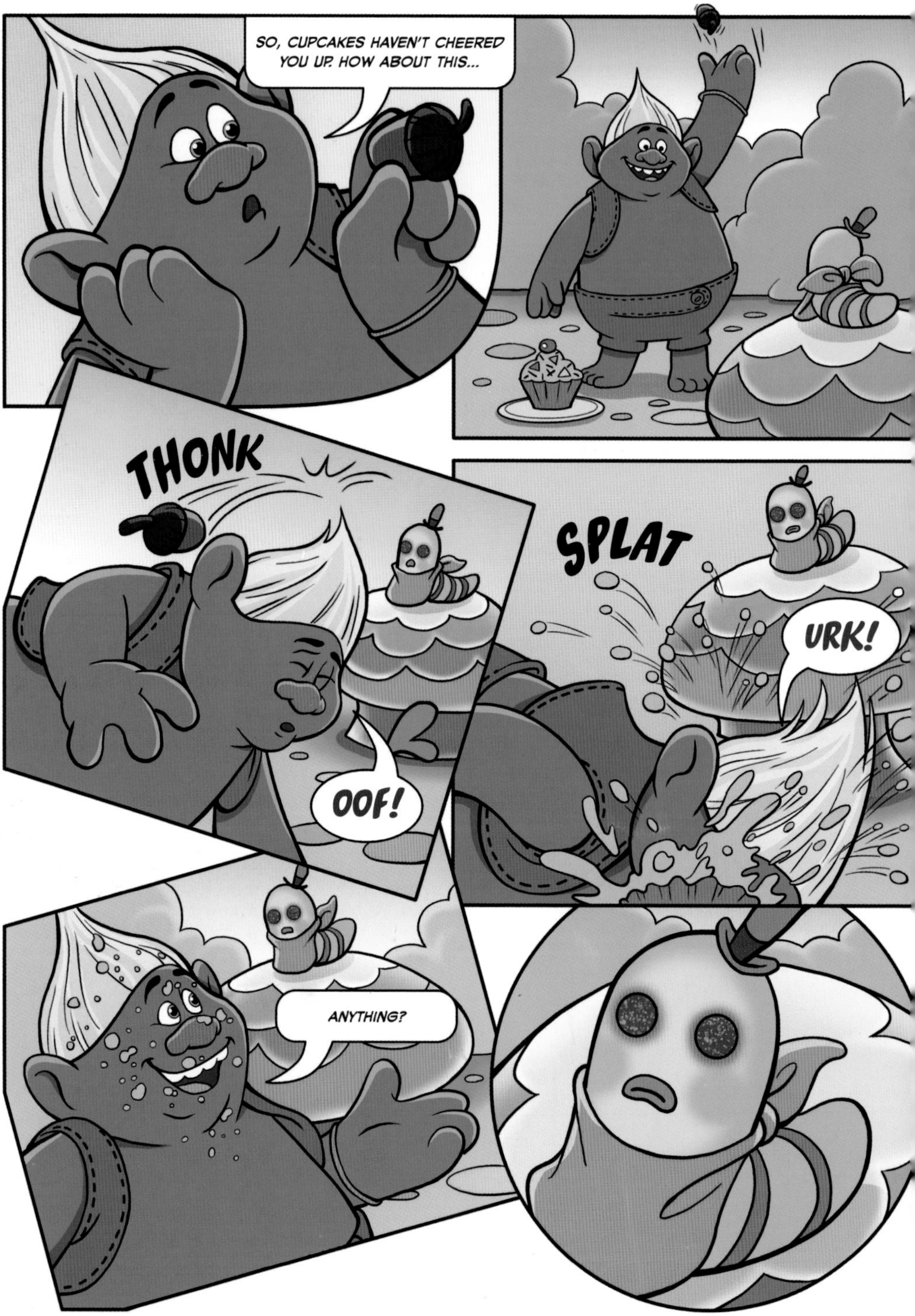
SO, CUPCAKES HAVEN'T CHEERED YOU UP. HOW ABOUT THIS...
THONK
OOF!
SPLAT
URK!
ANYTHING?

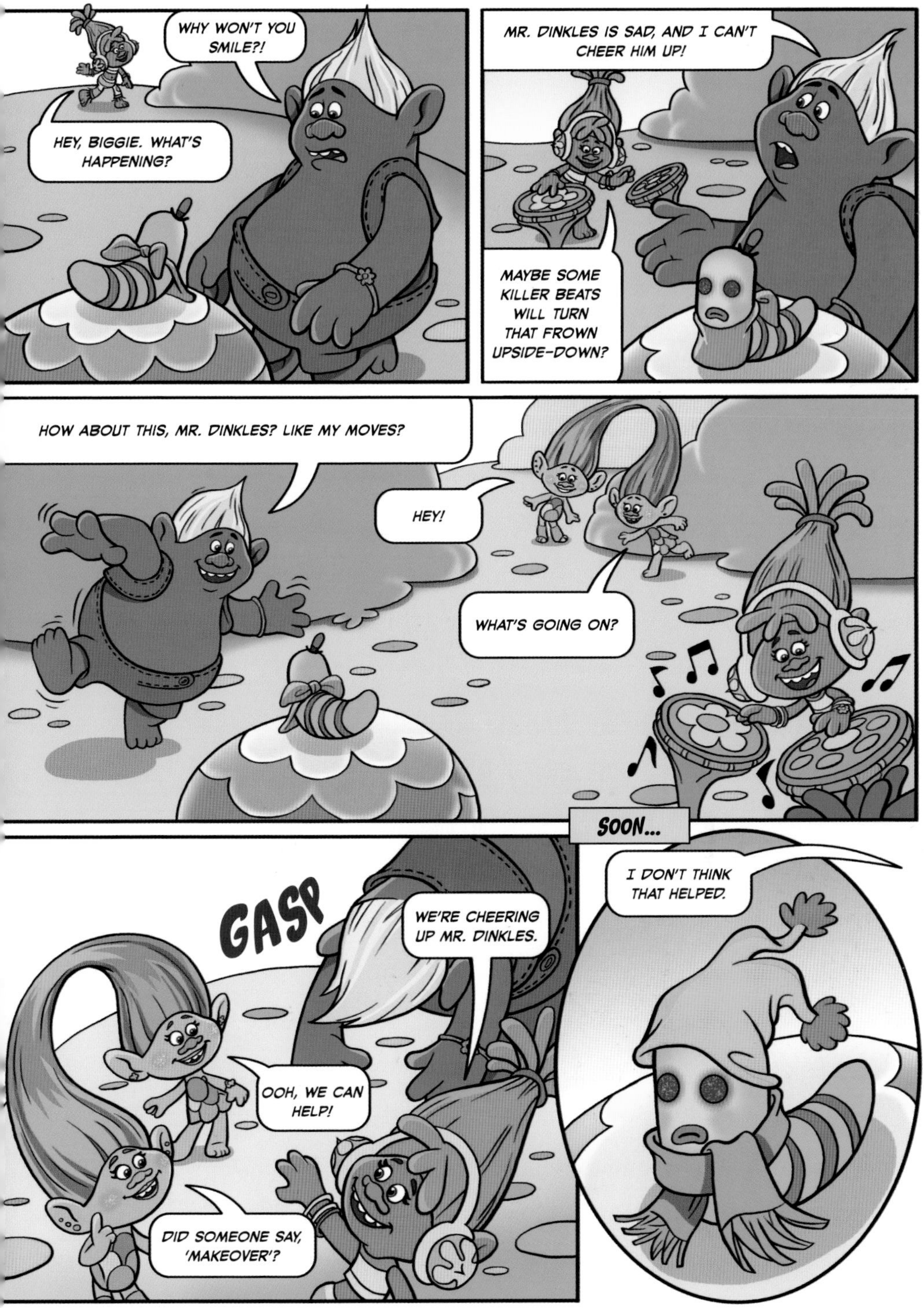
WHY WON'T YOU SMILE?!
HEY, BIGGIE. WHAT'S HAPPENING?
MR. DINKLES IS SAD, AND I CAN'T CHEER HIM UP!
MAYBE SOME KILLER BEATS WILL TURN THAT FROWN UPSIDE-DOWN?
HOW ABOUT THIS, MR. DINKLES? LIKE MY MOVES?
HEY!
WHAT'S GOING ON?
SOON...
GASP
WE'RE CHEERING UP MR. DINKLES.
OOH, WE CAN HELP!
DID SOMEONE SAY, 'MAKEOVER'?
I DON'T THINK THAT HELPED.

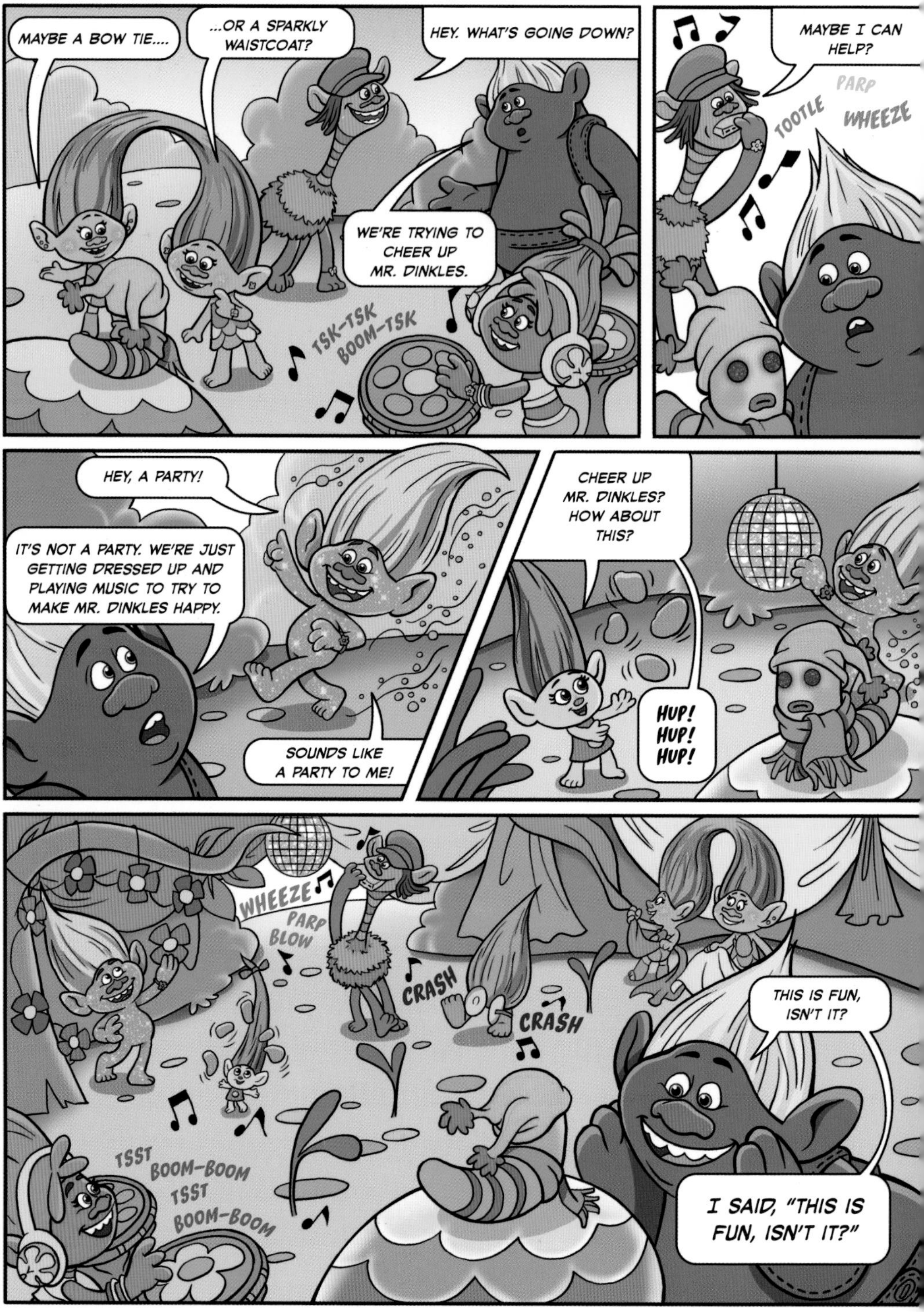
MAYBE A BOW TIE....
...OR A SPARKLY WAISTCOAT?
HEY. WHAT'S GOING DOWN?
WE'RE TRYING TO CHEER UP MR. DINKLES.
TSK-TSK
BOOM-TSK
MAYBE I CAN HELP?
PARP
TOOTLE
WHEEZE
HEY, A PARTY!
IT'S NOT A PARTY. WE'RE JUST GETTING DRESSED UP AND PLAYING MUSIC TO TRY TO MAKE MR. DINKLES HAPPY.
SOUNDS LIKE A PARTY TO ME!
CHEER UP MR. DINKLES? HOW ABOUT THIS?
HUP! HUP! HUP!
WHEEZE
PARP
BLOW
CRASH
CRASH
THIS IS FUN, ISN'T IT?
TSST
BOOM-BOOM
TSST
BOOM-BOOM
I SAID, "THIS IS FUN, ISN'T IT?"

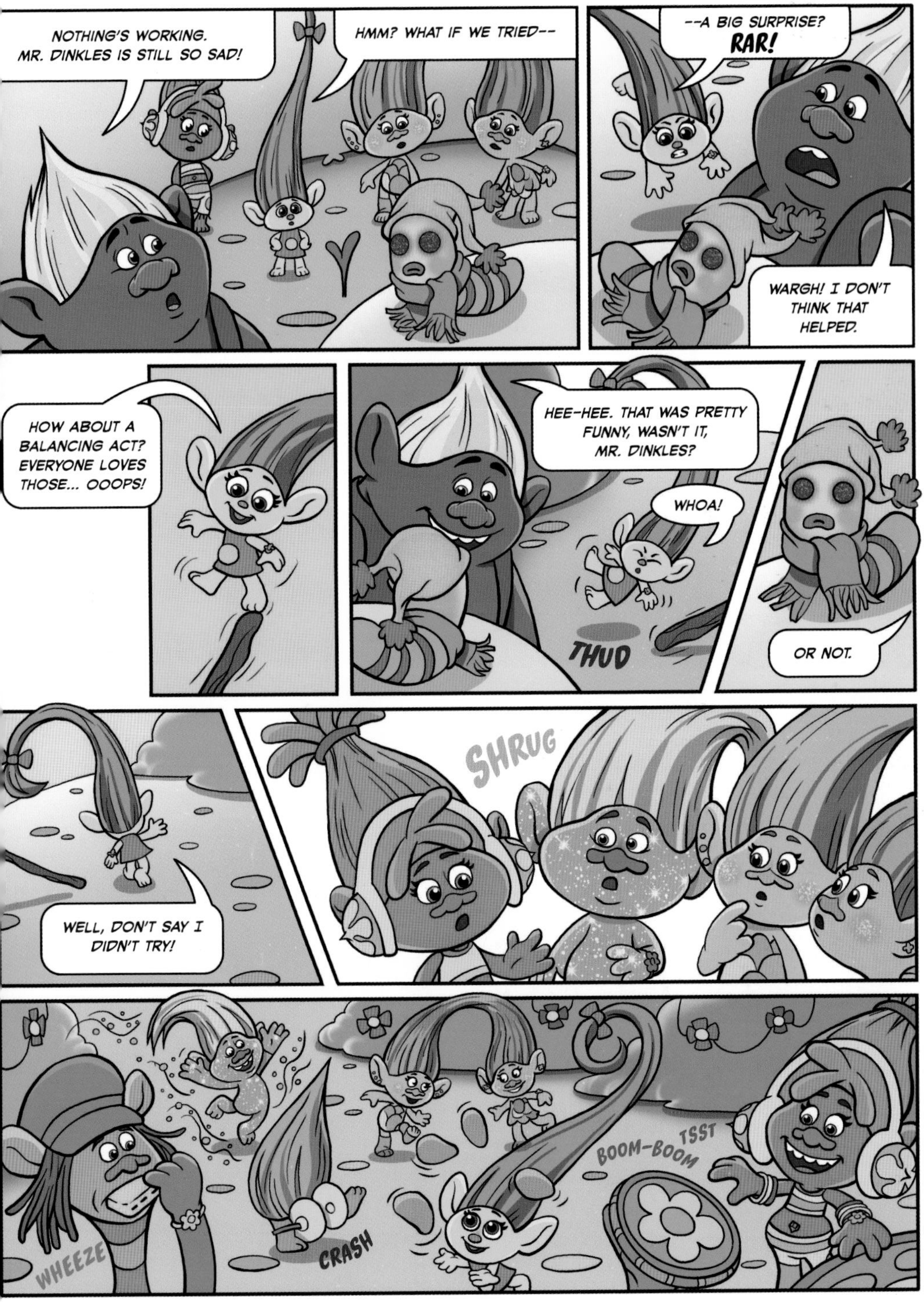
NOTHING'S WORKING. MR. DINKLES IS STILL SO SAD!
HMM? WHAT IF WE TRIED--
--A BIG SURPRISE? RAR!
WARGH! I DON'T THINK THAT HELPED.
HOW ABOUT A BALANCING ACT? EVERYONE LOVES THOSE... OOOPS!
HEE-HEE. THAT WAS PRETTY FUNNY, WASN'T IT, MR. DINKLES?
WHOA!
THUD
OR NOT.
WELL, DON'T SAY I DIDN'T TRY!
SHRUG
WHEEZE
CRASH
BOOM-BOOM
TSST

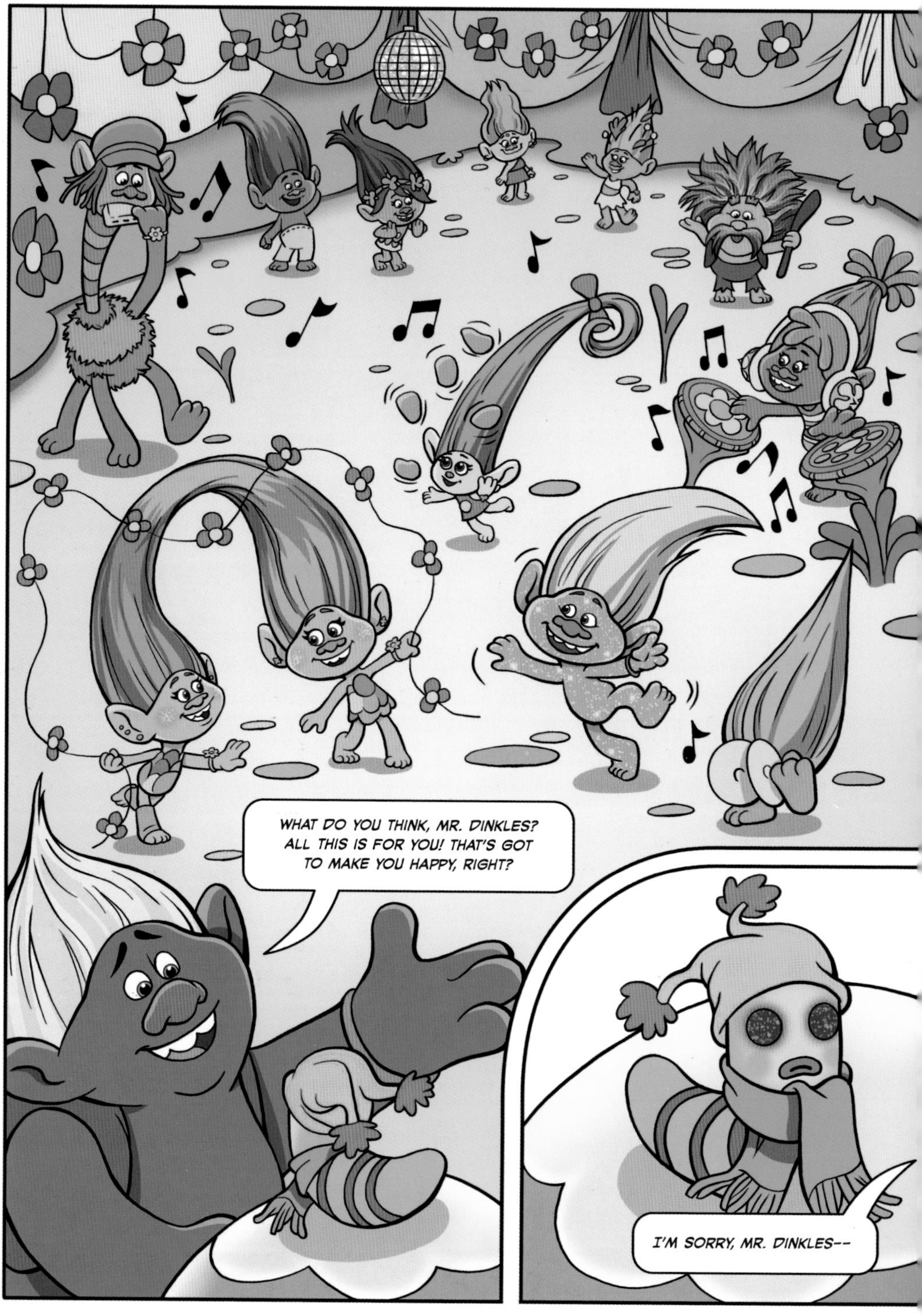
WHAT DO YOU THINK, MR. DINKLES? ALL THIS IS FOR YOU! THAT'S GOT TO MAKE YOU HAPPY, RIGHT?
I'M SORRY, MR. DINKLES--

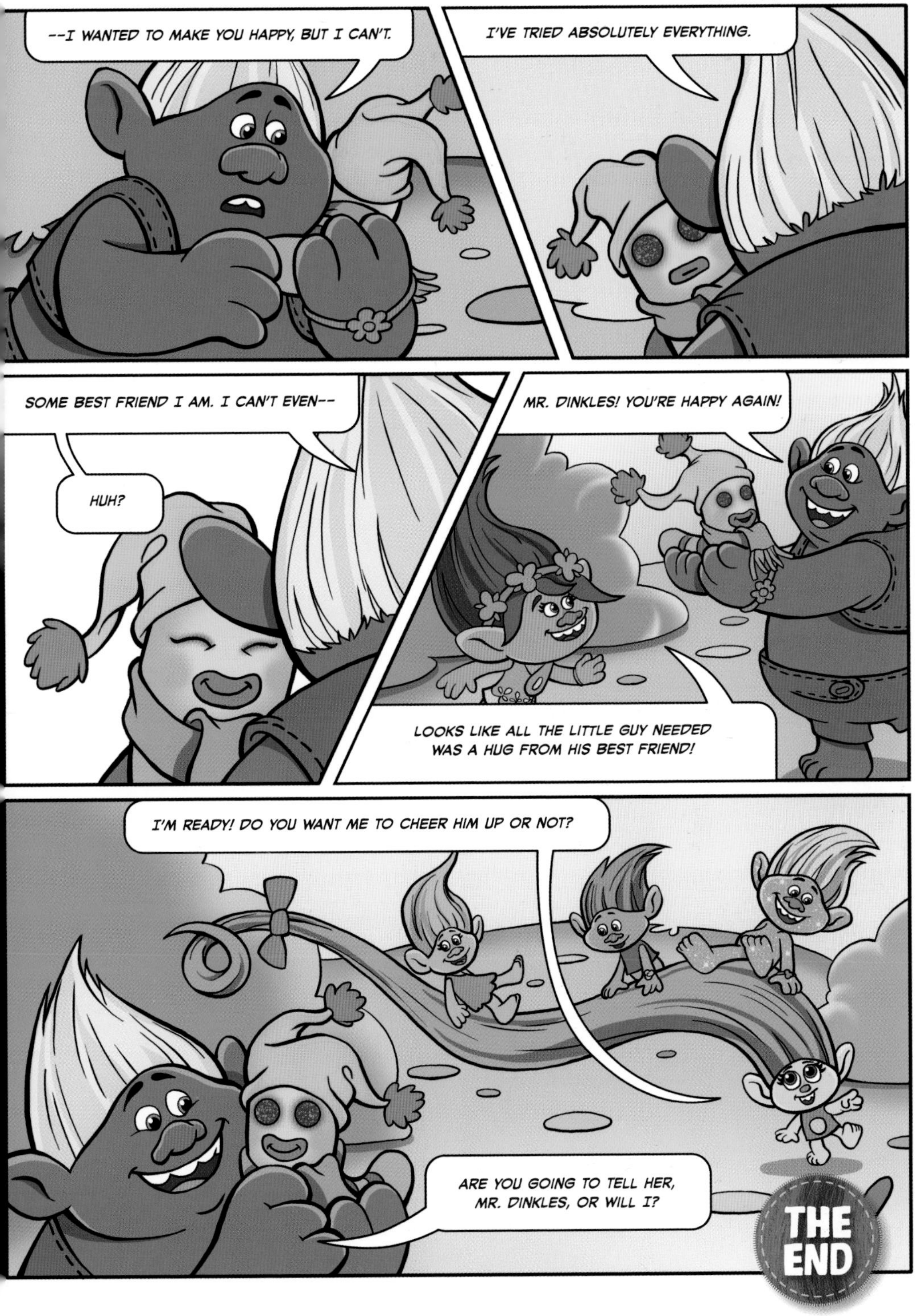
--I WANTED TO MAKE YOU HAPPY, BUT I CAN'T.
I'VE TRIED ABSOLUTELY EVERYTHING.
SOME BEST FRIEND I AM. I CAN'T EVEN--
HUH?
MR. DINKLES! YOU'RE HAPPY AGAIN!
LOOKS LIKE ALL THE LITTLE GUY NEEDED WAS A HUG FROM HIS BEST FRIEND!
I'M READY! DO YOU WANT ME TO CHEER HIM UP OR NOT?
ARE YOU GOING TO TELL HER, MR. DINKLES, OR WILL I?
THE END

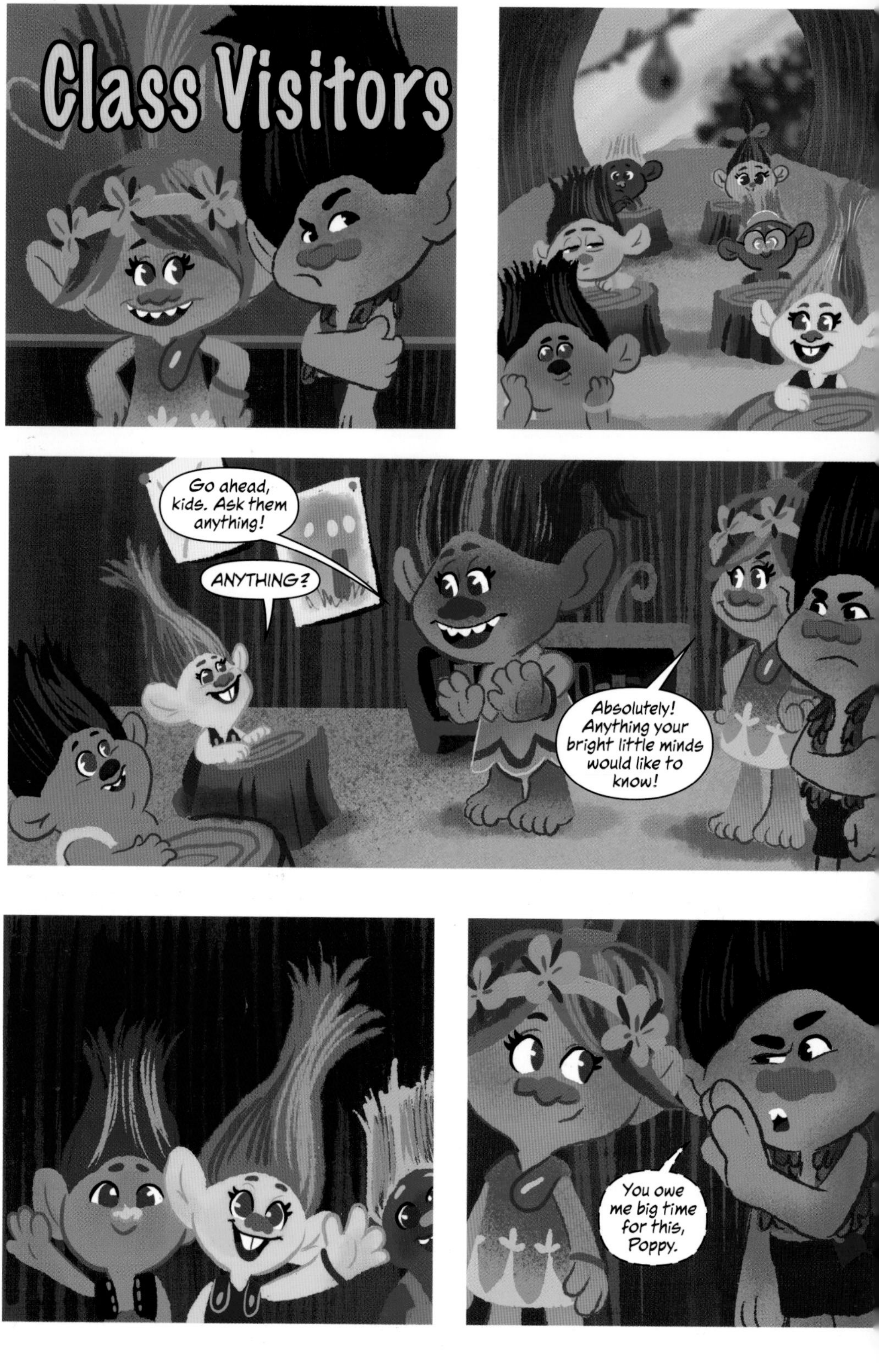
Class Visitors
Go ahead, kids. Ask them anything!
ANYTHING?
Absolutely! Anything your bright little minds would like to know!
You owe me big time for this, Poppy.

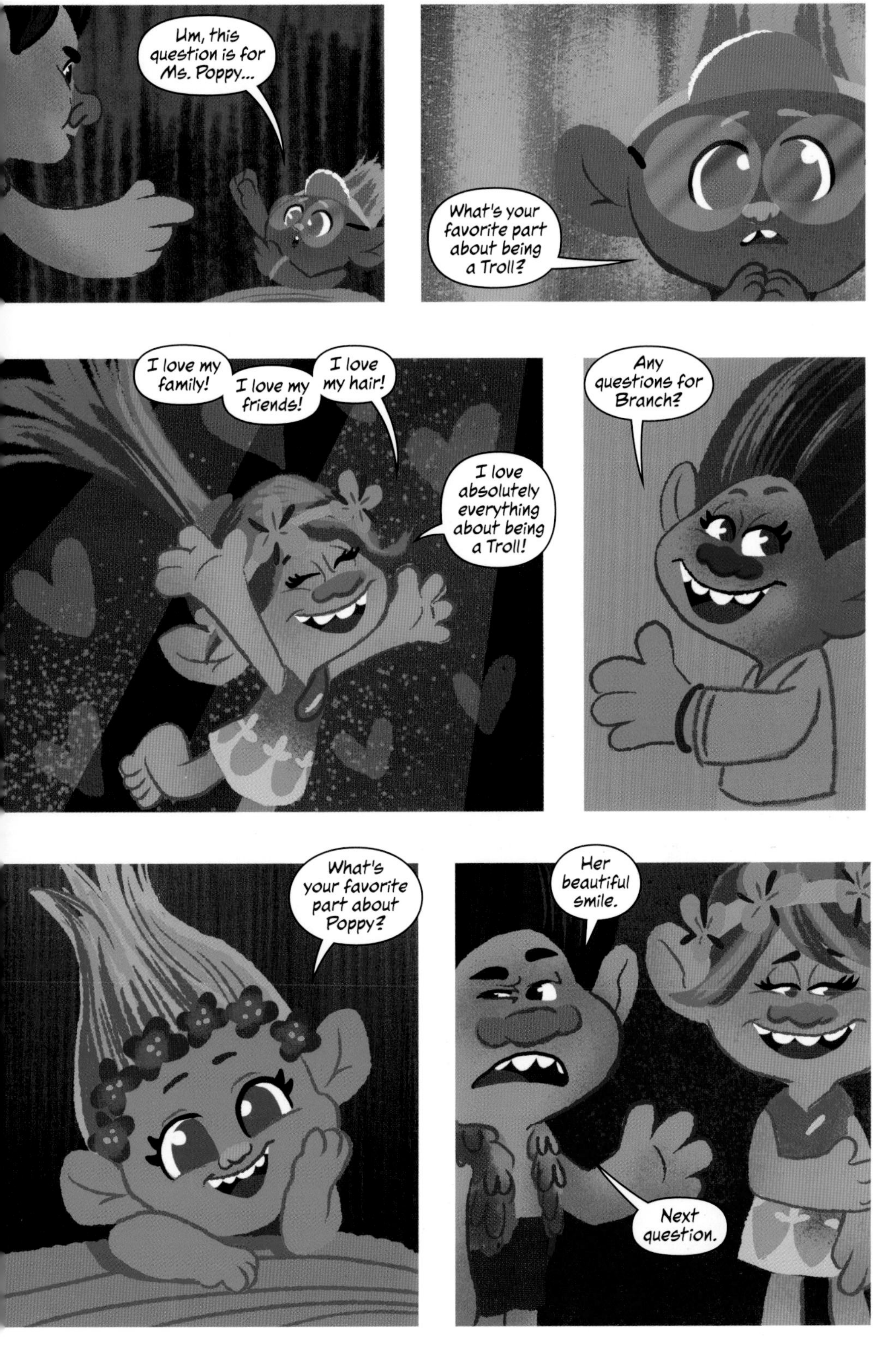
Um, this question is for Ms. Poppy...
What's your favorite part about being a Troll?
I love my family!
I love my friends!
I love my hair!
I love absolutely everything about being a Troll!
Any questions for Branch?
What's your favorite part about Poppy?
Her beautiful smile.
Next question.

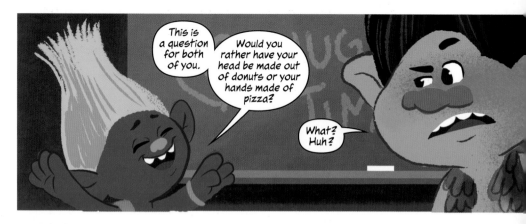

This is a question for both of you.

Would you rather have your head be made out of donuts or your hands made of pizza?

What? Huh?

I would rather have a donut for a head because then everyone would know how sweet I am!

This question is for Branch!

What's your question?

Can I go to the bathroom?

Um, sure.

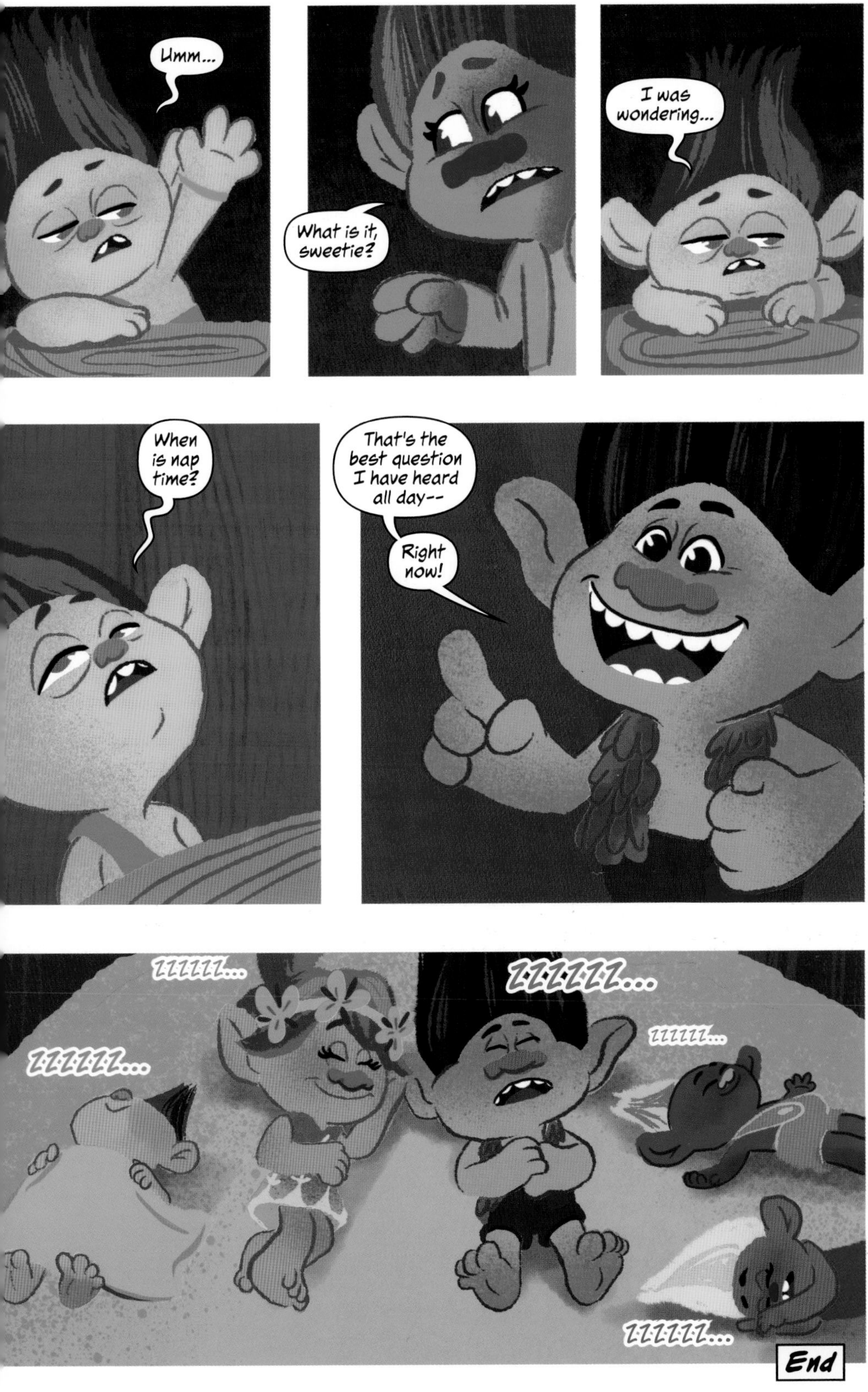
Umm...
What is it, sweetie?
I was wondering...
When is nap time?
That's the best question I have heard all day--
Right now!
ZZZZZZ...
ZZZZZZ...
ZZZZZZ...
ZZZZZZ...
ZZZZZZ...
End

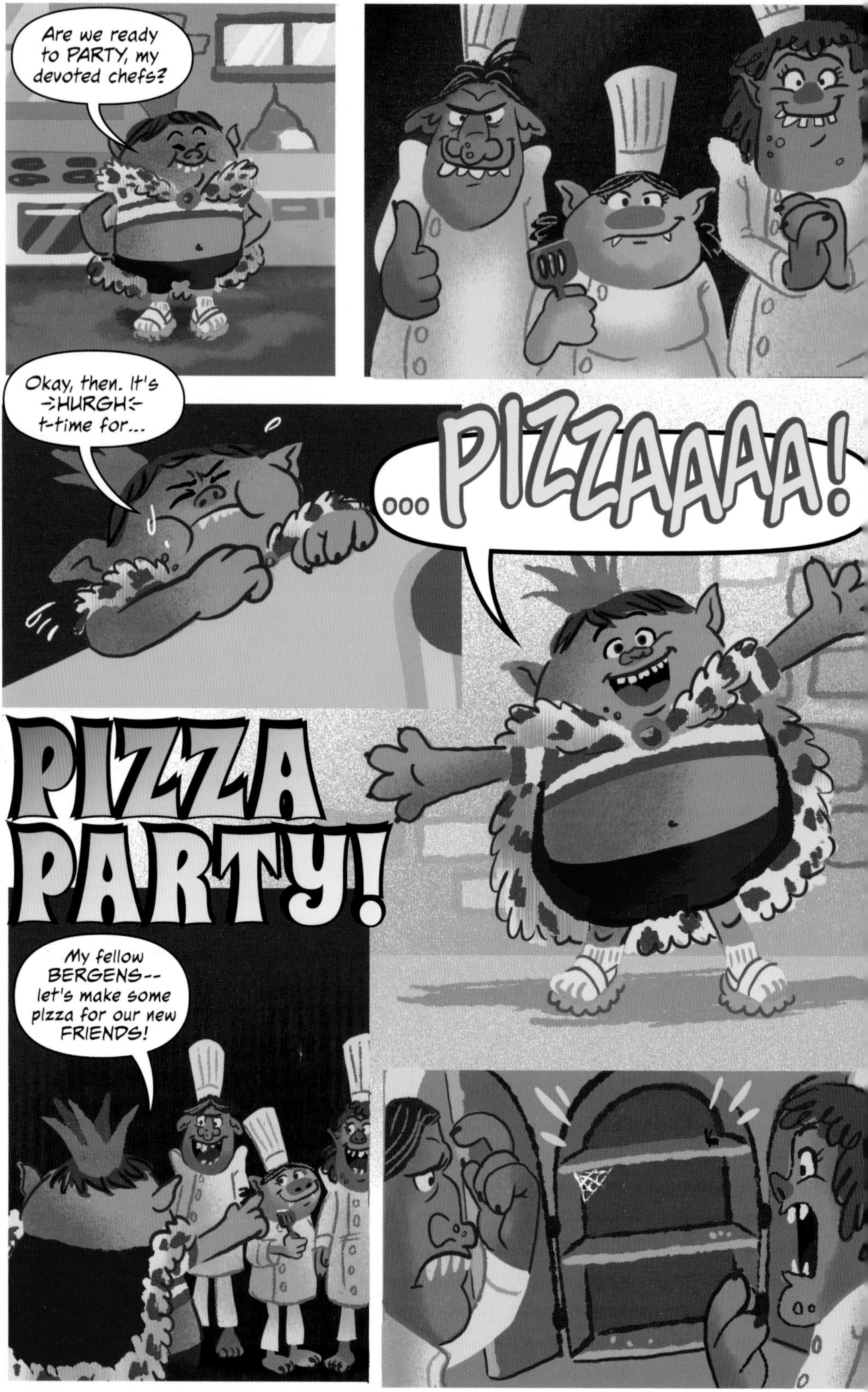
Are we ready to PARTY, my devoted chefs?
Okay, then. It's -HURGH- t-time for...
...PIZZAAAA!
PIZZA PARTY!
My fellow BERGENS-- let's make some pizza for our new FRIENDS!

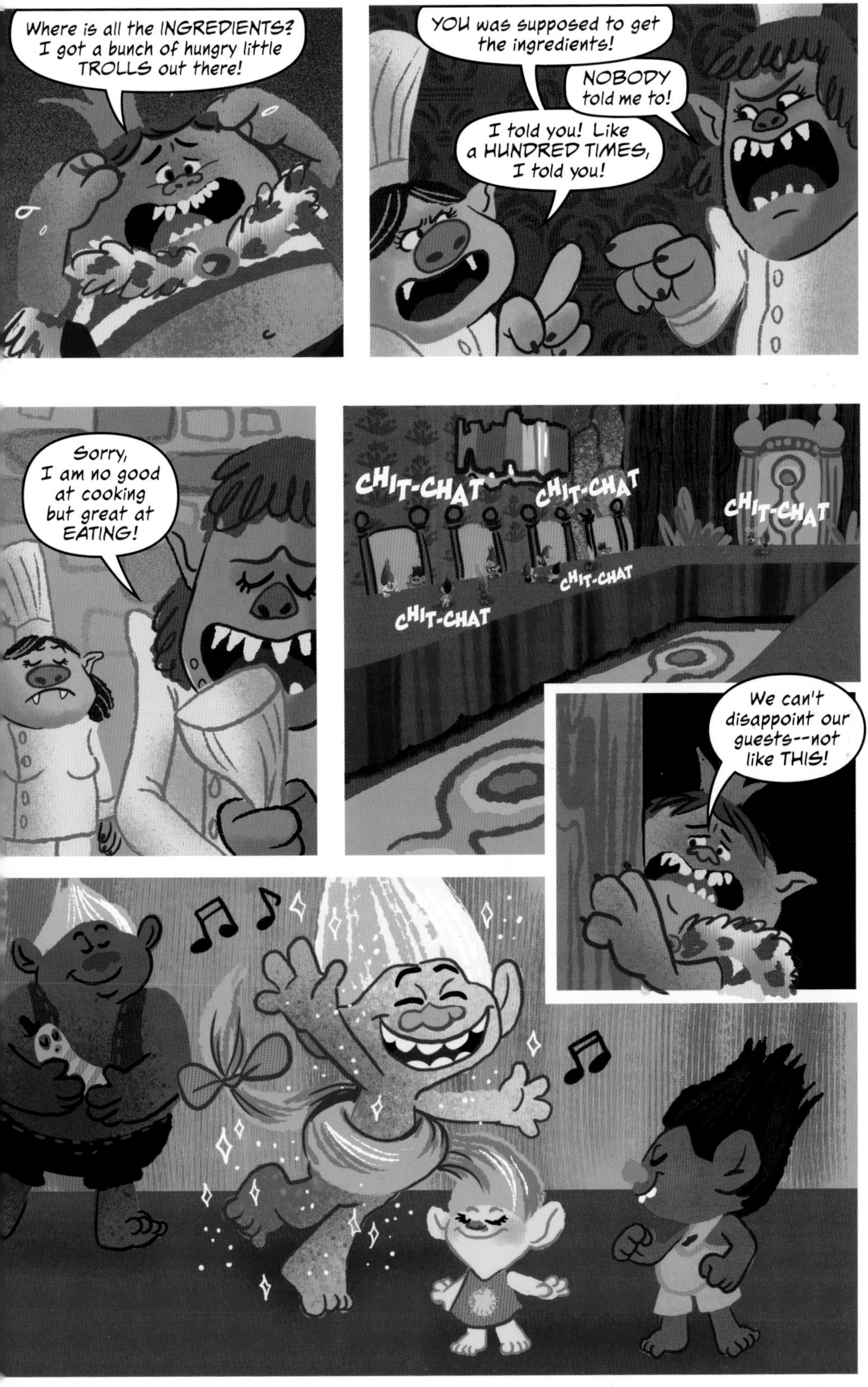
Where is all the INGREDIENTS? I got a bunch of hungry little TROLLS out there!
YOU was supposed to get the ingredients!
NOBODY told me to!
I told you! Like a HUNDRED TIMES, I told you!
Sorry, I am no good at cooking but great at EATING!
CHIT-CHAT
CHIT-CHAT
CHIT-CHAT
CHIT-CHAT
CHIT-CHAT
We can't disappoint our guests--not like THIS!

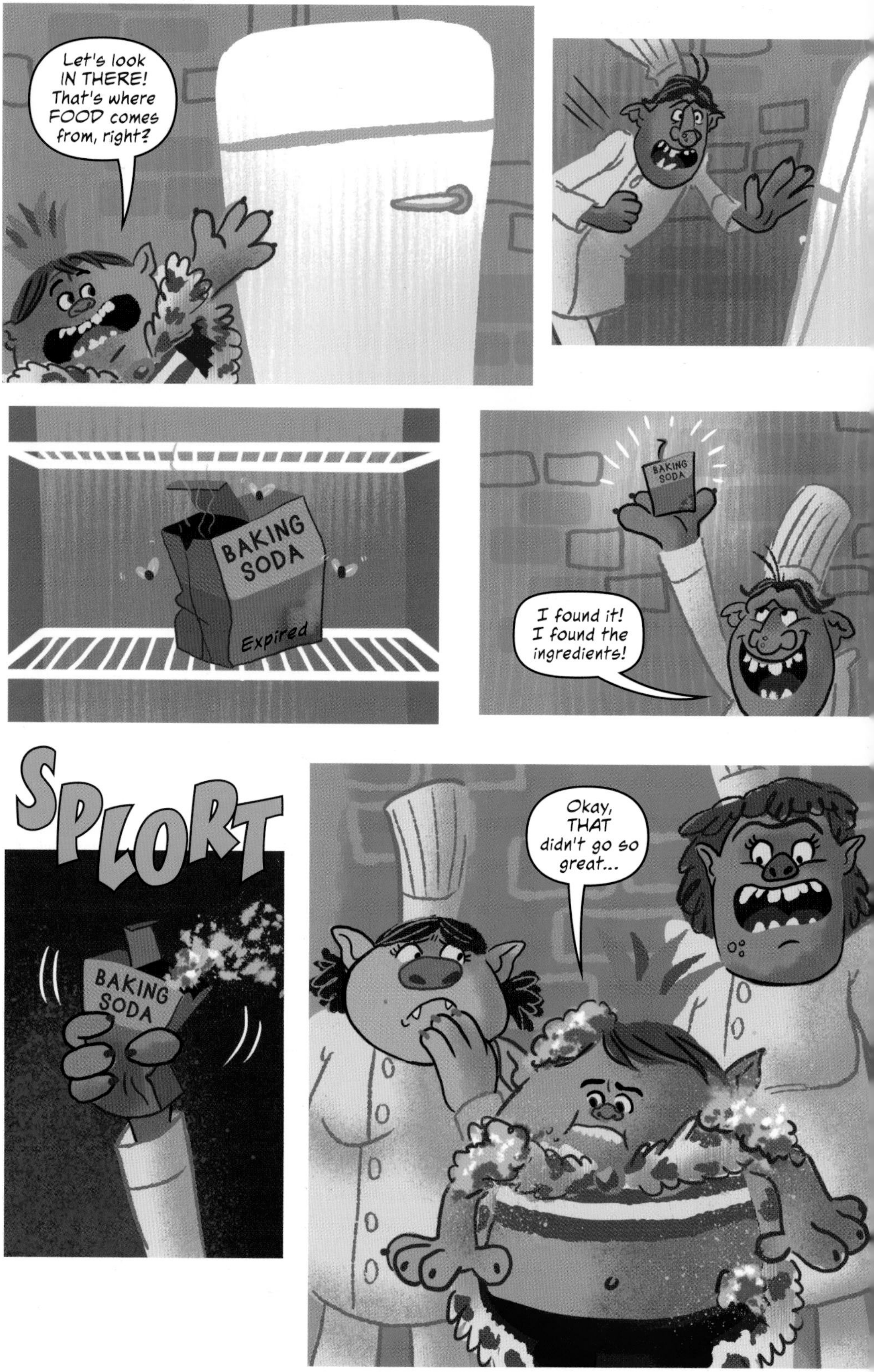
Let's look IN THERE! That's where FOOD comes from, right?
BAKING SODA
Expired
BAKING SODA
I found it! I found the ingredients!
SPLORT
BAKING SODA
Okay, THAT didn't go so great...

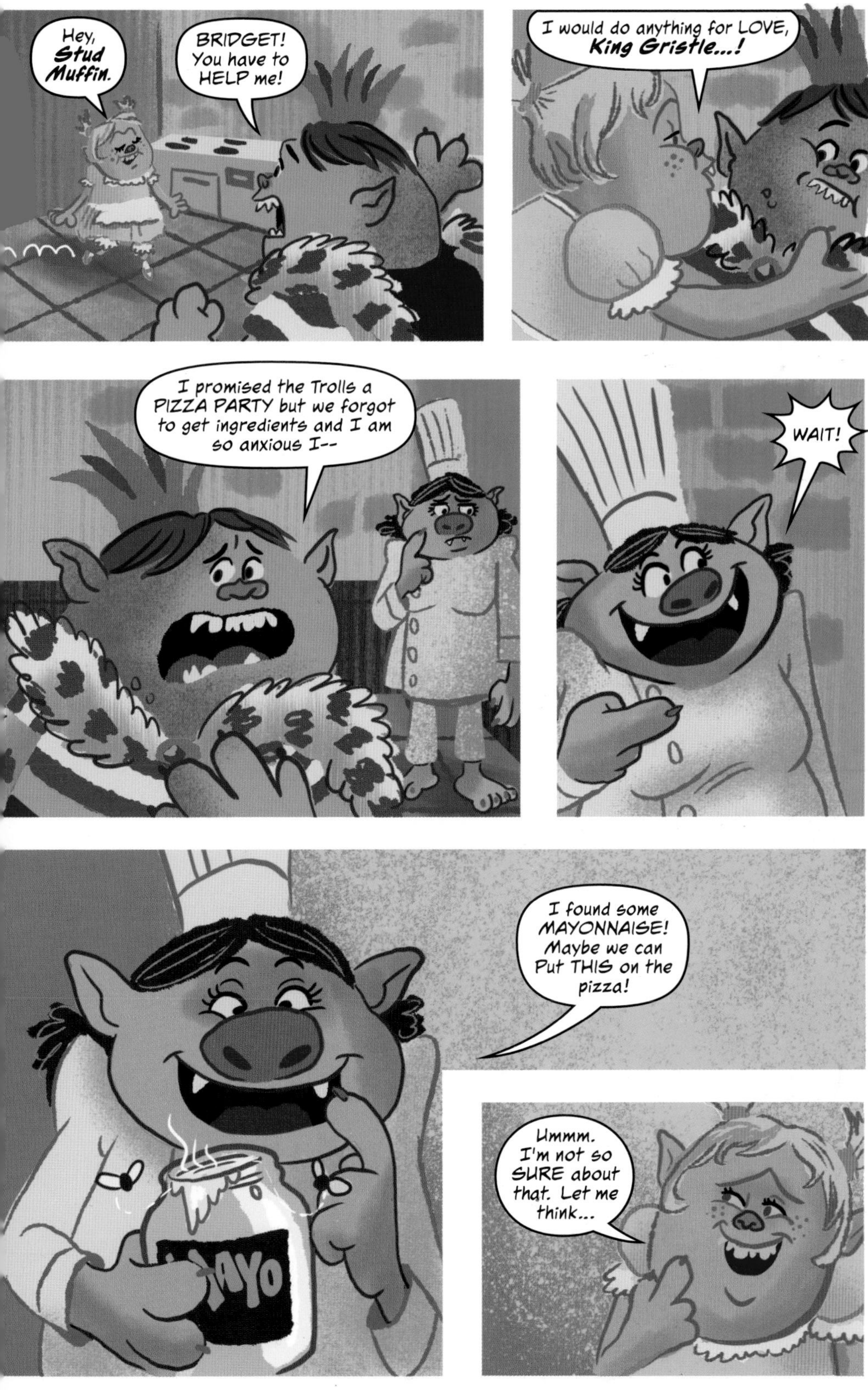
Hey, **Stud Muffin.**
BRIDGET! You have to HELP me!
I would do anything for LOVE, **King Gristle...!**
I promised the Trolls a PIZZA PARTY but we forgot to get ingredients and I am so anxious I--
WAIT!
I found some *MAYONNAISE!* Maybe we can Put THIS on the pizza!
MAYO
Ummm. I'm not so SURE about that. Let me think...

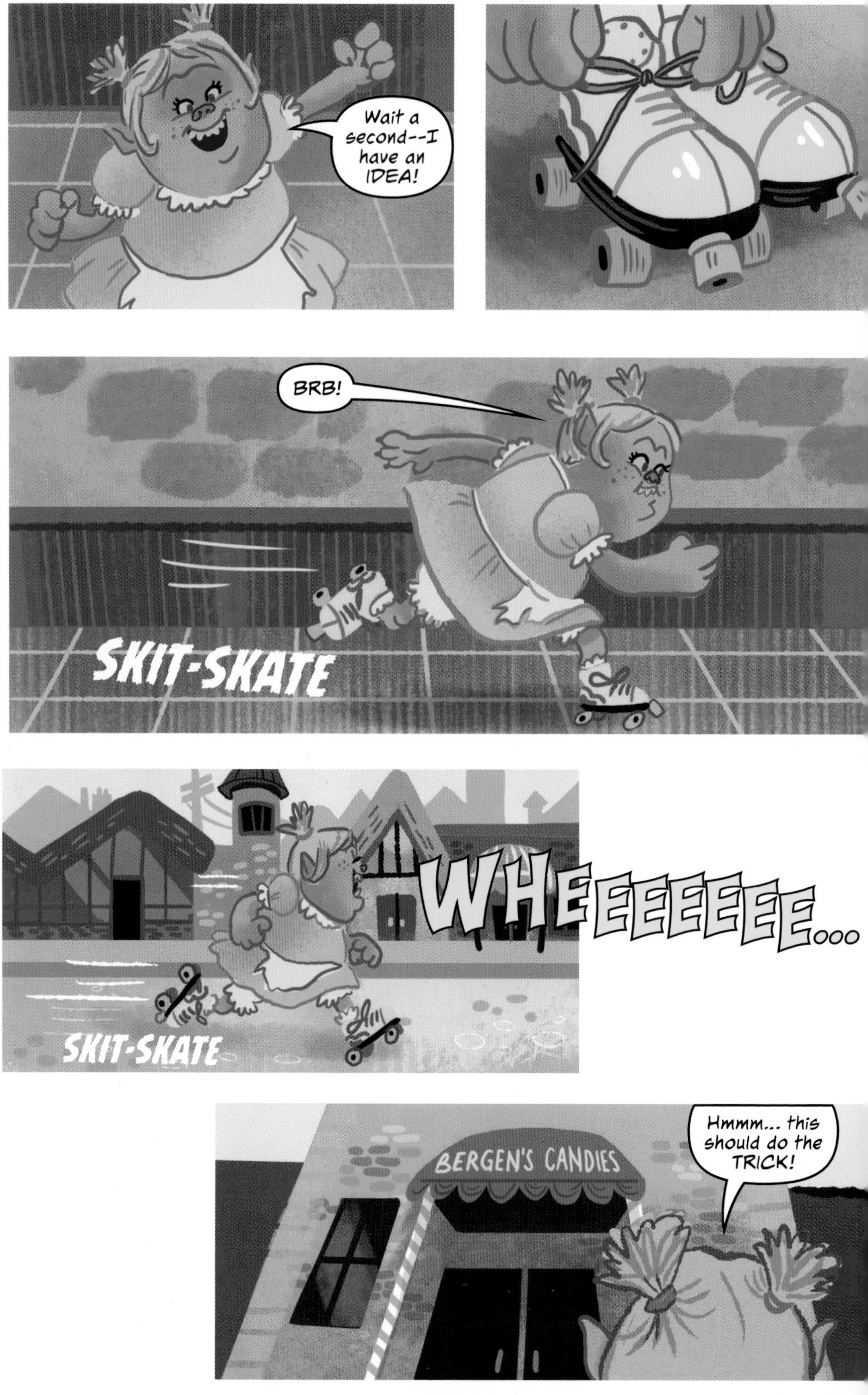
Wait a second--I have an IDEA!
BRB!
SKIT-SKATE
SKIT-SKATE
WHEEEEEEE...
BERGEN'S CANDIES
Hmmm... this should do the TRICK!

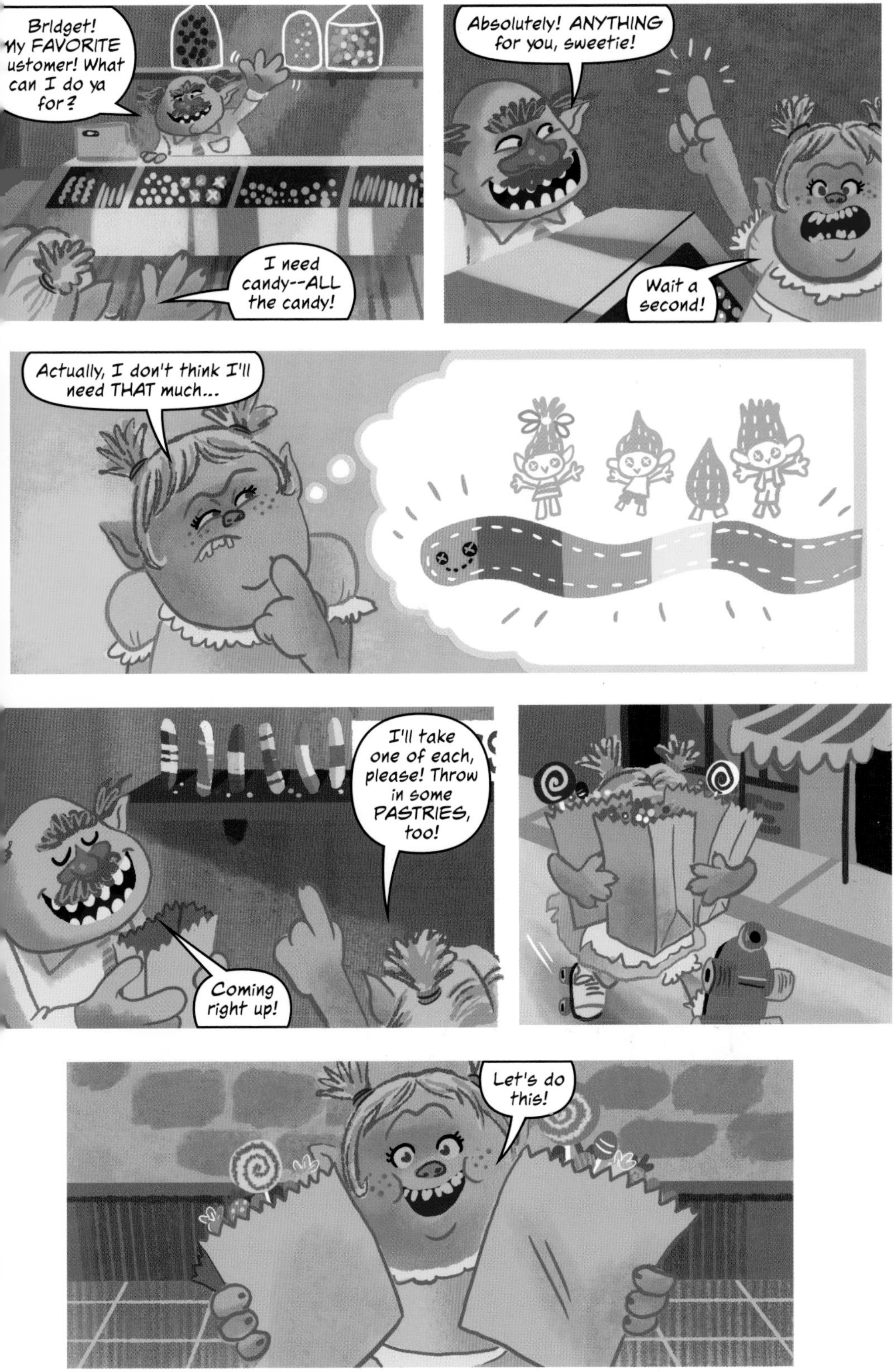
Bridget! My FAVORITE ustomer! What can I do ya for?
I need candy--ALL the candy!
Absolutely! ANYTHING for you, sweetie!
Wait a second!
Actually, I don't think I'll need THAT much...
I'll take one of each, please! Throw in some PASTRIES, too!
Coming right up!
Let's do this!

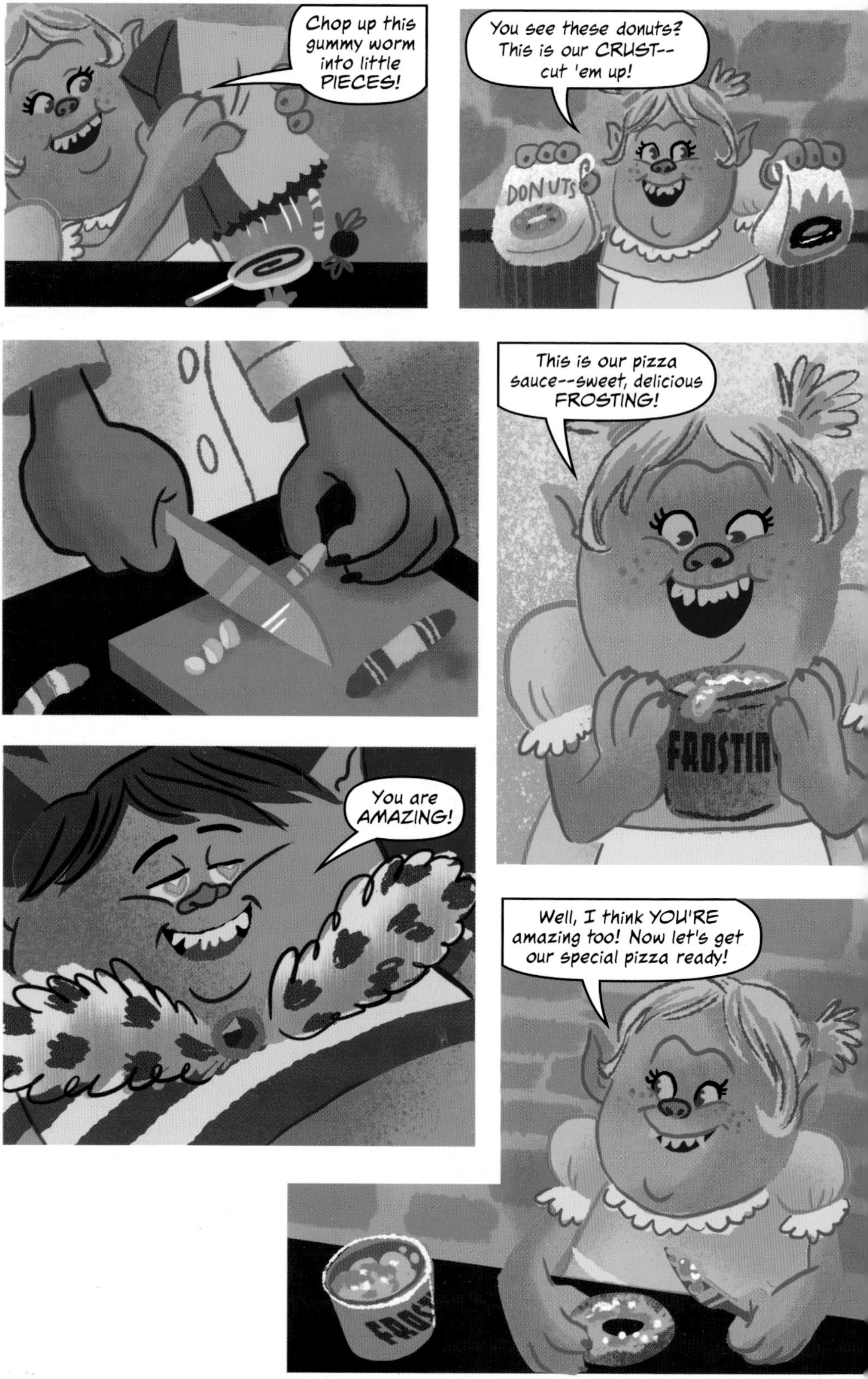
Chop up this gummy worm into little PIECES!
You see these donuts? This is our CRUST--cut 'em up!
DONUTS
This is our pizza sauce--sweet, delicious FROSTING!
FROSTIN
You are AMAZING!
Well, I think YOU'RE amazing too! Now let's get our special pizza ready!

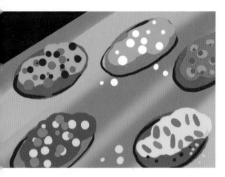

PIZZA!

PIZZA!

PIZZA!

Huh?! This doesn't LOOK like pizza...

It's a CANDY PIZZA! I repeat! It's a pizza made of candy!

You sure know how to throw a SWEET PARTY!

YOU are sweeter than candy, baby.

End

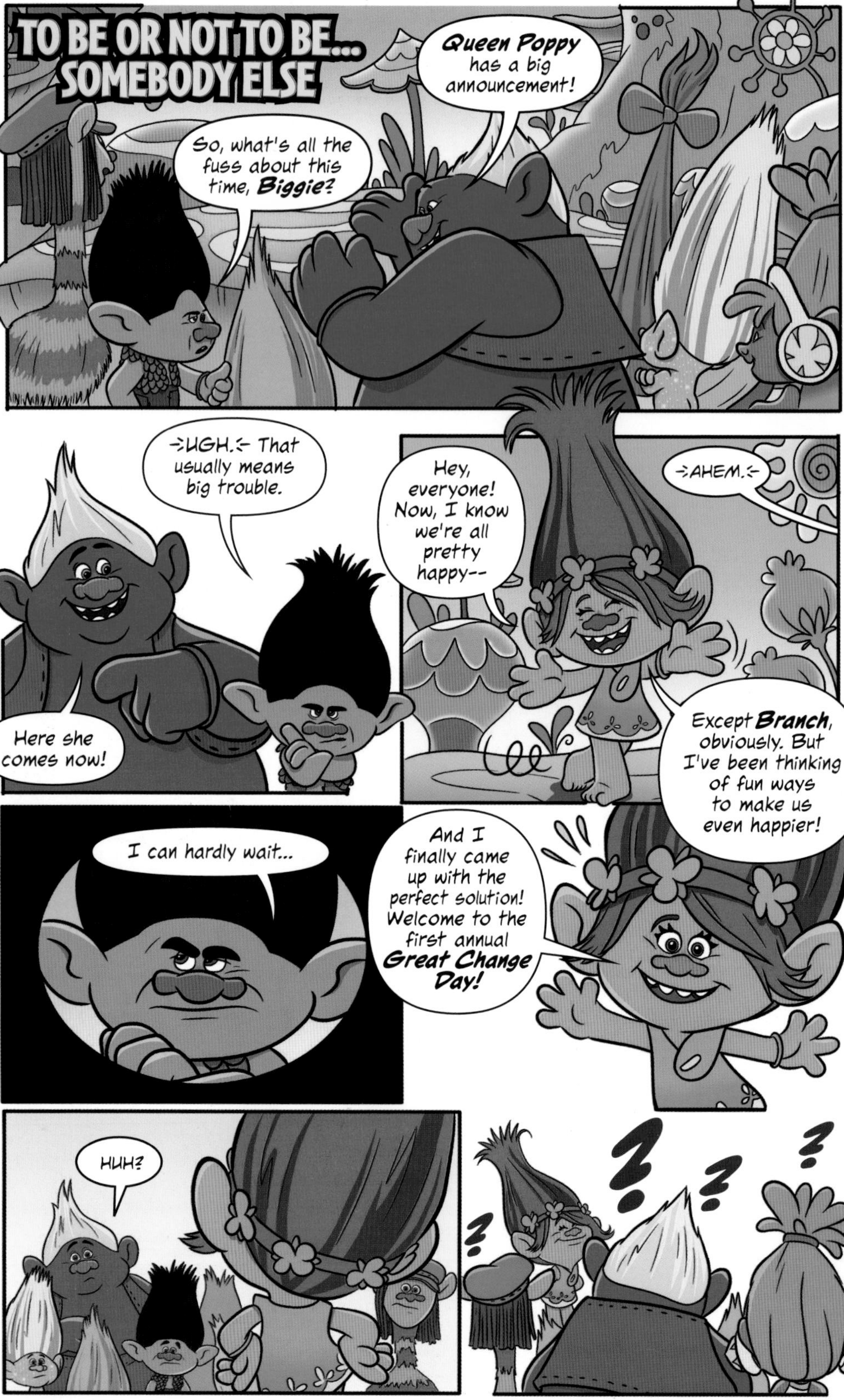
TO BE OR NOT TO BE... SOMEBODY ELSE
So, what's all the fuss about this time, Biggie?
Queen Poppy has a big announcement!
UGH. That usually means big trouble.
Here she comes now!
Hey, everyone! Now, I know we're all pretty happy--
AHEM.
Except Branch, obviously. But I've been thinking of fun ways to make us even happier!
I can hardly wait...
And I finally came up with the perfect solution! Welcome to the first annual Great Change Day!
HUH?

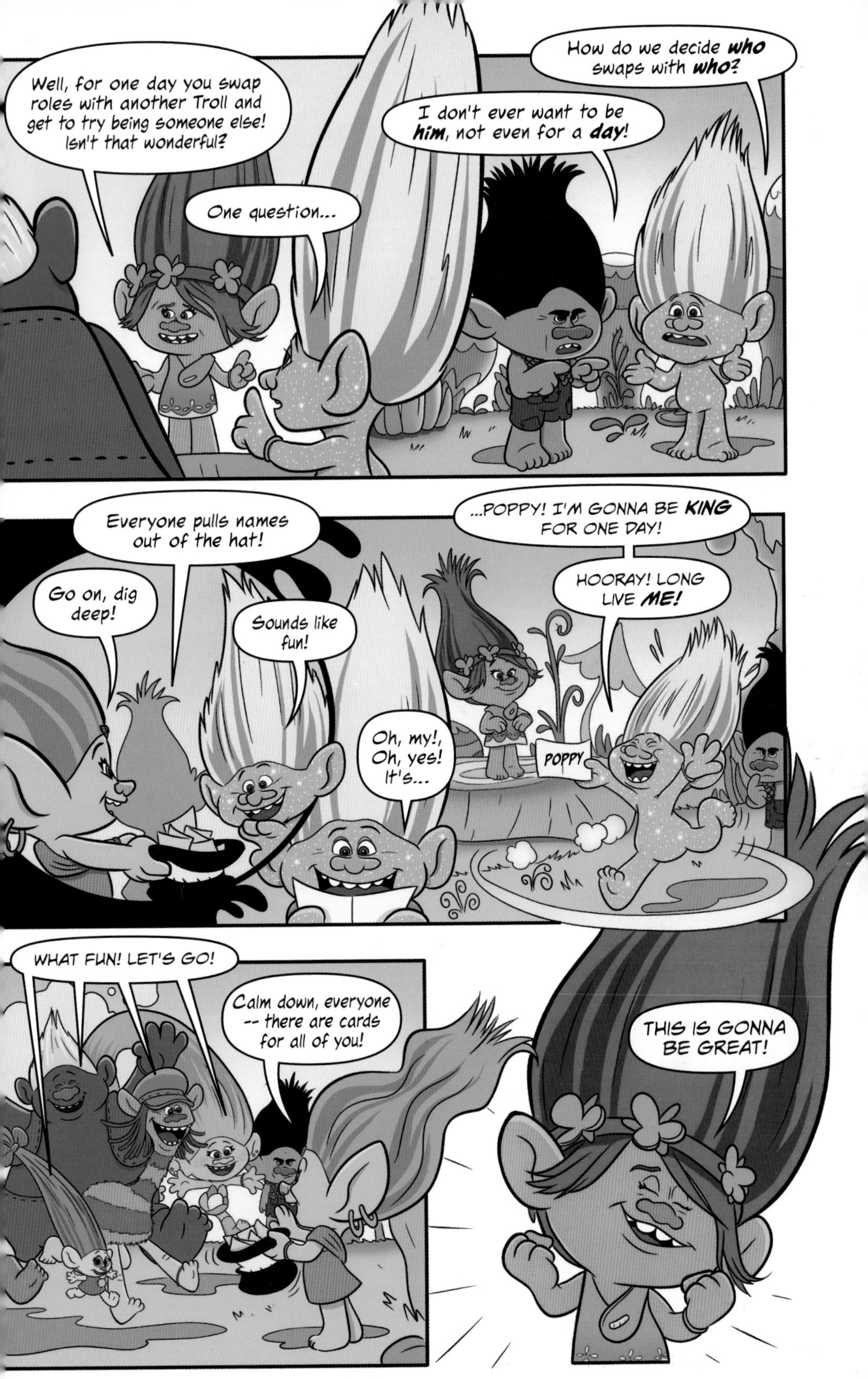
Well, for one day you swap roles with another Troll and get to try being someone else! Isn't that wonderful?
One question...
I don't ever want to be him, not even for a day!
How do we decide who swaps with who?
Everyone pulls names out of the hat!
Go on, dig deep!
Sounds like fun!
Oh, my!, Oh, yes! It's...
...POPPY! I'M GONNA BE KING FOR ONE DAY!
POPPY
HOORAY! LONG LIVE ME!
WHAT FUN! LET'S GO!
Calm down, everyone -- there are cards for all of you!
THIS IS GONNA BE GREAT!

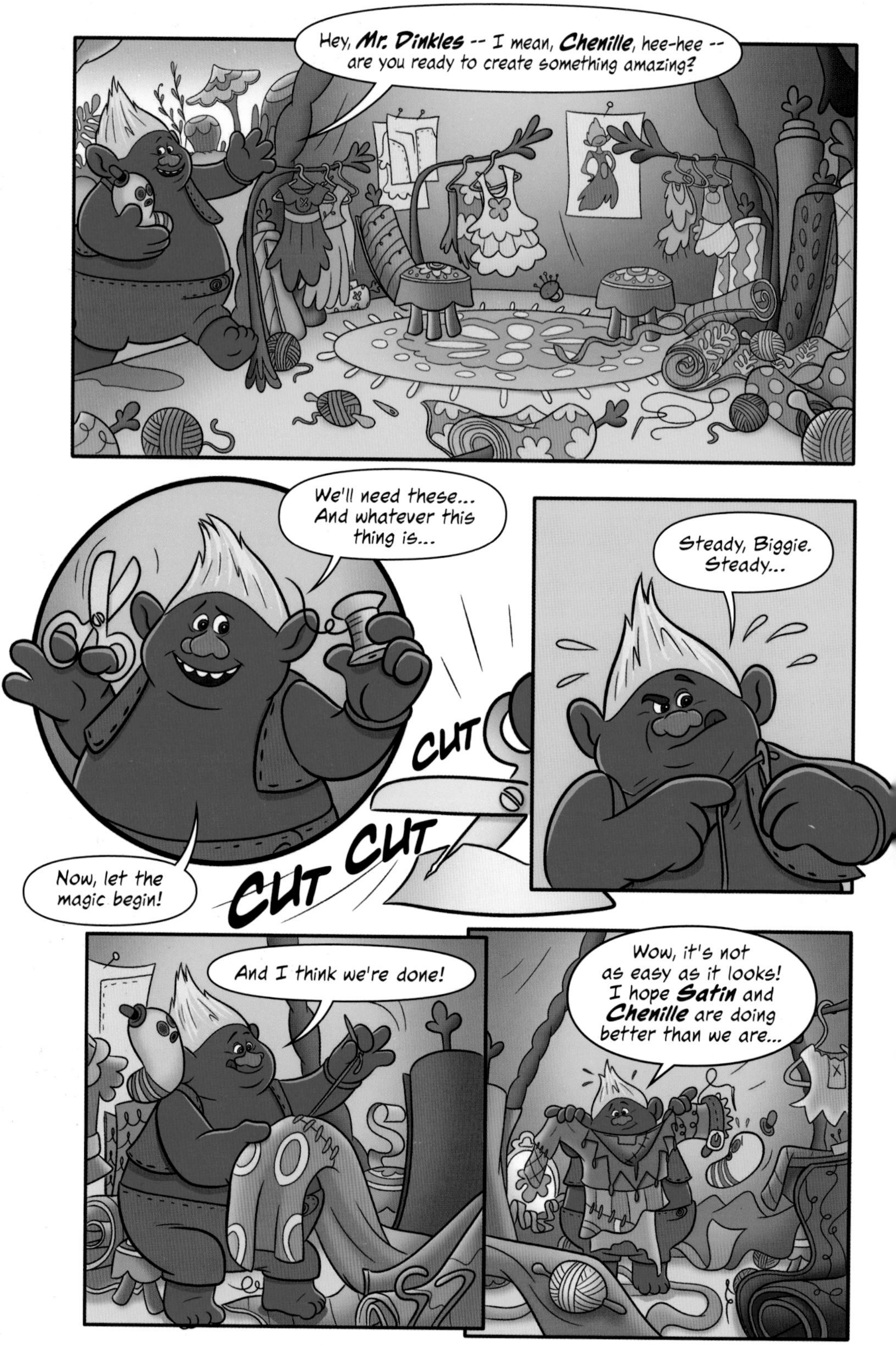

Hey, **Mr. Dinkles** -- I mean, **Chenille**, hee-hee -- are you ready to create something amazing?
We'll need these... And whatever this thing is...
Now, let the magic begin!
CUT CUT CUT
Steady, Biggie. Steady...
And I think we're done!
Wow, it's not as easy as it looks! I hope **Satin** and **Chenille** are doing better than we are...

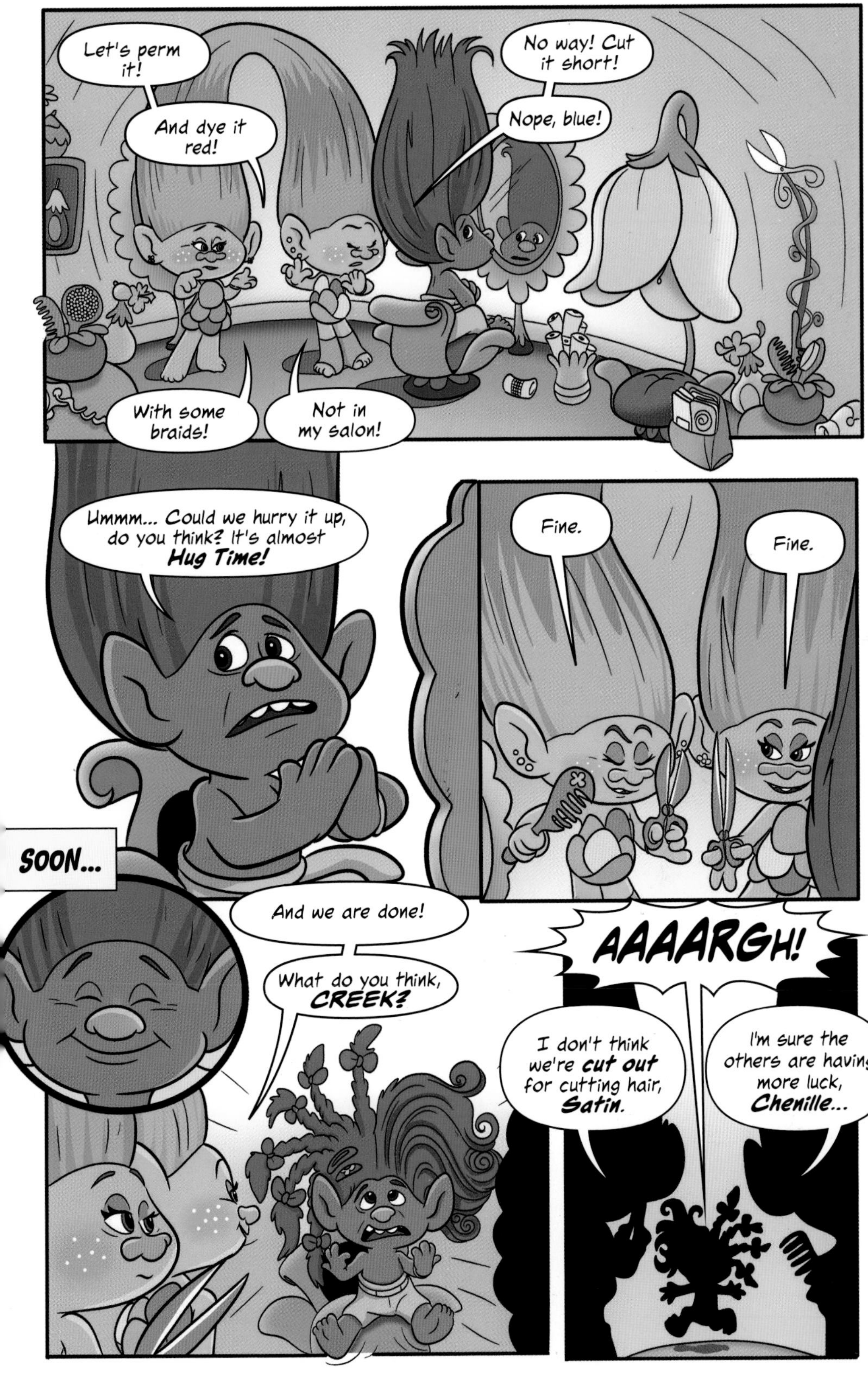
Let's perm it!
And dye it red!
No way! Cut it short!
Nope, blue!
With some braids!
Not in my salon!
Ummm... Could we hurry it up, do you think? It's almost **Hug Time!**
Fine.
Fine.
SOON...
And we are done!
What do you think, **CREEK?**
AAAARGH!
I don't think we're ***cut out*** for cutting hair, ***Satin***.
I'm sure the others are having more luck, ***Chenille***...

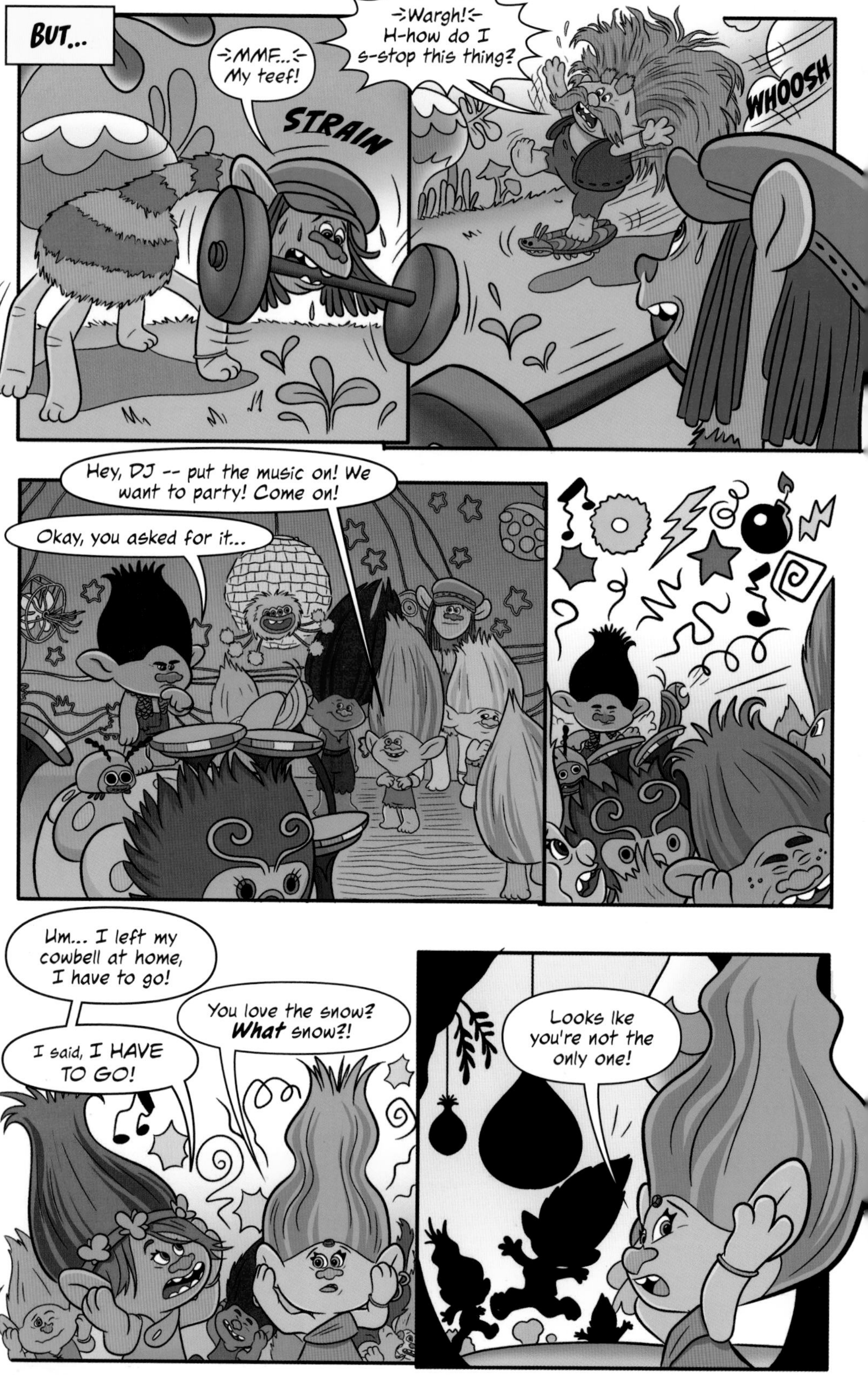
BUT...
MMF... My teef!
STRAIN
Wargh! H-how do I s-stop this thing?
WHOOSH
Hey, DJ -- put the music on! We want to party! Come on!
Okay, you asked for it...
Um... I left my cowbell at home, I have to go!
I said, I HAVE TO GO!
You love the snow? What snow?!
Looks lke you're not the only one!

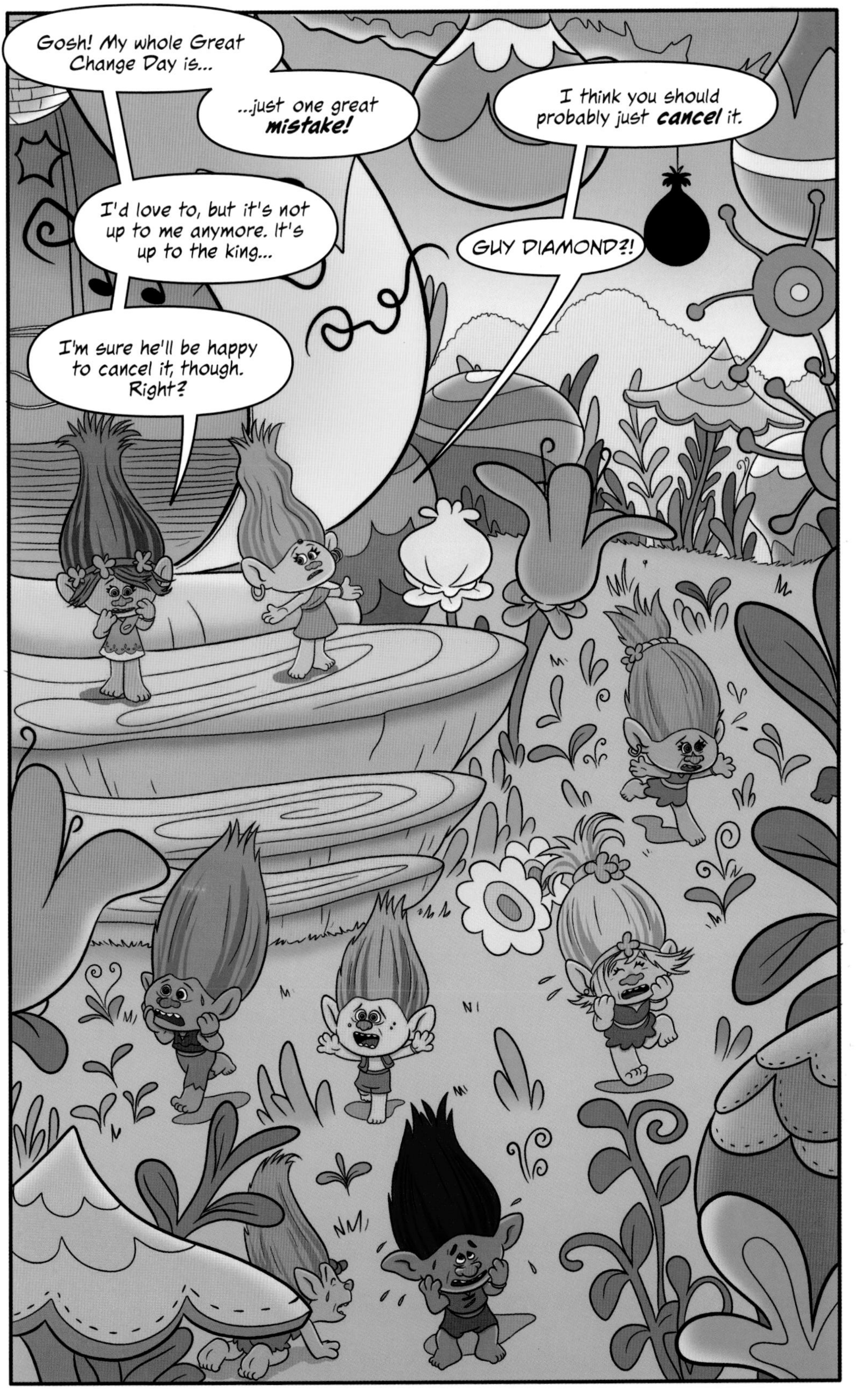
Gosh! My whole Great Change Day is...
...just one great mistake!
I'd love to, but it's not up to me anymore. It's up to the king...
I'm sure he'll be happy to cancel it, though. Right?
I think you should probably just cancel it.
GUY DIAMOND?!

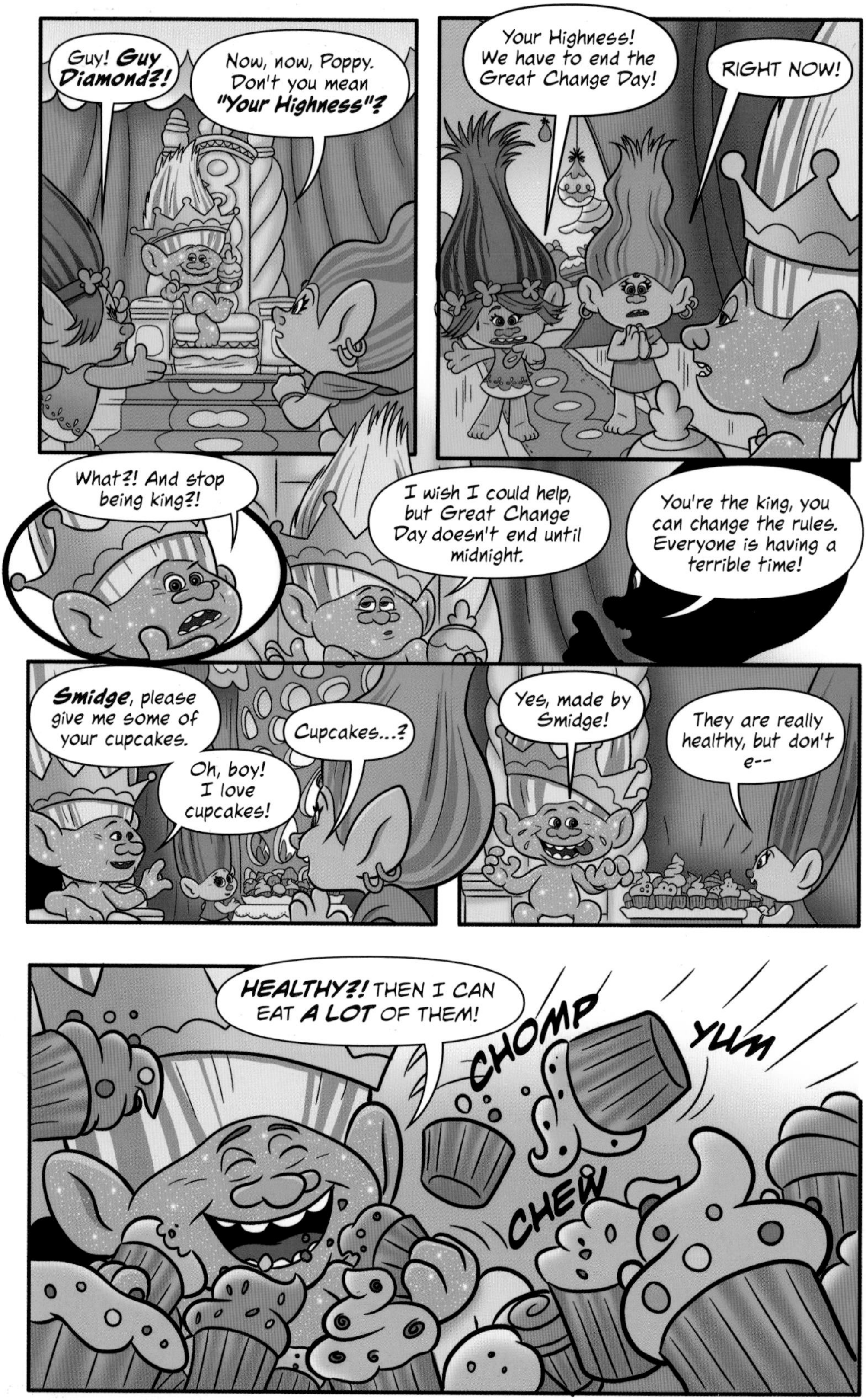
Guy! Guy Diamond?!
Now, now, Poppy. Don't you mean "Your Highness"?
Your Highness! We have to end the Great Change Day!
RIGHT NOW!
What?! And stop being king?!
I wish I could help, but Great Change Day doesn't end until midnight.
You're the king, you can change the rules. Everyone is having a terrible time!
Smidge, please give me some of your cupcakes.
Oh, boy! I love cupcakes!
Cupcakes...?
Yes, made by Smidge!
They are really healthy, but don't e--
HEALTHY?! THEN I CAN EAT A LOT OF THEM!
CHOMP
YUM
CHEW

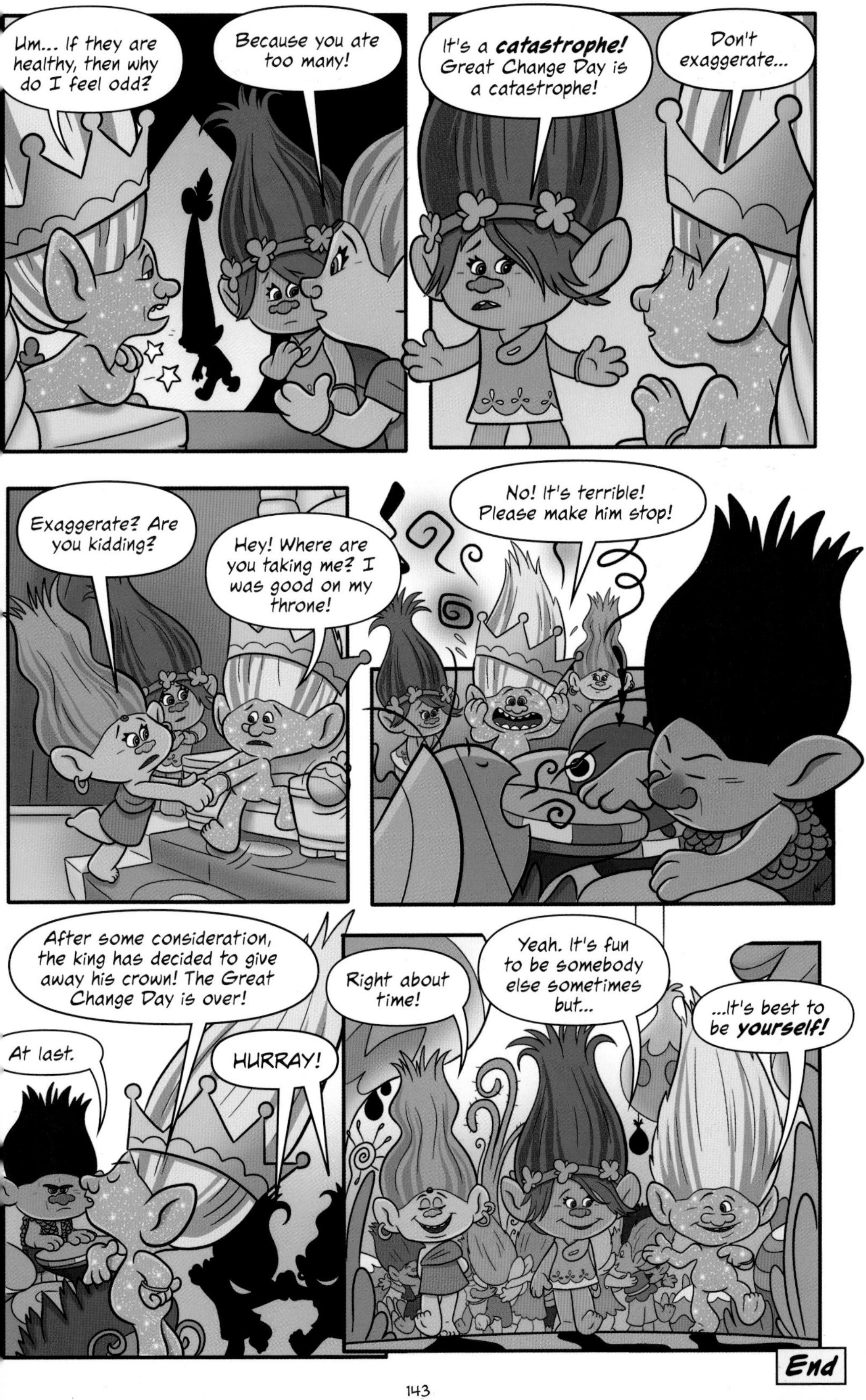
Um... If they are healthy, then why do I feel odd?
Because you ate too many!
It's a **catastrophe!** Great Change Day is a catastrophe!
Don't exaggerate...
Exaggerate? Are you kidding?
Hey! Where are you taking me? I was good on my throne!
No! It's terrible! Please make him stop!
After some consideration, the king has decided to give away his crown! The Great Change Day is over!
At last.
HURRAY!
Right about time!
Yeah. It's fun to be somebody else sometimes but...
...It's best to be **yourself!**
End

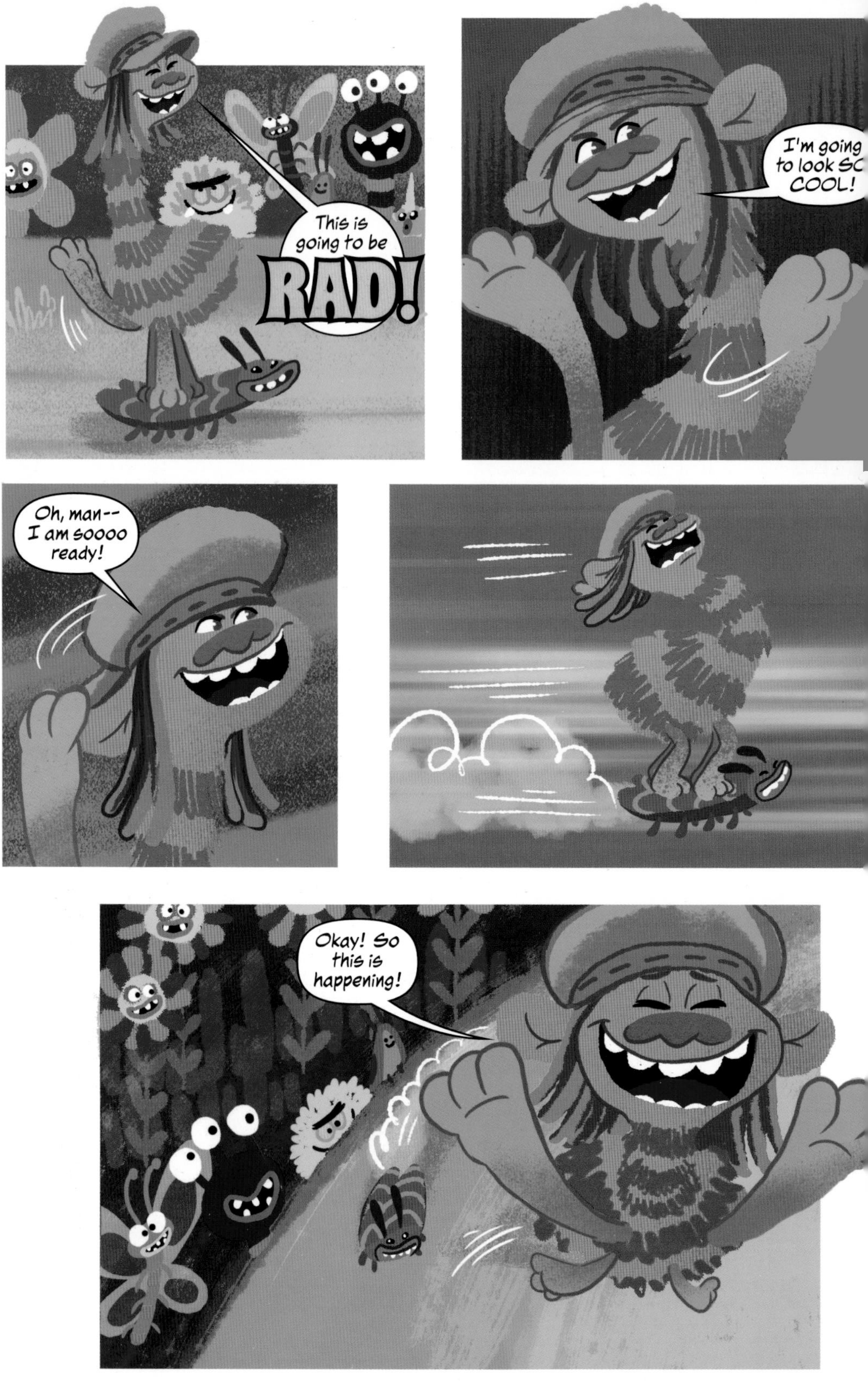
This is going to be RAD!
I'm going to look SO COOL!
Oh, man-- I am soooo ready!
Okay! So this is happening!

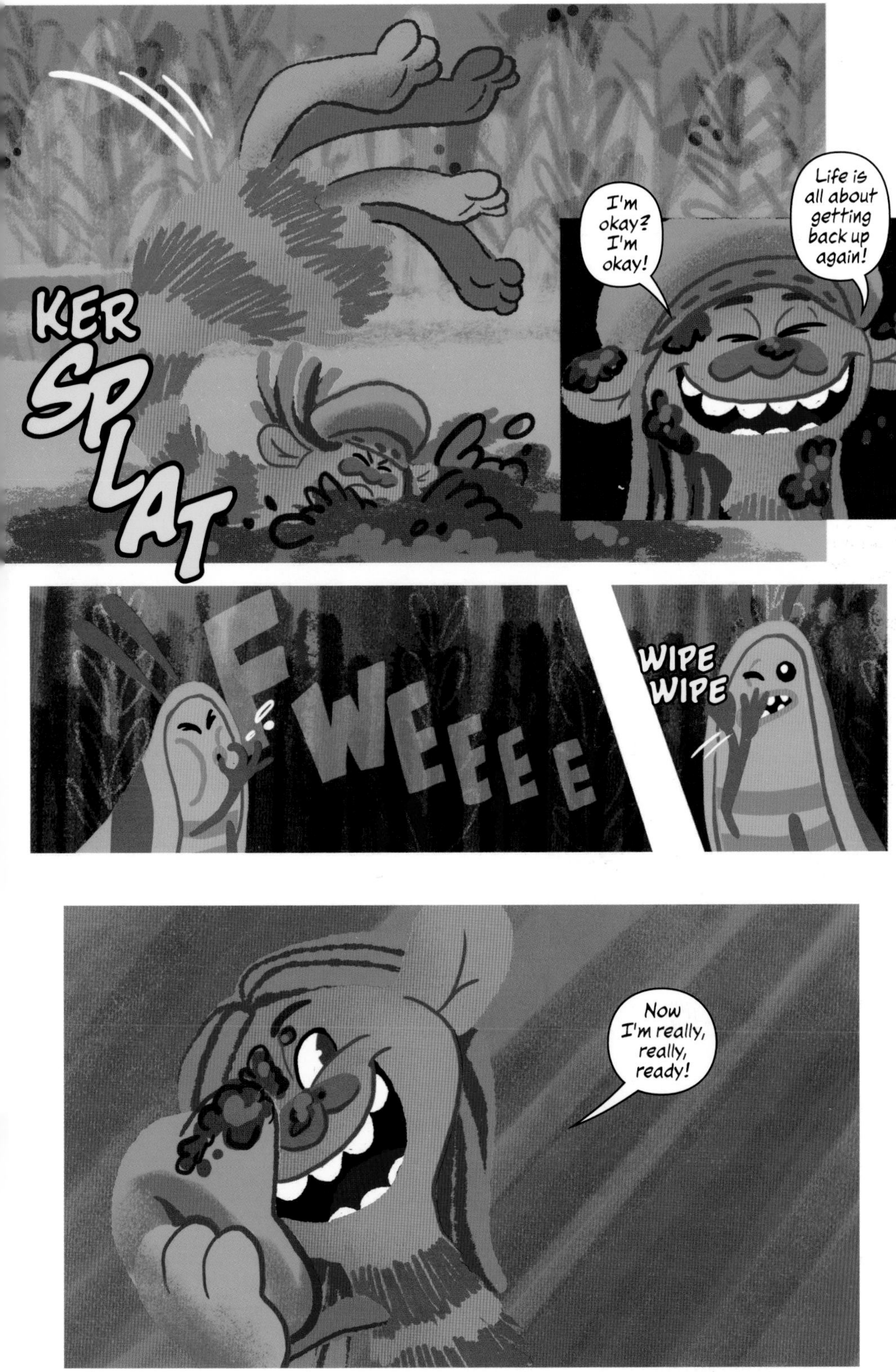

KER SPLAT
I'm okay? I'm okay!
Life is all about getting back up again!
FWEEEEE
WIPE WIPE
Now I'm really, really, ready!

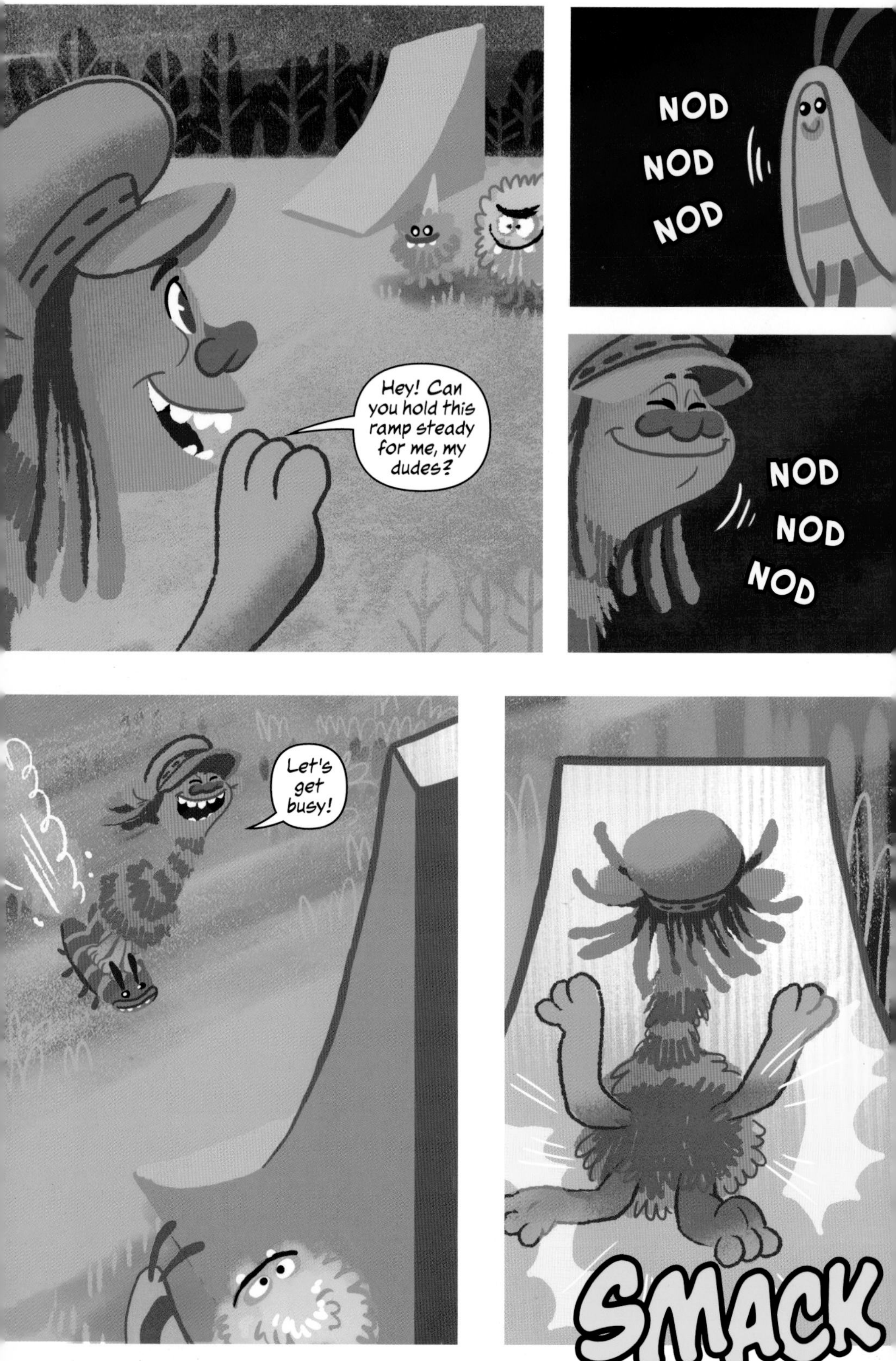
Hey! Can you hold this ramp steady for me, my dudes?
NOD NOD NOD
NOD NOD NOD
Let's get busy!
SMACK

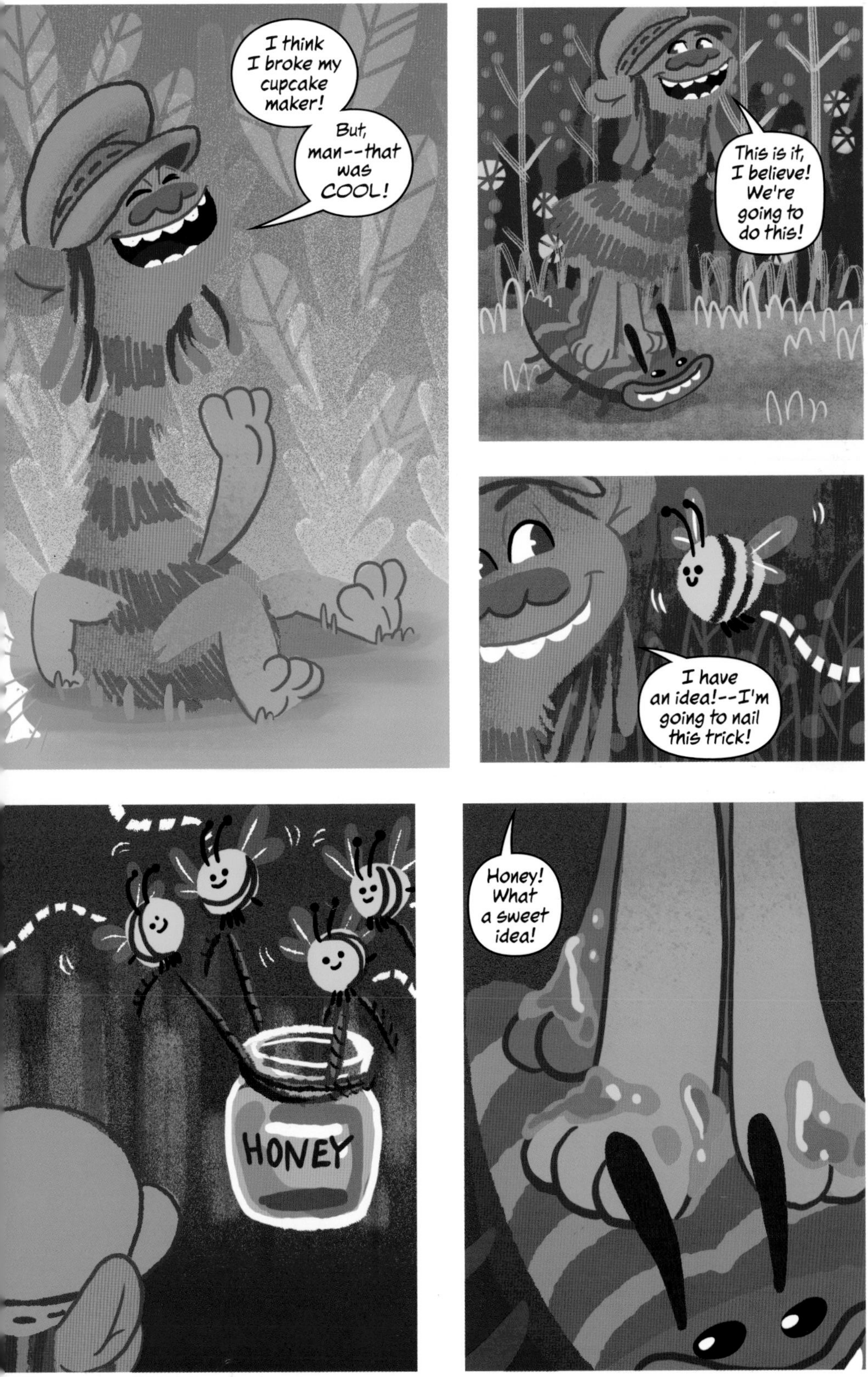
I think I broke my cupcake maker!
But, man--that was COOL!
This is it, I believe! We're going to do this!
I have an idea!--I'm going to nail this trick!
HONEY
Honey! What a sweet idea!

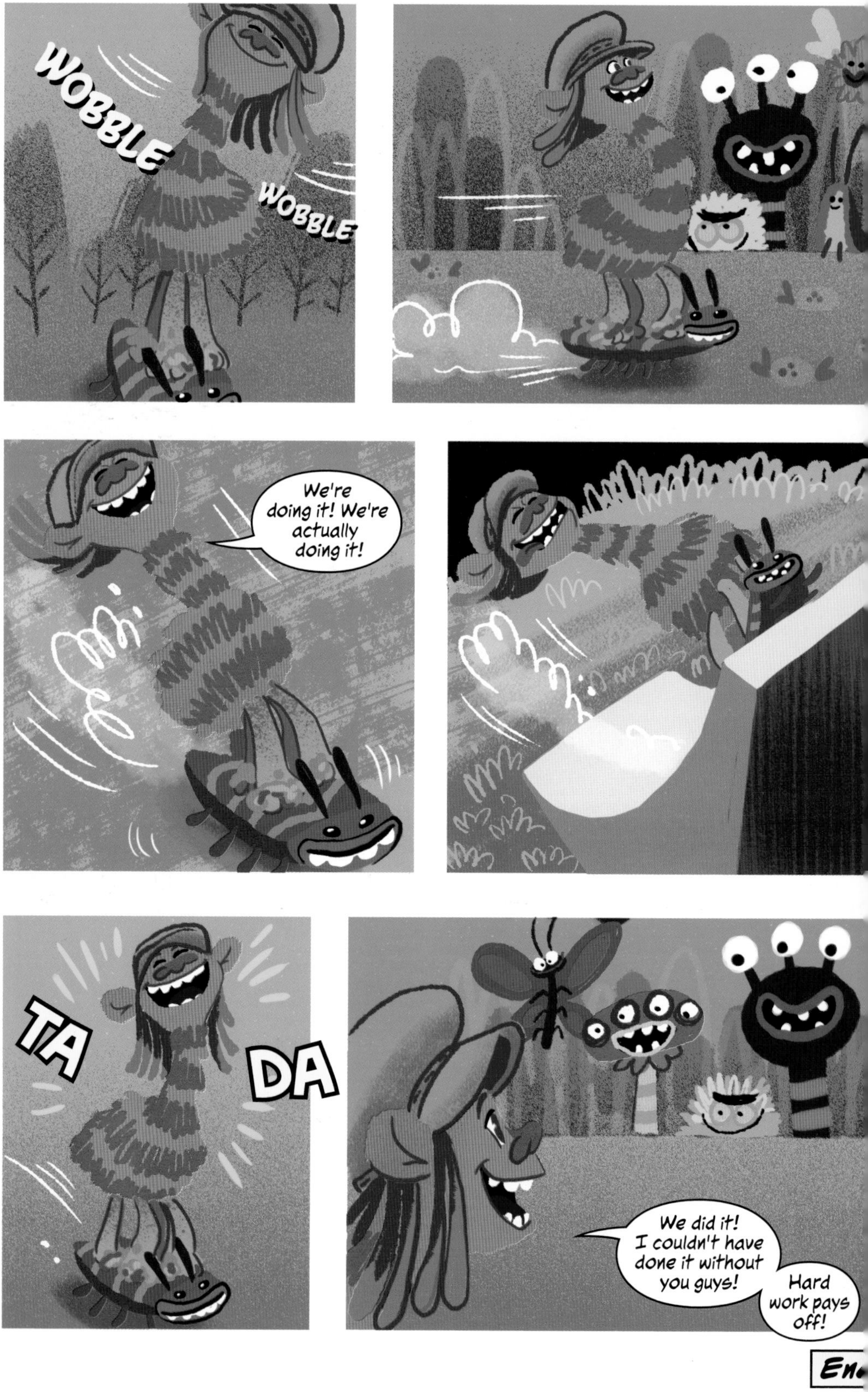
WOBBLE
WOBBLE
We're doing it! We're actually doing it!
TA
DA
We did it! I couldn't have done it without you guys!
Hard work pays off!
En

ROYAL PORTRAIT

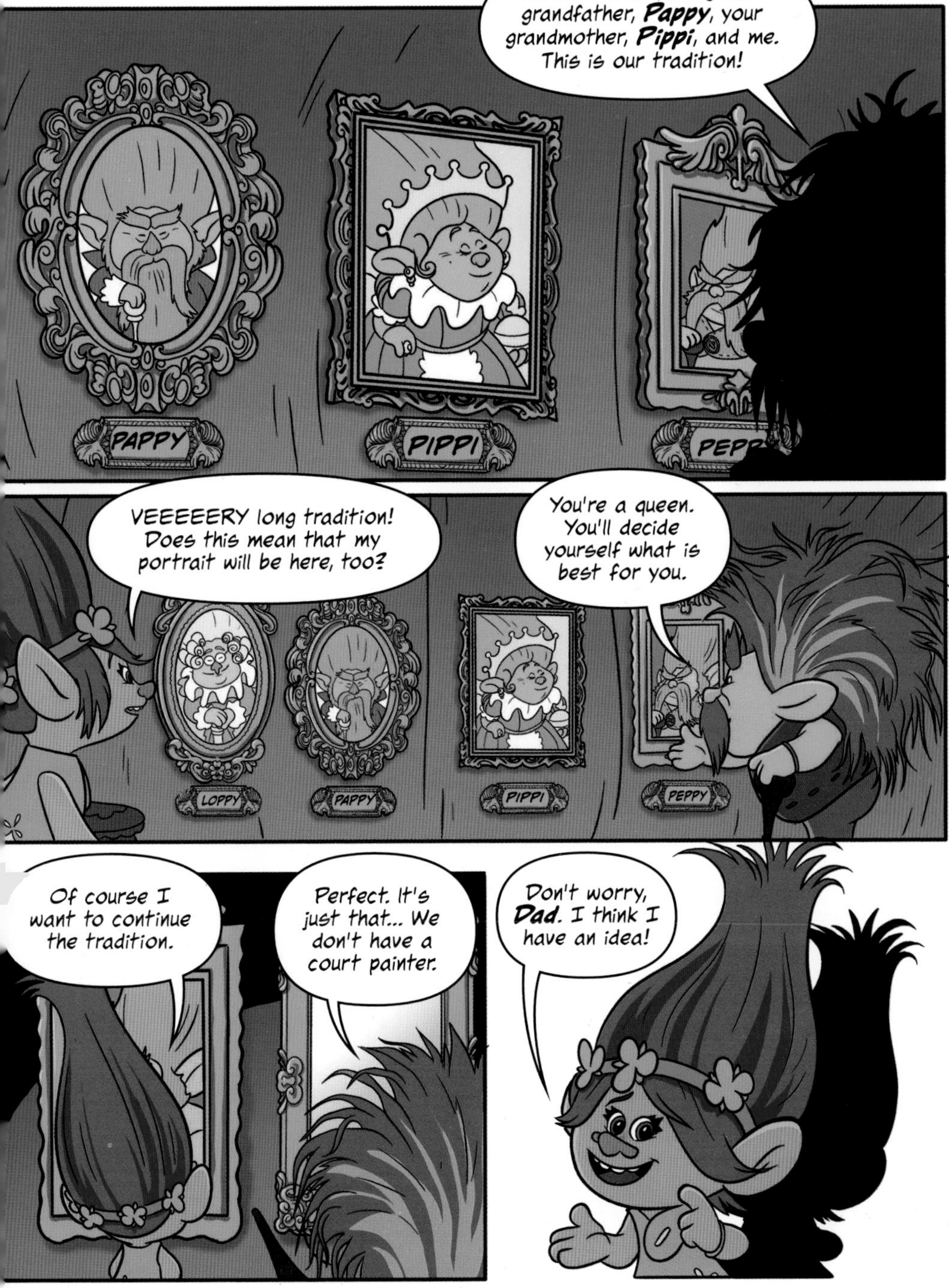
...And this is your great grandfather, Pappy, your grandmother, Pippi, and me. This is our tradition!
PAPPY
PIPPI
VEEEEERY long tradition! Does this mean that my portrait will be here, too?
You're a queen. You'll decide yourself what is best for you.
LOPPY
PAPPY
PIPPI
PEPPY
Of course I want to continue the tradition.
Perfect. It's just that... We don't have a court painter.
Don't worry, Dad. I think I have an idea!

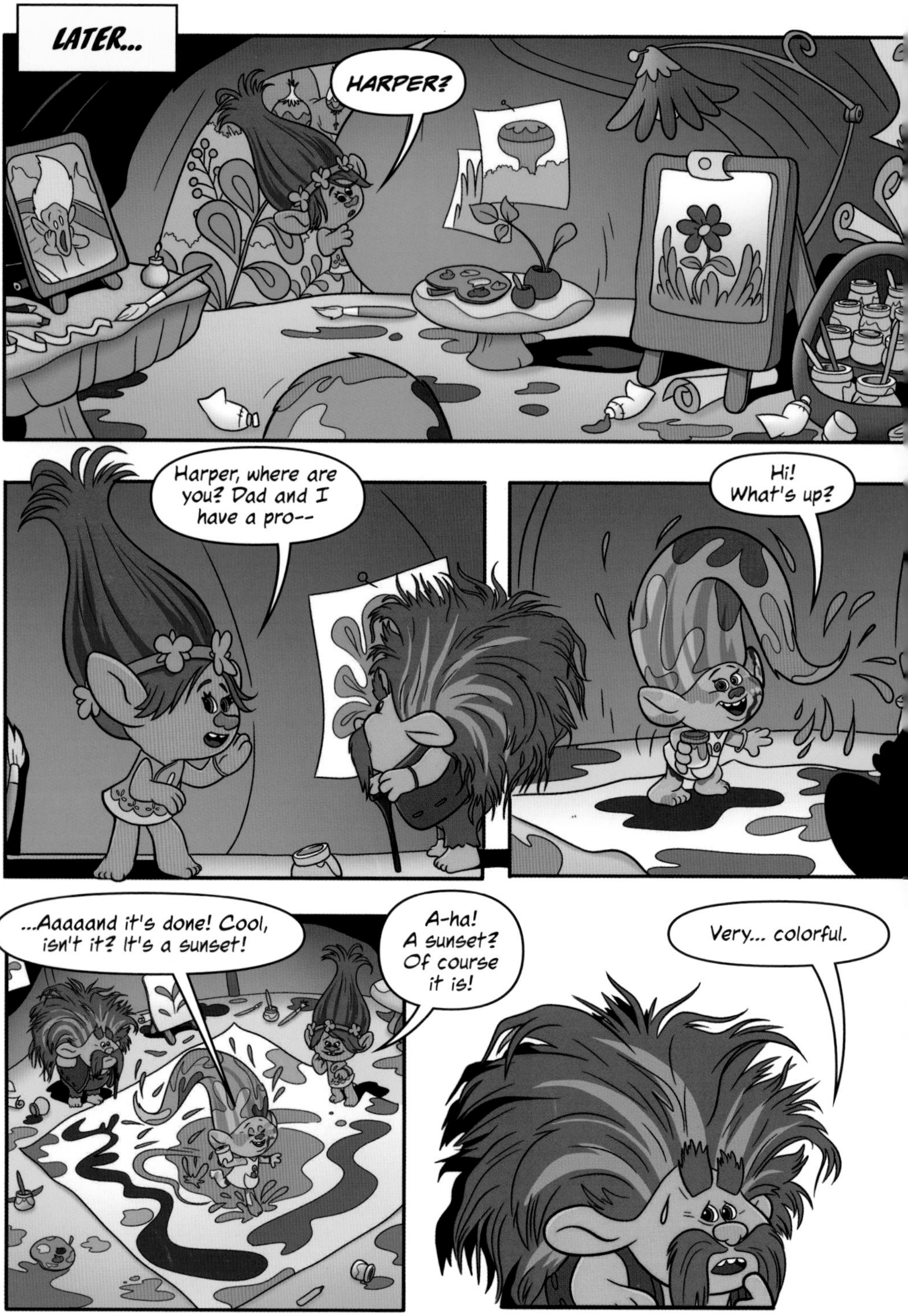
LATER...
HARPER?
Harper, where are you? Dad and I have a pro--
Hi! What's up?
...Aaaaand it's done! Cool, isn't it? It's a sunset!
A-ha! A sunset? Of course it is!
Very... colorful.

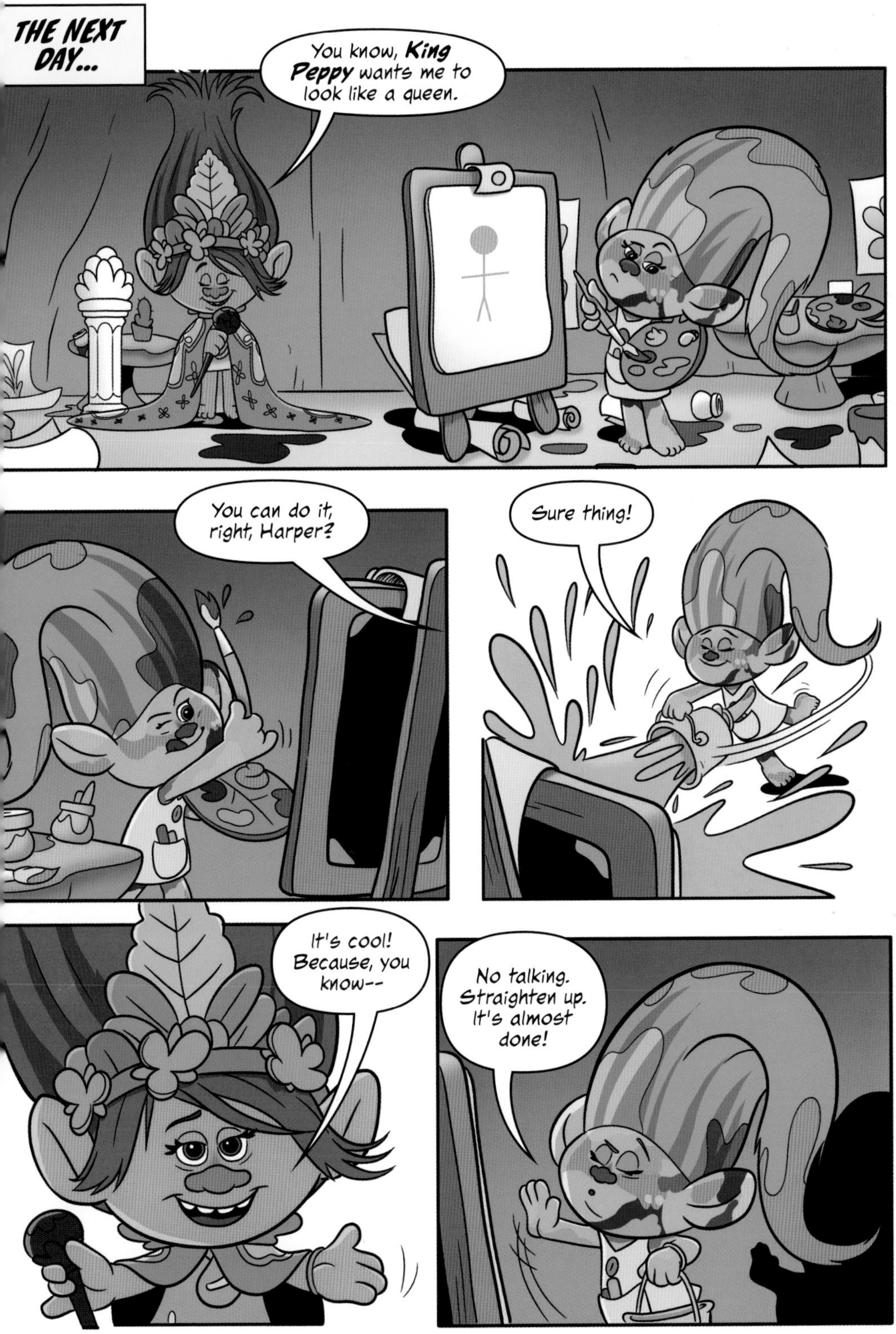
THE NEXT DAY...
You know, **King Peppy** wants me to look like a queen.
You can do it, right, Harper?
Sure thing!
It's cool! Because, you know--
No talking. Straighten up. It's almost done!

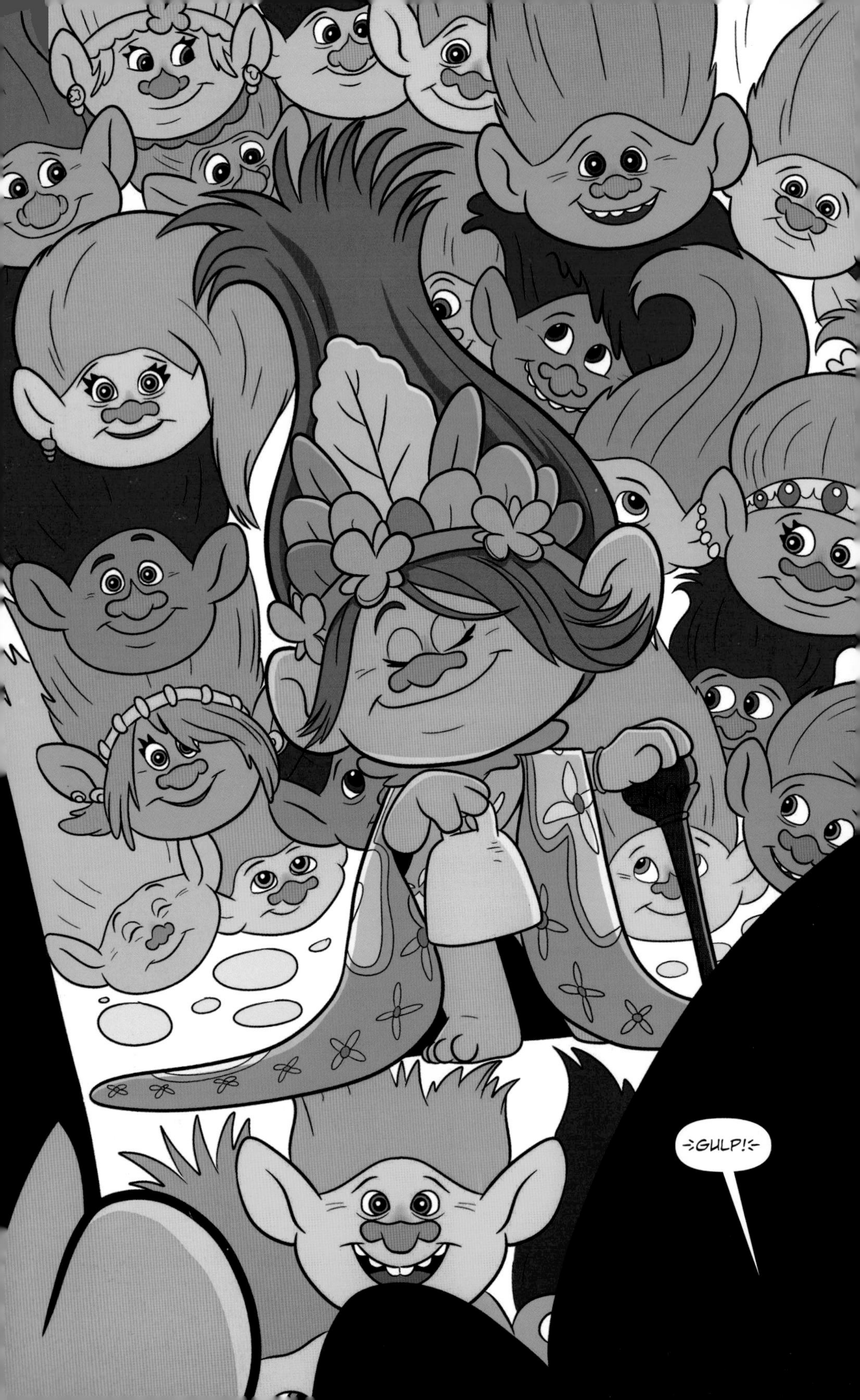
GULP!

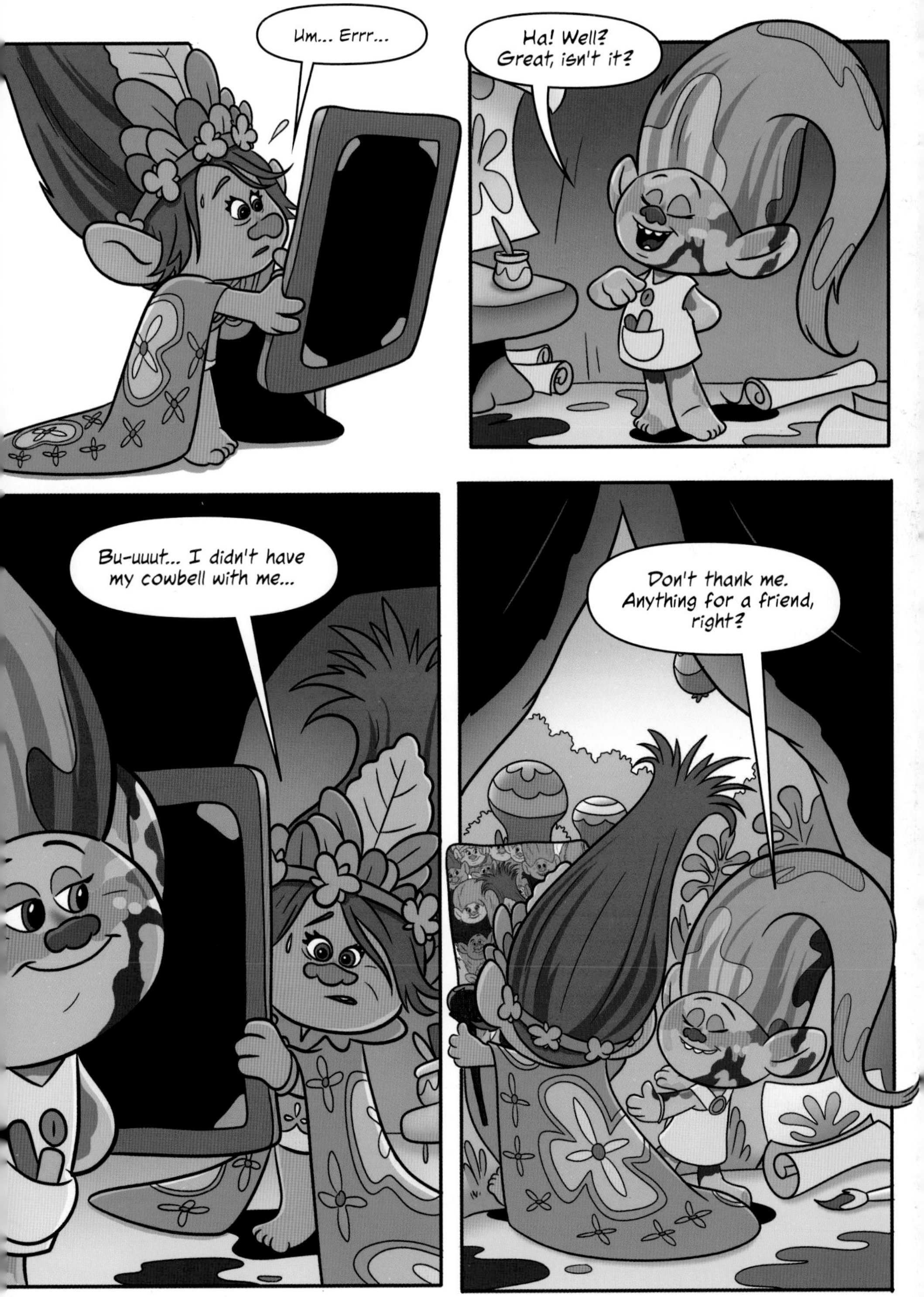
Um... Errr...
Ha! Well? Great, isn't it?
Bu-uuut... I didn't have my cowbell with me...
Don't thank me. Anything for a friend, right?

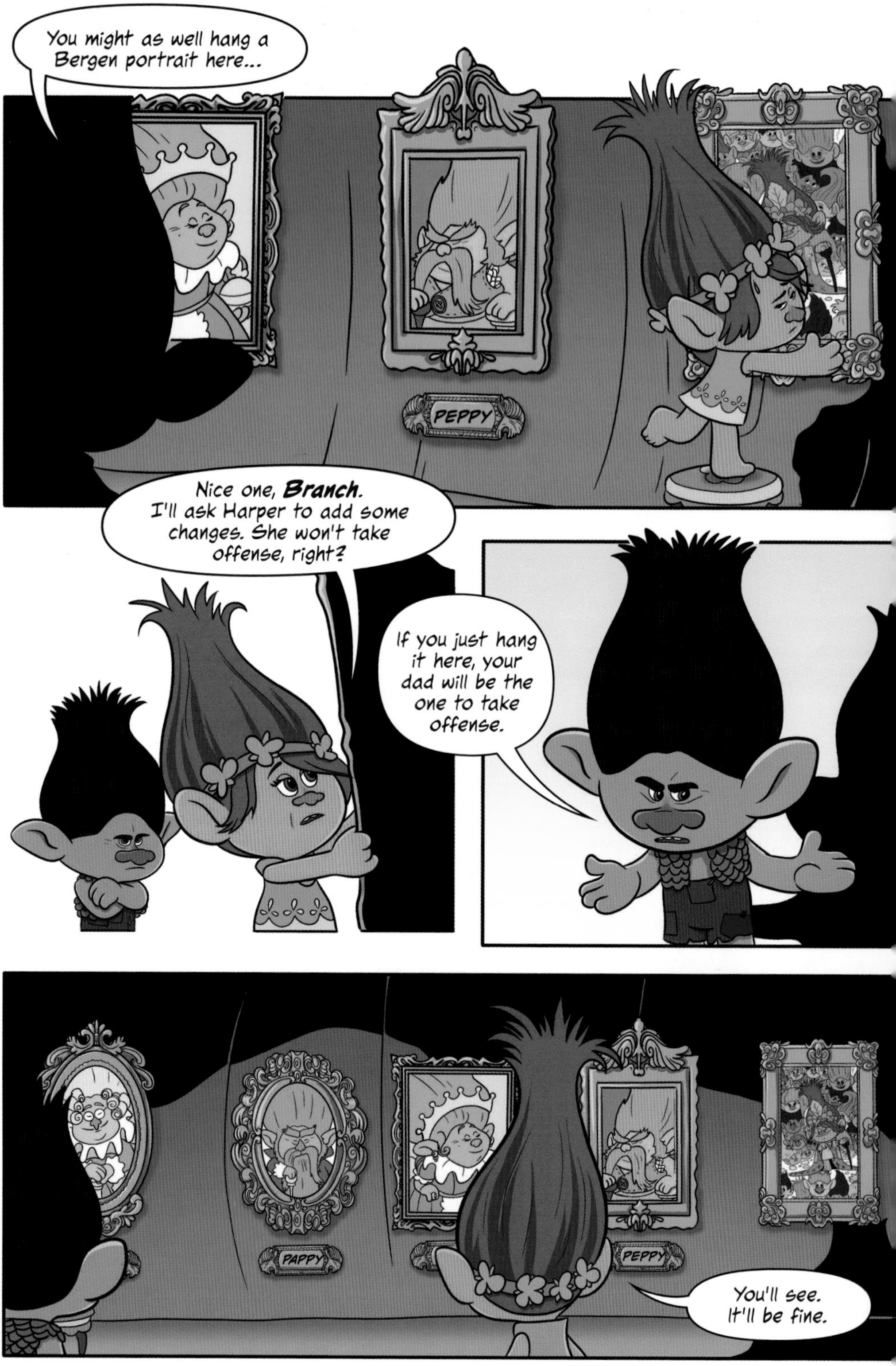
You might as well hang a Bergen portrait here...
PEPPY
Nice one, **Branch**. I'll ask Harper to add some changes. She won't take offense, right?
If you just hang it here, your dad will be the one to take offense.
PAPPY
PEPPY
You'll see. It'll be fine.

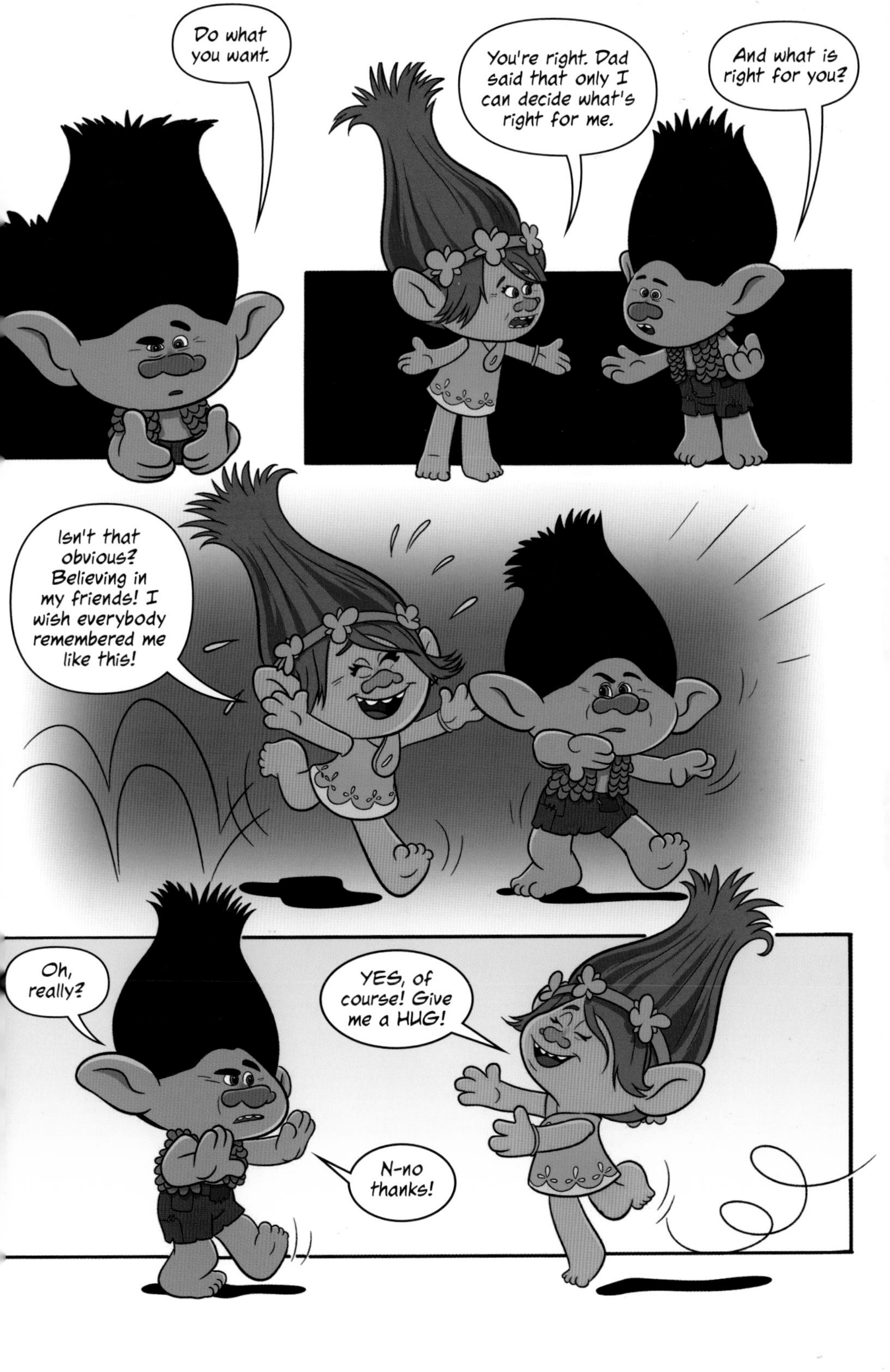
Do what you want.
You're right. Dad said that only I can decide what's right for me.
And what is right for you?
Isn't that obvious? Believing in my friends! I wish everybody remembered me like this!
Oh, really?
YES, of course! Give me a HUG!
N-no thanks!

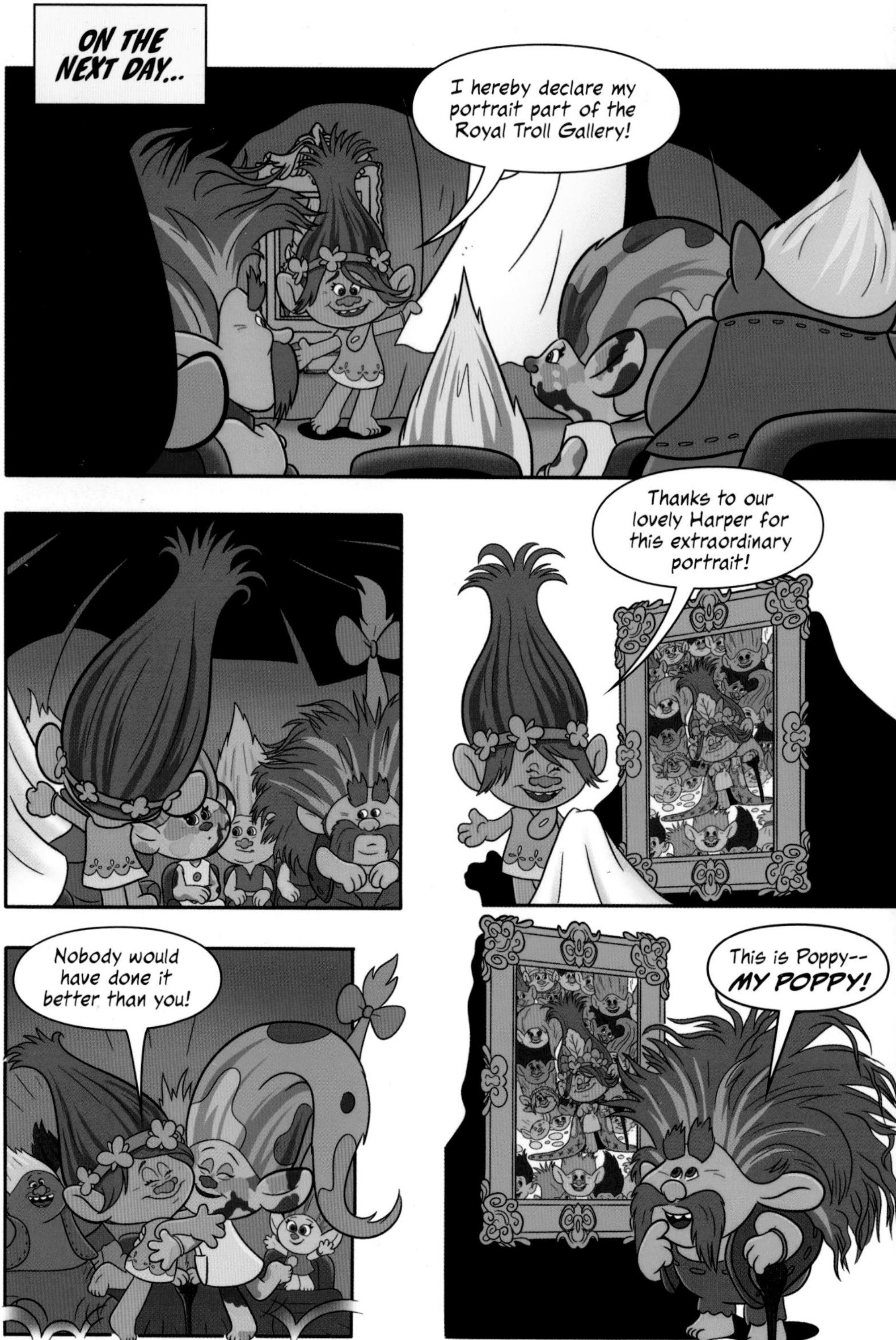
ON THE NEXT DAY...
I hereby declare my portrait part of the Royal Troll Gallery!
Thanks to our lovely Harper for this extraordinary portrait!
Nobody would have done it better than you!
This is Poppy-- MY POPPY!
End

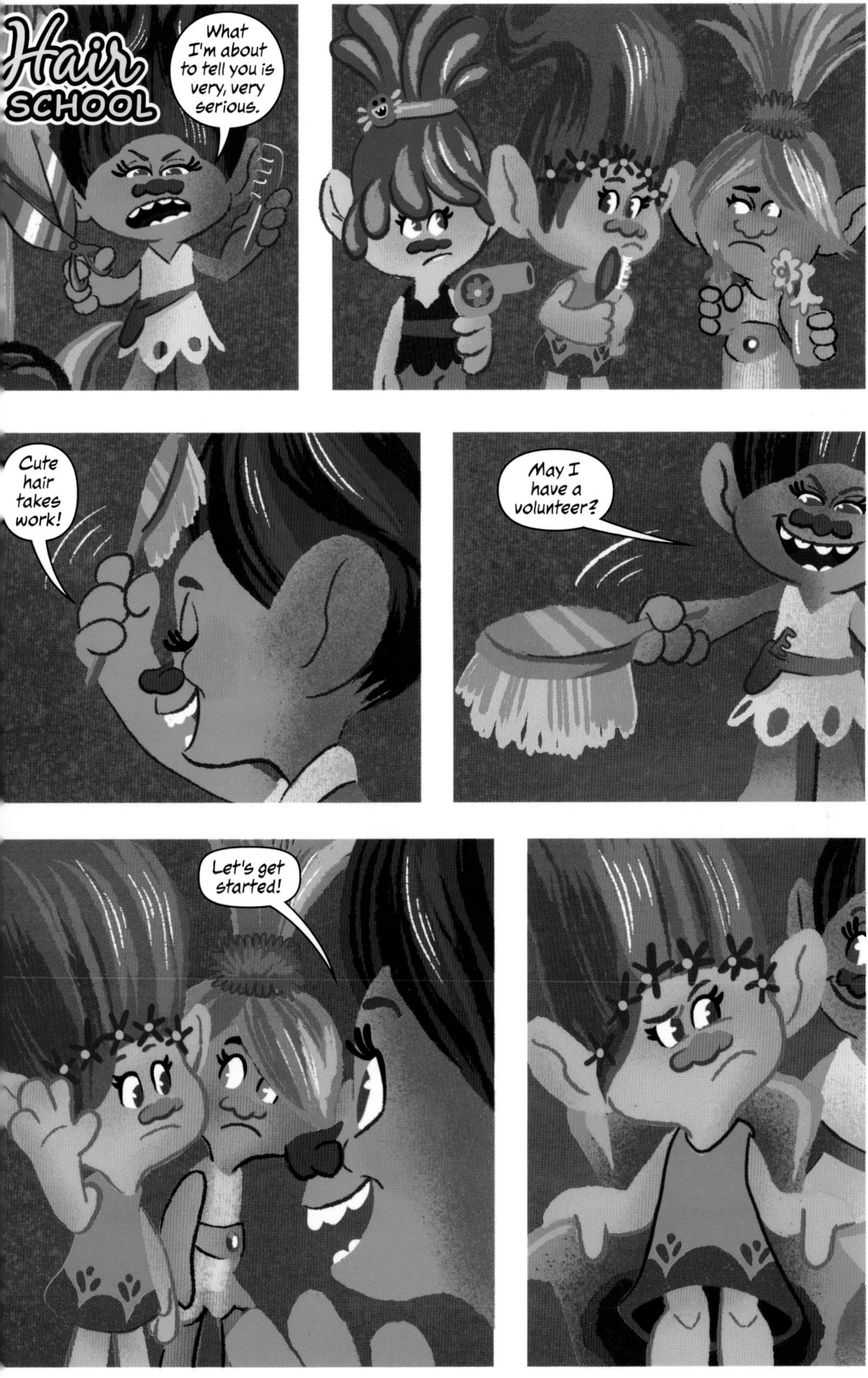
Hair School
What I'm about to tell you is very, very serious.
Cute hair takes work!
May I have a volunteer?
Let's get started!

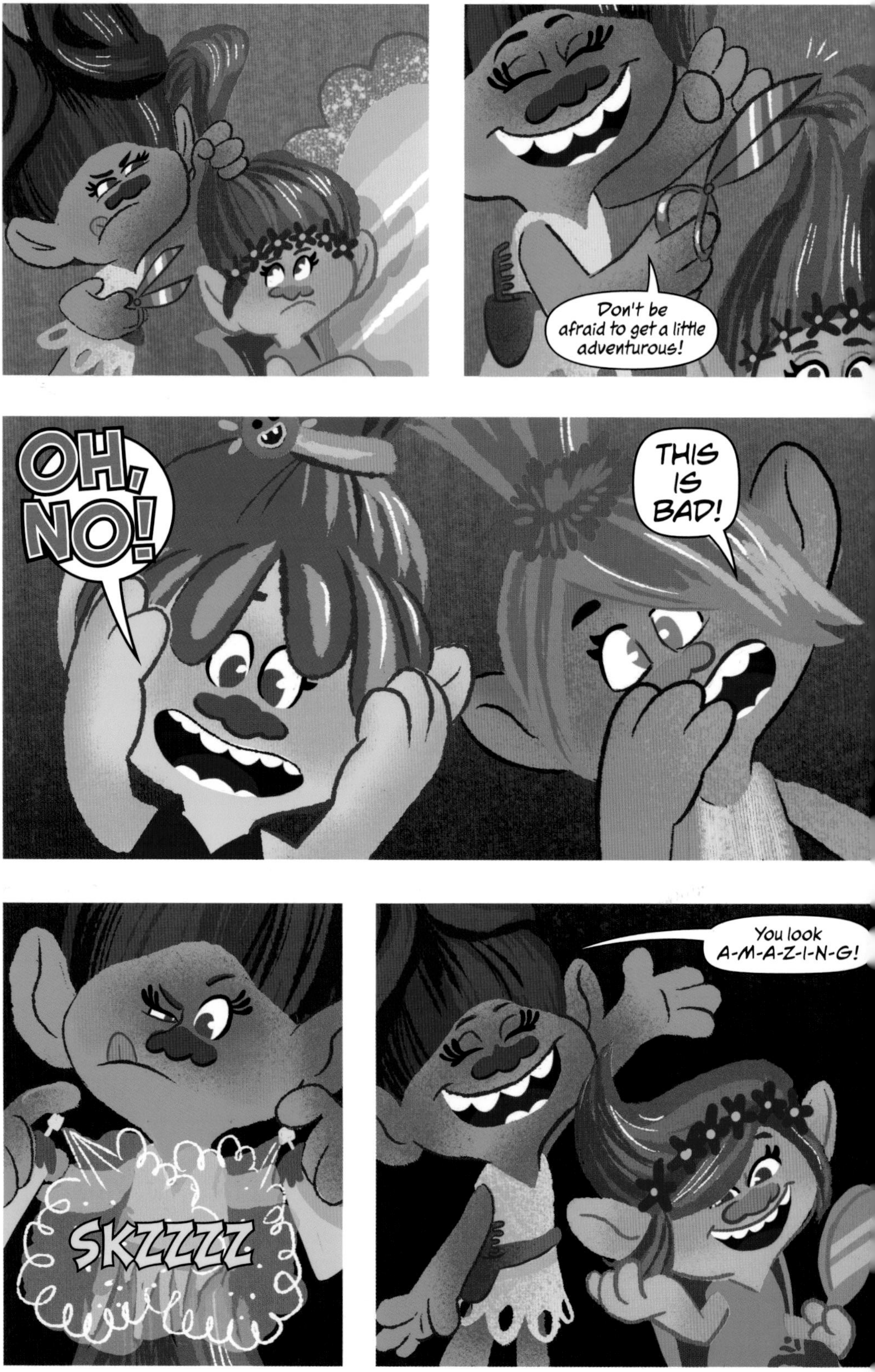
Don't be afraid to get a little adventurous!
OH, NO!
THIS IS BAD!
SKZZZZ
You look A-M-A-Z-I-N-G!

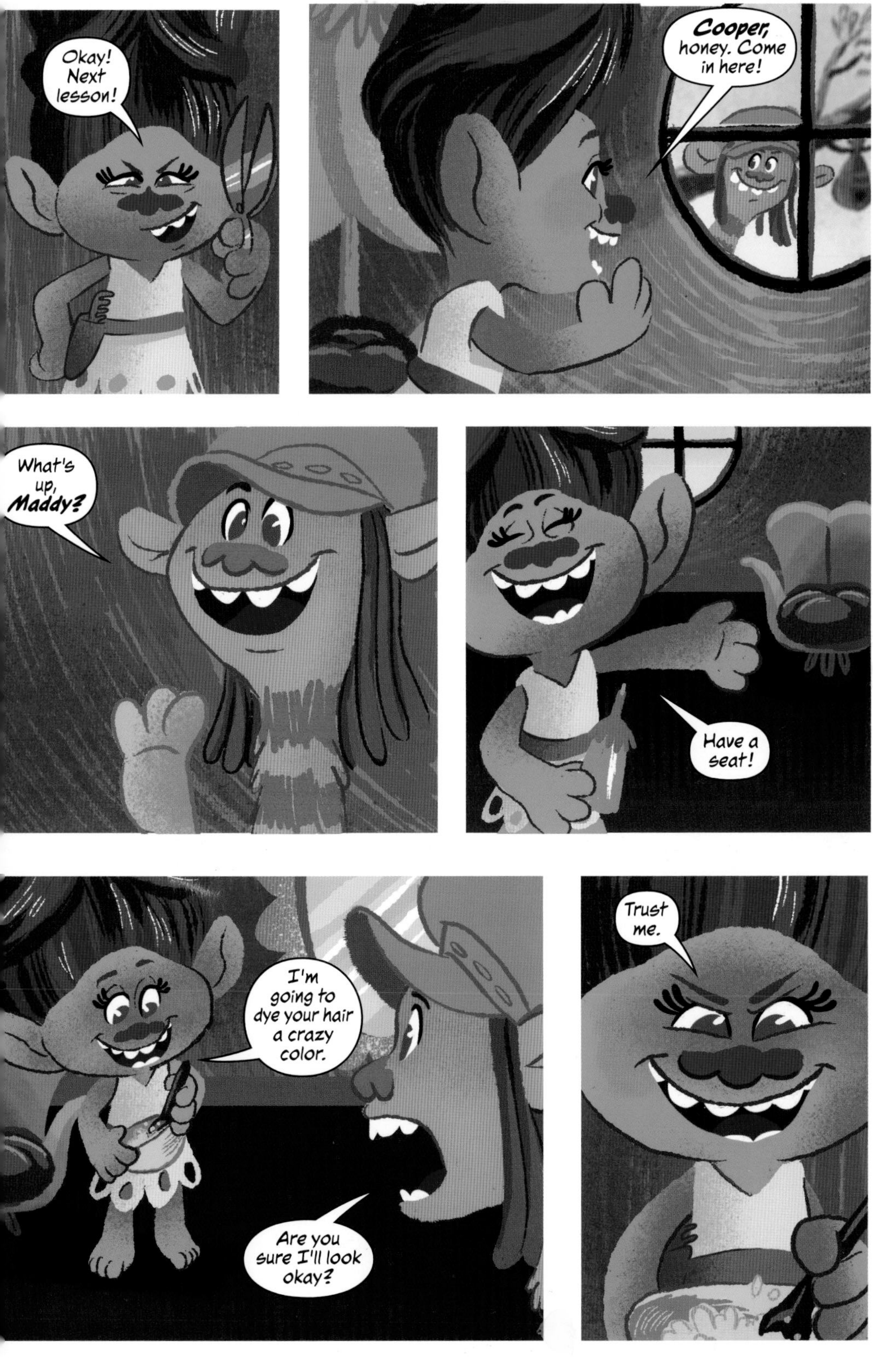
Okay! Next lesson!
Cooper, honey. Come in here!
What's up, Maddy?
Have a seat!
I'm going to dye your hair a crazy color.
Are you sure I'll look okay?
Trust me.

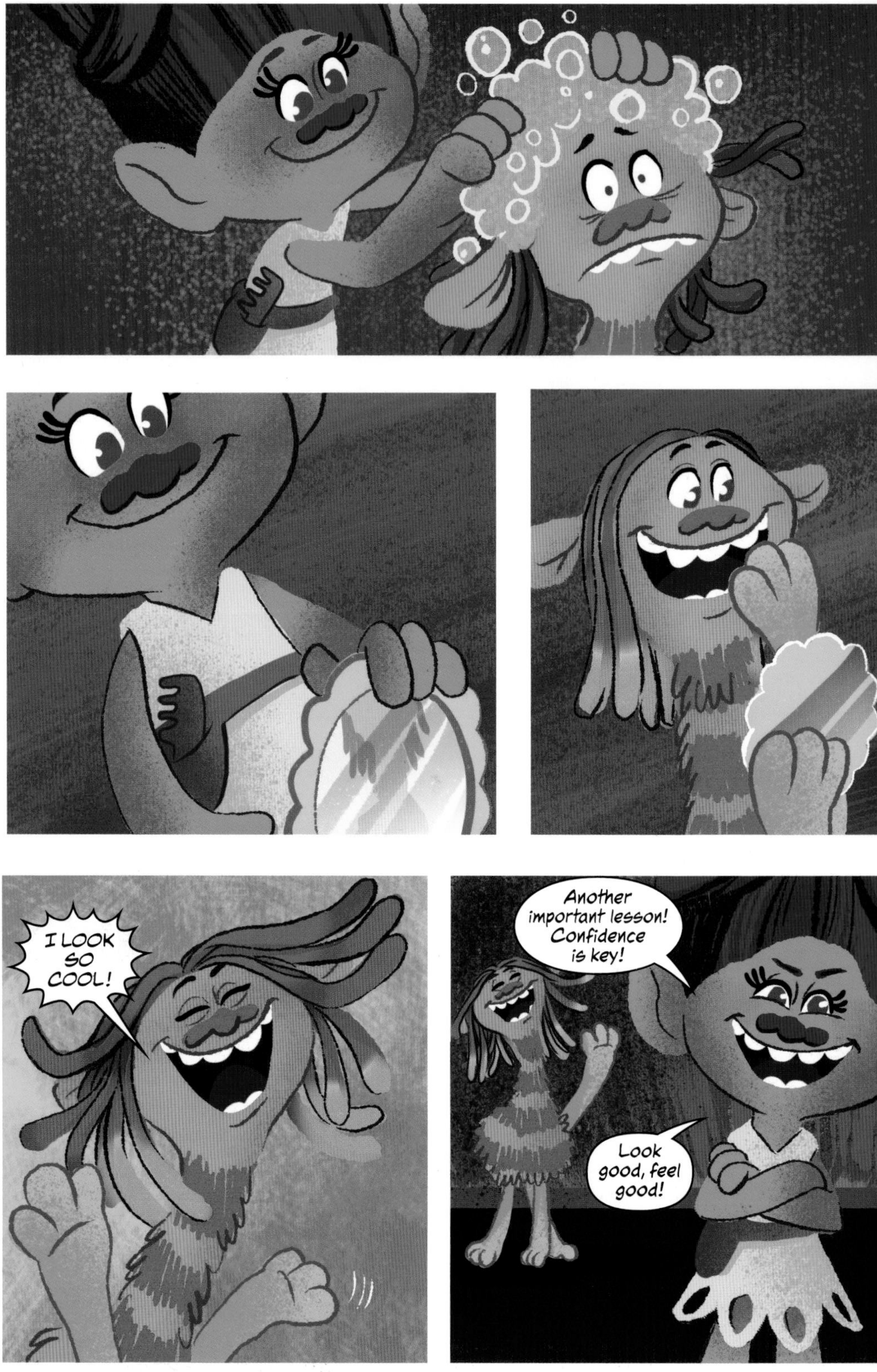
I LOOK SO COOL!
Another important lesson! Confidence is key!
Look good, feel good!

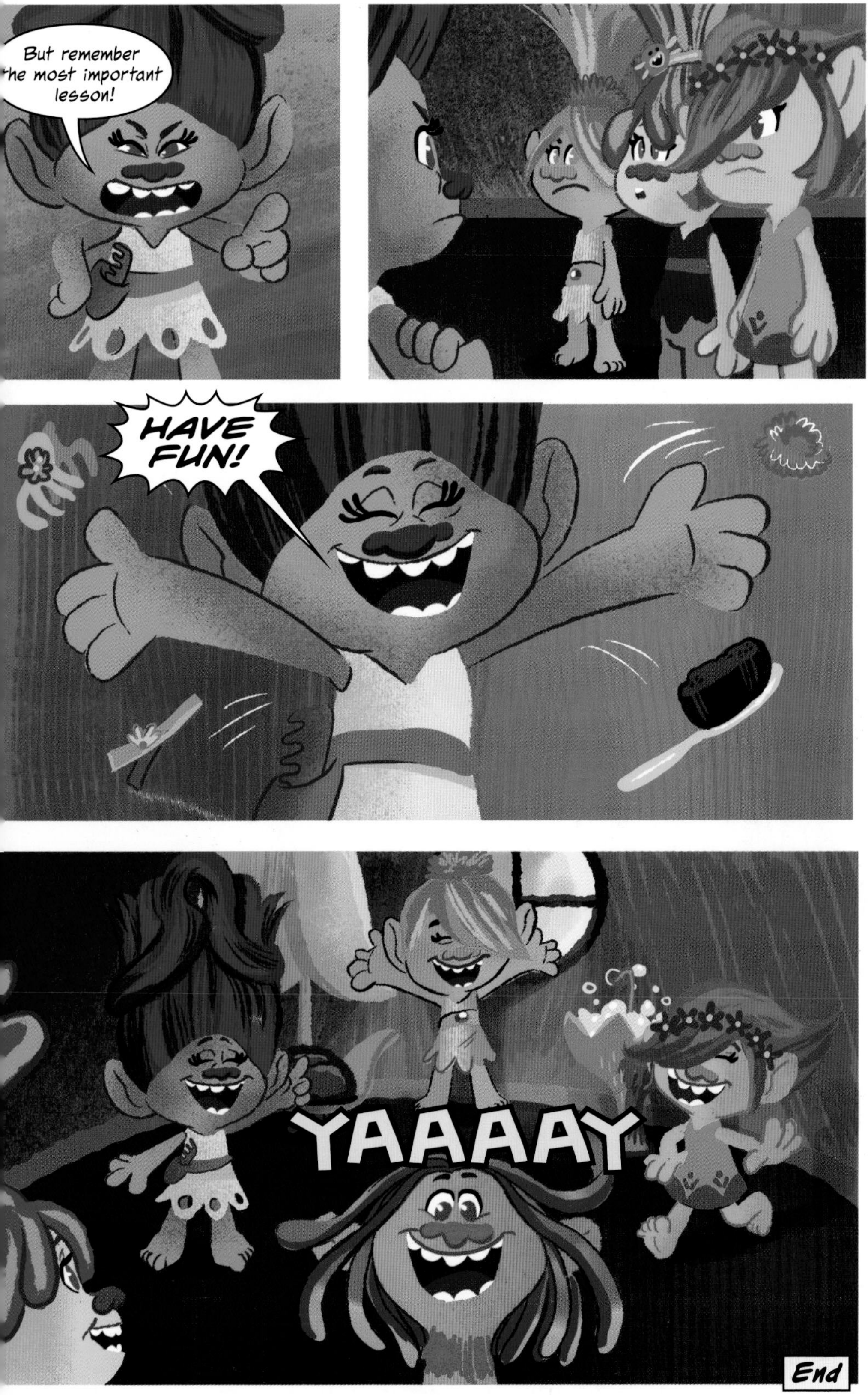
But remember the most important lesson!
HAVE FUN!
YAAAAY
End

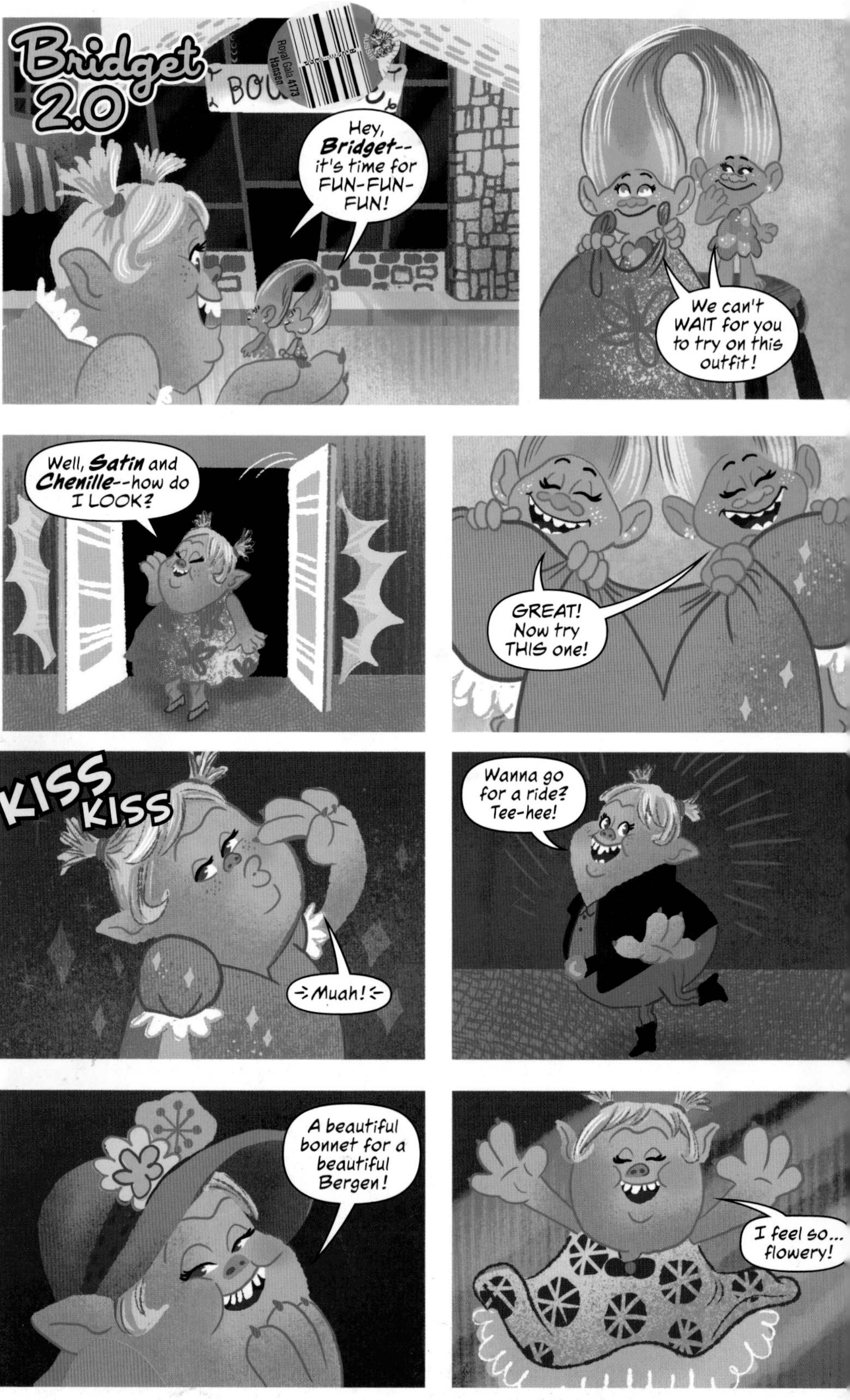
Bridget 2.0
Hey, **Bridget**-- it's time for FUN-FUN-FUN!
We can't WAIT for you to try on this outfit!
Well, **Satin** and **Chenille**--how do I LOOK?
GREAT! Now try THIS one!
KISS KISS
Muah!
Wanna go for a ride? Tee-hee!
A beautiful bonnet for a beautiful Bergen!
I feel so... flowery!

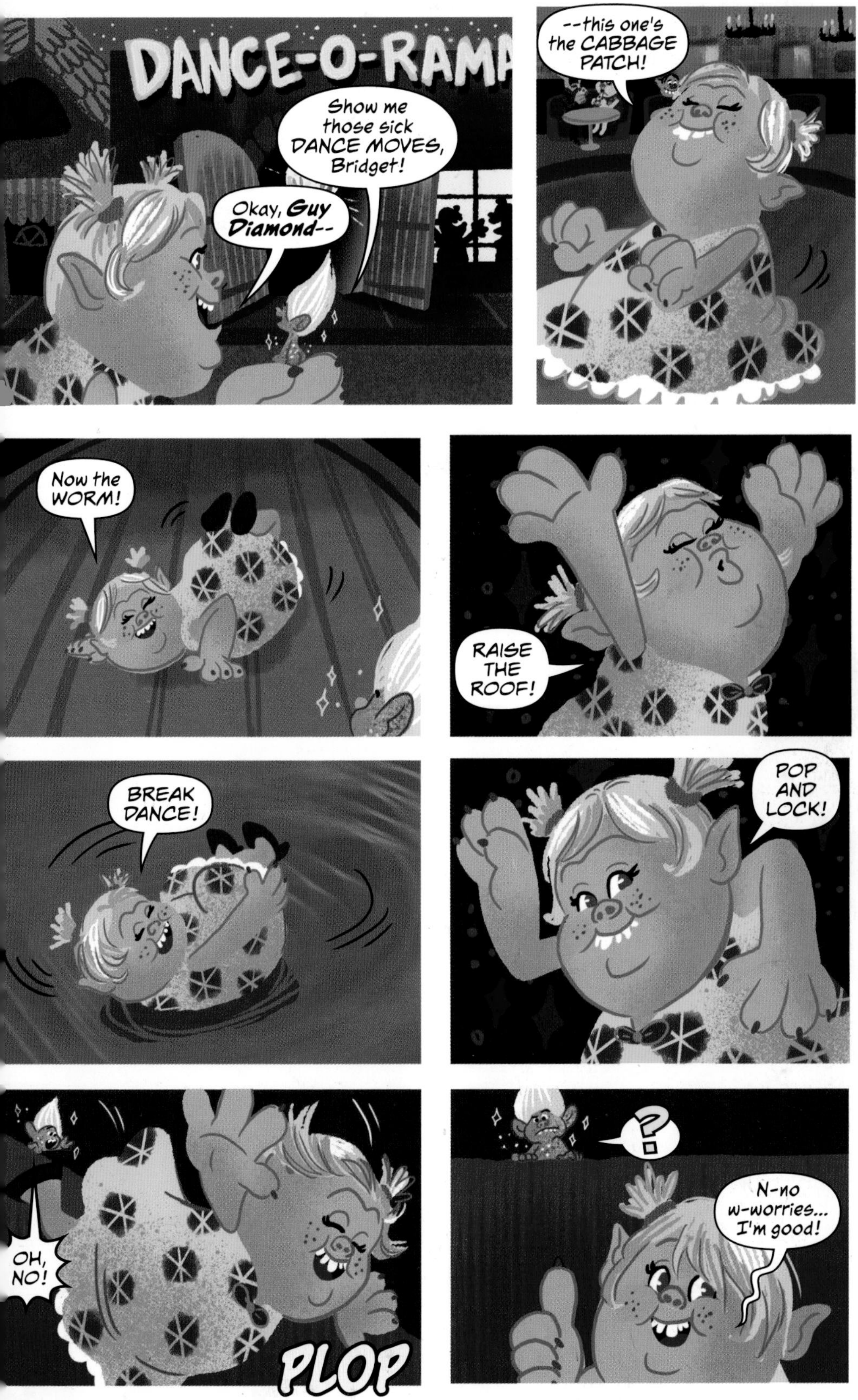
DANCE-O-RAMA
Show me those sick DANCE MOVES, Bridget!
Okay, **Guy Diamond**--
--this one's the CABBAGE PATCH!
Now the WORM!
RAISE THE ROOF!
BREAK DANCE!
POP AND LOCK!
OH, NO!
PLOP
?
N-no w-worries... I'm good!

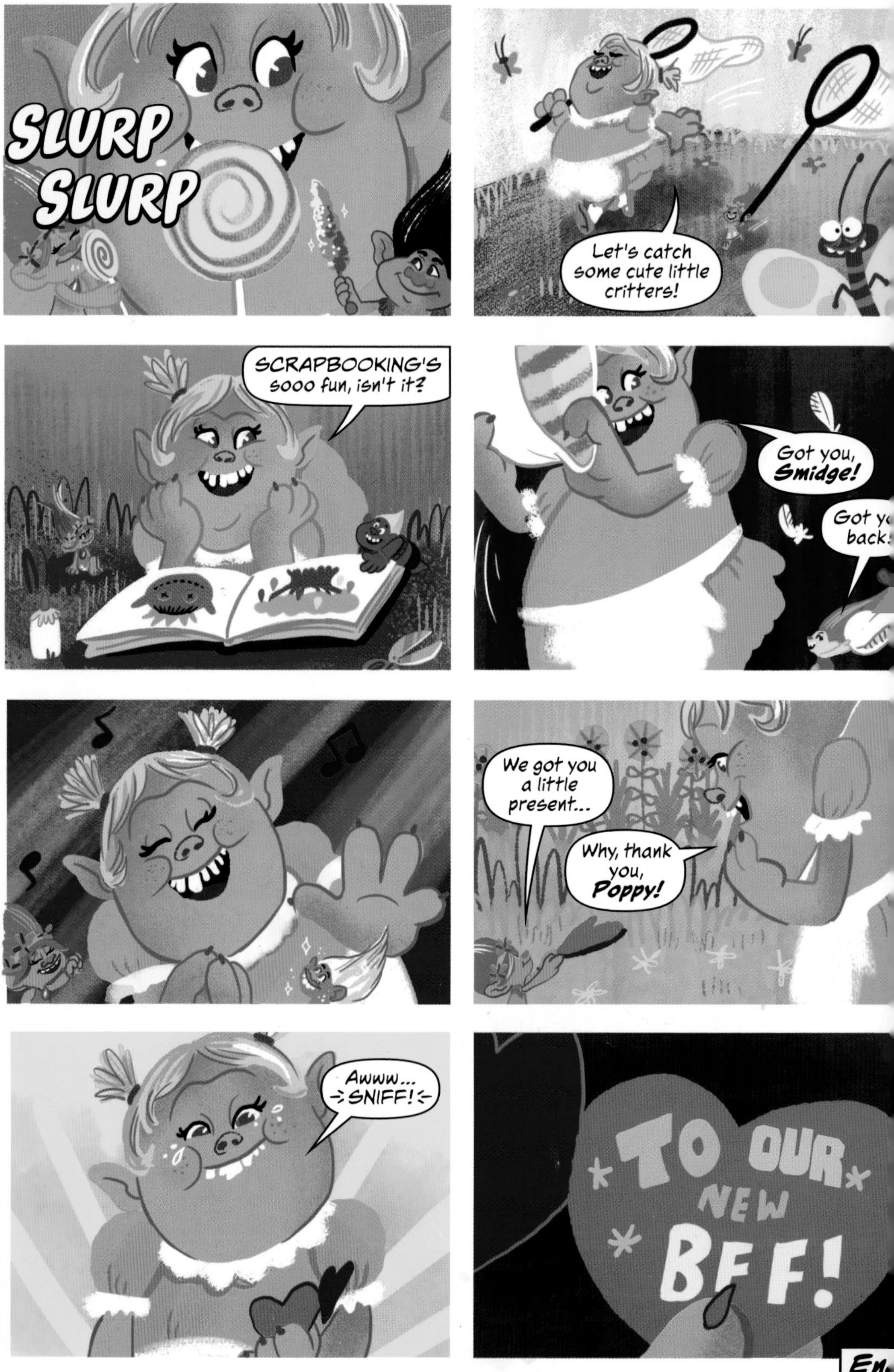
SLURP SLURP
Let's catch some cute little critters!
SCRAPBOOKING'S sooo fun, isn't it?
Got you, **Smidge!**
We got you a little present...
Why, thank you, **Poppy!**
Awww... SNIFF!
TO OUR NEW BFF!

SECRET MESSENGER

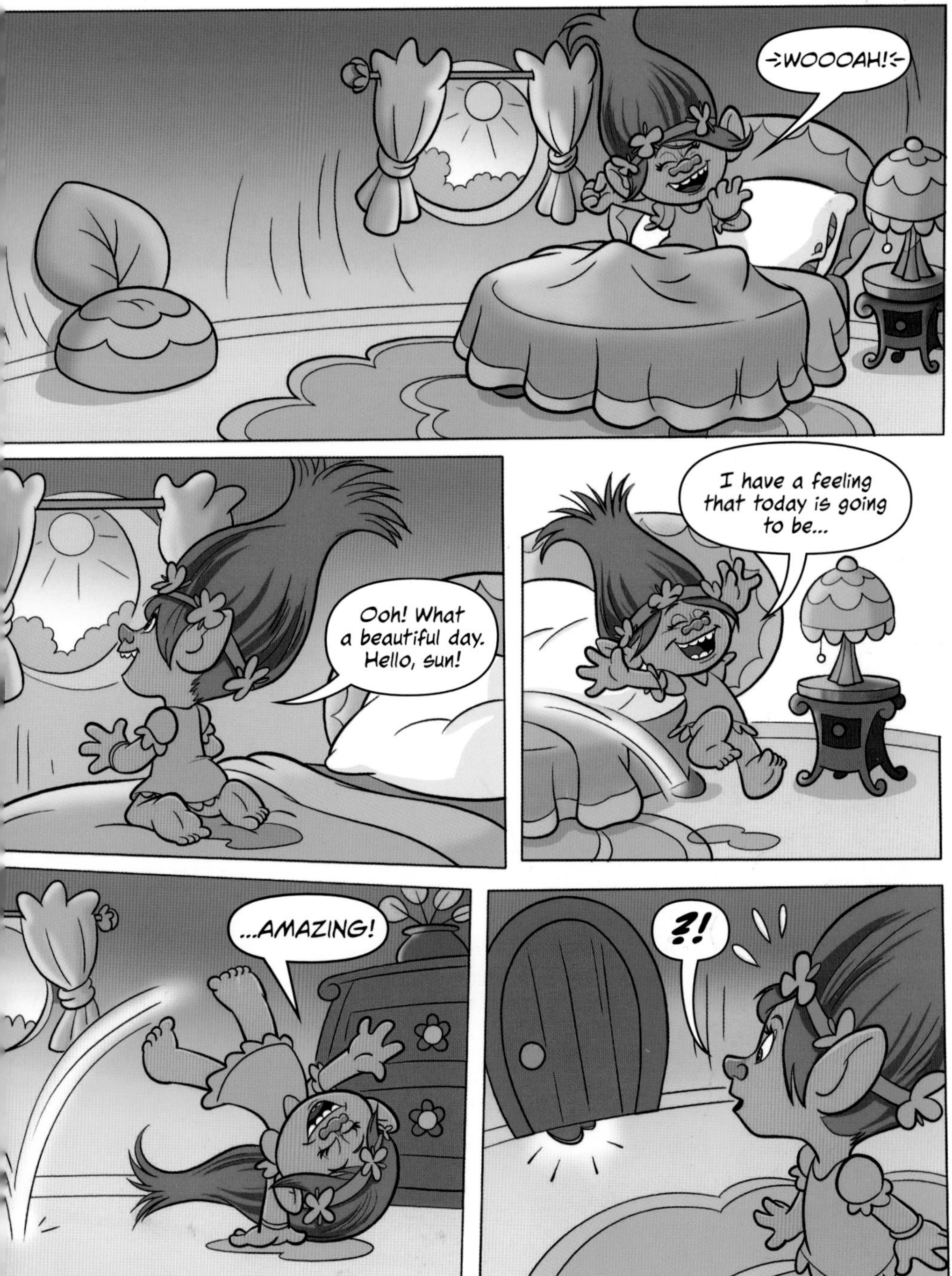
WOOOAH!
Ooh! What a beautiful day. Hello, sun!
I have a feeling that today is going to be...
...AMAZING!
?!

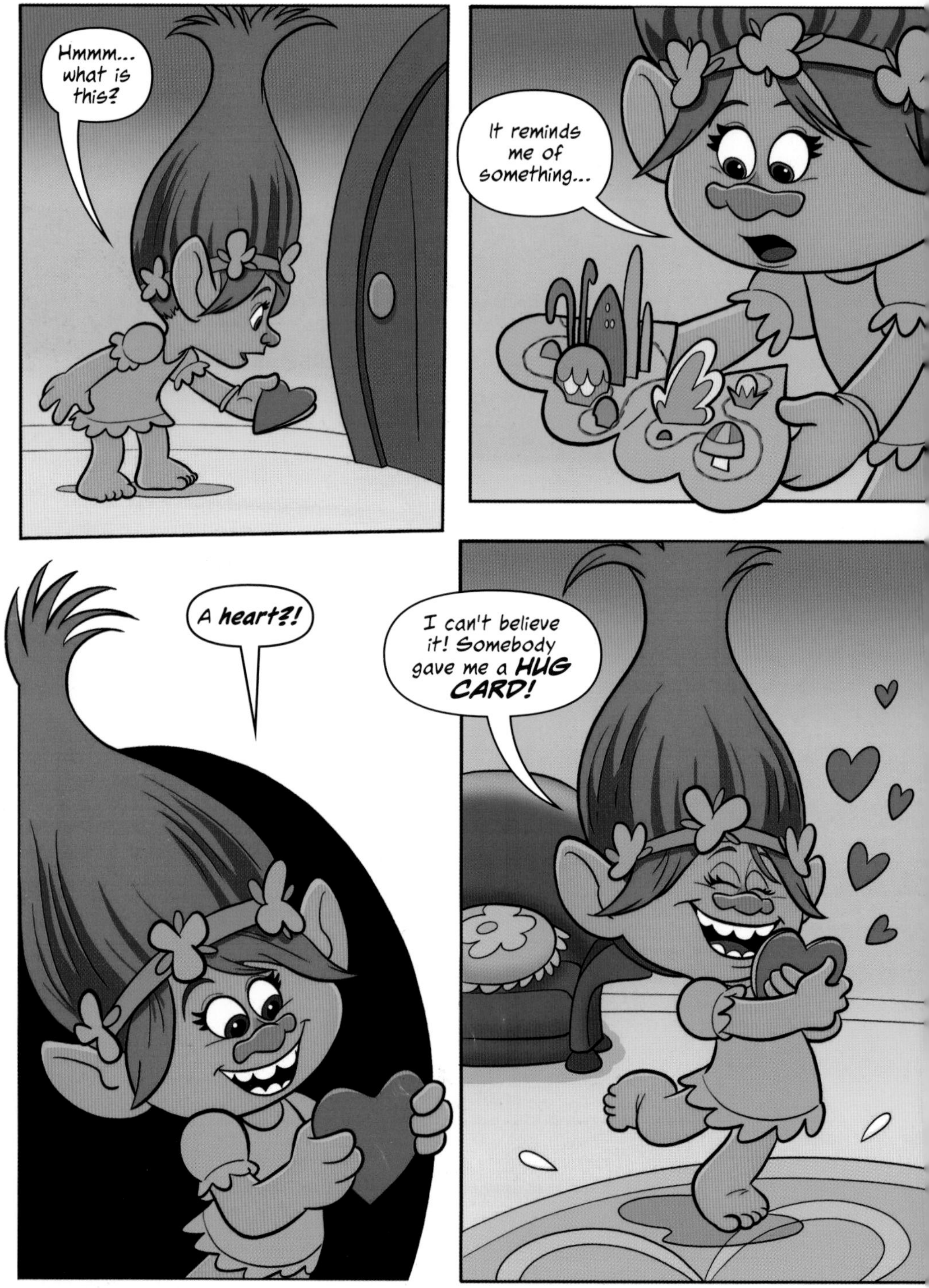
Hmmm... what is this?
It reminds me of something...
A heart?!
I can't believe it! Somebody gave me a HUG CARD!

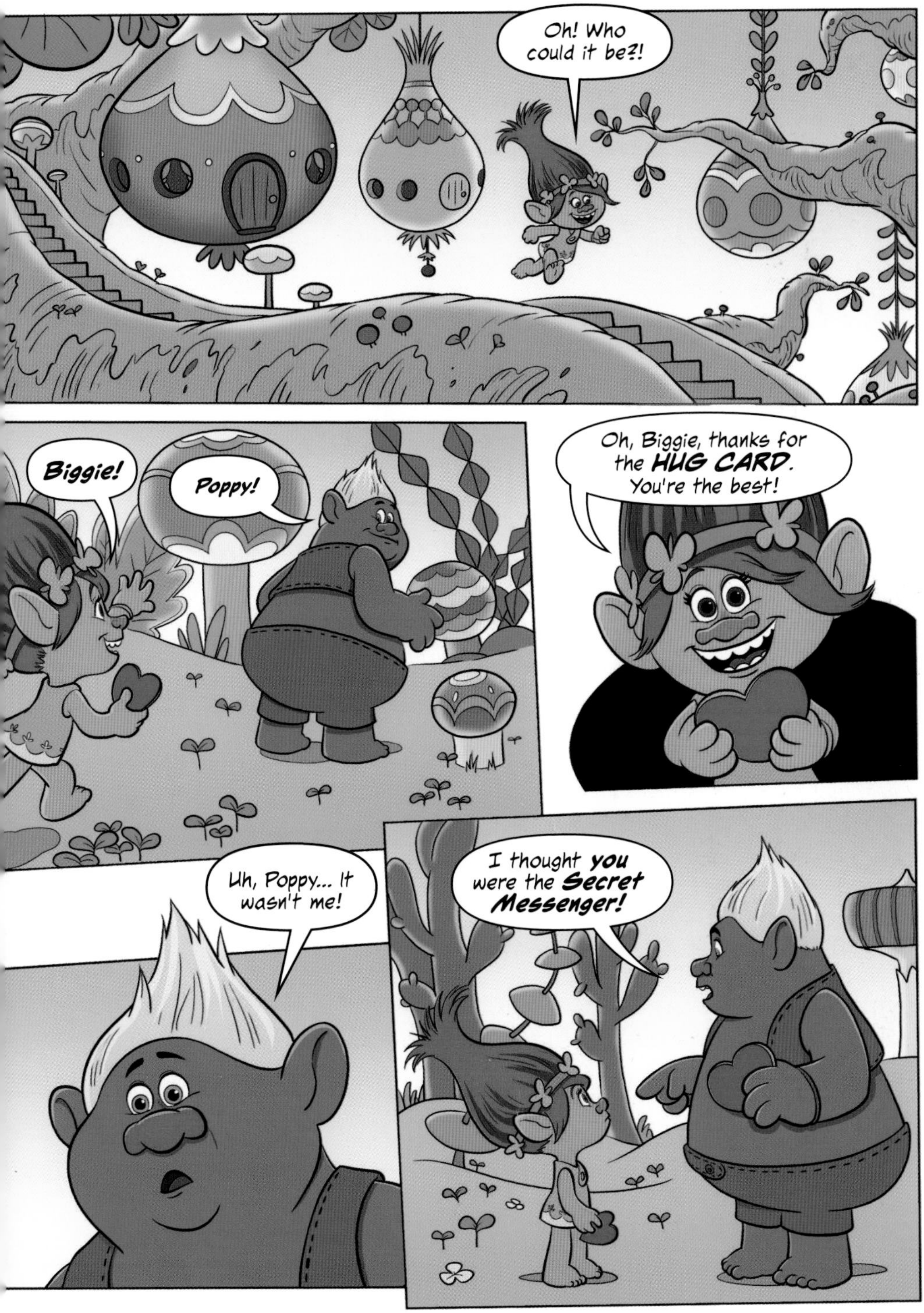
Oh! Who could it be?!
Biggie!
Poppy!
Oh, Biggie, thanks for the HUG CARD. You're the best!
Uh, Poppy... It wasn't me!
I thought you were the Secret Messenger!

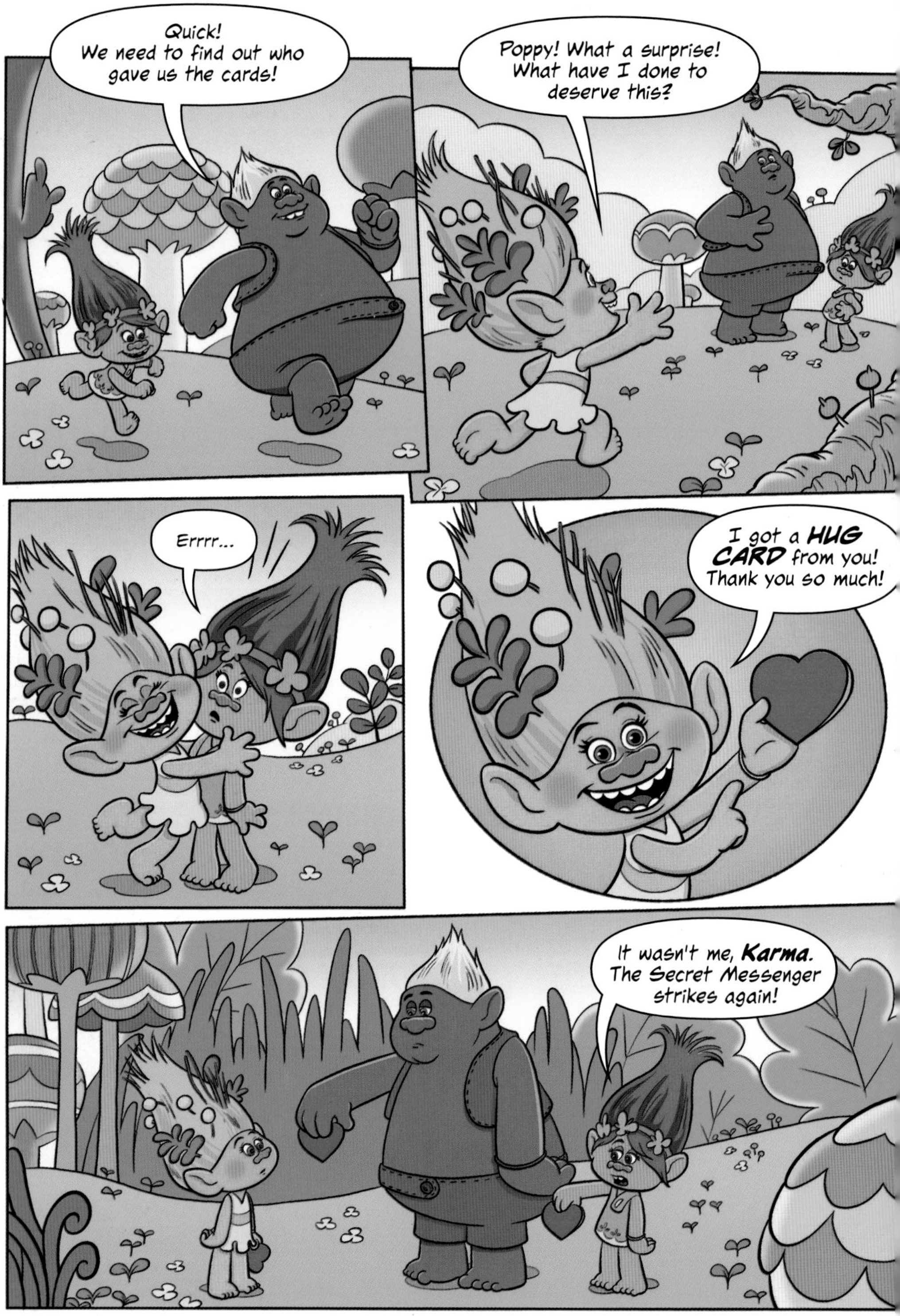
Quick! We need to find out who gave us the cards!
Poppy! What a surprise! What have I done to deserve this?
Errrr...
I got a **HUG CARD** from you! Thank you so much!
It wasn't me, **Karma**. The Secret Messenger strikes again!

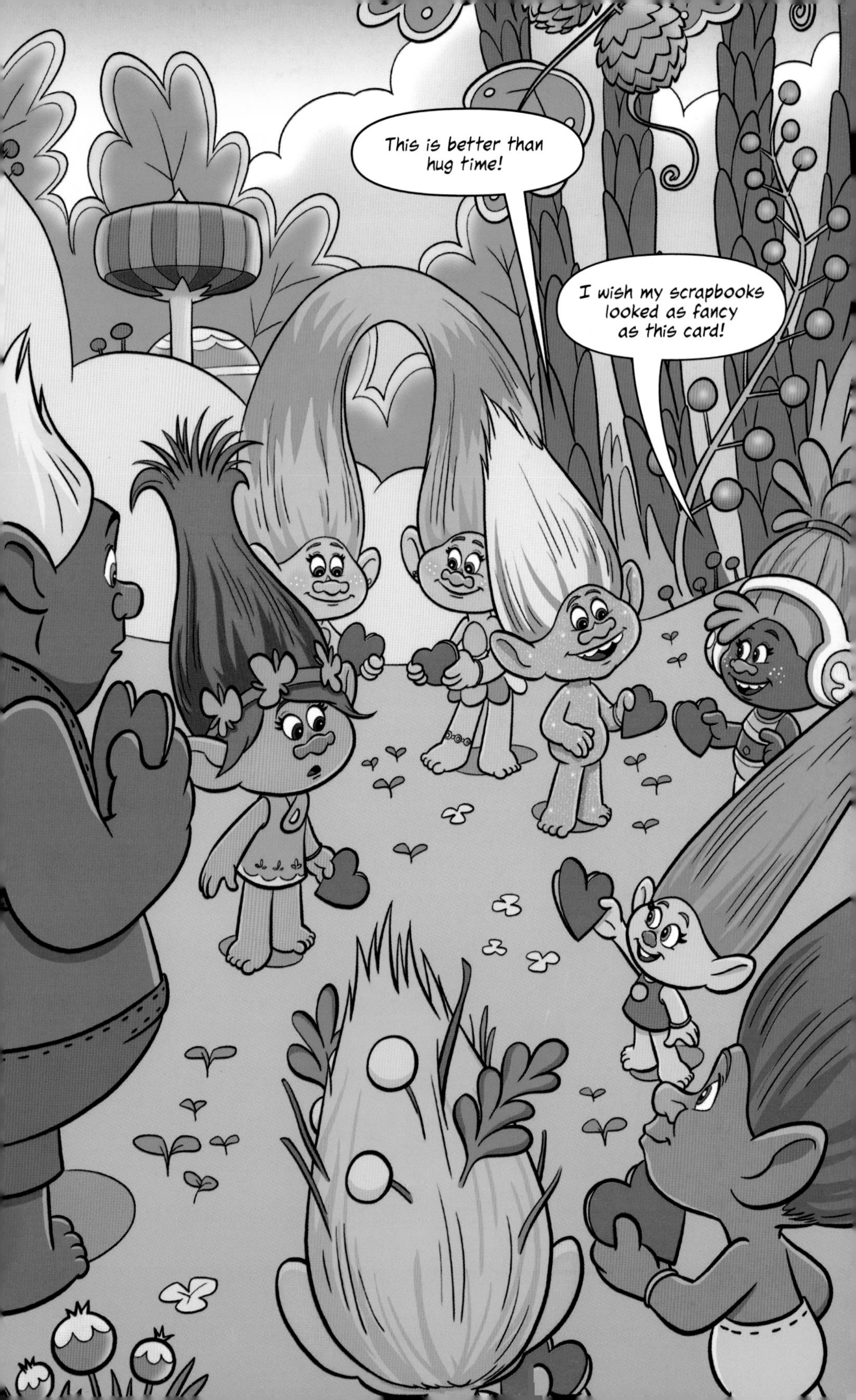

This is better than hug time!
I wish my scrapbooks looked as fancy as this card!

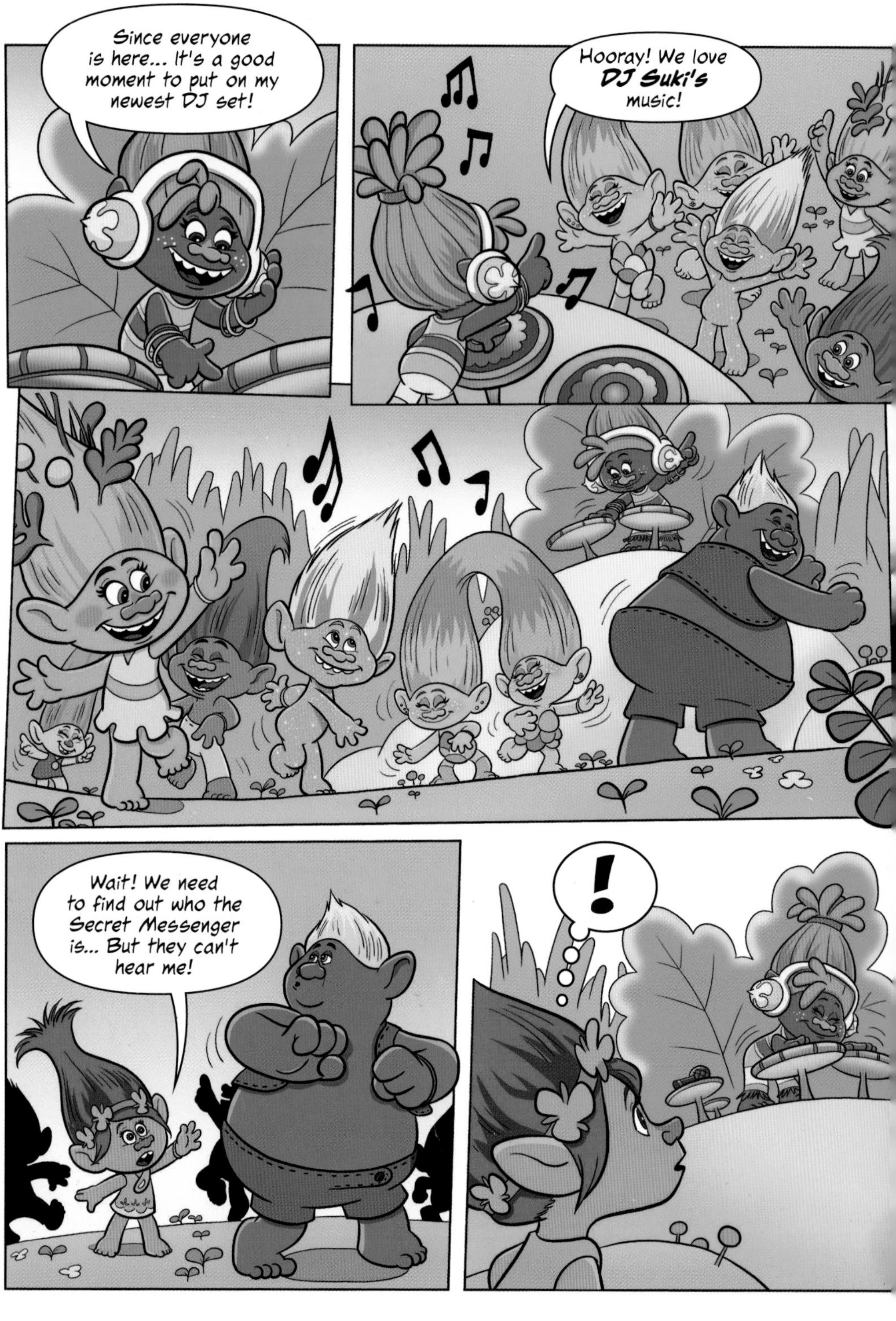

Since everyone is here... It's a good moment to put on my newest DJ set!
Hooray! We love DJ Suki's music!
Wait! We need to find out who the Secret Messenger is... But they can't hear me!
!

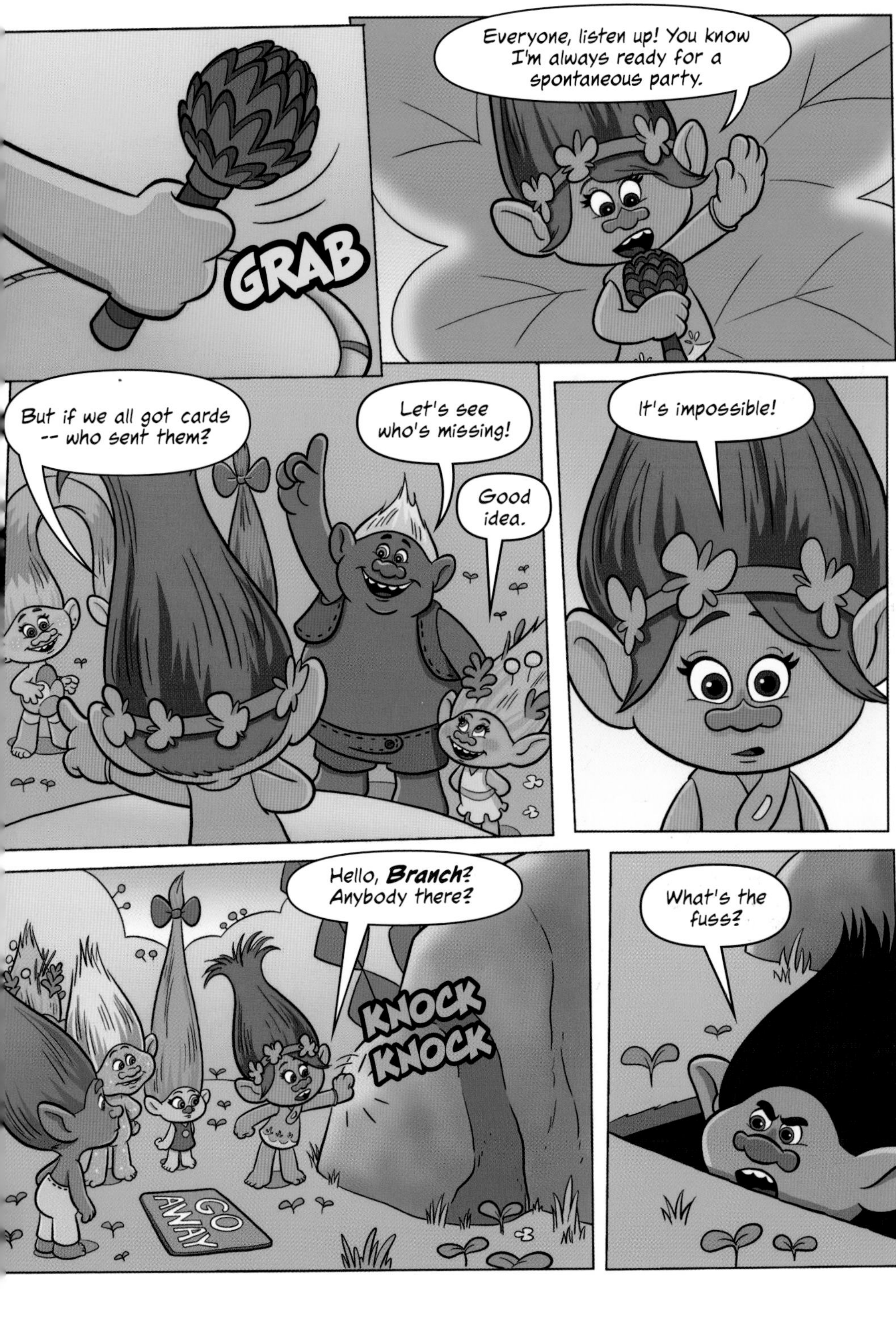
GRAB
Everyone, listen up! You know I'm always ready for a spontaneous party.
But if we all got cards -- who sent them?
Let's see who's missing!
Good idea.
It's impossible!
Hello, **Branch**? Anybody there?
KNOCK KNOCK
GO AWAY
What's the fuss?

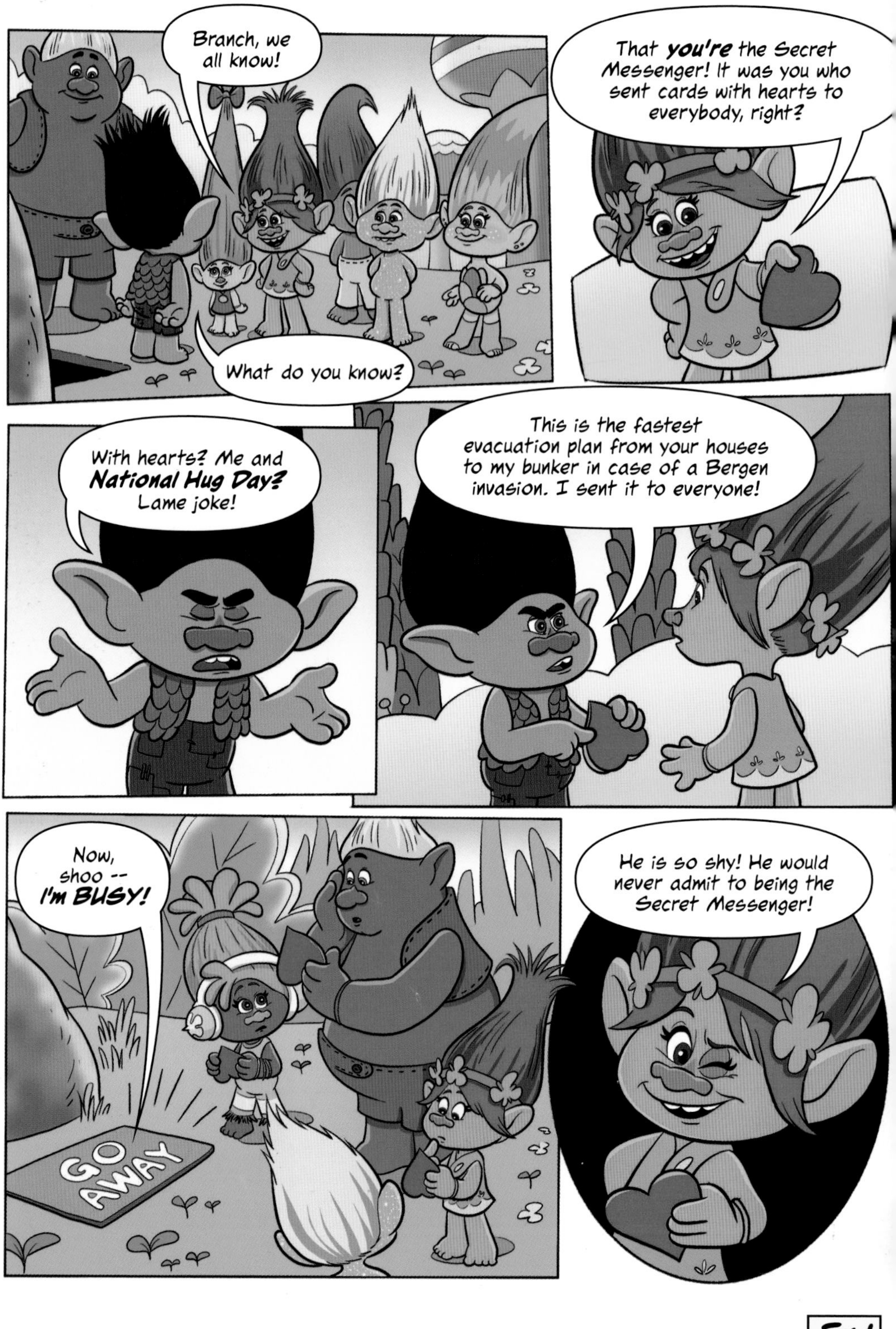

Branch, we all know!
What do you know?
That you're the Secret Messenger! It was you who sent cards with hearts to everybody, right?
With hearts? Me and National Hug Day? Lame joke!
This is the fastest evacuation plan from your houses to my bunker in case of a Bergen invasion. I sent it to everyone!
Now, shoo -- I'm BUSY!
GO AWAY
He is so shy! He would never admit to being the Secret Messenger!
End

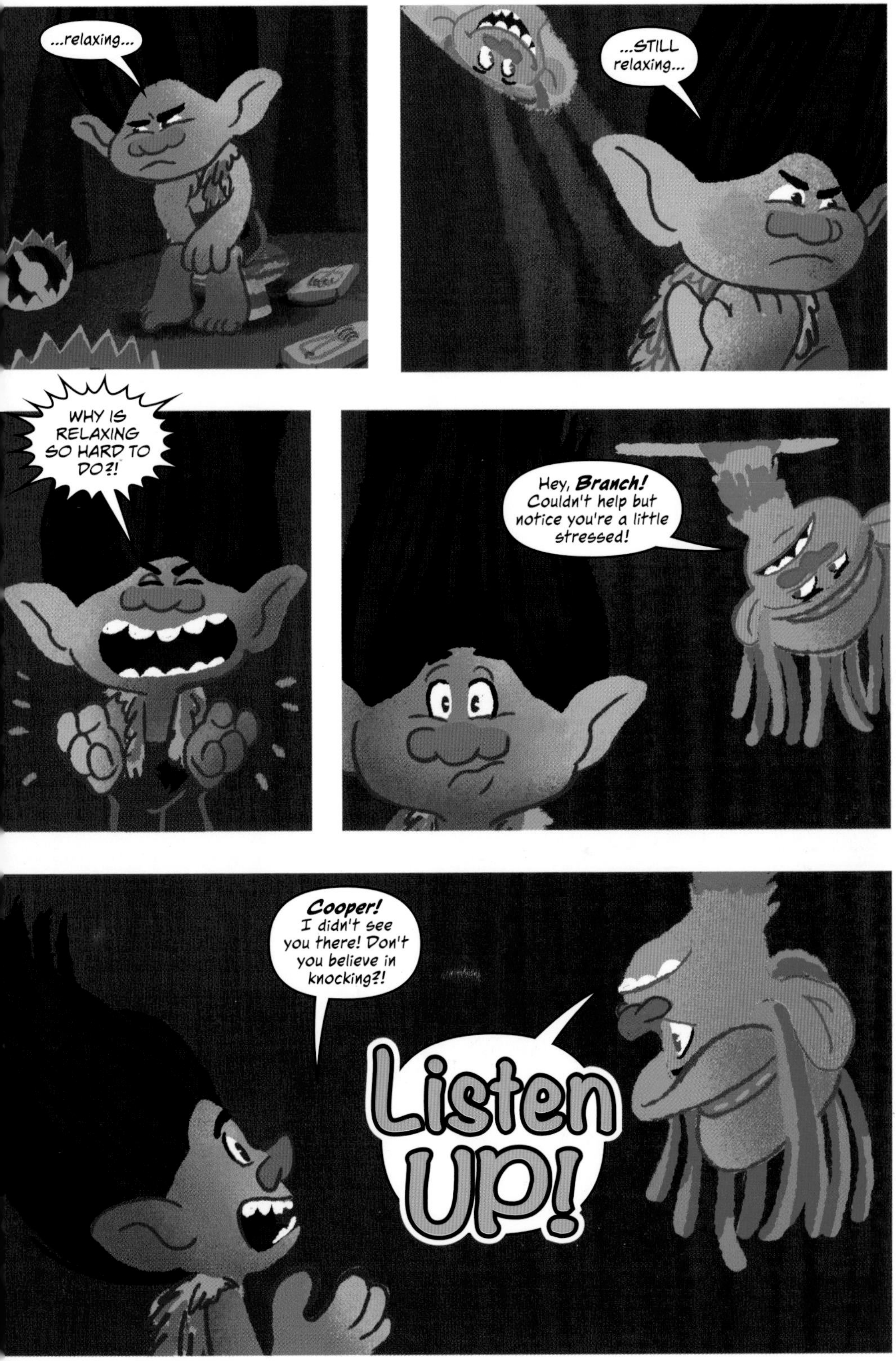
...relaxing...
...STILL relaxing...
WHY IS RELAXING SO HARD TO DO?!
Hey, **Branch!** Couldn't help but notice you're a little stressed!
Cooper! I didn't see you there! Don't you believe in knocking?!
Listen UP!

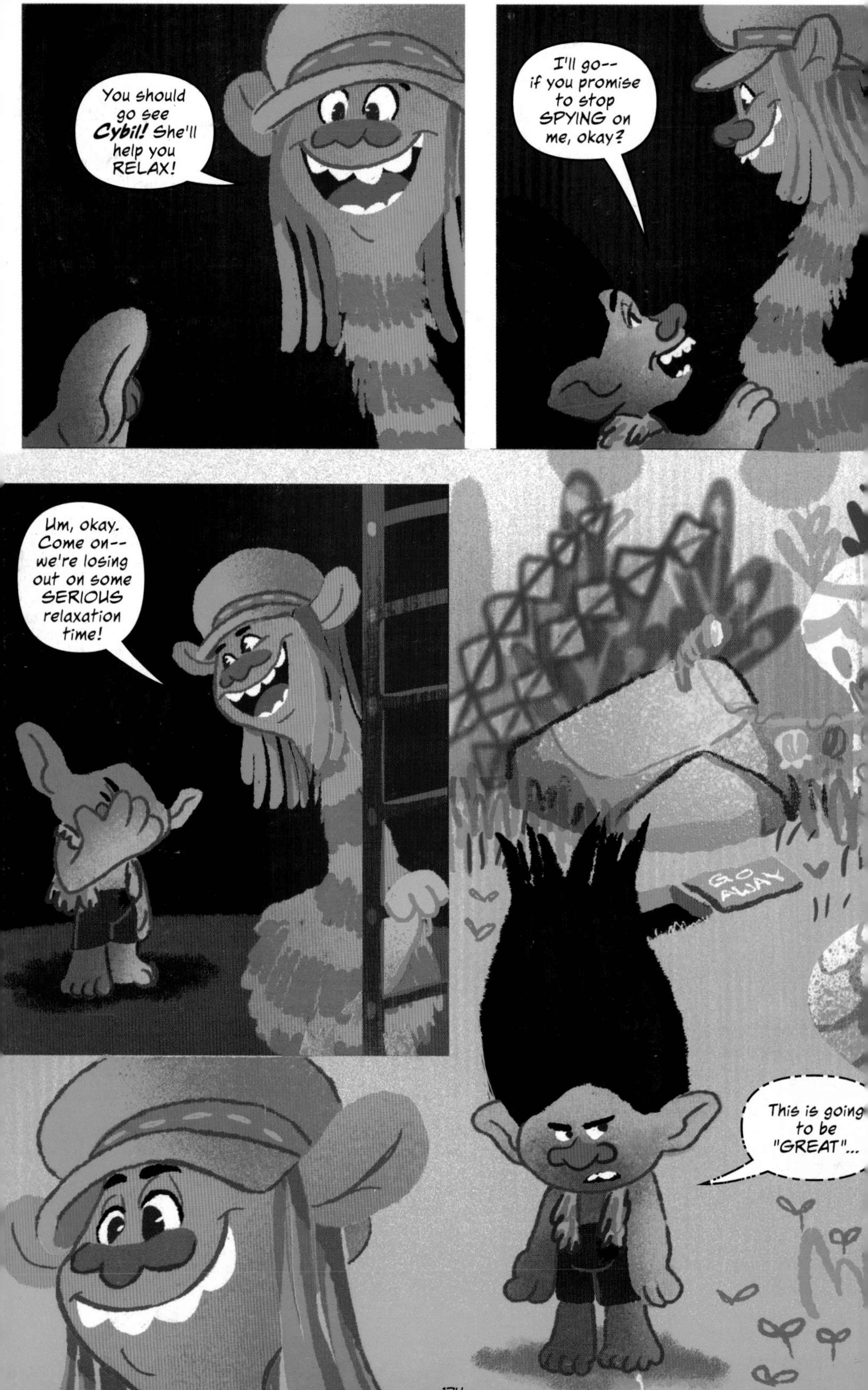
You should go see Cybil! She'll help you RELAX!
I'll go-- if you promise to stop SPYING on me, okay?
Um, okay. Come on-- we're losing out on some SERIOUS relaxation time!
GO AWAY
This is going to be "GREAT"...

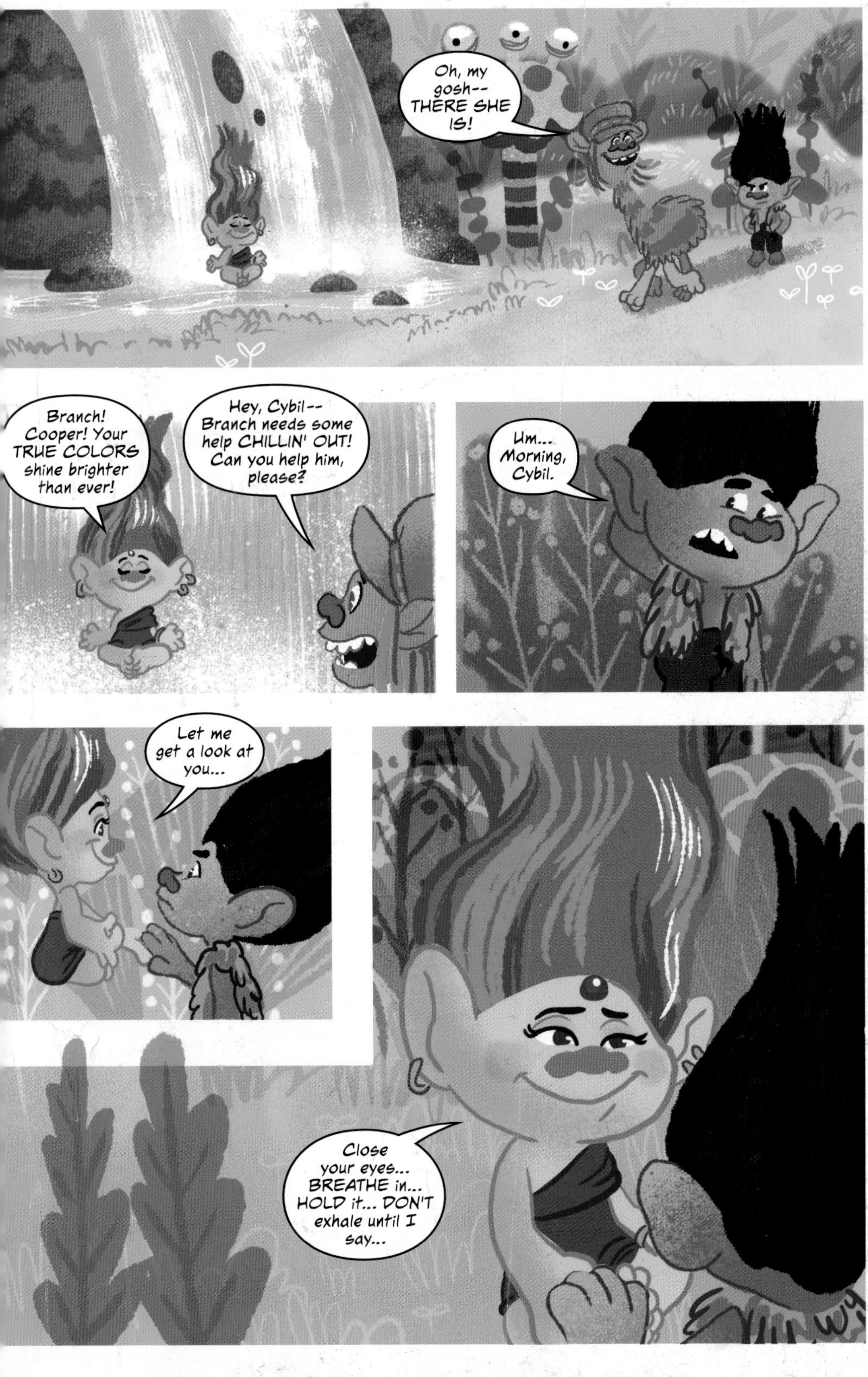

Oh, my gosh-- THERE SHE IS!
Branch! Cooper! Your TRUE COLORS shine brighter than ever!
Hey, Cybil-- Branch needs some help CHILLIN' OUT! Can you help him, please?
Um... Morning, Cybil.
Let me get a look at you...
Close your eyes... BREATHE in... HOLD it... DON'T exhale until I say...

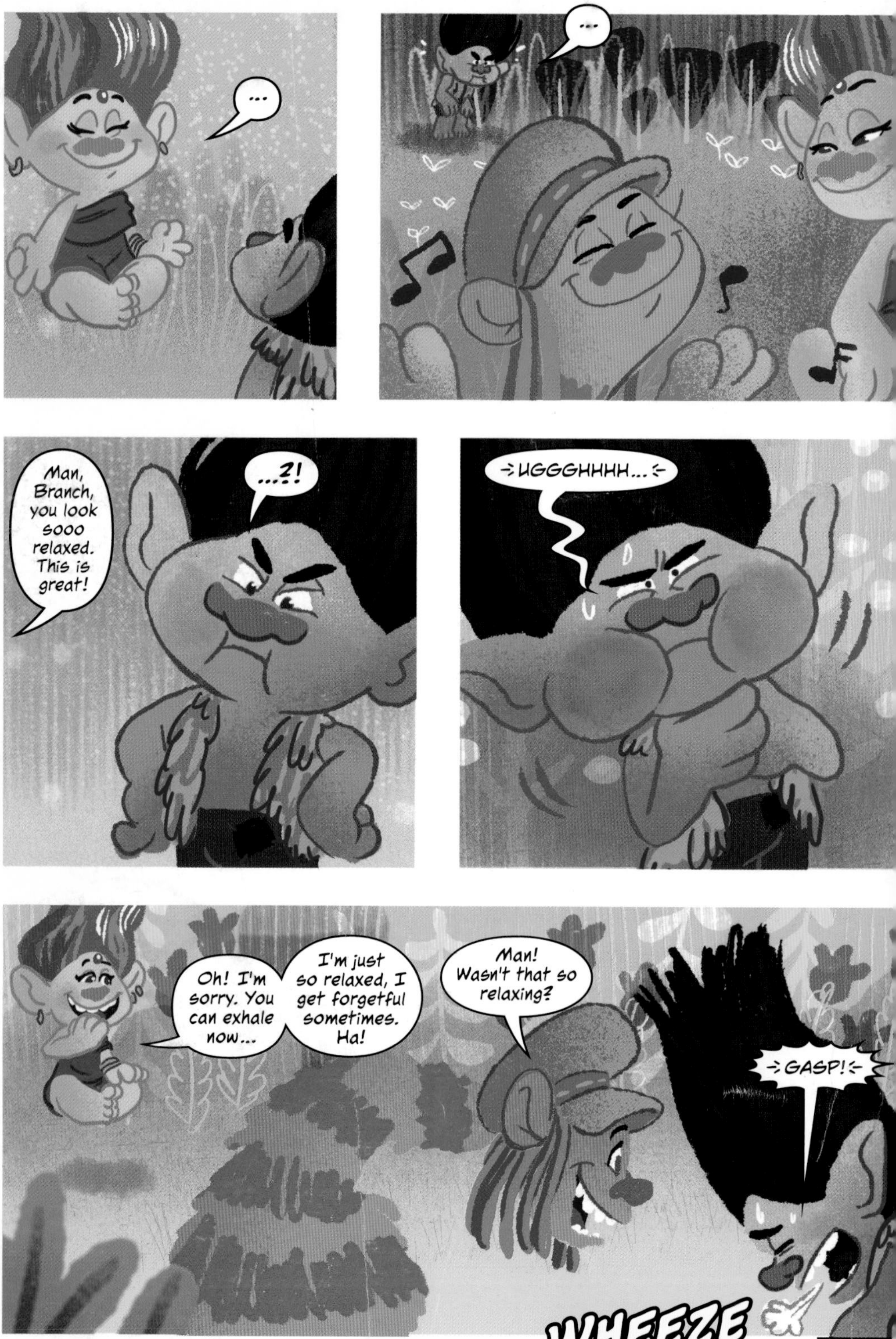
...
...
Man, Branch, you look sooo relaxed. This is great!
...?!
UGGGHHHH...
Oh! I'm sorry. You can exhale now...
I'm just so relaxed, I get forgetful sometimes. Ha!
Man! Wasn't that so relaxing?
GASP!
WHEEZE
End

SING, DANCE, LAUGH, REPEAT!

Based on the beloved movie from Drea[illegible] Animation. The Trolls are letting their hair down with more stories than you can shake a pet worm at! Poppy, Branch and all their friends are back just in time for Hug Time! Plus, more stories with those loveable (and miserable) Bergens. Featuring a handy guide to all the most popular Trolls in Troll Village and some Bergens.

DreamWorks
Trolls
Hugs & Friends
PAPERCUTZ

DreamWorks
Trolls
Put Your Hair in the Air!
PAPERCUTZ

DreamWorks
Trolls
Party With The Bergens
PAPERCUTZ

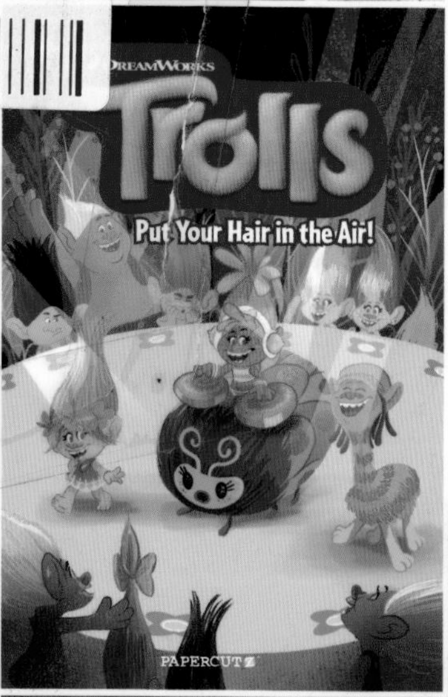

$14.99 US / $19.50 CAN
ISBN: 978-1-54580-124-6

ISBN: 978-1-54580-124-6
9 781545 801246 51499

PAPERCUTZ™
Dedicated to publishing great graphic novels for all ages.

www.papercutz.com

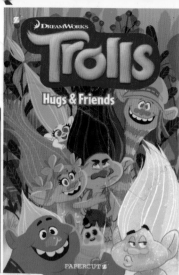

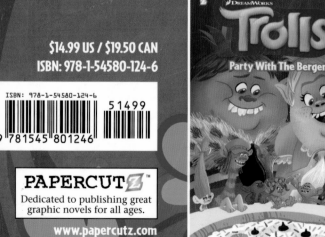